By the Light of Orion's Belt

By

Christopher T. Hunnewell

White Turtle Books

Canby, Minnesota

This is a work of fiction. The characters and events set down here are figments of the author's imagination. Any resemblance to any actual person or events is coincidental.

ISBN 978-1-933482-13-2

Cover & interior design by Joel B Reed
Cover photo: Child in canoe © Elena Elisseeva | Dreamstime.com

White Turtle Books
Canby, Minnesota
WhiteTurtleBooks.com

This book is for Carolyn, Christy, Billye, Bobbie,
Doylene, Jan, Jaymie, Mary Ann and Trudy

This above all: to thine ownself be true,
And it must follow, as the night the day,
Thou canst not then be false to any man.

William Shakespeare, Hamlet

CHAPTER 1

That spring we got lost on the Brazos River and found Tarzan Charlie. It was my last year of elementary school and I had the grades necessary for advancement to middle school. Yet, if a gun were put to my head, I couldn't recount any of the academics. Just personal betrayal, bitterness and abandonment compounded with a home life no one should endure.

Thankfully, my problems, particularly the numerous and loud disagreements between my mother and daddy, were fading by the Thursday afternoon. It was the eve of the long Memorial Day weekend. So like a puppy scratching to be let out, I could hardly wait before my mother stopped in front of the familiar two-story house. This was my safe haven and, for a while at least, I could forget what had become life's norm for me. One of the reasons that house was the most beautiful place in the world, at least for me. Even before I opened the car door, it seemed to nod welcome in various ways. The most noticeable being the two backyard live oaks waving their ancient branches like an emperor's wreath above the pinnacles of the gabled copper colored roof.

During breaks at school other kids had bragged about how they would spend their long weekend. Some spoke of family home gatherings or going to popular parks and attractions. Others announced elaborate schedules designed to inspire envy in those not invited to attend, and therefore a possible fantasy. Combined, they made no difference, not compared with where my cousin Tommy and I would spend the weekend.

My grandparents were taking us to Bandy's Camp, a resort located on the Brazos River in north central Texas. The river's full Spanish name was *Brazos de Dios*, or arms of God, a name early explorers gave it because whenever they needed water, God stretched out his arms and blessed them with various branches of this river. Looking at a Texas map, I traced the Brazos River's blue line that meandered from its start in West Texas with multiple bends across the land turning south to the Gulf of Mexico. The Brazos had forks or tributaries, including the clear and salt forks. Papa said the clear was actually murky and differentiated from the Salt Fork, because it was said to be as salty as ocean water. Here was a river with diversity and character that appealed to my sense of the exotic. Most importantly, it offered distance between me and my so-called home town.

Bandy's Camp was located on the Clear Fork of the Brazos. It offered every summer recreational amenity and claimed to be the area's biggest Memorial Day weekend party to usher in the summer season. It was the "total experience," as expressed by a group of teens I overheard lamenting how they could only dream about it.

Aside from the imagined possibilities, the reality was we'd camp out under the stars, eat food cooked over an open fire, swim and play until we were too tired to stand. We would, explained Papa, my maternal grandfather, have the opportunity for more fun than should have been legal in any of the fifty states and territories.

"Hell even the United States Constitution only guarantees the pursuit of happiness," Papa said laughing. "You rug rats will hit the deck running to a spot designed totally for that purpose."

Papa was the man to know, too. He'd been to lots of places like Bandy's Camp, some better, more worse, as he like to tell it. His was first-hand knowledge from being the lead guitarist of a rock and roll band. A band contracted to provide the entertainment for that magical weekend.

My maternal grandmother Ana had asked our parents back in April about us going. This was when hostilities were seemingly quiet. Surprisingly, when presented with the offer, my mother accepted immediately with no outward objection. However, my mother's delight turned caustic after we called my daddy and received his immediate approval, along with his love. After gushing my repeated thank you daddy, my mother grabbed the phone and told me to go outside and play.

Over the next month my mother avoided the trip's topic unless necessary and then groused about what I should pack. The morning she took me to Ana's, I was up early and ready to go even before she harped for me to hurry up because she had other things to do. "Things," I knew didn't exist, after overhearing her telephone conversation lamenting the exact opposite regarding "all this free time" after dropping me off.

On the drive to Ana's, she silently gripped and twisted the cover on the steering wheel and, even after stopping, she stared ahead before throwing the car door open like it had offended her. I waited for her and together we stepped to the sidewalk and her stride reminded me of those teachers we'd learned to avoid. She didn't help me with my bag, which was bulky to the point of ponderous, particularly after she had stuffed it with too many necessaries she thought I needed.

"Girls always need more personals for overnight trips than boys," she told me when the bag was in danger of bursting.

Later, half of its contents would be left at Ana's. But getting out of the car, I didn't even have time to slip on the bag's shoulder strap before my mother strode up the walk, oblivious to my struggle. Still, I knew better than to make a fuss that would give her an excuse to forbid me from going. Contented, I lumbered along carrying the bag low, swinging my torso in rhythm and losing energy the closer we got the front door. For with every third step it was necessary to shift my torso and head like a pendulum to compensate the bag's upswing. That's how I noticed my mother's clinched fist competing with her mouth, the later resembling a healed scar as she twisted her purse strap. Despite my mother's hostility, lugging my bag the short distance was a small price to pay to reach freedom's door.

At the front porch, my mother squared her shoulders, took a deep breath and took out a new coin to rap solidly on the front door. She stepped back as the door opened and Ana's broad smile beamed at us. I dropped my bag and ran into Ana's open arms while my mother stood, ramrod straight, before greeting her mother with strict formality. Decorum that was instantly broken with news of my Uncle Theo.

"I got a letter from your brother," Ana announced.

A veil seemed to fall from my mother as she raised trembling fingertips to her chin in a gesture she only used in times of extreme emotion. Lines that had been etching into the sides of her mouth relaxed and she was transformed to the woman I'd known before the trouble with my daddy.

"Theo, Theo," she cried. "He's all right isn't he?"

Ana confirmed Uncle Theo was indeed "fine as new wine" and invited my mother to come inside to read the letter. Instantly, my mother reverted to her armored self, declining because of an appointment, I knew didn't exist. In a voice reserved for telemarketers, she said she would read the letter later, though I would have given almost anything to read about Uncle Theo now.

My Uncle Theo is the second of Ana's three children and an officer in the U.S. Navy Reserve. He went to college by agreeing to serve in the Navy and after graduating with honors, the only way I thought Uncle Theo did anything, he was assigned to a ship just as the Gulf War erupted.

Before he went to his ship, he came to Ana's house wearing his uniform. We all said how proud we were, especially Ana, but seeing her hug him, I noticed her mouth scrunched and her eyes squeezed shut. I thought it was because of how grand and handsome he looked in his white hat and dark double-breasted blue suit with the gold racing stripe and star on his sleeves. This meant he was an IN-sane, which was the only way I could pronounce his title of ensign back then. Everybody laughed except Uncle

Theo, who snuggled me into his arms with all his loving and put his hat on my head, which he called a cover. He told me I was the only one who knew what was going on.

Ana read aloud the letters he wrote from his ship, cruising in the Gulf of Oman, saying he saw fireworks, what he called the fighting, but not much. To Ana's relief he never got close enough to get burned and came home unharmed. When he returned, he wasn't an IN-sane, but a lieutenant junior grade and inactive reservist. He found a job as a teacher in a nearby town and in a short time people were talking about how well his students scored. These same kids vied for his class and their parents were glad. About the time I set a future goal to be in his class, he married my Aunt Michelle and a short time later gave me two more cousins.

When the Second Gulf War started there weren't enough soldiers to fight and reserves were called up, including the navy. Uncle Theo explained they needed sailors to bring groceries and supplies to the soldiers fighting hundreds of miles from the sea. So he was recalled to active duty. Which meant the reason to go wasn't so much a problem for Uncle Theo as it was telling Ana.

"No, not again," she cried. "Please God, oh please, not again."

Uncle Theo tried to underplay the seriousness of "that briar patch," as Papa called the overseas countries with names we both couldn't pronounce. My uncle insisted there was no need to push the panic button. That he would only be responsible for ferrying supplies and would be miles and miles away from any fighting. News that disappointed my cousin Tommy, but Ana wasn't buying any part of his argument.

"Why can't they find someone else?" she shouted. "Why you? I can't go through this again. I won't, I won't!"

As before, he came to Ana's house to show us his uniform, and I was disappointed with its drabness. Instead of a white hat, double-breasted blue coat and shiny shoes that I could make funny faces in their reflection. He wore a loose coat over a brown T-shirt and equally baggy pants, which were beige and spotted with dark spots that reminded me of the old tea my daddy poured from his thermos onto the concrete of our front driveway. A stain that marred the concrete for a month even after hard rains and after I sprayed it with a water hose.

Unlike his white hat with the crest with an eagle and anchor, his floppy hat looked like a cartoon character's with a string that kept the hat on his head on windy days. He demonstrated rolling it up and stuffing it into one of his big thigh pockets. Pants similar to the pictures of men in pantaloons I had seen in my Arabian Knights book.

"Perfect," cried Uncle Theo scooping me into his arms, "because that's where I'm going."

"I thought you were going to I-rack," I challenged.

"Iraq is the new name for Persia," he said swinging me to the ceiling. "Maybe I'll bring back a magic carpet or Aladdin's lamp."

How could he bring back carpets or lamps, I thought? He certainly wasn't wearing curled slippers. Just his pantaloons, or BDU pants as he called them, were tucked into the tops of velvet tan boots. The only way I knew he was a sailor was the "U.S. Navy" embroidered in black letters above the left pocket of his shirt.

Still, Uncle Theo looked tough and I pitied any Haj, the name he called the enemy soldiers, who crossed his way. But I couldn't help but laugh as he strutted around the living room like those skinny girls we'd watch on the fashion channel. The similarity ended as he stomped across the living room with wide strides and stopped suddenly looked at the ceiling with, to me, a perfect, super-model-pout-mouth. Taking off his four-pocket coat, he swung it over his shoulder, gripping his canvas belt with lips pursed as he jerked his head from one side to the other. All the time dead pan serious, before he skipped off to the bedroom with a giggle.

Rolling on the floor, I laughed so hard my sides ached while Papa howled and pounded the couch arm so hard small clouds of dust erupted. Ana didn't laugh or clap and when we had quieted down she told Uncle Theo to give her all his clothes and she would have them tailored and his boots fitted.

"This is for comfort more than style," she said on her way to the kitchen. "What the government won't do, a mother must."

For me, I wanted Uncle Theo to be in his classroom before I got to that grade. His class, I predicted, would be a treat, particularly after he explained, in language I could understand, glimpses of military life. He repeated that he was not assigned to a "combat unit," that is, he would not be near the fighting.

What I didn't understand was how my Uncle Theo, the smartest man I knew, could not find what Papa called a legal loophole, and not go. Those were options, he told me, he never considered because he given his word and would keep it. He said to do otherwise he could not face his family, students or even look himself in the mirror. Meantime, Ana was just as adamant that he had done more than his share.

"You've got your patriotism stir fried with ignorance," she said.

That might also have been why Uncle Theo's family, my Aunt Michelle, and my other cousins didn't visit or call Ana as much as we did. But despite the raw feelings, anytime one of our family received a letter or call from Uncle Theo, everything else was forgotten and, for a while, forgiven. In our family, any news about Uncle Theo was shared immediately without reservation.

CHAPTER 2

Ana provided my mother with what she called the Reader's Digest version of Uncle Theo's letter. When Ana finished, my mother closed her eyes, smiled thinly. Without moving from the spot, she nodded and offered Ana her visitor-from-another-country embrace. Ana didn't seem to notice and told me to take my bag to my mother's old bedroom.

Rounding the corner of the hallway to the bedroom, I heard a low rumble from the front door. It was a sound similar in pitch to the back throat growl uttered by Ana's white and black cat, Sophie when another cat dared enter her territory. As hard as it was to believe, I knew that sound came from my mother. Yet, only a short time ago, store clerks had to lean forward to hear my mother's requests. On occasion, I'd heard friends and strangers ask my mother to please speak up. Though, lately, she refused to repeat herself and no one could say they didn't hear her, particularly when my daddy was home. On the contrary, my mother's voice was even louder at Ana's house. She reminded me of television commercials that rose by three octaves higher than the program they sponsored. The commercial makers, like my mother, wanted the viewers' total attention. Both had loud messages, only I didn't know what my mother was trying to say.

Stopping to listen around the corner was not an option. While my mother had no trouble being heard, her hearing was equally acute. Particularly to stealthy footsteps on a hall she had grown up walking. So I gave the door knob a noisy twist and heaved my bag to the bed like a shot put before stepping into the hall. Still standing in the hall, I pulled the door closed with a slam and kicked off my shoes before sliding silently toward the front door.

"Don't worry about it, Mother," said my mother even sharper than usual. "We are sorting things out and will talk to a family counselor. For once, be on my side."

Ana's response was a low and controlled murmur in contrast to my mother's tone. I tiptoed nearly to the end of the hall as my mother's voice increased to the pitch of two ducks I'd seen fighting in a park over a piece of bread, before it rang out like a physical force.

"Jackie, come tell me goodbye," my mother barked.

Mouthing curses and nearly losing my balance, I slid in the opposite direction and swung the bedroom door open hard. Jabbing my feet into my sneakers, heels out, as the door banged against the wall. I clomped nosily toward the front and rounded the corner. My foot missed a step at the expression on my mother's face as she glared at Ana. She was double twisting the strap of her purse again, but noticing me, a mortified expression crossed her face before she bent like a pocket-knife and hugged me. My nostrils filled with her ginger and orange body wash fragrance, stirring memories of first days of school and being tucked into bed. That was the mother I remembered and wanted, so I hugged her tight while she pat-patted me before forcibly breaking our embrace.

"Have a good time now," she ordered. "Mind Ana and Papa."

Fingertip patting Ana's shoulder, she turned and walked toward my Uncle M.J., her younger brother, moving toward us with his son and my cousin Tommy. She paused long enough to hug Tommy and M.J. and strode to her car. Her car was out of the driveway before M.J. was inside the front door and, as usual, he carried my cousin's backpack. Wordlessly he placed Tommy's bag on the floor of the front hall. He hugged Ana and she patted him like my mother before ordering us kids to go to our room. Tommy kept his head down as he shuffled down the hall ignoring the bag.

"It's the bell boy's day off," said Ana dryly stopping Tommy in his tracks. "The butler and maid quit yesterday and the gardener and chauffeur are home sick. Welcome to the Jump Up and Do It Yourself Hotel."

Ana glared as M.J. avoided Tommy's gaze until the boy u-turned and grabbed his bag by a shoulder strap dragging it after him. With his head bent, only I could see the small smile pulling at his lips and a twinkle in his eye. Of course, this was standard behavior for Tommy since M.J., or I should say my Aunt Sonia, Tommy's mom, never forced him to do anything. She believed in reasoning with children to utilize what she called progressive parenting. What she called the only true path parents of the modern age should raise a child in an ever changing world.

I was prepared to escape these lectures with appropriate excuses of illness or previous appointments if she even mentioned her studies of Jean Piaget or Maria Montessori. I didn't have a clue what she was talking about and judging by the expressions around me, I wasn't alone. I could only wonder why those people were so important to Aunt Sonia. After all, they passed away before I was born, weren't related to her by blood or marriage. Yet, I could have won big money betting that sometime during any visit with Aunt Sonia she'd launch a diatribe about "today's kids."

To me those "learned people," as Aunt Sonia called them, were malicious ghosts, haunting the rest of us for a "mission statement." A plan to assure Tommy had a natural childhood. Whatever that was supposed to be! I could only scratch my head in confusion about as to what my childhood or anyone's, besides Tommy's, was supposed to be.

Not that Aunt Sonia didn't try to explain that the main parental role was to monitor environment and remove any impediment interfering with a child's natural development.

"He will be free," she said with a raised chin. "and fully provided for his self-directed learning activity."

Listening to this "tripe," as Ana called it, for even a little while, inspired most listeners to shuffle toward the door. She supported her calling by quoting men and women of science who had dedicated their lives to helping modern parents raise happy, healthy and mentally adjusted children without pain.

"These are scholars," she bragged, "whose offices are covered, floor to ceiling, with academic diplomas and certificates of recognition for all their great work."

Certificates didn't impress Ana. She said they could have been recipes or awards for perfect attendance or regular bowel movements. Besides, she added, these dead friends sounded more like ingredients for a stew than experts. It was a dish she had serious doubts as to the nutritional value of, particularly since the main ingredient was it was dangerous to "burden a child" with any unnecessary responsibility during their formative years.

"It's like leaving out salt pork from a pot of pinto beans," Ana said. "It might be healthier, but overall, it's a very unappetizing meal."

"This is not the industrial age," Aunt Sonia said. "Childhood shouldn't be a punishment, it should, no, it must be, an extra special time onto itself."

"Horse pucky," Ana snorted.

Undaunted, Aunt Sonia recounted studies that proved potential geniuses had been lost in their formative years as the direct result of improper parenting instead of an infusion of pure love. "Children don't come with instructions," Aunt Sonia lectured. "Therefore, we must use any constructive help to avoid the mistakes of the past that have ruined so many."

"Horse pucky on a broom stick" Ana said. "And that which doesn't kill me, only makes me stronger.

Aunt Sonia demanded Ana not talk like that in front of us kids. "Children's developing personalities are affected and shaped by the behaviors of parents," Aunt Sonia said. "Temperamentally-easy children also enable parents a sense of competency. You might even say good children often create good parents".

"But I would never say that," Ana said. "I raised three kids with love and a switch and they all turned out to be damn fine, better than good specimens, even if I do say so myself. Look at them, not one in jail, the nut house, or on drugs."

"But Ana…," began Aunt Sonia, eyes shinning in the way they always did when she was anticipating an argument.

"I might think different if your frog and wop had been here when I was about to pull my hair out when my kids were puking and shitting yellow. No they wrote about raising, while I actually did the job."

"B-b-but," Aunt Sonia stuttered.

"Besides, and you'll find this out, if you live long enough, when you become a so called expert at raising kids, you're out of business," Ana said. "But you guys never opened shop."

Aunt Sonia left and Papa pounded the arm of his recliner. "She nearly wet herself," Papa howled. He laughed so much he fell out of his chair and rolled on his back. I climbed on top of him and Ana couldn't keep from laughing as she swatted us with a magazine telling him to hush and act his age.

My mother's car was around the corner before M.J. hugged Ana and Tommy trudged after me, backpack slung over his shoulder. But once out of sight of the adults, Tommy grinned sheepishly, knowing what to do with his bag. To say otherwise was like saying he didn't know where the bathroom was or the cold sodas in Ana's refrigerator.

In our room Tommy beamed, as he had again successfully tested and reassured himself of the consistency of order always present in Ana's house. It was a commodity Tommy rarely found at his parent's home since he was just as likely to get a new toy for admitting he broke something as punishment, but not so with Ana. He knew, even when it was rough, what to expect. For his part he was glad his father said nothing in defense of Tommy's defiance.

We made settling-in-noise in the bedroom as M.J.'s gravelly voice could be heard in the backyard.

"Mom, things are under control. All right? We're working it out. OK? We need some time, a little break. Understand? Try not to worry about it. Would you? Put the issue on hold. Sonia will pick him up Sunday. All right?"

Ana answered with the same low tone she used with my mother and added something else unheard.

"So, Theo is OK," toned M.J. in the same too loud voice.

We didn't hear Ana's reply and M.J. didn't call Tommy to say good-bye as he let the front screen door slam behind him. We appeared in the front hall with Ana looking after him, her right hand laying flat against the wall. The nails of her left hand dug into the top of the front door while the muscles of her bare forearms bunched as if she were preventing the hallway from falling in.

Without looking around she said, "Papa filled the pool. Go put on your swim suits."

CHAPTER 3

Ana, my maternal grandmother, came into the world as Jaclyn Kay Cooper. As her first granddaughter, I was bestowed the honor of her name, or almost. I got a J for Jo, instead of a K and Carmichael from my daddy. Nothing unusual in that, I was told Ana had many names during the course of her life. Though, I was warned to never repeat most of them. Together, we shared her shorter "Jackie."

"It's a good name," she always said. "So good there was more than enough for two women in this family."

As for matriarchal titles she absolutely refused to be called grandma, mawmaw or meemaw. Monikers she associated as "old lady with regrets."

Another reason she insisted we call her Ana, was that it was a modified version of Nana, one more word I couldn't pronounce when I was small, and came out "Ana." This mispronunciation was considered so cute that the rest of the family used it by habit as much as I did. However, our names were similar in other ways. She was more of a sister than a grandmother and not only because of our physical appearances either. Still, she never left any doubt as to who was the kid and who was the adult. Most of the time, anyway.

At Ana's house Tommy and I shared a mutual bond similar to refugees from different theaters of the same world war. We shared that mutual bond at Ana's house, our personal neutral zone or little Switzerland, as Papa called it. Though, after reading about neutral countries, I would have compared it to Argentina for climate and hospitality. Regardless of geography Ana's was our address for comfort and escape from the self-destruction of our parents' marriages. It was where, traditionally, when bad words flew, we were brought and everyone agreed was the best place.

Nestled in its conventional neighborhood, Ana's house was anything but ordinary. Nor was I alone in my conclusion since home and yard made tongues wag. Some, like Emily, the oldest daughter of Ana's neighbor, were beyond praise.

Though older than us, Emily always appeared when we visited. In the coming years, she spent less time with us and more with friends her own age. Yet, she never lost her fascination for Ana's backyard or missed the opportunity to pass the back fence.

One afternoon Emily stood with us at the base of one of the two live oaks watching a powerful afternoon summer storm fill the sky. Clouds dimmed from dove gray to the color of blackberries while forked lightning illuminated their centers and a rising wind shook the treetops above our heads. She would tell us later that it was that very moment she finally found the right word to describe her feeling for Ana's backyard.

"Mystical," she screamed, throwing her head back and stretching her finger tips skyward while thunder shook the ground under our feet and lightning seemed to rip the sky to shreds. When another thunderclap boomed so close it shook leaves loose from the top branches, we ran into the rain drops squealing in delighted terror to the back door, drenched before we could reach the step.

Emily was the first girl, though not the last, to ask permission to be married in Ana's backyard. Tommy and I witnessed this first of many ceremonies from the security of our tree house that Papa had built between two live oaks. At the conclusion of the ceremony, we showered the couple with flower petals from Ana's garden as guests gathered for the reception on Ana's half moon porch.

Just as Ana left nothing to chance in the back yard, Papa was equally meticulous to the particular trees for our tree house, taking days walking with his head thrown back. This was not as easy a decision as it might sound, either, considering that, in addition to the two monarchs, a dozen other trees in the back yard were equally potential candidates. We could only stare open mouthed at the immense joy Papa took as he completed the project.

"You would have thought he was making it for himself," Ana said laughing. "I thought he had a girl friend up there."

The result was a tree house that was the envy of any boy or girl, and more than one adult who saw it. There was room enough inside for five kids, two adults, and a cat, and covered with a green plastic roof along with a gabled front porch. Entrance was gained through a trap door in the floor's center via a rope ladder. A rope, pulley, and bucket let us hoist up bulky items from the ground to the porch.

PVC pipe offered the luxury of at least a trickling faucet that drained into a converted cook pot for a sink and dispersed to the farthest branches. Yet, we still had to come down to use the bathroom in the house. A feature I believe Papa left out at Ana's insistence.

From that tree house we got a bird's eye view of Ana's gardens and the carpet of Bermuda grass. The flower garden to my left hugged the red wooden fence that separated the yard from the alley. It took up that entire corner of the yard where rows of azalea blooms, camellias and blood red roses competed to produce the brightest colors. Nearby trumpet vines draped the fence with their bright green vines, seedpods thick as a baby's fist, and orange blooms like miniature jack-o-lanterns. By contrast, the opposite side of the yard was a vegetable garden with its annual harvest of corn, onions, beans and tomatoes.

Of course certain critics, in particular the ladies' city's tour of homes committee were caustic in their criticism. Whatever their reasons they offered, "tsk, tsk" slim chance of an otherwise lovely home of being listed on the tour of homes.

"Those old gals have a better chance of getting crushed ice in hell," Ana growled. "I nursed those gardens like my kids and I don't recall any those old hens offering a spare tit or a gooseneck hoe when I needed it."

Roaring with laughter, Papa slapped his knee and said Ana's attitude was the result of growing up on her grandfather's Texas Hill Country ranch. She'd always taken obstacles by the tail and horns and made them into opportunities. Which gave him the opportunity to tell a story I never got tired of hearing, about Ana as a teenager, not much older than me. A time when she brought down a 500-pound hog with a single shot from her grandfather's Winchester Commemorative rifle while wearing only a nightgown.

"How it got in my night gown, I'll never know," said Ana on cue changing her voice to a high, nasal tone as she gyrated her eyebrows and held a pen or some other long object above her head and waggled her free fingers. She was supposed to be imitating someone called Groucho Marx, but she was quicker to dismiss the story in a normal voice.

"Porky was plowing up the front yard and I nearly became a Jackie-burger," Ana said. "I didn't have too many choices."

Ana still had the Winchester Commemorative rifle, too, and as guns go, I considered it very pretty, in a rough, shiny, old time, neat sort of way. Along with Tommy I always got excited when that rifle was brought out. With its butt on the floor, I found the end was no higher than my underarm standing just over three-feet long. It held five "special" bullets in the tube magazine located under an 18-inch barrel. I measured it with a yard stick and used pencil and paper to figure the individual length of those special bullets were 3.6 inches long. Of course in my short life that was the closest I came to the actual size that didn't include occasional glimpses of actual bullets. Rounds taken briefly from their box and held aloft between my grandfather's thick fingers in the time it took me to blink seven times.

This was after Papa's friend brought two boxes of Commemorative ammunition when he stopped by one evening. I happened to be there as Papa took the two long red boxes. His friend explained they were part of a cache of a dozen different bullets he'd won at an auction. Since the friend didn't have a gun that shot Commemorative bullets, he gave them as a gift, though Papa tried to pay him, and the friend refused. Papa graciously accepted them before opening a box and extracting a single bullet. He held it to the light and I saw it was as long and broad as his forefinger. Sighing deeply, he thanked his friend before slipping the round back into the box's plastic holder. I never saw those Commemorative bullets again.

Later, when I told Tommy, he was furious that I'd seen even that one because it was a rare treat for Tommy or me to touch the Commemorative. I loved to run my fingers over the checkered wood of the fore grip and stock. For luck, I tweaked my thumb on the cute little side ring and made faces at my murky reflection shimmering on the dark barrel. On the other side, where the bullets were loaded, was the portrait of the cowboy etched on the silver surface who, in the right light, seemed to smile and wink.

The rifle was kept in a case in my grandparent's closet and only brought out on special occasions. The unspoken rule was the Commemorative was not to be used to hunt or shoot targets. Papa explained it was a one of a kind whose value decreased if it were fired. A concept that confused Tommy and me, for what good was having something if you couldn't use it?

"The Commemorative was made for aficionados," Papa said. "People who pay big money to hang guns, like these, in their collections. The same way a museum might pay for a valuable statue or painting."

This idea confused me since everybody knew pictures were hung on walls and statues set on coffee tables to left alone. Rifles were made to be shot, so it really made no difference since Ana had already fired it. What if it ate a few more bullets? Still, I didn't want to shoot the Commemorative. Its importance to me lay in the fact it was Ana's gun. It had been given to her by her grandfather as a wedding gift. Only it wasn't given when she married Papa.

The Commemorative was a connection to my great-great-great-grandfather, our royal family jewel from another time and a direct link to the present. The rifle had been given to Ana's grandfather at a special ceremony because his daddy had been a sheriff back in the cowboy days. Only the Commemorative wasn't from another century, as I sometimes thought Ana was, and it was not around when the pilgrims, conquistadors, or cowboys and Indians owned America.

Beyond its historical significance were the technical features that intrigued me, particularly in the way it chambered a bullet into the breech from its tube magazine. A process made into a visual extravagance when our nearly seven-foot tall grandfather stood in the back yard. Well away from the house and any other obstacles, he held the rifle in his right hand and threw it forward, with his fingers curled in the big D-ring lever. The momentum twirled the rifle in a complete circle between his arm and chest. In theory this revolution loaded and cocked the rifle.

"It's like the state lottery," Papa laughed, "designed to impress the ignorant and tax the stupid."

Jacking the rifle's lever with the rolling action opened the trap door on top of the rifle and peeled a bullet from the magazine at the same time. Yet, as the rifle turned upside down, even temporarily, there was nothing to keep the bullet from dropping to the ground. Despite this knowledge it was always fun to watch Papa twirl the Commemorative in a circle and it always made me take a step back. By contrast Ana performed a half-nelson version of the trick, a method that Papa assured us would load a bullet into the chamber.

Its bullets were the equivalent of fairies or ghosts to us, and why Tommy made it his quest to find the mythical ammunition and fire this legendary weapon. During each of his visits, with or without me, he was meticulous if not relentless in his search. He whispered to me how he believed with all his heart there was a secret ammo stash, supported by the discovery of an empty red bullet box.

Fortunately, when he found an actual bullet, it was the wrong caliber. Yet for Tommy it was the granting of a genie's wish. It measured the prescribed three inches and matched the red box bullet I'd told him about seeing in Papa's hand.

He hid his prize, even from me, though I knew something was up. He was just too excited and could hardly contain himself. He also didn't hear Ana's approach as he unsuccessfully jabbed that wrong and too big bullet through the Commemorative's side slot. Ana yanked him squealing to his feet with bullet and Commemorative clattering to the floor. She jack-walked him down the hall to the kitchen and, with each step smacked a wooden spoon on his bottom, disregarding his false howls of pain. At the kitchen table she ordered me to pull out a chair and. without being told. Tommy plopped down.

She disappeared and returned carrying the Commemorative and the bogus bullet. Leaning the rifle against the counter edge, she placed the bullet a foot to its side and ordered Tommy to move his chair to within an arm's length of both. From this position he could only see the bullet and rifle, and for the rest of the afternoon he was forbidden to speak or move.

Of course, I was as much a prisoner as Tommy was, since he was the only one I could play with. In this case, I was also his trustee. If he had to go to the bathroom, I had to escort him and wait outside until he was finished. It was the dullest and most silent afternoon I could remember until Aunt Sonia arrived.

She was not a happy camper, as Papa liked to say, and she didn't wait to hear the whole story before she grabbed and dragged him to the door. Silently, Ana watched them go as Aunt Sonia vowed never to bring her child back to such a household.

Her threat didn't last and Tommy's exile was temporary. Yet, when Tommy came to visit again, it was like nothing had happened and he stayed as far as possible away from Ana's bedroom. Not that it stopped me from discovering the Commemorative was in a new locked case.

In an effort to make peace my mother invited Aunt Sonia to go to Wichita Falls for lunch and shopping. Tommy and I were also invited to enjoy a lunch that included chocolate milkshakes with whipped cream and cherry on top. By the end of the day, the car trunk was filled with purchases and Tommy and I lay in the security of the back seat. Both of us were grateful to stretch out after walking all day. Tommy scrunched on the floorboard and I, being taller, lay face down on the back seat, though I wasn't sleepy.

I soon reaped the reward of my sleeping appearance when I heard the compression of material on the front seat and knew someone was leaning over to check the backseat. The radio was turned down, the herald that adults wanted to talk and my senses turned to full alert.

No one spoke for a full minute until Aunt Sonia asked why Ana kept the Commemorative. It was obviously a dangerous threat to her grandchildren, she reasoned, and any reasonable person would get rid of it. Besides, she added, she had heard the rifle would bring a lot of money, even if it had been fired.

I felt the car swerve slightly, coupled with another crossing of the front seat for a double check that the back seat passengers were asleep. Tommy I knew was out, since he could fall asleep anywhere. My head was turned to the seat where I was careful not to move.

"Besides being a family heirloom," my mother began, "the Commemorative is more than just a rifle. It's a talisman, a symbol of taking back control of her life."

"From whom?" My aunt whispered.

"The sperm donor," my mother replied flatly.

"The who?" said Aunt Sonia voice rising and catching herself from almost shouting.

"My biological father," said my mother with more control, "Momma's first husband. She called him Ed, but in my mind, he'll always be the sperm donor, because that was the only good thing he ever did."

I didn't know what a sperm donor was, other than something special, but talk about being glad my head was turned to the seat. My eyes felt as if they would pop out against the seat.

"Theo wasn't even a year old and I had started kindergarten," my mother said. "Ed worked on a cattle ranch."

Even at an early age my mother knew her biological father was lazy and cruel by nature. He was also a liar and a thief. Worse, the ranch owner and the men he worked with, knew it.

"I heard the boss yell one day, 'Your wife could do a better job,'" my mother laughed. "And she did too. Momma moved cattle, mended fences and everything in between."

Rather than appreciate her help, the sperm donor resented his wife's assistance. He pointed out any short-coming, no matter how meager, and only when the boss wasn't around. He never thanked her, just emphasized that if he had a little help he could get some things done.

"His pastimes were complaining about his boss, drinking beer and beating his wife. He didn't need an excuse for either, though his justification for the beating, was that she made him do it."

Whatever reason, it was a miracle, or lack of one, when he left, which was to go drinking. Returning home late, he staggered into the house crashing into anything in his path. Woe if someone was not awake, a door closed, a toy on the floor, or no hot food was on the table.

"That was time of the black dog," my mother said, "of open handed blows and screams and never getting out of bed when that man came home."

These were Ana's instructions, but that couldn't stop the little girl who became my mother from listening to the beating in the nearby bedroom. Heavy snores were her signal to creep out and help her mother to the bathroom. The following morning the man clomped into the kitchen, dressed in the clothes he'd slept in, and whining apologies while trying to make nice with the children. Theo suckled his mother's bruised breast staring with big eyed fear.

The scene repeated itself the following night and the next. My mother recalled that, even at that age, she knew the violence would never stop and something had to be done, or he was going to hurt Ana, bad.

A short time later, my mother remembered playing with her toy cars in the dirt beside their car and keeping an eye on Theo in the back seat. Nearby her mother had completed another of the chores the Ed could not do. When she finished, she told Ed she had to go feed her kids and couldn't do it with all the men around. The men looked away, peeking from beneath their hat brims. Looking up from her play, my mother noticed Ed stiffen and knew he wouldn't have tolerated any disrespect if they were alone. Glancing quickly at other men, Ed shrugged indifferently and told her to hurry back, if she knew what was good for her.

Ana said she would and drove to the rent house provided by the ranch to made a quick supper, but didn't bother with the dishes or to go back.

"She pulled out suitcases and said we were going to visit grandma," my mother said. "She told me to help Theo."

Being early winter the sun was setting as Ana finished loading. She stuffed bags and stuff into the trunk as if the house were on fire. When she closed the trunk my mother said Ana stood smiling a look of relief, and hope on her face. That is until they heard the unmistakable sound of an approaching truck.

"She grabbed Theo and told me to follow her," my mother said. "That was the one time I know I was truly afraid. I knew he would hurt her, he would hurt all of us to teach her a lesson."

The sun was nearly down when Ana closed the front door. With a strength that surprised my mother Ana pulled the living room couch away from the wall and directed my mother to get behind. She handed her Theo and told her to be still and keep the baby quiet. Behind the couch, my mother felt as much as heard movement of other furniture before the rasp of locks being thrown on the front and back doors made her ask what was happening. Ana shushed her that it was time to play the quiet game and mind Theo.

"Then the lights went out and even Theo got still."

It wasn't too long, my mother recalled, before she heard the brake to an unsteady halt in the front yard followed by curses filling the night. Footsteps resounded on the front porch punctuated by the unmistakable crunch of a toy being broken in their path.

"I felt like the little pig in the fairy tale whose house was built of sticks," my mother said. "Only I would have preferred the wolf from the fairy tale."

A gentle testing of the door graduated to violent vibrations and hoarse shouts. Soon door pounding threatened to take it off its hinges. My mother remembered how Ana had warned Ed if he broke the door, they'd lose the cash security deposit they'd been required in advance before they could occupy the house. Money was always short, my mother explained, and Ana tried to protect even the pittance they had. Using this knowledge to his advantage, Ed threatened major damage if she didn't let him in.

It was at that point the man outside the door said in a nearly civilized voice that he needed to get to bed, so he could be ready for work the next morning. An oath he had always made with a crossed heart that he would be good. At least until the door was unlocked and he burst in and sent Ana across the room with his fist.

"He always made those promises," my mother said, " and momma fell for it every time."

But Ana didn't open the door and Ed's demeanor eroded as he shouted that Ana was already in trouble for not coming back to work. He reminded her of what happened the last time she defied him and rattled the door with threats of if she knew what was good for her she would open up like yesterday. In response Ana demanded to know why he was drunk even earlier than usual.

"None of your business, woman," mimicked my mother in a slurred voice. "Jackie darling, my old buddy Denny here gave me $300 for the Winchester. You know we need that money for the kids."

"It was more like beer for him and Denny," my mother recalled, "and telling mother was a very big mistake."

Ana hadn't bothered to pack her personal belongings. She had packed only the essentials in the car. The Commemorative was still in the house.

"My grandpa's gun," Ana said. "That was a special presentation he got from his daddy."

"Yeah, and now it's going to bring a fine cash reward, so open up," slurred my mother in imitation. "Let's give Denny his gun, then we'll all go out for ice cream."

"That gun is worth ten times that amount," Ana answered. "It isn't yours to sell, grandpa gave it to me."

"Ever hear of community property," Ed crowed. "Even my old buddy Denny here knows that much about the law, don't ya?"

"Sure do," answered a man's squeaky voice my mother always associated with the squish-pop sound of a beer can. "Come on darling, give me my gun right now, pretty please, especially since I already gave him the money. I got places to go and people to see."

"Then you can get your money back," replied Ana in a shaky voice. "My gun isn't for sale."

"I've spent it," moaned Ed before catching himself. "Jackie, just open the dammed door wide enough to hand out the dammed gun, then we'll go get ice cream."

Ana's breath, my mother recalled, was like she was carrying a heavy load as the man at the door howled and rattled the front of the house.

"Know what, forget ice cream and forget you," Ed screamed. "Get that dammed gun right now, and get Theo dressed and ready to spend some time with his old man."

"Theo," said Ana in a voice my mother had never heard before. "Theo isn't even out of diapers, what on earth would you expect to do with him?"

"I'm losing what little patience I have woman," Ed said. "What I do with my son is my business, open the damned door, give me the gun and my boy in that order, or you'll wish to God you were never born."

"All right," Ana replied. "Denny, you like my gun?"

Oddly, Ana's voice was without the quavering warble of fear my mother always associated with these incidents.

"Sure do," Denny cackled. "That's what I'm here for, my property."

"All righty, just one little bitty minute," sang Ana jubilantly.

As if to hurry her along the front door rattled in a machine gun staccato. Ana returned and the sound of her voice made children and men jump.

"All right, I've got it."

With those words my mother remembered feeling baby Theo's heart pounding in unison with her own. Squeezing her eyes shut, she hugged him tight and bit her lip to keep from screaming as she prayed for someone to save her mother from the awfulness to come.

"It felt like even the house held its breath," my mother recalled, "I just tried not to cry."

"Now open this damned door, you stupid bitch," bellowed Ed after a short pause and wood rattling. "Do it right now Jackie, today, this very second, you hear me? I'm not going to say it again."

It became quiet inside and out and my mother remembered tensing for the expected sliding lock sounds. Instead, she jumped at the unexpected double chuckle of the Commemorative's lever being worked from the middle of the room.

"What was that?" Ed cried. "Dammit, what the hell was THAT?"

"Potato chips, bet you can't eat just one " Ana said. "So Denny, want a demonstration of this gun?"

"I told you I'm not kidding," burbled Ed rattling the door again. "Open up or I will break this door down."

"Talk, talk, talk," Ana teased. "Break it down already, the deposit's gone, just like you and so are we. What have I got to lose?"

In a drunken whisper, Ed ordered Denny to go to the back of the house and climb through the window into my room.

"Now Denny, you be careful," chided Ana in a sweet voice. "Don't trip over anything and hurt yourself."

Foot falls reverberated through the thin walls outside the house, followed by howls of pain punctuated by curses echoing from my bedroom. The floorboards shook in unison with Denny's moans while Ed shouted for him to shut up and turn on a light.

"Please do that Denny, dear," Ana sang. "I'll see you soooo much better, and keep in mind that a hollow-point through your liver is only half as bad as it sounds.

"You won't shoot anybody," shouted Ed over Denny's squeals. "Even if you had bullets, which I know you don't."

"You don't say?" Ana said. "What about the box Grandpa gave me on my last visit? That was the trip you wouldn't come on because you said you were tired of my grandpa riding you about being a bum. Well, he knew you and that's why he gave me that box of shells, or didn't I show you those bullets?" Clucking her tongue she added, "we've had so much fun, the thought must have slipped my mind."

No reply came from the porch as Ana continued in a tone like she was comparing cake recipes.

"Grandpa was concerned with this country abounding with varmints and rattlesnakes, " Ana said. "Still, you probably have nothing to worry about and there's a chance I'm lying my stupid bitch ass off and have no ammo. So, how can I kill you? You only have to come in to find out."

There was an emotion in those words my mother said she wouldn't be able to put a name to until years later.

"What was it?" Aunt Sonia whispered.

"Take a cup of utter disgust and add two heaping tablespoons of loathing! She had nothing to lose! Even if the gun wasn't loaded, Ed would have walked into a tiger's den, and I think he knew it too."

"It only holds five rounds," Ed argued. "You might get off one shot before I rip your stupid head off."

"I needed only one bullet for that other pig," Ana responded. "By the way Denny, this gun is so easy to reload."

Beyond the walls, my mother heard heated words, punctuated with curses, and growing in volume until Ana interrupted.

"Did I mention I called the sheriff," said Ana and the argument stopped.

"The sheriff," Denny yelped, "why, what for?"

A fresh chorus of pain resounded from my bedroom followed by the sound of a window shutter and the sound of a mass hitting the earth outside.

"Why did you do something so stupid?" Ed whined. "I knew you were dumb, but this is beyond brainless. Did you eat a double bowl of dumb ass this morning?"

Ana didn't reply and my mother heard Ed laughing at his own joke accompanied by back or palm slaps.

"Don't you remember this is my house?" He crowed with new confidence. "I'm the one that pays the rent, that's my car, those are my children."

"I told that nice dispatcher, a really nice woman, that two prowlers are trying to break in and I feared for the safety of my children. She said a deputy is on his way."

"I'm your husband and their father," Ed whined.

"Now there's the problem," Ana said. "Is that really you? Who's to say in the dark and do real husbands and fathers break the doors down to their own houses?"

For an answer more curses followed until Ana interrupted them again.

" What were you going to do with Theo?"

"Let him experience some quality time with his old pappy and good buddy Denny."

The open fraud of his words induced my mother to hug Theo even tighter to prevent him from being taken.

"I'm sure the deputy will understand," Ana said. "Besides you're home early."

"Fine, bitch, we'll all wait here until the deputy shows up, then you'll have to let me in. After all, in this country, a man has rights."

"Denny darling," Ana called. "You might want to check on that stuff in the storage room in the garage."

"Stuff," Ed squeaked. "What stuff? I warned you to stay out of the garage."

"How'd she know?" Demanded Denny, his voice rising. "You said it was safe."

"You know, I might never have looked if it wasn't for that warning," Ana replied. "But I found lots and lots of boxes with expensive price tags from a store I shop in town." She paused before continuing. "In fact there's boxes from lots of stores, some from here to Fort Worth. There's also that green leafy stuff behind the garage beyond those trees. Knee high, ripe, full of oil and ready for harvest."

Denny cursed Ed to give it up and clear out. Both stopped arguing at the sound of an approaching vehicle.

"All right darling, but mind you, this ain't over, not by a damn sight," Ed called. "There's going to be a come-to-Jesus- discussion real soon, you can take that to the bank. I promise that on your sorry life, sweet little Jackie girl."

"Write when you get work," Ana replied. "Just don't use me as a reference."

They left, my mother recalled, slamming truck doors and startling Theo to nearly jump out of her arms. Unable to contain his wails any longer, the baby boy howled with the squealing tires.

"Before I knew it, momma pulled the couch away from the wall," my mother said, "she took Theo and gave him a breast."

"What did the police do?" Aunt Sonia demanded.

"The deputy seemed to take forever. I could tell by his heavy footsteps on the front porch that he wasn't happy. When momma opened the door, I will never forget the look on his face as long as I live."

My mother giggled, the way she always did, when she thought something was really funny.

"The door opened and the deputy stood there, belly out, back bowed like he was about to deliver a serious talk. Only before he could get it out, his mouth puckered and his cheeks flushed beet red as he stammered for something to say," my mother said. "Nobody could blame him, either, not with Theo on momma's bare breast and me dressed only in shorts and hanging on her skirts."

The lower buttons of the deputy's khaki shirt looked as if they were about to pop off, if not that they were reinforced by a wide gun belt separating his shirt from pressed blue jean pants. He gripped a big flash light in his left hand and used it to push a wide brimmed straw hat back from his forehead. With more coughing, he put his other hand over his mouth and cleared his throat.

Oblivious to Theo's suckling, or the man's embarrassment, Ana told the deputy about the burglars, only leaving out their identities. The deputy mumbled he'd have a look around and moved off the porch turning on the flashlight in the same motion. My mother stood in the living room, her attention drawn to the open bedroom doors where the flashlight's beam danced across the open windows of her parents' bedroom. Curious she went to the bedroom she shared with Theo to get a favorite toy just as the deputy appeared through the open window.

"He smiled with tobacco stained teeth and warned me not to leave my window open," she said. "I wanted to say I hadn't opened it, but he was gone to the other side of the house before I could say a word."

Ana finished feeding Theo and wrapped the Commemorative in a baby blanket just as the deputy knocked on the door. Seeing Theo dozing on the couch and the breast covered, the deputy smiled easily and said he'd found no sign of the intruder. Ana thanked him and asked if could wait long enough for her to finish loading the car so she could follow him to town.

He nodded and took the diaper bag from Ana's arm while she cradled Theo in one arm and wedged the blanket wrapped bundle under her other elbow. The deputy laid the bag in the back seat as Ana laid the Commemorative between the driver's and Theo's car seat. My mother remembered standing to one side holding her toy while Ana talked almost nonstop, strapping Theo into his car seat, prattling about how unsafe it was to be alone.

With another bag in the floor board and all children settled, the deputy got into his squad car and took the lead with Ana following not two car lengths behind him. Their mid size car wasn't made for the hard packed dirt road that meandered to a paved road at the bottom of a hill. My mother stood on the backseat looking behind and into the darkness where she imagined the glimmer of the eyes of monsters, their shapes hovering just beyond the edge of the headlights.

"I told momma about the monsters' eyes and she told me to sit down because it was a known fact that monsters couldn't catch a moving car, just like they couldn't get under bed covers," my mother said. "I think that's why I sleep so well in a car's backseat, even today, because I know the monsters can't get me back there."

At the intersection to the paved road, the car bounced over a bump and my mother tumbled to the floor board. She climbed back up and stood in the seat looking behind and into the darkness that swallowed the road. What wasn't her imagination were the vehicle headlights moving toward the direction of the rent house.

"Don't ask me how, but I knew it was him, and I was so grateful we were headed in the opposite direction," my mother said. "I told momma about the lights and she said lay down and go to sleep or I might end up like that woman in the Bible who turned to salt."

My mother went to sleep and remembered waking with the sun on her face and pulling to a stop in the front yard of Ana's grandfather.

"That was such a long time ago and you seem to remember so many details for a girl barely in kindergarten, " scoffed my aunt, pausing to let this logic sink in. "I have colleagues who would conclude that in order to mask what really happened your mother told you this fantastic story repeatedly, and to herself, as a vindication for leaving her husband and your biological father."

The seat fabric creaked the way it does when a body leans against the passenger car door and I recognized a familiar fingernail tapping the headrest.

"She's repeated that story many times, hasn't she?" Aunt Sonia said with her all knowing tone. "The Lot's wife simile was clever, though she chose to leave out the final chapter of that story."

"No, momma never spoke about that night again, "replied my mother in a cold voice, "and your colleagues might also find it interesting how events, like losing a parent and your home, can sear themselves forever into a child's memory."

"Ana divorced him," said Aunt Sonia quickly changing subjects. "Did he try to get custody of you kids."

"Yes and no," my mother replied, "shortly after we left, he went to jail and refused to sign the divorce decree. Momma paid a deputy sheriff to read it to him. Later, Ed called to 'express his love' and say the divorce papers weren't legal because he didn't listen."

He also never responded to several court summons either, she added, saying he had parental rights and threatened to drag us back from the ranch. Only Ana's grandpa got on the phone and told Ed if he showed his face within 50 miles he could count on being hung face down from a fence post as warning and example to other varmints.

"But he provided for you?" Aunt Sonia asked,

"My mother told me he cleaned out their bank account and sold everything that wasn't chained down."

"Everything?" Aunt Sonia said.

"Anything," my mother confirmed, "but they had to finalize their taxes together. He told her if she'd meet him to sign some papers, he'd return her jewelry she left behind. He stipulated she had to bring Theo and me to see him and Ana's grandpa wasn't invited."

"How'd that go?" Aunt Sonia whispered. "Surely he knew the law was on her side?"

"Surely, you jest," sneered my mother with false mockery, "that was about the time momma heard that Ed's drinking buddy, Denny, was much more, he was his special friend."

"Special friend," repeated Aunt Sonia with my lack of comprehension, "what does that mean?"

"Extra special, close and personal as in the ultra Biblical nature," muttered my mother acidly. "Poor momma was so ignorant about such things back then, she had to ask someone to explain the concept of men with men. She thought it was physically impossible."

She found this out from a ranch hand she'd befriended. He called and told her Ed and Denny were in deep financial and legal trouble. He heard them talking about a guy in a bar who'd told Ed about a law requiring mothers to pay fathers for any kids they had together. Ed planned to take us until Ana paid what he thought she owed. It was also a physical opportunity to repay Ana with a beating, the excuse being Ana tried to steal his children.

"Which was the main reason the ranch hand called. He had heard Ed say if he couldn't get money from momma, then he would sell Theo and me in Mexico."

Ana called Ed and cancelled the meeting without explanation or an offer to set up another and told him to mail the tax papers to her. Talk about mad, my mother laughed. Later, Ed called back long distance, reversed the charges, and bragged how he'd hocked her jewelry and spent the money. Ana told him if he didn't want to deal with the Feds, then send her the tax documents and hung up on him in mid-curse.

"I had just walked into the hall when she slammed the phone," my mother said. "She looked like she was about to cry and swept me into her arms saying, 'It's a small price for something so precious!'"

My mother explained that Ana took a long time to recover from that part of her life, and for some reason, she blamed herself. Lying there, I couldn't understand, since Ana hadn't done any wrong. My mother added that with help from family and friends Ana eventually got her head together. She enrolled in a state training course that helped her land a job.

"That's how she met Papa, my real daddy," my mother said. "That's the closest explanation I can give as to why she keeps that gun."

"Do you think she would have shot your, I mean the...those men?" Aunt Sonia stammered. "Is...was she capable?"

My mother was quiet for a long time and I thought she was ignoring Aunt Sonia.

"Papa used to hunt or shoot targets with different guns. He taught me and the boys how to shoot guns. Momma always went along, but we never took the Commemorative. Yet, any time Papa had to stay away overnight and I 'd come to say good night, the Commemorative was always lying just under her bed, within easy reach, just like her hugs and kisses."

"So," Aunt Sonia said. "What's your point?"

"Make your own conclusion about Ana and the Commemorative," said my mother turning up the radio. "I never saw Ed again and can't say I even remember what he looks like."

"Studies have shown that behavior of that nature is self destructive and associated with insanity," Aunt Sonia lectured. "If you asked me I believe your mother should seek professional help. There are some wonderful experts in the field that have made strides...."

That was when I "woke up" with a hundred questions I couldn't ask.

CHAPTER 4

On a very cold Sunday morning when I was small our church choir sang "A Mighty Fortress" before we went to Ana and Papa's for dinner. I remembered how clean and warm the inside of the house was. So I always associated that hymn and lyrics with my grandmother's house.

It was my sanctuary since nothing was secure about the rest of my world. My parents' marital tiffs could erupt at any time and in small town tradition, everyone knew each other's nasty business, sometimes before the central parties involved knew all the details themselves. These "unfortunate misunderstandings" as they were dubbed over morning coffee and telephone conversation had precedence seconded only by weather.

Neighbors passed on sordid details in a manner the national weather service would have envied. Our family situation seemed to have the allure of an overflowing toilet, a prime topic, as long as it was someone else's toilet. With talk unabated and growing like a mountain avalanche, my classmates parents took steps to insulate their children from contamination of character deficiency. Girls and boys I'd known since kindergarten got quiet at my approach. Others, less familiar, laughed behind their hands, eyeballing me, whispering into their neighbor's ears. The honest few were direct and brutally invasive.

"I can't play with you anymore," said Joyce, whom I'd sat beside in the first grade. "I can't come over to your house and you can't come to mine."

"Why, what did I do?" I called. "What are you saying?"

Without answering, she ran back to a gaggle of girls that included her twin sister, Jerri. They'd watched us from beneath the eaves of a building.

"You told her?" Demanded Jerri in a tone confirming an order had been carried out more than a question answered.

Joyce bobbed her head and a twitter of laughter erupted without anyone looking toward me. They chattered like chickens and I was about to drag Joyce across the play ground to teach everyone a lesson about treating me or anybody this way. Then I saw Mrs. Planter, or the Weed as we called her behind her back. She was our teacher and was standing in the shade of a nearby building. Her salt and pepper hair was pulled back into a traditional schoolmarm's bun that couldn't distract as she scanned the playground through bottle thick glasses. She was dressed in a red pantsuit that hung on her wrath thin figure like a crumpled wrapper. Her sour expression never changed as she glanced my way.

Thankfully, the Weed was the only teacher I knew that wasn't aware of my home life. She had been lauded as one of the best teachers in the school district mainly because she'd been around longer than some of the buildings. For those in the upper grades the happiest day they could remember had been the last day in her class. She wasn't disposed to treat bus drivers any better. This was probably the reason I overheard discussions of how she should have retired a hundred years earlier. They said they heard she was holding out another year for the passage of the state legislature's fat teacher's retirement package.

"The school board," muttered one man, "should make her retire and would have if the Weed didn't have something else besides lint in her pocket." All agreed she had two faces: one for visiting parents and colleagues and the other for bus drivers, kids and stray cats.

Officially, her self-proclaimed mission was producing students well prepared to take on the next grade and, ultimately, higher aims. That meant college and only if the student could meet her canons of excellence. Those standards didn't always require academic superiority as much as financially secure parents. She liked to say some children knew how to take tests and for those who didn't or couldn't cut the mustard, "Somebody has to dig ditches and wait tables." The Weed said unofficially, "Why fight destiny?"

This was reason enough not to waste time with dull children. It was a category I had been placed into, without my knowledge, at the onset of the Fall semester, the same time my parents started arguing.

It didn't matter that I couldn't always complete my homework because my parents screamed while I hid under my bed. There was also, in the Weed's room, no excuse for students to stare into space during a fill-in-the-blank examination. While I wrestled with my home disaster, she rolled her eyes when I failed to grasp a math problem or science project such as the function of the human heart.

True, it was interesting to learn that a person's heart beat more than 3.5 billion times in a lifetime, but it happened whether I was aware of it or not. I just didn't see any reason to memorize the names of the four chambers that pumped the blood. Again, they pumped whether I knew their names or not, so why learn that the upper chambers are called the left and right atria, and the lower chambers are called the left and right ventricles. Flustered, I would stammer the information inaccurately to the giggles of my classmates. For all I cared, they could have been called Larry, Moe, Laurel and Hardy. Thus, I was rarely called to participate in classroom group activities.

The audacity of the lower digestive system was another matter. This part of the body actually produced something silly, disgusting, and funny. Its titles included something besides Latin names and it was referred to as an air twist bandit.

I also looked up the definition of a fart, which was to expel intestinal gas through the anus. Though they are formally called breaking wind, according to the big dictionary in the school library. Anus certainly sounded better than a butt-hole, though I didn't know what it was until I found the word in the same dictionary. Further information flushed my cheeks red and filled me with superiority in processing more information about that part of the body. A by-product of my research inspired a fascination with how the human body processed food and drink put into it.

With the help of the librarian at the public library I found some medical journals with articles offering detailed expressions, both medical and the type boys used like "cut the cheese", "rip one", "poot", and "toot", along with the less socially offensive "backfire", "barking spiders", and the innocuous "great nothingness", and "air twisting". Equally delightful and disgusting was to find they were ranked according to the actual sound or the lack of it. There was the "fizzy fuzz", the "goose", "growler" and "thunder". All these, regardless of volume, were minimal and all groveled in fear and trembling at the feet of the infamous "silent, but deadly".

By straddling the fine line between gross and cool I was elevated to a higher intellectual-social level. Regardless, these were forbidden subjects along with toilets, digging boogers and picking scabs. I was a freak, for only a freak would want to know such information, so I lost points. But, no pun intended, curiosity overpowered civilized norms for a few girls in my class. Particularly, after I explained, to their squealed denial, that contrary to popular opinion, girls winded just as much as guys. Their outrage was buttressed by the social difference that boys were proud of theirs, also accompanied by stifled laughter. Other information was given a blind ear, such as that girls could be as nasty as boys, not passing gas resulted in death, and that, regardless of how socially detestable, air twisting was a normal function proven by medical science.

Why the outrage? This information was considered high knowledge and not intended for dissemination to the masses. Meaning all those outside our group and particularly boys. But once the girls got past the initial grossness, they reveled in the freedom I brought of innocent sounding expressions whose true definitions would have earned a face slap. Joyce and Jerri were delighted to discuss the great nothingness, especially when the Weed walked past. More than one tacky boy crinkled his brow listening to us talk about air twisting. So I was urged to find more medical journal incantations to integrate into our secret language.

For a time, my parents indiscretions were forgotten and I had a minor seat in the circle of a small tribe among a room full of tribes. Where the only thing worse than being least was belonging to no tribe at all. From this exalted position I was urged to continue my research. All that ended a few weeks before end of school on an abnormally hot Friday.

Just after lunch a knobby-headed boy named Monte Cosper raised his head, sniffed and said, "Who cut the cheese?"

The Weed blinked myopically behind her thick glasses looking confused until she jumped to her feet at growing outbursts uttered with noses held. Oddly, I never caught the whiff of "it" and, I learned later, neither did any of the kids around me. Still, grateful for the interruption of an otherwise dull class period was the opportunity to moan and hold noses at the unknown presence in our mists.

"What is that vile, disgusting odor?" demanded The Weed waving both hands in front of her face causing her flabby underarms to flop. "That's horrible!"

She rushed to a row of windows to my left opening them in succession. Sliding the last up with a slam she whirled and glared across the room. No one spoke as she returned to her desk, but instead of sitting down, she opened a nearby filing cabinet and ordered everyone to get ready for an exam.

She took test materials from the cabinet and handed them to the kid at the front of each row. We took out paper and pencil and wrote our names at the top of our paper. Midway through the test the Weed walked down the center aisle glancing at the test takers' progress. She was at the back rows when my pencil broke, so I got up and moved toward the pencil sharpener located at the other end of the room.

"Where are you going Jaclyn?" she challenged.

I held up my pencil and she impatiently waved me on along with a finger to her lips not to make any noise. I smiled at such an impossibility since the pencil sharpener had to grind loud to get a point. Much like something else I thought and repressed a smirk as I returned to my seat. That was when the back row kids moaned and held their noses with gagging noises.

"That is just disgusting," the Weed cried. "Whoever is making that filthy odor must stop now. In fact leave the room."

A twittering of giggles drowned the complaints of the back rows, the least being the girls of my crowd. The others couldn't help themselves, I knew, because as every kid knows, farts are mysterious, embarrassing, unmentioned and funny. Especially if the "flatulence," as it's referred to in the medical books, was somebody else's. Funnier still was the Weed's contention that toots were somehow controllable, unlike coughing, itching, sneezing or breathing. She might as well have asked us to stop our hearts from beating.

"Whoever this child is has poor health habits."

"Yeah, give us a break," moaned Monte waving his hand in front of his face. "That last one hung on my eyebrows."

The room erupted and the Weed slapped a desk with the edge of her metal ruler. "There is nothing funny about this situation. It's unhealthy and threatens the health and personal safety of everyone in this room. He or she needs to admit they have a problem and seek proper help."

I tried not to laugh, thinking whoever they were had probably had a can of cheap chili with beans with green chilies and ground cabbage mixed with super hot sauce the night before. Someone, I concluded with a leer, would visit the rest room very soon and reveal their presence.

Before that could happen the Weed paused and everyone became quiet avoiding eye contact and the spotlight of total humiliation. Yet, the Weed wasn't finished. "Someone knows who this unfortunate person is!"

Monte turned around and opened his mouth as if he was going to say something, but turned back and folded his hands looking straight ahead. No one could blame him since being labeled "pooty" was a fate no kid wanted. But there was nothing lower than a rat-snitch. Only the Weed gave the rats a way out.

"We'll do this democratically," she announced looking around the room. "Everyone take out a blank slip of notebook paper and write who you think this unhealthy individual is. Fold it and I'll collect them."

"Popeye the Sailor," I scratched in wide script on my paper, "toot-toot."

I placed my vote with the others in a cardboard box Mrs. Planter held. After the votes were cast she sat the box on her desk and resumed the lesson finishing just before the recess bell.

In the girl's bathroom, I inhaled, but couldn't keep from snickering at how silly I was trying to identify the stinky culprit in one of the stalls. It didn't matter because the odors were standard. Though as I left my stall I noticed different girls walking slowly past the stall rows. Trying not to burst out laughing I quickly washed my hands and went to the playground forgetting about the vote for the rest of the day.

Typically, before the last bell rang, the Weed moved to the back of the room and stood by the door. She announced what to study for the next day's lesson just as the bell rang. Everyone gathered their backpacks to leave. When I reached the door the Weed touched my shoulder and told me to stay behind. Other kids shot sidelong looks, but said nothing as they left. With the last child gone, she closed the door and turned to me.

"I wanted you to know that according to the vote virtually everyone believes you made those smells."

"But, I didn't," I stammered in shock. "I, I, I..."

"They believe you did," she added with emphasis. "So, you might want to watch your P's and Q's really close from now on."

"But I didn't," I said louder. "I haven't done anything!"

"Don't raise your voice to me," she said over her shoulder as she returned to her desk. "Go home now Jaclyn, think about this and don't let it happen again!"

It was like being simultaneously kicked in the mouth and stomach. As much in shock as pain I forced myself not to cry as I passed other kids.

"Do you know what she reads about?"

"You should have heard what a girl told me about her."

"It had to be her!"

Why, I demanded, why? Why did she take that stupid vote? She certainly didn't have to tell me about it. Yet the worst part was realizing how much mean there was in the world and how helpless I was against it.

That day I stayed at Ana's house until my mother got off work. As always Ana had a snack waiting for me, only I said I was tired and wanted to lie down. I carried my bag to my mother's old room resisting the urge to throw it against a wall. I found a corner and slid to the floor with my fists pressed into my eyes, moaning low until the door opened. Before I could pull my hands away Ana was on the floor in front of me, legs crossed Indian style

"All right, what happened? Spill it!"

My first response was the all purpose "nothing," and I was just tired or sick. Only those never worked with Ana, so I told her everything. When I looked up her fingers gripped her knees as she stared at a spot above my head.

"That hag," she said.

"Ana it wasn't me, I swear it. Besides, from what I read, it's not something the intestines can help."

"I know sweetie," she said placing her hands on my shoulders and pulling me into her lap. "What wasn't written in those medical magazines was there was only one set of guts in your classroom that could have produced that kind of stink."

My face pressed into her shoulder, I cried and she held me as I poured out my wails. Then she told me to dry my eyes and got to her feet pulling me up. We returned to the kitchen for my snack and feeling better.

I still dreaded going to school the following Monday. When the day arrived few people talked to me, but by chance I was alone with Joyce in the rest room. Without a word, she checked the stalls like a character from a bad movie and stood watching the outside door. She told me her mother had brought her to school early.

"That's when I saw your grandmother coming out of the Weed's room," she said. "Did you know why she was there?"

I shook my head, dried my hands wondering if I would be the first girl to drop out of the sixth grade. Yet the school term ended, though not soon enough for me, and I learned I had been passed to middle school. Not that my classmates were happy.

"The Weed passed you only because she didn't want to fool with you another year."

So, that was my life when I got to Ana's, betrayal and change crashing through my life like meteorites, with neither friends, parents or school to trust and the world whirling out of control faster than I could comprehend. Worse, I was changing and didn't understand the how and certainly not the why or the way to control it.

The only constant was my gun toting, garden growing grandmother, whose arms I ran to during thunderstorms. Where she melted fears by telling us about ancient Indian chiefs beating their tom-toms among the clouds to make what we called thunder.

At Ana's house, the boogie man was afraid of her. But she didn't believe in a "there-there" approach. Life was to be faced like the time she drove us through a cemetery in the middle of the night as a lesson that there was nothing to fear from the dead.

She was my Ana, I would proudly tell anybody, including Aunt Sonia's colleagues, dead or alive. She didn't need professional or any other help because she feared neither man, woman, child or demon. Nor could she be accused of being the stereotypical gray haired granny baking cookies. We were expected to pull our load, as she called it. At her house, we made up our beds, helped with dishes and house work to her satisfaction.

On the eve of this particular weekend we were prepared to help load the camper and do anything to get ready for the trip. Instead, to our happy surprise, she directed us to put on our swim suits. This was a treat we generally earned after at least an hour's worth of work. Yet, she offered no explanation other than that she had a headache. This was odd to me, because, headache or not, Ana always finished a job. Still, nobody had to tell me twice to go swimming.

Before Tommy could touch his backpack, I was in the bathroom with my new silver and red bathing suit my mother ordered from a catalogue. After making double sure the door was locked, and even bracing the vanity chair against the door knob, I pulled off my clothes. I couldn't avoid the intrusion of my reflection in the big mirror.

Like a bystander at a car wreck I gaped at the catastrophe that had once been me. There were my daddy's eyes, my mother's mouth and Ana's chin. Yet, there was also a big nose, chubby squirrel's cheeks and droopy ears. Then add ribs that could be counted, bumps, sharp pointed elbows, knobby knees and thigh bones that a coat hanger could be hung on and the whole package about as appealing as a string puppet. Between my legs was a tuff of dark wispy hair, its color and texture poising questions if wombats hung in our family tree. Worse, the pelt, with Johnson grass tenacity, was spreading in a spiraling line toward my navel and my mother wouldn't even let me shave my legs.

Looking into the mirror reminded me of the words written on the side mirrors of Papa's truck, "Objects may appear closer than they actually are." The same expression I'd seen in a cartoon with a bespectacled character wearing glasses and a big nose driving a car with three fingers. On the cartoon car's rear view mirror was the same caption as Papa's truck. The image totally filling the cartoon mirror was the angry, red eye of a monster.

Was I real or illusion? With no answer I broke my concentration and looked at the toilet as I pulled on my bottoms. After an adjustment to my top I stepped into the hall and found Tommy leaning against the wall. Nonchalantly, he sighed before moving down the hall and increasing to a fast walk toward the kitchen and back yard.

Outside on the half moon porch, we broke into a full sprint and dove into the blow-up pool. We hit the water together, howling like monkeys as we surfaced to converge at the pool's center for a grapple and tussle. We'd fought like this since we could walk and experience had taught me to use my leverage and height over Tommy's strength. Sliding my right foot behind him, I pushed and we fell out of the pool spilling half its contents into the surrounding grass. Tommy, who would never accept defeat by "a girl," rolled to his feet and took off. I gave chase anticipating Tommy's standard evasive routes around the yard. To my surprise, instead of the usual sprint for the tree house rope ladder, he zigzagged to the porch and into the house. Right behind him again, I knew he'd head straight to our room to hide under the bed. Instead, he scooted down the hall to our grandparent's room and in our blind delight we failed to hear the music playing from the room ahead of us. I nearly collided with Tommy when I realized the music's source was a stereo located on Ana's dresser. Breathing hard neither of us moved as the words of one of Ana's favorite songs filled the room. A catchy tune, I always remembered the repetition of "united we stand," which was the title of an Aesop fable I liked almost as much.

"It was number one on the charts," she explained the first time she played it for me. "After I heard it on AM radio, I had to have the record."

I didn't know what AM radio was, only that this song was special to Ana. She played it, like many others, on the turntable of her sound system resembling an old time radio I'd seen in an antique shop. It was from Ana's collection of 45-rpm records that she kept along with CDs, cassettes and "long playing" vinyl records she'd collected over the years. The difference between this song and others was that Ana played it particularly when she was alone. I didn't know all the words, but Ana knew the song by heart from start to finish.

From the record player a female voice crooned about wanting to be no place but with her love. A male singer answered, wanting nothing else but her smile, followed by a chorus of scratchy singers filling the room. Normally we would have added our voices, but we were hesitant watching Ana silently mouth the familiar words. It was like when she was on the telephone and we'd been told to never bother her on the phone. Only she wasn't holding a phone and her lips creased with a smile as her eyes shone.

Nearby on her dresser lay a stack of objects arranged neatly on the long, dark and very old box that had been in Ana's bedroom since I could remember. Barely six inches tall and wide, the box's three-foot length stretched across Ana's dressing table. The lid and sides were inlaid with rich burnished teak wood scrolls along with mother of pearl leaves. Inside it was lined with plum colored velvet faded with age.

I was always thrilled by its mysteries since family legend deemed the box had belonged to Ana's grandmother, a gift given to my ancestor by a sailor who had returned from the mysterious shores of the Far East. Papa told us that, according to family legend, the sailor arrived with the box under his arm and wrapped in satin. He walked into the church on the very day of my great-great grandparents' wedding. When the sailor realized he was crashing his sweetheart's nuptials, he placed the box in her hands and, with tears streaming down his face, kissed the bride's closed knuckles and shook her husband's hand before returning to the sea.

That ancient family chronicle made the box unique and its contents treasures and only to be opened for special occasions. This is why I learned early that, while there were many liberties in my grandparents' home and few hard rules, one iron clad canon for everyone was "Don't touch Ana's memory box!"

I watched Ana pick up an embroidered patch with a musical note symbol that had been beside a stack of picture postcards. The top photograph depicted people dressed in strange clothes with an alien background. Whipping the flopping patch like a baton, Ana raised her voice above the chorus emphasizing every word.

"For united we stand, divided we fall, and if our backs should ever be against the wall, we'll be together, together, you and I." Nodding her head to the beat, Ana's smile faded as her lips quivered and she wiped her eyes. Other items from the box had been arranged in neat piles on the dressing table including scraps of paper, photographs and trinkets. Each, like the music, had it's own special story for Ana. If we were good, she might tell us about them. Only she still hadn't noticed us as the last chorus of "You and I" filled the room until Tommy sneezed and Ana blinked her eyes as if waking up.

"Tommy, Jackie! Were you running in the house, wet?"

"Yes ma'am," we chorused.

She grabbed a tissue from a nearby box and blew her nose. Turning she switched off the stereo and glared with what Tommy called "The Stare."

"I suppose you were in the pool without sun block too," she chided. "What have I told you about that?"

Our silence shouted volumes, provoking a sigh, though she wasn't angry. Ana told Tommy to fetch a towel and the bottle of sun block from the adjacent hall bathroom. She motioned for me to stand in front of her. When Tommy returned she dried my body with the towel and took out a hairbrush.

"You're getting taller, and bigger," she said looking at our reflections in the dresser mirror. "How did that happen?"

"Ana," I said. "You know I turned eleven last week."

"I'll be eleven next week," Tommy piped.

"Is that right," Ana said. "Funny, it wasn't too long ago you were turning ten and Tommy was nine. For that matter, it wasn't that long ago your mom was eleven and your daddy was ten. I was just saying so this morning when they dropped you off."

Straightening up, she held a damp strand of my tawny brown hair that fell to the middle of my back. She liked to say we were blondes with brunette hair.

"It curls at the ends the way mine used too," she said leaning over to place her face beside mine. I thought how beautiful she must have been, when she was younger, which is not to say she wasn't still attractive, just… older.

"The hog plum don't fall far from this tree," she said with a laugh. "I used to have to bend over to do this."

It was the mention of what Ana "used to be," that drew my attention to the objects set on the box.

"Who are they?" I asked.

I pointed to a stack of grainy old color photographs, the kind with too much light in the background of the picture. A photo from another era and place showed four boys and three girls panning for the camera. It wasn't difficult to recognize my teenaged Ana. Though like the other girls in the photo, she had thick bangs and hair the color of mine flowing over her shoulders. Pimple-cheeked, shaggy-haired boys wore checkered pants or jeans along with turtleneck sweaters or flowered shirts with beaded necklaces or medallions hanging from necks.

I pointed to the boy my teen grandmother snuggled with, a possessive hand on his chest. He sported sheaths of dark blonde hair along with mutton chop sideburns that extended to the center of his face completing a bushy frame. Tinted aviator sunglasses hid all but the shape of his eyes.

"These old Kodachromes didn't do him justice," she said tapping the boy's picture. "Those eyes were soooo blue and even dreamier. "

Her green eyes shone in the photo and were considered another family trait I had inherited. Not wanting to consider body parts I placed my finger on the photograph.

"That isn't Papa," I said

"No, sweetheart," she said looking away. "He was a boy I knew in college. Those are some talented people we hung with."

"Talented?" I asked.

"She was a poet," said Ana tapping her finger on the photo of girl with apple cheeks and freckles. "And he, " she pointed to a sleepy eyed boy with a ponytail, "crafted fabulous creations from metal."

He was an artist, she added, whether it was a sculpture or tools and household items like the big triple-pronged meat fork twisted like a braid we saw every Thanksgiving.

"He made knives out of old files, saws or car springs," she said, "like the one I gave to my aunt for Christmas. He made it out of a rasp, a tool used to clean horses hoofs. ”

"Ewww," I said. "I wouldn't want one of those in our kitchen."

"Silly, yes you would," Ana chided. "The metal holds a sharp edge and he always put such beautiful handles on his work."

"What about him?" I asked pointing to an odd looking boy with frizzy hair and glasses so thick they were opaque.

"He crafted leather," Ana said. "He made bags, vests, belts and holsters of every kind.

"Holsters? Tommy asked. "You mean like for guns?"

"Yes," Nana answered, "also for cigarettes, lighters, knives and hair. He made this for me."

Reaching into her memory box, she pulled out an oblong piece of dark red leather skewered with a small stick through holes on either end. On the smooth side of the leather were three raised symbols.

"What's that?" I asked.

"A leather hair stay for keeping long hair on girls or boys in place.

"What kind of writing is that?" I asked pointing to the symbols.

"Alpha," she said pointing to the first emblem, "the beginning."

Her finger moved to what looked like an upside down triangle with an upside down number 8 in the center.

"This represents a pyramid, a two dimensional building and communication symbol crossed with infinity."

Her finger slid to the final symbol on the far right. "This is omega, the last or end. Together they stand for the infinite goal to build and spread beneficial ideas and enlightenment."

Fingering the leather, I ran my finger over the sharp point of the stick. Turning the hair stay over I found initials stamped on the underside of the leather.

"JKC + CTW"

Ana plucked the hair stay from my hand, reinserted the stick and put it back in her box.

"You went to college?" I asked. "What was it like?"

"I only went two semesters, " said Ana voice dropping. "I never went back, I meant too and I wish I had."

"Why didn't you go back?" Weren't you good in school?"

"Oh, I loved it," Ana said. "It was a new world and learning was fun. But, I wanted to get away from home though I didn't know what I wanted to be when I got there."

Again she looked away before replacing the other items into the box.

"What about him?" Asked Tommy with his finger hovering over the blond boy.

"He went away to fight a war," she said, "the last person they should have called."

"Did he die?" Tommy asked hesitantly. "In the war, I mean?"

"I don't know, I hope not," she said. "He always said he had great things to do, places to go, and would make a name for himself. He said a little thing like a war couldn't stop him."

She looked up, staring beyond our reflections in the mirror. "We all had that attitude," she added and tied my hair into a pony tail with a rubber band. "Later another boy asked me to marry him."

"Was that Papa?" I asked with romantic hopes.

"No, he wasn't your granddad," she said voice dropping. "Things didn't work out. We married too fast and soon." Ana became intent on my hair.

"Did you like him?" I asked tapping the picture with the talented people. "Him I mean!"

"Yes," she said disinterestedly. "I always wondered what happened to him."

I was going to ask if she'd ever tried to find him when she announced, "Time to butter up."

This was one of our favorite summer expressions that always made Tommy and I giggle. Tommy squeezed the sun block bottle mouth onto Ana's hand and a farting sound preceded the white glop on Ana's hand. Tommy and I broke into fresh giggles as Ana smiled and spread the cool gel across my neck and back. Satisfied, she turned me around and dabbed my face like she was applying war paint. I felt my neck blush as she smeared my upper chest lifting the swim suit straps off my shoulders.

Swirling the goop over my belly with both hands she gathered the excess and smeared it over my right shoulder to my fingers. With more goop she repeated the application to my left arm. Only when she turned my left hand up her eyes narrowed. Frowning, she wiped her hands and snatched up her half-moon glasses lying on the dresser. After placing them on her nose, she held my forearm with both hands and peered closely as she turned my wrist.

"You've got an *Orion!*"

"A what?" I asked with no need to look at my arm.

"An *Orion*," Ana repeated laying her index finger on a spot just below my wrist.

I knew she was talking about the linear dots I discovered only days before all the other changes began. Unlike my chest, it was too obvious to cover my wrist, particularly during the summer since the dots were on the underside of my arm, a knuckle's width from my wrist joint. Five small moles barely bigger than pepper seeds, a shade darker than the skin on which they lay.

Never wanting to stand out, I always tried to keep my arm turned down even when I knew there was no reason to cover them. Other people had moles, and they weren't unusual. Yet, for me, these moles made the mistake of appearing at the wrong time. They were centered freakishly on my wrist where a wristwatch band or bracelet could hide them, if I had one. Still, I would have preferred to cover my entire arm to the elbow.

Three of the moles were parallel to my wrist joint and perfectly spaced apart like they'd been drawn there. Two other moles were located below the three at a left angle. Together they reminded me of the dotted arrow on the top of a juice box with instructions to "Put straw here."

"It gets its name from the belt of the constellation named after Orion the Hunter," Ana said. "Those five moles are like the five stars that make up his belt and scabbard."

"Constellation? Tommy asked. "Who's an Orion, and what did he hunt?"

Ana told us Orion was an ancient Greek hero, a mighty hunter with a little dog, who hunted animals nearly to extinction. He was unfortunately famous for being stung and blinded by a giant scorpion. Mention of stings reminded me of my chest and I wondered if scorpions or some other bug had left their mark. It seemed a plausible explanation, and why I avoided contact with any surface because of their tender nature and the painful consequence.

By contrast my wrist moles were prone to itch at inopportune times, an unpreventable characteristic. They had started itching just as Ana began telling us about Orion's best friends, the Greek goddess Diane. She was a friend who placed him in the night sky with the other constellations, along with his dog and the scorpion. Wow what a friend, I thought, and why would anybody want to be a constellation?

Ana explained that constellations were "connect-the-dots" images of star patterns devised by the ancient Greeks and many other ancient civilizations. Each picture was a story about heroes, monsters or legends. The night sky acted as a tapestry for these tales.

"Like your memory box?" I asked.

"Something like that, only on a much bigger scale," Ana said. "These memories are for everyone, though different to specific cultures from around the world in other forms. They all have a story to tell."

"They also remind us that change is inevitable," she added, "because people are always changing. Just as constellations tumble through the sky, mortals struggle through life and, like constellations, mortals have consistency like love, family and wisdom."

"But why are these on me?" I demanded, "What did I do to get an Orion?"

Ana squeezed out more sun block and concentrated on rubbing it into my skin before she answered. "I can't say because it's your Orion, " Ana said. "And it's not what you've done, it's what you will do. "

But why me, I wanted to know? Secretly, I was delighted with my special marks. Here was proof of my sole citizenship and royal title as undisputed ruler of a secret kingdom. Yet with the unknown, I was unsure how to rule my realm. Uncertainty vied to usurp my crown and displace my kingdom's most loyal, though confused, subject.

"Orion is also useful for locating other stars," Ana said. "Astronomers found that by drawing a line from the belt southeastward, it was easy to locate Sirius, the brightest star. So it's also a direction finder used the way ancient civilization like the Mayans, Egyptians and even the Hopi Indians built their pyramids and structures. They built them with Orion's belt as a terrestrial sign post, a straight line to their sacred places miles beyond the horizon."

When Papa was in the Air Force, she recalled, particularly after a hard day, that looking up at night for Orion her heart warmed knowing Papa was on the other side of the world and would also be looking at Orion's belt.

"Momma said they'll have to be taken off," I said feeling even more confused. "She says moles are tacky and dangerous."

My cheeks burned as I turned my eyes to Ana's memory box to avoid looking at Tommy.

"Moles are cool," Tommy whooped. "My best friend Jeff said moles are almost as good as tattoos. I wish I had some."

I stifled the urge to crawl under Ana's bed wondering if the word "freak" was appearing on my forehead.

"Tommy," Ana said, "go get that bottle of aloe vera under the sink in the other bathroom."

Tommy made ready to sprint for the hall only to be stopped at the gate. "Don't run in the house," Ana warned.

Tommy sidled around the corner as Ana removed her wrist watch and, without looking, laid her index finger on her left forearm. Looking down I stared at a spot just below her wrist, my embarrassment fading like smoke. Her nail tip rested below a series of three beige dots, parallel to her wrist, straight across while a fourth and fifth splayed footed to an outside direction.

"It's never bothered me," she said, "besides many cultures consider these marks to be a sign of good luck, a blessing by the gods."

She rubbed more sun block on my right arm just as Tommy returned to report he couldn't find the aloe vera in or near the other bathroom. Ana shrugged that it was OK, though I feared Tommy knew there was a secret afoot if we were quiet.

"Are we lucky?" I asked. "Are we Greek?"

"We're very lucky," said Ana smearing sun block on my legs and feet. "I'm lucky to have you and Tommy here. We're not Greek, but I am a New Athenian."

"A mew aunt themian," I asked fascinated.

"A New Athenian," Ana repeated "Builders of new worlds."

Drying her hands with a tissue she retrieved a green cord from the pile of stuff next to the photographs. At the end of the cord was a bright red tube with a black collar and tapered on one end.

"This is called a beacon," Ana said. "A symbol of the New Athenians' simple approach to life."

She held up the tube for closer inspection. At its top was a compass, on one of its sides was a slender mirror, on the opposite side was a thin piece of metal nearly the length of the tube. Below the black collar the tube's tapered end was a whistle. Ana blew a sharp note before twisting the beacon's collar, separating the halves and pouring its contents to her dressing table. Among items was a small wedge of gray metal with a hinged metal hook that nearly bounced off the dresser. Ana caught it and, with the longer section of the tub in other hand, used it to scrape the tube's thin metal strip. A shower of sparks erupted and we squealed jumping out of their way. She explained the little metal hook was a can opener with a variety of other uses.

"We could make fire," she said dropping the can opener and picking a saran wrapped little bundle. "Of course we only used this method as a last resort since we had these."

The bundle consisted of kitchen matches with a piece of sand paper wrapped around its center with a rubber band. The blue heads of the matches flaked against the saran wrap since they had somehow been exposed to moisture. Tossing the ruined matches to one side, she picked up a small baggy containing several small hooks and lead shot sinkers and laid them beside a roll of nylon fishing string wrapped tight around its middle with a single strand.

"We could fish for our supper, or lash together a shelter."

Other items from the tube I recognized included a card of needles speared through paper with streamers of different colored thread swirled through their eyes. A folded sheet of lined paper was wrapped around a pencil stub along with two birthday-cake candles and three adhesive bandages secured with a rubber band. She had to tap the tube's smaller end to dislodge two tarnished quarters. Though a wrinkled clear plastic wrapper containing a red swirled mush plopped out by itself.

"What's that?" I asked, extending a tentative finger to the plastic package.

"That," Ana snorted, "is either an emergency ration or a really old piece of peppermint candy, whichever you like."

"Rats and onions?" Tommy said. "I don't like rats and I sure don't like them with onions."

"Rations, Tommy," Ana laughed. "Like regular food only much smaller. Everything needed to build a better world."

"Wow," I said reaching for a tissue to wipe away excess sun block. "What did you build?"

"Nothing of wood or stone," she said. "We mostly had fun, made monthly meetings and went out for drinks and movies. We would talk, listen to music and dance even more. We built each other up according to our pledge."

"A pledge?" I repeated. "What kind of pledge?"

Ana squeezed more sun block into her palm and motioned Tommy to step forward. In no time he was sweet smelling and glistened. I thought Ana had forgotten my question until she motioned me to stand beside Tommy. She raised both her hands with palms out and the joints of her thumbs touching.

"*I pledge my hands*," Ana began and placed the tips of her fingers on her temples.

We stared at her until she indicated us to hold our hands like she was following her motions and repeating, "I pledge my hands."

"*My head and my heart*," she continued and brought her fingers down to the center of her chest before again thrusting her arms up and crossing her wrists. "*And I consecrate myself to truth, justice and humanitarian service.*"

I was taken by the solemnity of the words and actions and the way my grandmother's eyes shone. I was also irritated that my Orion began to itch. Still, I was happy to at least have a name for it now.

"As the first Athenians gave the world architecture, science and government, I will leave my world better through my personal gifts."

The words echoed in my ears and mind and I felt hesitant, actually fearful about repeating or completing the rest of the oath.

"I render freely my talents and fully avail my resources without wrong to man or nature."

Ana sat with her head bowed for what seemed like too long until she crossed her hands over one another and took our hands in hers.

"Congratulations," she intoned, "I welcome you into the sacred mysteries of the New Athenians."

"This is so cool," Tommy said.

He reached for the tube to blow the whistle and I picked up the photo of the New Athenians.

"What did you build?" I asked. "Is it something somewhere we can go see?"

"Oh yes, " Ana said. "I built your mommy, M.J. and Theo. So, I kept my pledge."

Ana told us the New Athenians believed spirit and the mind projects were more important than material and secular ones. They engaged in "building quests" that might involve the whole club or just one. They lifted each other up and intervened to help a member clarify his or her existence by making priorities and seeking true answers to life questions. Sometimes it was necessary to get away and seek solace in silence and isolation, a project the New Athenians sometimes helped with cash donations.

"We called it touching the mountain top," Ana said. "A time to differentiate between buttercups and raccoon poop."

"Of course some sojourners' idea of mountain top touching," she added smiling, "included visits to popular night spots."

This was a side of my grandmother I'd never seen or heard about. I admit I wasn't able to accept or understand it, particularly since I'd had her on a grandmother pedestal for so long. She had been in a club, a posse, a gang whose existence I could only imagine.

"Did you go to secret meetings," I asked. "Are there any New Athenians nearby that we know?"

"We weren't secret, even then," she said. "In fact, we were down right loud. Still, I never saw those boys and girls again after I left school."

"Who told you about *Orions*?" I asked.

Unwittingly, I had revealed there were two *Orions* were in the room. I glanced at Tommy, only he hadn't noticed.

"My grandmother," Ana answered. "She had an *Orion*, just like yours. Her lost sailor told her about the constellations and those marked with a

Divine gift of destiny. He told her how Orion had abused his skills and was blinded. Yet, by loosing his sight he tapped new skills and discovered a fresh outlook about himself and the world."

Pausing, Ana seemed to collect her thoughts from afar.

"My grandmother said that like Orion, there are no guarantees that life would be rosy," Ana said. "Orion certainly had love and joy, but also trials and tribulations."

She stared at the mirror as she had when Tommy and I first entered the room. I wondered if Ana's mirror would speak to her like the story of Snow White. For an answer Ana reconnected the two halves of the beacon and draped its cord around my neck.

"Let's start a chapter of New Athenians right here," she said. "You've already taken the pledge, so why not become a full member."

"How come Jackie gets to wear the bee-can," Tommy whined.

"Because she can say beacon!" Ana said. "Now put your hands on it and repeat after me."

Following Ana's example we put our hands on the beacon. Ana crossed her arms and held out her hands to shake our free hands.

"I welcome you into the fellowship of the New Athenians," she said. "I now charge you to go forth, honor your pledge and fulfill your destiny."

"What's my destiny?" Tommy demanded.

"It's to get to the pool for the rest of the afternoon," said Ana tickling him, "and have as much fun as you can."

Tommy ran out of the room giggling and Ana took the beacon from my neck and opened it to reinsert the other items.

Ana?" I asked. "May I wear the beacon to Bandy's Camp?"

"Why don't we save it for special times?" Ana said. "You can wear it when we go on our first building-quest."

"Couldn't I wear it tomorrow?" I pleaded

Ana didn't answer, only stared at me in an odd way.

"All right," she finally agreed, "just let me update a few things, some of that stuff has been in there for years."

Ana threw the old candy wrapper in the trash and returned the other items to her memory box. Tommy called to know what was keeping me. I followed the sound of his voice into the den and found him bouncing on Papa Mike's leather easy chair.

"I'm *Orion,*" Tommy declared, "a mighty hunter."

"Well I'm a goddess," I said. "You stay away from my wild animals."

"Not if I don't want to," he said. "You can't make me."

"Scorpion," I called and pointed behind Tommy. "Get him!"

Squealing, Tommy fell bottom first, into the seat and his hand accidentally smacked the television remote control housed in a sheath draped over the arm of the chair. We jumped as a choral chant filled the room and black and white images of sneering little men painted with black makeup flickered on the screen. I recognized it as one of Papa's movies "Tarzan of the Apes."

"That's like the zillionth time he's seen that."

Tommy grinned as, for the zillionth and one time, we watched stubby armed little men, called pygmies in the credits, lasso tall people, both black and white and pull them into a pit where someone wearing a cheap gorilla suit rushed the camera growling. Screams and chants were silent briefly before Jane, the only chick in the flick, as Papa called her, got yanked into the pit. Gorilla Suit was on her and she screamed before fainting. An old man with a thick white moustache, who was supposed to be Jane's father, jumped into the pit to fight Gorilla Suit and got knocked down.

As always a thick-chested man wearing ripped shorts and a big knife swinging on his hip ran barefoot across the screen faster than I thought was possible yodeling, "EeeYAH, EeeYAH, EeeYAH!"

This of course was Tarzan, who with apes and elephants not far behind, arrived and, for the zillionth time, Tommy tried unsuccessfully to imitate the Tarzan yell. For the zillionth and one time he shouted, "Umgawah, pacee, pacee!"

Papa said that was jungle speak for "move your butt," or just about anything Tarzan wanted it to mean.

Papa called these movies "vintage," and he had hundreds that we'd seen more times than I could remember. Which made even less sense for Tommy to stare at this "classic" like he was seeing it the first time. I continued bouncing as he slipped down to the seat still staring.

"Do you think Tarzan was a new Athenian?"

"Maybe," Ana answered from behind us, "and if Papa catches you in his chair and playing his movies you'll be a baboon. "

"Why's that?" said Tommy slipping off the chair.

"That's how red your butt will be after Papa gets through wearing you out."

She swatted the bottoms of Tommy's cutoffs and we ran, squealing, for the back door.

We stayed in the backyard until Papa came home. He and the other band members loaded two trailers with their equipment from the garage. By the time they finished it was dark and they adjourned to the living room to talk. We'd had our supper and Ana lead us to the backyard to spread a blanket where the sky wasn't blocked by trees. She pointed and called the star constellations by name, recounting their Greek legends. To my disappointment, Orion wasn't visible at that time of night. Ana explained it was typical of Orion to appear later.

By the time we returned, the men had left, so we bathed, but instead of putting on pajamas, Ana had us dress in our shorts and T-shirts. In this way, she said to our delight, we could be up and gone.

In my mother's former bedroom she read from a book we'd never seen, its pages yellow with age, filled with stories about ancient Greek myths. She showed us the old drawings with captions about Hercules before reading about the adventures of Jason and the Argonauts. Too soon she closed the book, despite our pleas for more, and promised to complete Jason's voyage the next night. We said our prayers and Ana kissed us both on the forehead. Tommy was asleep before I was snuggled between the sheets and Ana turned off the light.

"Ana," I called. "Are there still heroes in the world, like those Greek stories or Tarzan?"

"I'd like to believe so," said Ana kissing my forehead. "I want to believe so."

Chapter 5

Orion's belt was briefly visible as Ana guided me by my shoulders out the front door to Papa's van in the front driveway. Understandably, my only interest was the pallet spread in the little space behind the van's backseat. Tommy was already there curled with his knees to his chest pressed against the back seat as I snuggled against him.

I fell back asleep and it seemed my eyes had just closed when my chest bumped Tommy's shoulder blade. The sting brought me wide awake. Looking up, I saw the van had left the pavement for a dirt road and dust billowed behind us while Tommy slept on. The van rolled to a stop at the entrance to Bandy's Camp and a man leaned out of a little house to talk to Papa before we drove into the camp. He stopped long enough to direct the trucks with instruments and sound equipment to a bandstand located on the far side of a field. The other vehicles followed us to a line of travel campers and tents on the far side of the camp.

Scrambling to the back seat I found a piece of thread and used it to tickle Tommy's ear from my new perch. He woke grumpy and swinging. Ana hushed us to settle down with the threat of being tied to a tree for three days. Never doubting her, we contained ourselves as Papa slowed the van to a crawl to allow dozens, maybe hundreds of people to walk in front of us. The crowd streamed toward a series of colorful booths pitched on an open field across from the campground. In passing, I spotted face painters and inflatable playgrounds. There was also a Shetland pony ride and I was surprised at my disinterest. Maybe it's because I'm too big for ponies, I thought, so give me a horse.

Not soon enough, Papa stopped and we piled out and stood away from the van while he navigated it into an empty campsite. Two other band trucks took the spots on either side of us and unloaded huge boxes, bundles and tents.

There was much to do besides setting up camp. Wives of other band members joined Ana awaiting her orders since her job included getting the locals motivated. She organized the other women to sell T-shirts and other band stuff when they weren't screaming their heads off after the songs. The other women waited for her at a nearby picnic table, talking, stretching and smoking cigarettes.

" Cheerleaders for the band," Ana muttered. "Go team."

However, she was our grandmother first and lead us in the direction of the booths. Out of earshot of the others, she opened her purse and gave us each a zip-lock plastic sandwich bag. In it were Kleenex tissues and a $10 bill. We would have taken off running for the booths if it hadn't been for Ana's hand on our shoulders. She draped the beacon's cord around my neck.

"Blow the whistle only in an emergency."

Ana added other instructions Tommy didn't want to hear. "Don't go near that river for any reason," she said. "Under no circumstances are you to get any closer to that water than you can throw a small rock."

She knew Tommy could throw a rock far for his age because she'd taught us, so there was no getting around the boundaries. Tommy didn't like the idea, but together we echoed, "Yes, ma'am."

Ana turned and we ran across the road to the booths across the field. By the time we got to the first booth crowds had clustered so thick I couldn't see where one booth began and another ended until we pushed our way to the front. Between the first rows of booths were a pair of box elder trees offering shade. A young man and woman dressed in shorts and matching Polo shirts stood under one tree while an artist sketched them. Beyond the trees was a pudgy man dressed in a multicolored tie-dye T-shirt and shorts sitting on the plank of a dunking booth. A pimple-faced boy with a cigarette dangling from his mouth wound up and pitched a ball at a red target to the left of the booth. Nearby two children stood mesmerized as a clown in baggy pants made balloon animals while a woman sat behind a table piled high with colored T-shirts that read "Old Guys Rule."

Moving on I saw other booths with elaborate metal and wooden crosses, jewelry, paintings and photographs. One sold dog and cat collars and I thought of Ana's cat Sophie, before remembering she didn't like collars.

Still, it was interesting to watch a woman knap a piece of flint into an arrowhead. On the table in front of her were a set of finished examples tied with strips of leather for necklaces. I thought it might be fun to learn how to knap flint, but didn't care to at that moment. I looked at the toys advertised as "hand made" and pondered how anything got made unless somebody used their hands. Still, I had no interest in string drawn cars, marshmallow shooting PVC guns or wooden whistles.

There was a collection of DVDs and VHS tapes featuring old western movies I thought Papa would like in his collection, though no title jumped out with a must have-appeal.

All this stuff, I realized with a shock, I would have given my eye-teeth for last year and spent my $10 quicker than a snot slick slide, as Papa liked to say. I would have been happy with my purchase too. Yet, kid or adult stuff seemed like so much useless clutter. This was a realization about myself that fascinated yet saddened me.

The other booths seemed to blur as we made our way down the line and the sun climbed midway into the sky. I was not only disinterested, I was bored. Past the booths, I saw a makeshift stage made of plywood and boxes. A man dressed like a Caribbean pirate stood at the edge of the stage and introduced himself as "Captain Rupert." He called and motioned for kids to "join his "scurvy pirate crew."

Scurvy was another word I'd found during my air twist research. Only, the definition wasn't my inspiration to join the crew. Yet, Tommy nearly ran over me to get to the lady pirate. A woman Captain Rupert called his first mate, Mrs. Captain Rupert.

I noticed more boys than girls were drawn to Mrs. Captain Rupert with her red hair flowing from under a blue bandana tied back above small ears with huge hoop earrings. She wore a man's white shirt, its sleeves ripped off exposing freckled arms and the tails tied at her waist, with three buttons open from the collar. She motioned for kids to form a line, handing us bandanas and vests showing us how to put them on.

When all hands were dressed, she lined us up and demonstrated how to step when Captain Rupert sang his sea chantey. Our job was to shout "YO-HO" at certain times and jump up. Mrs. Captain Rupert also jumped causing her chest to try to escape through the open top buttons of her shirt, prompting parents, particularly daddies, to rush forward and snap cameras that temporarily blinded most of us.

For me the song could have ended sooner as parents clapped too much, waving at certain little pirates and taking continuous photographs. When the song finally ended, Mrs. Captain Rupert walked our line again and I noticed the fourth button of her shirt gapped open. To my mortification she revealed more cleavage than I'd seen in my life as she thanked each of us and draped the props over her arm. She also shoved a pillowcase under our noses, with a skull and cross bones drawn on the side, telling us to take a prize. Dipping my hand into the bag I barely pulled out my arm before she moved to Tommy. Even after he grabbed his prize, he continued staring.

"What are you looking at?" I hissed elbowing his ribs.

"Her chest," he whispered. "She's got hair in the center just like Papa."

Face flushed, I turned and studied my prize: a rubber dagger with a wiggly blade. Resisting the urge to throw it, I pushed it into my back pocket. Tommy held out a plastic candy dispenser with a skull and crossbones hat on top of the plastic head. Unwrapping it from its package Tommy popped out a candy pill for each of us from the pirate's chin by flipping a lever located under the beard.

Nearby, other entertainers were setting up including jugglers, hula dancers, trick roping cowboys, and tumbling cheerleaders. They arranged themselves at a respectable distance from each other forming a wide circle. Mrs. Captain Rupert chatted with a perky cheerleader, and Captain Rupert, with a clown with a painted face and broad tie. More than anything, I wanted to go back to our camp and turned, expecting Tommy to follow me. Instead, he ran past the entertainers to the edge of a slope.

Joining him I looked down the hill to a level plain. Beyond a cleared field was a dense thicket of twisted trees and bushes. Separating the thicket from the field was a stack of hay bales forming a wall longer than Ana's backyard fence and taller than Papa if he stood on his twin brother's shoulders. That is, if he had a twin.

It looked as if the hay bale wall was a backstop for a baseball diamond. However, no one was holding a bat though two groups of kids stood facing one another. "Dodge ball!" Tommy yipped. "Dodge ball!"

CHAPTER 6

Tommy was a towheaded child with very fine almost invisible eyelashes and had started combing his dark blonde hair into a cow lick only the year before. Slender as a ruler, he had no hips or butt and was always the last chosen for any team games. He had no favorite video game, though his mother insisted he play chess. He liked action movies that inspired him to take martial arts and join the boy scouts. His mom discouraged both with a one-size-fits-all excuse that he was too young and might get hurt.

But if there was ever a recreation designed with my cousin in mind, dodge ball was the game. He fell in love the first day on the schoolyard when a pink ball slammed him in the back of his head knocking him to the grass. On the verge of bursting into tears, as he usually did on these occasions, he forgot everything when the kid who threw the ball told him to bring it and come join the game. From that time he was hooked, and regardless of the age group or game version, Tommy played.

We knew if my Aunt Sonia knew she would have declared it too violent and might launch a protest to get it banned from the whole school. So Tommy knew better than to mention it to her. He told Ana and Papa and mentioned it off-handedly to his dad when he came to pick him up. For once M.J. showed actual interest in Tommy as the boy explained and his father listened without comment.

When M.J. came to Ana's early the next day to pick Tommy up, he had a new dodge ball. Actually he had four dodge balls that we took to Ana's backyard. Yes, I wanted to play dodge ball too, so we stood in Ana's backyard where M.J. explained that dodge ball had two versions. The primary required six balls placed in the center of a court. At the sound of a whistle two teams dashed from opposite directions, grabbed a ball and hurled it at their opponents. Once hit, a player is out and a point was scored for the other side unless the opponent caught the ball.

The availability of a wall allowed participants to adapt the game to a lesser variant requiring one team to stand against the wall while the opposition threw the balls. Other than the wall, the difference in the later version was that receivers could not catch the ball.

In preparation, M.J. ran laps with us around the yard stopping at intervals to crouch or sprint. With Ana's wooden fence as a backstop he tossed old tennis balls at us and demonstrated how to pivot, dodge or skid. He taught us to sidestep, trunk twist, duck and jump. At first we got hit, though with each succeeding round the balls found their mark less and less.

Using an old laundry basket tied between two trees M.J. coached us to throw dodge balls from different angles, including on the run. Soon, Tommy could hit a plastic milk jug, half filled with water, and swinging from the tree house. He set soda cans atop sticks at different heights with the objective of hitting only the can without disturbing the stick. We scooped ground balls at a trot, transferring them to opposite hands like loading a slingshot.

Post training briefs were used to discuss tactics over Ana's fresh limeade. "Look to see who's laughing," M.J. said. "Those are the ones having fun. That's the team."

With his father's instruction, Tommy climbed the playground hierarchy of dodge ball eminence and, for a time, was considered the dodge ball master. At least, until Aunt Sonia made an unannounced visit to the school one afternoon during recess. Tommy didn't see her waving, but he smiled as he received the highest accolade of dodge ball honors. Both teams tossed balls at him at once and while he evaded most of them, through sheer numbers he was eventually tagged head and trunk. He was bestowed with the highest tribute of respect to his skill.

Like an Olympian athlete, Tommy's glory was brief as all heads turned to look at Aunt Sonia crossing the playground screaming about assault and battery. To his shame, she dragged Tommy into the administration office squalling threats of going to the school board as the playground monitor trailed in their wake. Her outrage was compounded when she discovered M.J. had signed the permission form allowing Tommy to participate in "a barbaric torture of a beautiful little boy."

Thereafter Tommy's school recreation was restricted. Being benched didn't stop him from offering advice or participating in after school or Saturday bootleg games where neighborhood kids were glad to see Tommy take the court. His existence was a state, or at least, a street kept secret. As our school's undisputed dodge ball czar Tommy possessed not only talent, but the foresight of a sports bookie for assessing dodge ball players and teams.

"This isn't a game," Tommy muttered under his breath as we stood there looking. "Look who's laughing!"

I followed the incline of his chin from three throwers toeing the foul line to a boy with shaggy blonde hair. His bare arms revealed sunburned skin not covered by a stained T-shirt that had once been white. Throwing the ball, the boy turned and grinned at the bystanders, displaying teeth too big for his mouth wiping his palms on the front of jean shorts that might have been cut off with a chainsaw. Nearby, two older boys regarded him without expression and with crossed arms.

"Lonnie Fant," said the largest boy, loud enough for everyone to hear. "He's as useless as his daddy Arlie."

"Probably worse," his friend concurred. "It's a family tradition. You should hear the nasty stories my dad tells about his uncles and grandpa."

Lonnie heard them, along with everyone else, but instead of getting mad he beamed another crooked grin with his chin held high as if he took more pleasure in the harsh words than praise. He also made an obscene sucking sound from the side of his mouth before returning his attention to the game.

The two boys talked for less than a minute before starting up the hill. Lonnie happened to look around as they were leaving. His eyes widened and his mouth drooped with an expression of severe disappointment looking after them. I thought he might call, "don't go, wait, please stay," but instead he scowled and howled. "Let's get this show on the road!" He heckled, "Who's the first victim?"

The object of the game was to score points by hitting an opponent with a ball and scoring two points, while a miss eliminated the thrower. The inning continued until everyone was hit or the last thrower eliminated. When innings ended with an excess of throwers or receivers, that team got a point for each player still in the game. As in regular dodge ball, in this version game points were gained by combinations of individual and team effort. But the only driving force in this particular game was Lonnie. It took no time to realize he lacked any real skill for the game as he jumped and crowed like a mutated frog winning points through intimidation. Should one of his own team pick up a ball close to Lonnie, he had no shame in yanking it from their hands.

"You couldn't hit anything any how," mocked Lonnie without apology.

I saw that throwers were unenthusiastic and kids against the hay waited with the expectant expression of wanting to be somewhere else. Throwers and receivers glanced enviously up the hill at the prancing entertainers. Lonnie dug the ground with his sneakers, like a dog doing its business, and combed his greasy hair from his eyes with his fingers before he lifted his head and brayed like a donkey.

When the other team had been eliminated to one, in record time, Lonnie demanded the latest score before dispatching the last player. His team shuffled toward the fence to defend and strutted kicking dust and clapping hands, capering from one side to the other.

"Take a break guys, this won't take two minutes, not two minutes, do you hear?"

The white haired boy reacted like a squirrel as the balls flew. Lonnie jumped behind other kids to avoid being hit and, regardless if the ball was meant for him, he taunted and screamed for throwers to try their luck with him. At one point two throwers simultaneously launched balls and missed Lonnie by a breath as he belly flopped to the ground. Jumping to his feet, he leveled a dirty forefinger at the throwers with a silent promise to return the favor. And while it took longer to eliminate the other team, Lonnie was the last standing at the end of the round.

During the next inning a red headed girl with a freckled face stepped out of bounds to avoid being hit, an automatic point without hitting her. Hitting above the shoulders wasn't allowed and points were automatically lost. Yet, Lonnie paid no attention to the shouted warnings and nailed her hard in the ear as she stopped to keep from running into a hay bale. Instantly her face screwed into pain and she ran squalling up the hill with another girl behind her.

"Lonnie we've told you about that," said a boy. "Do it again and you're out for good."

Lonnie gave his "I'd like to see you try" smirk and added an apologetic expression as shredded as his shorts. When none of the other bystanders stepped forward to replace the two girls, Tommy and I raised our hands and Lonnie donkey brayed raising a dirty finger to the sky. The other team took their place against the wall. Tommy stepped to the foul line and I found a spot six positions to Tommy's right. Lonnie took a stand at the far end of the hay fence, hands on his hips and thin lips curled, revealing yellow teeth.

"Ever play this game before, son?" Lonnie called to Tommy. "You're awful pretty, so be careful or somebody might try to kiss you."

Tommy and I exchanged nods and in contrast to our team members, waited with anticipation to pick up a ball. The others threw their balls with lifeless effort as our opponents moved with equal fervor the length of the hay fence. Before long a kid three places to Lonnie's left was eliminated and a ball bounced toward me. Lonnie watched me retrieve it and a puzzled look crimped his face. Just as Uncle M.J. had taught me, I stepped to my right, caught the ball with my left hand, my torso pivoting to fire it parallel down the foul line to Tommy. Just as we had practiced, he received the ball leaning over the foul line with his right palm. His body twisted like a wound spring with the momentum of the ball before he rifled it toward Lonnie's chest.

The white haired boy was standing there making sucking sounds, much too preoccupied to hear a teammate shout a warning until it was too late. The ball hit Lonnie solidly in the mid section and bounced to the foul line. All activity ceased as both teams stared from Lonnie to Tommy.

"Lonnie never gets hit," whispered a girl to my right. "At least not by anybody smaller than him."

"Don't count," Lonnie squealed. "Not fair! No point! Not fair!"

"It is fair," said Tommy scooping up another ball. "Check with the National Dodge Ball Association. They use that play all the time."

Tommy didn't bother to say the National Dodge Ball Association didn't play the lesser version, but both teams exchanged confused glances before nodding their heads in Tommy's favor.

"I say it ain't fair!" Lonnie squealed. "It don't count!"

"Can't argue with the National Dodge Ball Association Lonnie," declared the boy who'd warned him. "It's legal. You're out." Everyone turned as one to stare until Lonnie stomped away eyeing Tommy.

The game resumed, but it was very different from what it had been. Throwers laughed along with receivers as the inning ended with our team gaining five points. We took our places against the stack as Lonnie elbowed his way to a position directly in front of my cousin. When everyone was in place Tommy leaned forward into the defensive stance M.J had taught him. Exchanging nods with another kid on the foul line, Lonnie looked around as if the broad choice of targets was too overwhelming. Absently, he wiped his arm across his nose and drew the ball back behind his ear.

"It's nap time pretty boy," Lonnie shouted. "Say good night!"

Together Lonnie and the other boy launched their balls in Tommy's direction. To everyone's surprise but mine, Tommy stepped forward and rotated his body like a swinging door. Both balls sailed past him to hit the backstop with a mocking "pa-pong-pong" and Lonnie's victory bray was cut off before he could say "ha!"

Our team's score rose from the basement with success unimaginable before Tommy's arrival. Other players copied Tommy's tactics tossing their balls down the foul line. A pair of kids snagged balls and tossed them ineffectively to each other. Others tried hiking the ball between their legs like a football center or hand passed a ball behind their backs all the way down the line.

Everyone seemed to have found a new sense of fun, except Lonnie. This didn't stop him from trying to snatch balls from other player's grasp only to have them taken back, sometimes with the help of two of his teammates. He also refused to coordinate any strategy, but his own. More than a few points were scored on both sides with a team play. Yet, Lonnie refused to concede if he didn't get sole credit for making the point. The results were a massive loss by Lonnie's side of otherwise easy points.

That's not to say Lonnie's team laid down. It became every man and girl for themselves as Lonnie's intensity increased and threw balls that left bruises if they'd connected. Yet his greatest frustration was the inability to hit Tommy, even once. Others tagged him, but not Lonnie and it seemed as if the balls themselves rebelled, though Tommy wasn't the only one he couldn't hit. His threats were ignored and everyone read his telegraphed throws by the abuse he shouted. Still, Lonnie had to blame someone, anyone or something.

"These balls are messed up," said Lonnie during a change of sides. "They need air."

No one paid any attention and took their places as Lonnie repeated his complaints like he was delivering divine guidance. What was missing was his signature sucking sound and menacing tone as he became more frustrated.

"Be careful now," said a girl on our team with her eyes darting in Lonnie's direction. "He's mean as a stepped on snake. You saw what he did to that red headed girl."

Kids standing a few feet away leaned toward us nodding their heads.

"His daddy is even meaner," she hissed. "Lonnie said his daddy just got out of jail and if we cross him." She paused and looked around twice. "His daddy will stomp a kid's whole family, even babies." She added how Lonnie bragged that even if his daddy went back to jail, he never forgot, or forgave a wrong. Eventually he would track down the offenders, making them sorry for being born.

"Lonnie says he's done it before," she said to accompanying nods of other kids. "Watch yourselves."

Lonnie eyes were always looking at one of us, and he wasn't alone. The number of bystanders had grown since Tommy and I started to play, with clapping and shouts of encouragement that made Lonnie physically cringe. Desperately, and without warning, he fired a ball at Tommy's nose. It was another violation of the rule against hitting above the shoulders and could have done some real injury if it connected. That is, if Tommy hadn't effortlessly bent his neck hard left as the ball closed, letting it pass within a freckle of his right ear.

"I got him," Lonnie howled. "You saw, I hit him You tell them kid, I got you?" Lonnie was shouted down as both teams voiced loud and firm disapproval. Tight lipped, he left the line and sat on his haunches, his face turned away from the bystanders.

By the last inning our team was behind by only four points. Lonnie and his friend were at the wall and Tommy was the sole opposition. The girl who'd whispered warnings about Lonnie, voiced her doubt at the obvious, that Tommy had to tag both players to win. By contrast, she added unnecessarily, the defensive players only had to dance to the opposite ends of the stack to cut the odds of getting hit by half. To hit one a thrower had to be skilled or very lucky, for two, he had to be blessed.

Tommy, as it turned out, was all three.

Chapter 7

Instead of going to the opposite ends of the wall, Lonnie and the other boy stood together in front of the wall. Toeing the dirt, they spat or squatted on haunches, their eyes always on Tommy as they stood and stretched.

"OK pretty boy, last call. Hurry up and miss us," Lonnie called. "I got things to do, places to go, people to meet."

"More like loot to steal and folks to maim," hissed the girl who knew about Lonnie.

Lonnie crossed his arms and kept a full arm's length distance from the other boy. He cocked his right leg at a right angle, balancing the tip of his sneaker in front of his left leg. The other kid copied the stance, looking similar to salt and pepper shakers, and called insults, insisting Tommy hurry up and throw.

Ignoring them, Tommy gripped the ball in both hands, crab walking to his left, stopping nearest the other boy and dropping his left shoulder as if winding up a throw. Everyone tensed, but there was no throw as my cousin grinned and shuffled right, feigned again with equal results before frog hopping closer to Lonnie. He performed this ritual twice and even I became impatient for a throw, though I knew a battlefield setup cannot be rushed.

Tommy stepped far right, as if to repeat his skipping jig, and twisted forward on his right foot pivoting his whole body like a boxer throwing a right hook punch. Neither boy at the wall had time to disengage before the ball traveled three-quarters of the distance. The other boy slid to his left exposing Lonnie's left side to the oncoming ball. Wide-eyed, Lonnie staggered to his right. The ball whistled past the other boy, slamming Lonnie's shoulder joint with a solid "plong" and flew the short distance to smack the other kid's ribs with a final "plung."

No one had seen anything like it before. They could only stare in disbelief at the history that had been made, until a shrill scream of protest cut the silence. "It don't count," Lonnie shouted. "It hit above the shoulder! It don't count! You cheated! We win by default!"

Before he could repeat himself, Lonnie's voice was lost in the cheers of both teams. After all, here was the first double tag they had witnessed and, although our team won, the other team was equally ecstatic crowding around Tommy to pat him on the back. Girls asked me where we were staying and boys wanted to know when we'd like to get another game going.

Unsuccessfully, Lonnie continued to shout above the ruckus that the play wasn't fair. Finally, he stomped away to the L-end of the backstop opposite the fence with two other boys. The others took up positions leaning with their backs and one foot resting against the bales while Lonnie kicked a bottom bale repeatedly before folding his arms and yanking a straw from a bale above his head and stuck it in his mouth. The other boys also pulled out straws to put in their mouths as they glared in our direction. The celebration quieted down some, but more kids appeared to gather around Tommy.

Meantime, Lonnie's straw bobbed like a living thing until he spat it out and jerked another from the bale before hooking his thumbs into the loops of his shorts and swaggering toward us. The others fell in on either side of him and wedged their way toward us until Lonnie was within an arm's length of Tommy. Feet spread wide Lonnie showed crusted yellow teeth pulling the straw from his mouth pointing the gnawed end pointed at Tommy.

"You're lucky kid," Lonnie said. "I've never seen anything like you."

No one said anything as he shoved the straw's gnawed end at Tommy's nose emphasizing each word before shoving it between his canines.

"You are a very lucky kid. Of course luck ain't everything, so you'll need to watch yourself around here."

I was tempted to ask the redundant question, only one of the boys beside Lonnie spoke on cue.

"Really, why's that?"

"Because some guys don't believe in luck," Lonnie said. "They only see a smart punk who thinks he's better than everybody. So it ain't surprising that for punks around here, smart or dumb, are open season."

"I'll remember that," said Tommy turning to go.

Lonnie shuffled and blocked Tommy's way.

"Some people think I'm a smart punk," Lonnie continued, "and they'd be wrong too, I don't think I'm better than everyone else, I know. Only, I don't care what anybody thinks and you want to know why?"

Again no one in the crowd answered the rhetorical question and Tommy stared into Lonnie's eyes.

"Why? "Blurted the other boy, after Lonnie elbow nudged him.

"Because I know savate," said Lonnie loud enough to be heard up the hill. "Been taking it since I was six from Supreme Savate Master Mike DeGrief."

"What's that?" Asked a voice, "and who's Mike DeGrief?"

"Savate," said Lonnie unhooking his thumbs from his belt loops, "is French foot fighting. Master Mike DeGrief is an ex-Navy SEAL and the top competitive savate fighter in Oklahoma. He's never lost a fight, and neither have I."

Lonnie delivered his announcement the way I'd heard speakers on TV announce candidates for president. It was the same way some kids spoke of sports, musicians or professionals as the best, greatest or number one in their field. There was hint in Lonnie's tone that he wouldn't tolerate arguing the point either.

"That's like karate?" a girl piped enthusiastically. "My cousin took karate."

"No, stupid," Lonnie spat, "karate is for punks. Savate stomps butt and you can take it to the bank that if a karate guy meets savate, karate steps aside." Murmurs rose as he turned in full circle and said, "I'll have my black belt next year."

"How do you know this Mike the creep," a boy asked. "I never heard of him."

"That's Master DeGrief to you," snapped Lonnie as if that should answer everything. "I know him through my dad and he's head of the best security company in the country."

Seeing our opportunity, Tommy and I turned, but Lonnie and his friends moved into our path.

"It's a fact that there's no defense against savate," said Lonnie waving the gnawed straw like a baton again. "That's why I don't worry what other people think about me." The straw was back in his mouth as his thumbs hooked into the belt loops of his shorts before leaned down to Tommy and said. "I'll be happy to give you a free lesson. "

"No thanks," Tommy said. "We have to go."

"What's your hurry?" said Lonnie moving back a step. "You're about to get the benefit of what my daddy calls a life lesson. It could save your life some day, so you'll thank me."

Raising his fists to his collar bones, Lonnie pulled them down like he was tugging a rope to his middle and his left foot swung into the air reminding me of a playground teeter-tooter. As kicks go Lonnie's weren't any more special from any other kid's. The toe of his sneaker whipped within a double freckle of Tommy's forehead before it touched the ground and launched again, missing Tommy's nose by another freckle.

Seeing the other two boys step back winking and grinning as the crowd formed a circle, I knew a kick would "accidentally" catch Tommy square in the face. Yet, Tommy stood his ground and the crowd hummed "ahs" each time Lonnie's sneaker left the ground. I stepped to my cousin's side and Lonnie caught my movement. Twisting, he whipped a foot toward my chest and even without contact the tenderness rose to high alert with the color on my cheeks. Tommy waved a hand for me to stay back.

"That's right pretty boy," Lonnie said. "You don't need a girl for this lesson, because you are one."

I considered the option of a straight frontal attack and noticed that when Lonnie's left foot returned to earth, he always side stepped two steps to his right to regain his balance before kicking again. Tommy must have noticed this little dance too, his eyes gleamed and his mouth curved into a grim smile.

Braying, Lonnie launched a kick at me and when his foot hit the ground, followed by the obligatory right-double-step, there was Tommy's sneaker beside Lonnie's right foot. Lonnie crumpled over Tommy's foot like a sack of potatoes, without the sack. Stunned silenced soon fell victim to laughter as Lonnie scrambled to his feet, teeth bared and launched another foot at Tommy. It could have split a dodge ball, but the foot missed. Once more, Tommy scooted to park his foot beside's Lonnie foot before the left one hit the dirt. Again, to the roar of laughter, the white haired boy crumpled with the grace of a string-cut-puppet.

CHAPTER 8

Lonnie scrambled to his feet, legs apart and fists doubled. "Nobody does that to me! You're dead meat! Dead, dead, do you hear?"

Holding his fists below his nose Lonnie advanced toward Tommy making his sucking sound heard over the shouts. I dashed between the two boys, grabbed a surprised Lonnie by his shoulders, pushing with my right hand and pulling with my left, the way Uncle Theo taught me, and swept his leg with my right foot, letting gravity do the rest. His eyes bugged in shock as I released him and he fell, arms flailing and head bouncing on the packed earth.

"Owwww!" he howled. "Owww, I have a concussion!"

Everyone crowded around Lonnie, not offering help, but hopefully looking for blood or spilt entrails. My problem was the mob also blocked our way to the slope and the camp. I thought of pushing through and running for the hilltop. That would have been the wisest move if not for the memory of a boy I'd known in second grade. He was a new, a total stranger accused of stealing. I didn't know the particulars, but everyone knew stealing was wrong. So, as if drawn by a magnetic force, when I saw him running with a group of kids in pursuit, I ran after him without knowing why, but totally intent on catching him. The chase was like a snowball rolling down hill with more kids joining the mob the longer we ran.

And it didn't matter what he had done. He ran, we chased! To this day I can't say why I joined the hunt that might have hurt that boy if a teacher hadn't intervened. When she demanded to know what was going on, a righteous voice declared the boy was a thief, who stole money. Which was never proven, though someone said he'd taken five cents. Which I suppose is why we all laughed stupidly and tried not to look at each other after the teacher said, "Is that all?"

That situation stuck in my mind reminding me that given prey a pack will automatically give chase, regardless of the reason. Not knowing what else to do, I grabbed Tommy's hand and we ran toward the far end of the backstop. Glancing over my shoulder I saw Lonnie struggling to his feet.

"Get them," Lonnie screamed. "Nobody does that to me."

We ducked behind the hay backstop and found a corridor between the hay bales and a brush thicket. We ran past brambles and briars hanging from the trees like drapes. The thicket reminded me of the jungle vines Tarzan swung from in those movies Papa liked. Only these vines had thorns as wide and long as the nail on my little finger and I didn't need a jungle lord to know we could be torn to pieces trying to get through those stickers.

Still holding Tommy by the hand, we ran down the corridor that was just wide enough for us to run side by side. I thought we could run to the other end of the backstop and slip between the fence and the short side of the L where the freckled girl had been hit. Only the hay bales were flush against a barbed wire fence, leaving no room between bales and fence. Literally running out of path, I saw a break in the brush to my left and turned onto a path stretching into the thicket. With no time for me to consider how far this path extended we turned just as Lonnie appeared at the far end of the wall screeching like a demon.

Glimpsing the other boys behind him, Tommy and I sprinted down a knobby trail that slopped downhill zigzagging like a jagged scar through the brush. These brambles were taller than Tommy and I standing on top of one another, with overhanging tree branches shading the path to near darkness.

Tommy stumbled and I slowed so we could catch our balance and looked back to see Lonnie and his pals appear from around a bend. Screaming in delight, they moved toward us at a full run as I looked down the path as straight as a corridor at my school. They would catch us even if we sprinted.

Dropping my hand to my side, I remembered my pirate's prize in my back pocket and pulled it out as I ran toward the boys raising the fake knife above my head the way I'd seen knife throwers on TV. Wide eyed, their heads tilted in the direction of my raised hand, their feet skidded to a stop. When I swung my arm forward, they dove for the ground and Tommy and I ran ahead.

At the end of the corridor we turned left into a path broad enough for all of us to run side by side. Yet, there was no break on either side of the brush. Yet, the further we ran the more light filtered through the overhead branches and the sound of falling water grew louder.

My first thought was it must be the river we'd been told to stay away from. Yet, I reasoned, the river was thousands of yards, maybe miles, in the opposite direction. With no time to mull the facts I ran through an iron frame without a gate. Out of the shadow of the trees, the path sloped into a clearing the size of Ana's front yard. The area was clear with knee high grass and a beaten path that wound its way into a stand of trees. To our right was a narrow course way with high water that reached the lower lip of a concrete dam. The dam blocked what I realized was a creek flowing into the river.

Moving into the clearing I saw stone steps ascending to a concrete wide platform that was part of the dam. I mounted the steps two at a time. The water behind the dam was deep and green, which would have made it a nice place to swim or picnic because of a pair of cottonwood trees shading the platform. Yet the priority was escape and while the trees had climbable branches, none were stout enough for two.

Water flowed across the top of the dam in a steady torrent. At its other end was a huge L-shaped pipe, with a periscope elbow, that allowed water to gush in an arch as thick as I was and pool two yards below the foot of the dam. The pipe was big enough for us to hide on its far side, but to get to it we had to cross a narrow slab of concrete barely wide enough for our feet and covered with slimy moss while water pushed at our ankles.

I considered running farther up stream and realized how easily they'd catch us. Frantically, I looked for Tommy and ran down the stairs, spotting two stones the size of baking potatoes beside the bottom step. Grabbing one in each hand, I ran back to the path, shouting for Tommy to find a club.

Hot, sweaty and mad I decided whatever happened, it wasn't going to end without a fight and lots of pain for the other side. It looked as if the gate was our best defensive spot since they wouldn't be able to circle behind us. Satisfied, I looked for more weapons when Tommy crawled out of the barbed wire fence that was parallel to the creek. I was about to give him what for, for not finding a club when he motioned me to follow and dropped to his haunches and moved back through the fence where the wire was bent unnaturally wide. Squinting through the wire and bush revealed another slight trail on the other side. I motioned Tommy to keep going and I sprinted back up he dam's platform steps dropping my rocks.

"Come on Tommy," I shouted with my hands cupped to my mouth. "They'll never catch us on the other side."

Then I heaved the rocks like a shot put into the deep water behind the dam producing two deep "kerpunk" splashes I hoped would amplify off the hills. Shrieking, I ran all the way to the fence, dropped to my knees and crawled through the wire gap. Crab-walking downhill, the thick foliage closed behind me like a gate and the trail became broader and sloped toward the creek. More light filtered through the overhead branches, but I almost missed Tommy hiding below a rock ledge. He hissed and made room for me against the rock and we settled in to hold our collective breath. Before long, the sound of running feet grew louder then slowed to a silent creep betrayed by leaves on the bigger trail.

Peeking over the rock, I caught sight of cloth flashes through the leaves before ducking down and straining my ears against the wind blowing through the trees. Before long, we couldn't hear anything until a series of curses ripped the air from the direction of the dam. These were words I only heard in movies my parents forbid me to watch.

"Where are you punks?" Lonnie screamed. "Come out and face me like a man."

Turning to face Tommy, his mouth twisted into a smirk and mouthed, "like a man," before sticking out his tongue and rolling his eyes. I had to hold my hands over my face to muffle my laughter.

"Lonnie," I heard a boy's voice call. "Over here!"

We heard footsteps smack on the concrete of the platform and noticed, to our horror, the distinct outlines visible through small openings in the foliage. If we could see them, they only had to turn to see us, but they didn't. But Tommy and I inched down against the rock still seeing at least half of the dam and the pipe gushing water.

"They fell in," a boy's voice shouted.

"I hope not," spat Lonnie in the same loud voice. "Their souls may belong to Jesus, but their ass is mine."

"You heard the splashes, see the water here and the girl screamed," the other boy shouted. "Maybe they drowned. We can find their bodies and get a reward."

"Did you have extra bowl of dumb ass this morning?" Lonnie snapped. "Or are you stupid naturally? They're around here someplace and we can find them."

We heard them move off the dam and I wanted to thank Lonnie for being a jerk. We heard them return to the gate.

"I don't like this" said the first boy irritably. "I'm going back to camp."

"No you're not," Lonnie commanded. "They're probably just up the trail and not far."

"Then you find them," the other boy said, "I'm bored and it stinks here."

We caught glimpses of the other boys passing the entrance to our hiding place. Lonnie followed and stopped directly in front of the crawl hole in the fence. Foliage made it difficult, but we just made him out through the leaves looking after the boys. When he took another step up the trail, I could see his face clearly with the longing expression he had when the older boys left. He stared after them before finally dropping his head to his chest and running his hands through his hair. I thought he would follow, instead he raised his chin and spat in their direction.

"Fine, quitters, I'll do this myself!" he yelled. "You'll see!" and added in a low growl, "Nobody does that to me."

He disappeared and we heard sound from the direction of the dam. Straining our ears, we tried not to crunch the dead leaves around us that seemed loud as galloping horses.

"I know you're here somewhere, so you have to come out sometime. "

Tommy's eyes crossed again with a goofy expression. Together, we shook our heads and silently mouthed, "Oh no we don't."

"Come out now and it won't be so bad," Lonnie pleaded. "I promise I'll be fair."

Holding my nose with two fingers I wiggled my other hand in the direction of the voice while Tommy stuck out his tongue and shook his head side to side. His tongue flopping against the sides of his face which made laughter nearly impossible to control. I waved Tommy to stop, which he tried, but with a finger to his lips, he sputtered uncontrollably before we clamped our hands over our mouths and ducked to the ground in an attempt to compose ourselves. Cheeks in the dirt, we looked into the other's eyes and sputtered uncontrollably until I turned away. Twice I looked back only to catch a fresh case of the giggles rushing to my throat. Mercifully Tommy held up his pirate candy dispenser before I would look again.

Elated I concentrated on the little pirate, focusing on the painted grin and beard. My laughter subsided, and so nearly did my heart when gushers of water erupted from the creek just down the slope. Soon the trees around us shook as rocks bounced from their upper limbs falling to earth. Chunks of wood and more rocks followed, falling on either side of us, including a stone that plopped barely six inches below my feet. We scrunched tighter against the rock slope where I covered my head with my hands and lodged the beacon painfully against my right chest. The soreness was secondary and to hide it, I hissed through my teeth like I was laughing as more rocks fell. Before the rocks got closer Lonnie must have run out of ammunition, or got frustrated. To our relief the bombardment stopped. We wiped our brows with the backs of our hands, like cartoon characters, before giving each other a thumbs up and tapping fists. Then we heard a massive splash from the direction of the dam.

Bugged-eyed, we turned to one another for an answer. We heard frantic splashing along with even worse curses. Realizing what had happened. I thought of going to help, but hesitated as the sound of dripping water mixed with indignant mutterings grew steadily louder.

"By God you better be drowned," Lonnie shouted, stopping again at the entrance to our lair. "When I find you, you'll wish you were in hell where you belong."

The sound of dripping water noise and squishing shoes faded as flashes of a once white T-shirt moved ghost like beyond the foliage. Even when there was no sound, we didn't move, though Tommy popped two more candies.

"He's waiting up the trail," I whispered. "So, we'll sit here a little longer."

Nodding, Tommy turned and leaned his back against the big rock, his mouth working with the rhythm necessary for dissolving the hard candy. I found a comfortable surface and stared in the direction of the creek watching the ripples from the big water pipe in the last stages of existence. The ripples carried tree leaves from overhanging branches drifting along with mating dragonflies.

I was elated thinking about the dodge ball game, the fight and the race. For once, I was on the winner's side, but I also felt sad the way I had about the gift booths. Sighing, I turned and looked up the slope wondering how long we'd have to sit before Lonnie lost patience.

"Hey," exclaimed Tommy getting to his feet. "Look down there!"

CHAPTER 9

Tommy moved out of the shadows and down the slope to where sunlight and shadows dueled for supremacy of the shore.

"What? Wait, no, wait," I cautioned, trying to keep my voice down. "I don't see anything! Where are you going?"

He shuffled the distance to the creek bank and I considered whether to follow him.

"Wait," I repeated and as loud as I thought possible. "Where are you going?"

He didn't respond and I got up struggling to keep my balance as my feet slid on a carpet of dead leaves down the slope. Tommy stood against a tree, its trunk as thick as my leg, growing at the edge of the water. Unable to control my downhill momentum, I nearly ran into him before falling on my back. Tommy didn't seem to notice our near mishap. He was mesmerized with something below the tree he was holding.

"Look at this," he said.

I got to my feet, but before I could join Tommy at the tree he was holding he bent over and fell from sight.

"Tommy," I screamed.

There was no splash or thud in the mud or sand. Instead I heard a sound akin to a super-sized dodge ball bounced on pavement. Not caring who heard me I reached the tree, grabbed it to keep from going over the edge and looked down. Only there was no shore, merely a sheer bank to the water more like a short cliff with a straight drop off of three to four feet. I expected to find my cousin lying in a bloody heap on the rocks below. Instead, he looked up at me, the top of his head toward me, grinned and appeared to be floating on top of the water, or so I thought. Ripples moved around him, yet the water neither lapped or got him wet.

"Hey Jackie," he said, his hands folded over his stomach. "Look what I found!"

Grasping the tree with both hands, I looked down to where the tree's roots showed through the earth at the water's edge from where Tommy floated. Annoyed, I forced my mind to make sense of what I couldn't believe my eyes were seeing. That's also when I felt the rope tied around the tree. Turning to the tree, I grasped the rope that was the same color as the bark of the tree. It might have been mistaken for a branch. It was wrapped in a single loop around the trunk, its other end attached to the inflatable raft Tommy lay on. Like the rope, the raft merged perfectly with its background symmetry, making it nearly invisible.

Shaken, but relieved, I tried to imitate Ana's angry-look. I was unable to hold my mouth scrunched for long before curiosity over rode all other emotions. The raft was the kind of boat used in Papa's old movies, with soldiers hunched low, paddling, their faces smeared with black shoe polish while one man lay in the front with a big gun. This was the type of boat used for secret missions to land on deserted beaches on a moonless night, while enemy sentries walked the parapets of a fortified installation, its destruction vital to ending a war.

Looking toward the dam, I saw no enemy sentries, or anyone for that matter. Meantime, Tommy grabbed the rope attached to the front of the raft, and pulled himself up on the hood or top of the raft. What was amazing was that, while I could make out its oval shape, its color still blended in so well I had to keep my eyes fixed so I wasn't fooled by its camouflage.

"Ana told you not to go near the river," I said. " So you'd better come out of there before you get in big trouble."

His expression twisted with mock horror and he made no move. "This is not the river, it's a creek," he said. "They are different bodies of water, aren't they?"

"Not to Ana,' I said "now give me your hand!"

I bent down with my right hand still hooked around the tree and held out my left.

"Ahh Jackie," he moaned, "We just found it."

"And we're just going to leave it," I said wiggling my fingers. "It belongs to somebody, so come on!"

"First, let's paddle it across to the other side," he said not extending a hand. "It won't take 15 minutes."

"Have you ever paddled a boat?" I demanded. "Have you ever been in a boat by yourself?"

"I can dog paddle. It shouldn't be too hard. Come on, it'll be fun!"

"Do you plan on paddling with your hands?" I replied. "Because I don't see any paddles.

Tommy looked and saw nothing was in the raft. His shoulders slumped, until he turned to me smiling again.

"I could hang my legs off the back end and kick."

Frowning, I shook my head and Tommy climbed onto the raft's nose and held out his hand. The loose end of the rope dangled in front of him, he grabbed it with his other hand and stretched the open one toward me. Leaning down, I caught his hand and we both pulled. Only gravity, along with his weight, were on his side as he jerked my arm. Tree bark scraped my palm and I squealed as I fell on top of him and into the bottom of the raft.

The pain in my hand competed with my chest while Tommy wriggled out from under me, laughing and happened to look over my shoulder. The end of the rope he'd been holding slipped over the raft's front, and we were moving.

CHAPTER 10

We scrambled to the front of the raft as the rope slithered loose from around the tree and dropped into the water and trailing the raft like a trained snake. I pulled the rope in hoping it would catch on a root or submerged rock. Holding the dripping end, I tied a quick knot and tossed it toward the shore where it fell short by inches that grew to feet and yards. Gathering it again for another toss, my attention was drawn to the sound of rushing water. Looking around I saw the arching stream of water from the big elbow shaped pipe slam the water's surface below the dam with the impact of a belly buster dive.

"Jackie," Tommy cried. "What did you do? What will we do?"

The sound of falling water grew louder and seemed to pull us toward it like we were being towed. Droplets soon soaked the raft and I yelled to be heard above the roar.

"Lonnie, Lonnie," I screamed. "We're down here! Lonnie, come get us. Here we are!"

"Are you crazy?" Shouted Tommy, not two feet away from my ear. "that creep will pound us to hamburger if he finds us."

"If he does," I shouted back, "he'll have to get us back on land."

"Lonnie," yowled Tommy with his hands cupped to his mouth, "you ugly, snot-headed tub of butt holes "

My cousin looked crazy grinning his "whatever works" expression. Shrugging, I added my insults, hoping to draw Lonnie and thinking if the white haired boy wasn't mad before, he had no excuses now. We yelled every insult and vile expression we'd heard, on or off the play ground, taking particular delight in those filthy names we weren't even supposed to know and never, ever repeat.

Yet, help, good or bad, never arrived as the raft moved toward the frothy rings produced by the discharge. Wondering how fast a rubber raft could fill with water, I thought of swimming. But considered that the only time I'd seen rafts sink, in Papa's movies, were when the good guys stuck knives in them, and that was on purpose. What wasn't in Papa's movies was the thick moss covering the sides of the dam with a bright green curtain shimmering in the sunlight. On top of the water extending liked gray lawn from the foot of the dam was a compost of wood chips and dingy foam with oatmeal consistency. Its layer stretched from shore to shore and looked thick enough I almost thought I could walk on it. The adjacent tea colored water reeked with a nose wrinkling stench that, combined, wasn't close to my idea of an easy swim. There was also the reality that, until then, we'd only swam in water up to our waists, where we could see our feet.

Tommy grabbed the seat of the raft to brace for impact and I did the same. Looking at one another, we gritted our teeth, squinted eyes to slits and braced for the expected hard impact. To our surprise, we floated close enough for a good spray before the rippling momentum sent us downstream. When we were no longer being sprayed, I stood up in relief and joined Tommy on his end of the raft.

"We should bump against land soon," I said in a tone I wanted to believe. "First chance and we'll jump out."

The current moved the raft to the center of the creek and we joined carpets of leaves ambling downstream. These were provided by the broad cottonwood trees with thick trunks anchored high on one shore whose heavily leafed branches fluttered above or in the water. Scrambling to the top of the raft's side, Tommy waited impatiently for a very low branch to come within reach.

"It'll be just like Tarzan," Tommy said. "We'll climb up the branch to the top and down the tree."

With his bad Tarzan yell, Tommy wedged his rear against the oarlock and caught a branch that drooped into the water with both hands. He tried to pull himself up, only the thicker limbs were too high to reach and Tommy wasn't strong enough to pull himself up. Yet, he refused to let go even after the branch splintered and the current pulled. He almost fell into the water, but I wrapped my arms around his waist and yanked him into the raft's bottom. He stood up in a foul mood glaring at me and letting the leaves in his fists float to the raft's floor.

"I had us stopped," he whined.

Making a face I moved to the front of the raft just as the current swung us in a circle and the nose rope trailed behind us. Tommy moved to the back and we took opposite sides of the raft and scanned the shores. Neither of us saw so much as a paper wrapper to indicate human presence.

The knee high grass competed with thick bushes and vines I noticed, and trees hundreds of feet tall spread their broad limbs toward other trees like the fingers of giants holding hands. I wondered if we had passed through some weird inner dimension like I'd read about in science fiction stories or seen on TV.

My moment of dread was replaced with the secret delight of floating. Though I might be alone, sort of, I wasn't forlorn and actually in a better place than others. The greenery embraced my being with a magic I did not yet understand, but knew was there. The world before me seemed to regress two thousand years to the time of the ancient Greeks Ana had read about.

"Is this what Eve felt like?" I whispered.

Twisting around, Tommy demanded to know what I'd said and looked irritated when I shook my head. Silently, I reflected how the goddess Diane and friend of Orion might have been born in this very spot. My imagination made connect-the-dot constellation pictures among the bushes and trees. To my surprise, because I knew it was my imagination, there wasn't an armored Orion, giant scorpions, dogs, twins or bears. Instead, there were Indians, like the ones from the stories Ana said her grandfather told her. I blinked, seeing the warriors among the shadows or crouched beside a tree. There were also girls, like me, naked and unashamed wearing simple belts and necklaces hefting bows or spears.

"Come, join us," they beckoned in a silent language. "Forget school and home and all those silly fools. Be one among those like you."

Bows gripped in their fists they stretched their arms aloft displaying the Orions imprinted on their forearms. In response I placed the beacon's whistle between my lips without blowing and enviously watched these wild girls sprint beside the shore and bound up trees. Yet, like the monsters in my closet, these shadows offered only so much reality, that which I allowed them. With a blink or head turn they vanished, though I didn't want them to go. Only the thought of leaving Tommy alone stopped me from striking for the shore.

This fantasy was how I nearly overlooked the man wearing the bright plaid yellow shorts and dark blue football jersey standing near a copse of a tall trees. His unfamiliar form made me wonder if he was a wood troll or some other mythical creature, and a natural enemy of the wild girls. Never mind the contrast of colors against forest shapes, though I mistook the shorts for a bush or light reflection. Yet, the form didn't change or fade after I blinked my eyes or changed positions on the side of the raft. I even turned to look at the opposite shore believing the apparition would go like any normal phantom. But it didn't and instead hitched up his shorts over a protruding belly, draping the football jersey over his paunch.

"Look over there," I hissed. "There's somebody by those trees."

Tommy scooted to my side of the raft straining to see the spot I pointed to. From our position on the creek the figure seemed far away, but the distance closed and the shape changed into a man, increasing in size as we drew closer. We were carried in a serpentine route to the where the man stood and his features looked like badly drawn scribbles on lined paper. Eventually, I made out a shaggy yellow mane that flew in wisps when the man jerked his head to look nervously from one side to the other, though he never looked in our direction

"Finally," Tommy exclaimed, "the cavalry has arrived!"

Tommy put his hands to his mouth to make a shout when I stopped him.

"Wait, let's get closer and be sure he hears us."

Tommy agreed though that wasn't my only reason for delay. The wild girls on creek bank whispered danger. The man fidgeted and paced like a caged animal, yellow hair whipping with each movement. We got closer as the lion's head jerked in the direction of the trees. Clearly, I could see hoary eyebrows, curly as a buffalo's, shading black eye pits and a bulbous nose bent irregularly to the right. His mouth was covered by a full butter bean beard that also draped the upper half of his football jersey, blocking out the numbers.

I was about to tell Tommy to shout for help when a reed thin man stepped from the copse of trees. Beardless, with a thin mouth, the skinny man glanced around while his fingers twisted the threads of a hole in his oily jeans exposing a pale thigh. Butter bean stiffened and spoke low as the thin man moved cautiously toward him. Butter bean withdrew his right hand from his shorts' pocket, extending it toward the thin man's outstretched claw. The thin man's fingers shot out like a toad's tongue and disappeared into his jean's pocket. Butter bean stepped closer to the other man and hands extended again, briefly touching fingers. But not before a figure crashed out of the foliage behind Butter bean. Both men turned in the direction of the intrusion and a package, the size of a pack of gum, fell to the dirt.

With his rice colored hair twisted into dried rattails, his shirt a metal gray. Lonnie Fant stumbled forward talking too loud and fast. I heard only "Daddy."

The skinny man moved in a crouch, rat style, toward the gum pack. He barely moved his hand back before Butterbean's foot missed his hand by a hair. Teeth bared, the thin man backed into the trees with Butter bean crouching to brush the ground with his shank sized hand. In the same motion Butter bean stepped toward Lonnie swinging his open hand into the boy's face and knocking him to the ground. The boy rolled to his stomach and the man grabbed his hair and pulled his head up. Lonnie had his hands on his face and blood oozed between the fingers. The man's mouth nearly touched the clasped hands while his beard was stained with blood, turning strands into the color of old honey. But Butter bean didn't seem to notice as he shook Lonnie and shouted slurred words through broken, tobacco stained teeth.

Our raft moved to a position that gave us a front row, center stage view of this scene. I could see the trail where the thin man had disappeared along and the break in the weeds where Lonnie had emerged.

"Are you going to call to him?" Tommy whispered into my ear, making me jump. "You said any help was better than none."

Without answering I hoped the man wouldn't see us, though wishing I could do something as the boy's head dropped and the man stomped away through the weeds where Lonnie had emerged.

Was Lonnie dead? I wondered, holding my breath as the raft rounded a peninsula. Lonnie's shoulders shook spasmodically and I inhaled when I heard the agonized sobs. For an instant there was no rotten kid who'd chased us, just someone that needed help. I wanted more than anything for the raft to beach for the sole purpose of helping him.

When he raised his head I saw tears had cut streaks through the grime on his face. A single pink snot bubble expanded from his nose, popped and a flood of blood from both nostrils oozed over his mouth and chin down his shirtfront.

He got to his feet with obvious effort and stared at us. Thanks to the water level combined with the shore's embankment we could see over the tops of the short grass. From Lonnie's perspective, I imagined we resembled a Halloween spook house skit, like one Ana took us to the year before. Inside the spook house, the host appeared with his face covered with phosphorescent paint. He appeared to be a floating head, though his body was covered in dark clothes against a black background. Meanwhile, another player walked beside him, wearing regular clothes, his head covered with a black hood.

For Lonnie, we must have seemed like two ghost heads floating along the ground, open mouthed and staring wide eyed. After shaking his head, he shut his eyes, rubbing them hard before looking in our direction. Recognition crossed his face, and his expression of horror turned into rage. He snatched up a stick and raced across the open field to intercept us with knees and elbows churning. Meantime, blood flew about his head in all directions staining his shirtfront and hair. Closing the distance between us, he screamed and would have fallen into deep water if he hadn't seen the creek at the last second. He managed to stop himself, but couldn't help hitting the shallow water when he fell over the bank.

For the second time we watched Lonnie get to his feet and shake with amazement. Blood still poured from his nose as he got to his feet, screaming and launched his stick like a javelin. We pulled in the trailing rope as the stick arched and flopped in our wake. Howling, Lonnie climbed the bank and ran toward us along the shore.

"Come back and fight," he howled. " Damn you, you'd better stop or I'll kill you."

Mockingly, the current seemed to speed up and moved us along even faster, which only made Lonnie angrier as we moved further out of his reach.

"We want to," Tommy called. "Can you catch this?"

Tommy held up the rope in an honest attempt to explain. Lonnie searched the ground for rocks and sticks, ineffectively throwing one after the other until there were none within reach, so he dug into his pocket and a multicolored missile sailed toward us. We lay on the sides of the raft as the object sailed between us and bounced off the raft's seat to the floor.

Reaching down, Tommy held up a perfectly knapped arrowhead wrapped with leather that I recognized from the arrowhead lady's stall. Tommy held it out to me and it was the ultimate affront to Lonnie. Howling, he ran along the bank as if his life depended on it. He looked as if he intended to dive into the raft. He might have caught us too, if not for a tributary, too small for a name, but half as wide as the creek and high with water. Thanks to the saplings on either of its sides, there was no way he could get a running jump to cross. So, Lonnie disappeared inland and we heard him crashing while we were carried farther away. We had moved far enough down stream so that when he reappeared he was a white headed stick figure on the receding bank.

"I'll find you and I'll kill you," he howled. "I'll tear your living guts out. You're dead meat, no matter how long it takes. I will find you."

We could hear Lonnie's screams long after we rounded the next bend. Tommy still held the arrowhead and shivered before slipping it into his pocket. I coiled the rope.

"What did we do?" Tommy said, "What was that all about?"

"I don't know. I'm just glad to be away from him."

Grateful to be away from the angry boy and dangerous men, I moved to the raft's right side, scanning the opposite bank and silently calling for the forest girl tribe. They didn't appear and I fumed how even imaginary friends could desert a girl.

Tommy went to the front of the raft and cocked his head before stretching his arm and pointing a shaky finger. "The river!"

CHAPTER 11

We're going to get it from Ana now for sure," Tommy moaned. "She told us not to go near the river."

What a joy, I thought, to be in trouble with Ana. I would have given all the tea in China for a whipping from her, my mother or daddy. I longed for an hour's sit in a hard backed kitchen chair and to hear a familiar adult voice start a sentence with my first and middle name. Anything was preferable to the churning waters ahead of us.

Tommy tried to bounce his body from one side of the raft to the other in an effort to nudge the boat to the shore. His movement only made the raft twirl and lifted one side dangerously high. I shouted for him to stop and, not knowing what else to do, sat down on one of the raft's seats and braced my back and feet against its side. Tommy did the same, grabbing the rope and passing me an end. Feet propped and shoulders wedged against the opposite side, we gripped the seat for dear life.

Tommy yelled above the growl of rushing water, "Here it comes!"

More like here we come, I thought, straining my muscles as the thought of underwater jagged stones ripping the raft to shreds and sucking our helpless bodies to the muddy bottom. Gritting my teeth, I braced for the transition from creek to the river and...nothing. At least, nothing I expected.

With the graciousness of a hostess ushering expected guests into her living room, the river gently swept us toward the far shore. We were so close I could see cardinals and field larks feeding. The creek, by contrast, slapped the raft with a sloppy farewell kiss that pushed it into the flowing waters of the river's embrace. Waves hit the raft's sides dousing us with fine spray. I stepped onto a seat and my heart leaped seeing the flags flying on the Bandy's Camp buildings.

We shouted and I blew the beacon's whistle until we were out of breath. When I stopped, I heard the opening cords of a song Papa and his band practiced constantly in his garage. Combined with Papa's music were the shouts of a huge audience.

"They can't hear us," I said. "Everybody is at Papa's concert."

"Somebody will be by the river," Tommy assured me. "Not everybody likes his music."

The beacon's shrill single tune tried unsuccessfully to compete with my grandfather's music that grew louder as the sight of the building tops rose over the trees lining the shore. We flopped along and rounded a bend and I saw a bare shore and the roof of the pavilion where Papa played and I knew Ana was nearby. Hope surged higher at the sight of a dock connected by a long metal-railed dog run. It was not covered and offered slips for a dozen boats along and had swimmer's ladders on either side, but there were no swimmers.

On the middle of the dock sat an elderly couple in folding chairs placed at the front edge. An old man held a cane fishing pole, its heavy green line snaked across the water in front of him like syrup on a pancake, attached to a red and white plastic float dancing on the waves. Smoke from a half smoked cigarette curled from the old man's thin lips while a sweat-stained cap obscured most of his face

Beside him sat a woman in a bright orange sundress with her face hidden by a broad straw hat tipped forward. We floated closer and I saw the flesh of the woman's arms hanging like dough on the undersides. With hands covered with brown spots she held a big hardcover book on her lap.

Waving our arms, Tommy yelled and I blew the beacon long and hard. The old couple never looked up until we were nearly abreast of the dock. The old man pulled in his hook, glanced our way and his eyes widened in surprise. But he never slowed his cast to his right. Without indicating he'd seen us, he leaned over to the old woman and patted her hand gently. The straw hat flipped up revealing a pink, moist face with an irritated expression. Cigarette nub bobbing, the old man's lips moved and her face changed into delight as she followed the direction of his outstretched hand. Satisfied she was looking, he flipped the cigarette butt away with a spray of sparks and dug into the torn pocket of his plaid shirt.

Staring myopically, the old woman's glasses shimmered as we waved frantically and she pushed the plastic rims from the middle to the bridge of her nose. She leaned forward with spindly hands and the old man wedged the pole across his knees and into the chair. He steadied her with one hand and lit another cigarette with the other. When he leaned forward, like he was going to stand up, I whooped with expectation of rescue. Instead, he gripped the pole like a baseball bat and swung it to his right, the line away from our raft.

Tommy screamed, I blew the whistle and the old woman bounced in her chair like the guest of honor at a surprise birthday party. Clapping her hands little girl style, she tilted forward and stood up unsteadily. The book on her lap tilted forward and would have fallen into the water if the old man had not caught it. She didn't seem to notice as she bounced and waved. He put the book beside her chair and cast his pole in the direction we had been.

"Please help! Help us! Help, please!" I screamed. "We need help!"

"Have fun," she cackled in her high voice. "Be mighty careful because that water is awfully deep, keep your life jackets on."

The skin on her upper arm flopped like a wet flag and her straw hat fell off. She didn't notice the hat or the old man catch it as she waved. He didn't look our way as he settled the hat on her head and forced her back in her chair.

"Help! Help! We can't get off this raft! Help us, please!"

The old man's head turned with us and smoke haloed his head as the cigarette bobbed in his thin mouth. After waving the smoke away, he cupped a hand to his ear and cocked his head in our direction. We yelled until our voices croaked and I believed help was on its way. Then he cast the pole upstream and stared blankly in that direction while the woman's head dipped down to her book. The straw hat obscured her face and we rounded the next bend.

CHAPTER 12

My Orion itched and my chest throbbed from where I'd laid against the raft. Watching the flags on the tops of the Bandy's Camp buildings recede I grasped the beacon and whipped it over my head, intending to throw it into the river.

"Jackie," Tommy yelled, "if you don't want it, give it to me."

Angry, but in control, I re-draped the cord and the beacon fell to my chest, feeling no better or worse.

"Those old people will tell somebody," Tommy said. "They can't be so dense to believe it's normal for two kids to be floating in a rubber raft."

I didn't answer and slid down on the seat. Tommy stepped over and joined me

"If we could control the direction somehow," Tommy said, "maybe we could get it to shore."

If we could control anything, I thought, we wouldn't be here.

Tommy threw his shoulder against one side of the raft and his back against the other in a bouncing ball motion. The movement inched us closer to the camp side and again lifted the raft's bottom dangerously high. Feeling the raft teeter each time Tommy hit a side and the wind blowing in my hair, was warning enough. I told Tommy to stop, which he did, reluctantly, before he stood on the front seat. I sat on the back and we watched the opposite sides of the shores, ready to draw attention. Only no one appeared and the scenery blended into a constant repetition on either side, the only difference being another bend. Rippling water lapped dapple colored shores at the foot of hills carpeted with cedar trees. The scene was so annoyingly endless it gave me hope that we were floating in a circle. To my disappointment I saw the changes in the land that dispelled my hope.

Worse was the intense reflective sunlight that hurt my eyes and forced us to seek what little shade we could share inside the raft. Occasionally we stood on the seats and caught water spray on our dry skin from a particularly rough stretch of rapids, showers that lasted from a few seconds to a minute. Each time we held our arms out, mouths open and even raised our shirts for direct contact until the current steered us to another calm surface.

"How far does this river go?" Tommy asked. "Think we'll float all the way to the ocean?"

"No," I answered, "Ana said there are lakes between here and the ocean."

"Then somebody has got to find us before then," Tommy declared. "This is really getting old."

"They will," I said with assurance I didn't feel.

I felt angry at the river, the old people, Lonnie, and circumstance. Just like Jeri and Joyce and the air twists, I didn't understand what I had done to deserve this situation. To my relief my Orion had at least quit itching like a worm trying to burrow out of my wrist. With no other option I stretched out on the back seat and slept. Tommy did the same and together we lulled in and out of sweaty sleep until late into the afternoon. Without knowing what time it was I looked up and saw the sky wasn't moving, realizing immediately that the raft had stopped.

I blinked at the puffy clouds in the sky and swung my legs before climbing groggily on to the seat and saw we were beached beside flat piece of sandy shore with a side pool maybe two inches deep.

"Tommy, come on!"

Tommy woke with a jerk, his head wobbling and looked around. He climbed up on the seat and immediately bounced over the side. I followed kicking my feet with an "up and over" and rolled down the outer side. I fell butt first into the gritty water, the wetness welcome at first, though lukewarm and slimy. Further inspection revealed I was sitting in the center of a nest of insect larva. Screaming, I jumped up and in my effort to wipe off any bugs managed to paint myself with more muck. I slopped my way to dry ground just as Tommy dropped over the raft's side and landing flat on his back. Disgusted, I scraped a layer of goop from the side of my leg with a stick making "yuck" noises and reaching for a handful of sand.

Without our weight, the raft moved grudgingly away until a slight breeze caught it and it moved into deeper water as if it had grown tiny feet. Forgetting the muck, I splashed into the water to catch it. Despite my pleas, it moved toward the center of the river before I was waist deep and twirled it's way to the next bend.

Before I had time to be angry, my feet started sinking into the soft sand. Tommy was behind me and we screamed trying to pull our feet free. Instead, we lost our balance and fell backwards, which freed our feet so we could crab-walk to shore on hands, rear and feet.

"Now what?" Tommy demanded panting.

"I don't know," I replied trying to catch my breath.

Tommy splashed water over his head and without knowing what else to do, I blew a long sharp note on the beacon's whistle.

"What good will that do?" Tommy demanded. "Those old people certainly couldn't hear it."

"Maybe not," I said, "but they aren't the only people in the world."

So I blew the whistle with a combination of variations including shave-and-a-haircut, Marco Polo and Yankee Doodle. No one sprang from either shore, but the sound cheered Tommy and we laughed as we helped each other clean up.

I saw the sun drop to a hand's breadth above the horizon realizing the only sure direction was the one we'd come. I motioned Tommy to follow on ground that was either hard mud or soft sand. Both made walking difficult, though walking on the high ground wasn't possible because of the high grass that extended as far as I could see. It was also where clouds of flying bugs sent us squealing for the water. So we skipped from one safe area to the other and cautiously moved along the shore. When we saw a break in the grass that indicated a trail, I waved my hands to discourage bugs and we ran inland toward a line of cedar trees that seemed to extend to the horizon.

"There's got to be a farmer around here some place," I said. "Keep on the lookout for smoke, a tractor or something."

"Think they'll feed us?" Tommy asked.

"Sure," I said with a reassurance I didn't feel. "Farmers are famous for fixing great meals and being nice to kids."

Only we never actually found a farmer and my prediction diminished as the trail tilted uphill into the cedars. I don't think I'd ever been so hot and tired. Combined with my itching Orion and the soreness of my chest, I was not a happy camper. Yet, I had to put on a good face for my cousin.

"Come on," I said with forced bravado. "I'll bet we'll find a house just over this next rise. They'll have dogs and cats and horses for us to ride."

I supported my claims by using the compass on the beacon. From the direction of the needle, I knew which way north was and that we were walking southeast. A direction that meant nothing to me other than it was the same one as the trail we were following. It just lead to the next rise, the next and the one after that and after each we found bigger and wider expanses beyond. Worse, the sun was setting and gloom was beginning to close the trail behind us. Hot and dusty we sat down on a large boulder with a large cedar growing behind it.

"Maybe we should make camp for the night," Tommy suggested. "I can't walk much further."

"We've got to keep going," I insisted. "It can't be much farther, besides this doesn't look like a good spot to camp."

Not that I knew a bad one. I had never been camping and Tommy knew it, repeating for the hundred and something time how tired he was.

"But we have to keep going," I repeated. "Somebody is looking for us, I'll bet there's a search party."

"How would you know?" He demanded irritably.

Before I could answer our attention was drawn to the sound of an overhead drone. We looked up in time to see a single-engine airplane fly directly over us. Tommy ran after it waving his arms with me behind him, blowing my whistle and waving my arm to the receding plane. Tommy moved through a break between two cedar trees and down hill to an open field where the plane flew out of sight. The sun took that opportunity to disappear and shadows grew long.

Hands resting on our knees, we tried to catch our breath along with the last of my patience and energy. "What did you think you were doing?" I huffed. "You don't believe you could have caught that airplane!"

My cousin didn't answer, only heaved for air until his attention was caught by something in front of us and beyond the field.

"Just what do you think you are looking at?" I snapped again, realizing I had never talked to Tommy like this.

"Live oak trees," he yelled over his shoulder and ran in that direction. "Like Ana's house."

Sure enough at the far edge of the field was a huge live oak tree. Its waxy green leaves even in the growing darkness looked like a familiar painting. I followed wondering what Tommy expected the trees to provide. Yet, its presence seemed to instill an energy he didn't have five minutes earlier. I caught up with him where he stood just beyond the shadow of the gigantic branches of the huge tree. Stopping to lean on his knees again, he tilted his head up and stared up at the tree.

"OK," I said, "a live oak tree, now how is this supposed to get us found?"

"I don't know," Tommy whined. "I thought it was, you know, a sign!"

"A sign?" I yelled and an echo answered. Lowering my voice, I said. "It's almost dark, we won't be able to find that trail. If it's a sign, then it's a stupid sign, if you ask me.

"But can't you see?" Tommy begged. "I mean come on, Ana, live oak trees?"

"No, I can't," I snapped, "I only know that we're lost."

Wanting to scream, I walked to a dead log lying at the edge of the field. Tired and hungry, I wanted to tell the whole world what I thought of signs. Tommy left me and walked toward the tree and into its shadow.

"Just a second," he called over his shoulder. "I have to go the bathroom."

"Hurry up," I called. "I don't have all day."

How funny, I thought, since there was practically no daylight left and I had nothing else to do.

"I'm becoming my mother," I whispered to myself.

I needed to go too, and had suppressed the urge since we left the river with prospect of a clean indoor toilet. How I envied boys the equipage to go anywhere. Besides, I had never peed outside in my life and wasn't sure of the mechanics. I had tissue in my pocket and concluded that, minus an actual toilet, doing it "out there" could not be too different, or at least I hoped it wasn't, Ana always said, "When you have to go, you find a way."

"Tommy," I said. "I have to go too."

"So go," Tommy said. "No one is stopping you."

"Stay over there," I called, "and don't look."

"Why would I?" he replied tersely.

This was just another funny actually, since we'd been using the bathroom in front of the other since forever. Modesty wasn't the priority as it was my first time to go outside, but I was determined the event would not become the stuff of family legends or jokes.

I refused to have the event marked like "Yeah, you were born the year Jackie used the bathroom outside for the first time. She landed on her butt after doing her crazy potty dance in the woods and messed herself."

Taking every precaution, I stepped away from the log and pulled down my shorts. I realized I was standing in an open field and felt like I was on the auditorium stage at school. Patches of Johnson grass and green poke salad plants bobbed with a slight wind reminding me of an audience the way they leaned forward with the slight wind, like they didn't want to miss anything of my show. As creepy as it sounds I stepped over the log and scanned the spot where I'd seen Tommy disappear under the canopy of the tree. Satisfied I couldn't see him, and, therefore, he couldn't see me, I lowered too fast and promptly fell on my tail. Cursing, I struggled to my feet, dusted off my tail and let loose.

"Hey Jackie," Tommy said, "Quick, come here!"

Panicked I bunched my shorts at my knees and hopped like a baby chicken closer to the log. With my bare rear to the open field I cleaned up and pulled up my pants. Furious, I ran around the log and headed toward Tommy's voice with the intention of busting him. I found him in he tree's shadow standing with his head tilted back at the base of a trunk three times the size of the one with our tree house. I stomped forward, but Tommy didn't stir at my approach, his head was tilted nearly straight back as he pointed to the tree tops. Following his arm I saw a series of boards nailed to the trunk of the tree. Following these steps I saw bottom of a huge tree house, as big as ours, with a square entry in the center of the floor.

"I told you it was a sign," Tommy said, grinning.

"We haven't got time to explore tree houses," I said. "We need to get back to that trail before it really gets dark."

"It's already dark, and I'd rather be here than that trail," said Tommy. "Unless you've got a better idea?"

Tommy stepped toward the first board rung. I was about to protest when a long, high yipping cut the air like an electrical wire. Looking toward the log and the open field, I thought of all the open ground we'd cross to get back to the trail. From the direction we'd been walking toward, an answering wail stopped me and another howl from the direction of the river sent me scrambling up the ladder.

Tommy was at the top of the ladder before I grabbed the first board. He disappeared through the floor opening by the time I was half way up.

"Jackie," he called, "You won't believe this."

Cautious, I didn't let his enthusiasm hurry me. Soon my head and shoulders emerged into a spacious room and my hands rested on old carpet that lined the floor and sides. I pulled myself up and in and looked around.

"Is this neat, or what?" Tommy declared. "Wonder who made this?"

In the far corner of the house was a black box the size of a paperback book with "Winchester printed in red on its side. "Winchester .30-30 WIN. 150 GR, ballistic, silvertip," Tommy read. "Like what the Commemorative uses."

"No it's not," I corrected, all knowing. "The Commemorative is a .32 special, remember?"

"I'll bet this is where hunters shoot deer," said Tommy changing subjects.

Standing up we looked over the top of the tree house's side to a clear view of the open field we'd just crossed.

"OWWWWWWW! YIP-YIP-YIP-OWWWWW!"

"What is that?" Tommy hissed with a shiver and joined me to look in the direction of sound.

I dropped to the floor, happy to be off my feet, and said I didn't know. I was secure that whatever it was it couldn't get into the tree house. "You're right though," I said trying to sound bright again. "This is a better spot to camp than the trail."

Of course, having nothing makes pitching camp easy. Finding things, like the bullet box, was a welcome luxury. Dusk settled and I opened the beacon to carefully lay out its contents separating the kitchen matches and birthday candles. Using the Styrofoam bullet separator as a candle holder I lit a candle. To my surprise I found that, in addition to the stuff I'd first seen in Ana's bedroom, a tightly rolled piece of plastic had been included along with a little package of beef jerky and a roll of multi-colored candy.

"We've got supper and desert," Tommy said.

"Just wish we had something to drink,' I said.

"You could go back to river," he teased.

"Or not," I replied, "at least not now."

Not wanting to waste any of our fire making stuff, we ate a very quick supper by candle light. I put the other items back in the beacon and spread the plastic sheet. Tommy and I lay under the plastic making little tents, with twigs from the tree to prevent the plastic from touching our sticky skin. The candle finally burned out and the darkness was total. The howling seemed as if they were just below us.

"Wish they, whatever they are, would shut up," Tommy said.

Not knowing what else to do, I blew the beacon's whistle in a series of long and sharp notes. The howling stopped for a while, only to start again. I blew it again until I was too tired to do anything except fall asleep. Midway between sleep and waking, Tommy shook me awake.

"Hey Jackie," Tommy called. "Look, there's Orion's belt!"

Irritably I looked through a break in the trees and saw the distinct constellation turned on its end, the same way it was on my arm. The three biggest stars were straight up and down, instead of across, with the two footie stars pointing upward. Or, as up as you can get in the sky.

"Guess we're not the only ones in crash mode," I said.

Thinking of Ana, I blew the beacon with a long, shrill note. The howling stopped and I fell into an uneasy sleep.

CHAPTER 13

People say there's nothing like a good night's sleep in the great outdoors. I might agree, if I'd actually slept straight through the night we spent in the tree house. Tommy and I alternated using the plastic sheet until we got too sticky to keep it on. After kicking it off we slapped bugs, before pulling the sheet back for short periods. During the blackest part of the night, the temperature dropped, the bugs left and a chill forced us to scrunch together for our first night of camping, and the worst night's sleep of my life.

Dawn light filled the tree house too early with buzzing insects keening near my head. After hitting myself, but missing the irritating bug, I rubbed crusts from my eyes and smacked my lips to produce moisture in my mouth. My tongue felt like it had been glued to the top of mouth. My already nasty mood wasn't improved seeing Tommy flopped in a corner. Papa used to say Tommy could sleep through the end of the world, but even that old joke failed to make me laugh.

Getting to my feet, I looked across the field we'd crossed the previous evening and scratched fresh bug bites. Sunlight had almost dissipated light patches of fog hovering over the field like a party of ghosts. Turning my head toward the direction of the river, my spirits sank when I saw how close the river was. We seemed to have walked so long and it looked like we had barely come two city blocks.

Angry, I looked down at Tommy and, more for spite, shook him awake. He blinked up at me and I envied being able to sleep like that, but also knew rousing him was more trouble than it was worth. I had priorities, so I told him to stay put until I got back. After blinking once, he flopped on his side and back to instant sleep.

A full bladder inspired me to hurry through hole in the floor and down the tree. I returned to the log at the edge of the field, this time with no concern about who saw as I pulled my shorts down without interruption or complications.

"Practice makes perfect," I told the log as I cleaned up. "But let's not make a habit of this."

The packet Ana had given me only had two or three tissues remaining, along with the $5 and the handkerchief. It didn't take a genius to figure out I had material for one more potty. Hoping there wouldn't be another time, but having no idea what I was supposed to do when I ran out of tissue or money, I kicked dirt over my recent contribution to the environment, muttering at the unfairness that boys could go anywhere. Looking beyond the field, I considered returning to the trail we'd originally walked from the river. Instead, I returned to the live oak, walked in a widening circle to its far side and found a narrow trail. Being closer than the other trail, and with my mouth dry as cotton, this trail seemingly leading in the direction of the river, so my choice was easy. Memories of muck, bugs and old men's cigarette butts did not endear me to the river, but I realized I didn't have much choice. And it could have been worse, as Papa liked to say.

"There are parts of the world with water diseases that haven't been seen since the conquistadors," Papa told us. "Which is probably why there aren't any conquistadors anymore."

"Once those nasty germs got inside those Spaniards," he added with a wink, "they gnawed away at their insides leaving only helmets and breast plates with the seal of the king of Spain."

Memories of Papa made me laugh, but my temper refused to overlook my situation of being lost, thirsty, hungry and alone. At least, I told myself, I could wash my face and catch the attention of a boat or somebody on the shore.

I walked down the path, shaking off the bad night's sleep, and a parade of miseries fell into step with me. There were bloody streaks on my arms, the result of scratching insect bites. These attracted more insects and I thought of my last meal.

"Sustenance," the cafeteria lady at school would say. "That is not necessary nourishment for a growing girl or boy."

"Does anyone know where we are?" I asked aloud to shut up the cafeteria lady. "Other than a million miles from everywhere!"

Rehashing the events of the previous day, I believed my circumstances would not have happened if Tommy hadn't been along. I might be with girls my own age now, safely swimming in the proper little area with Ana nearby. This could have been a weekend to remember, heaped with peace and safety.

"So why me?" I screamed, "It's just not fair."

In answer, small bugs that had kept their distance, keened maniacally around my head. I shooed them, without effect, and they hovered in holding patterns beyond the length of my arms. Even after flailing my hands like a windmill, several stalwarts buzzed my ear and, again, I slapped myself solidly on the side of my head. Furious, I turned circles, waving both hands and broke off a branch from a dead tree for a club to swing.

"I just want a drink of water!" I screamed. "Leave me alone."

In answer, a bug landed on my neck and another on my forehead while the others buzzed their song. The air whistled with the swings of my branch and the bugs avoided it easier than my hand. Catching sight of a fat bug resting on a weed beside the trail, I swung, raking the top of the dew-wet-grass resulting in huge water drops catching a bug unaware and sending it flopping onto the trail. I stomped it into the mud I had created before turning to the grass and swiping my club through it again and even more water lurched out in great soaking splashes.

Water, I thought, cleaner than the river. But how do I gather it?

My socks were wet and I briefly considered sucking the moisture out of them. "Yuck," I said aloud. "I want strawberry jam, not toe for breakfast."

There were my shorts, underwear and T-shirt, but they were nearly as dirty as my socks. "It's not fair, not fair at all," I complained, " I just want a drink of water."

Stomping my foot, I struck the ground with my stick and slapped my right thigh. The plastic sandwich bag in my pocket crumpled its synthetic greeting. I pulled it out and removed the tissues, handkerchief and money. Without knowing what else to do, I wadded the handkerchief loosely in my hand and stroked the grass, the hankie was sopping before I brought it to my face. Gratefully, I sucked out the moisture in seconds, gleaned the grass again and got another swallow. It was just enough water to make me want a tall glass filled to the brim. Impatient with the efficiency of the little cloth, I remembered the plastic sandwich bag, balled the handkerchief again and squeezed the results into the bag's open mouth. After six gleanings I filled the bag half way. Seeds floated on top, but I picked them out and the water tasted wonderful.

I repeated the process collecting enough water to quench my thirst. Feeling better, I thought of Tommy and grimaced thinking of him sleeping while I found water.

"I'll do it when I come back," I said and drank the water.

Pushing the hanky into the bag, I stuffed it into my pocket as my raw insect bites reminded of their presence again. I knew I wasn't supposed to scratch them and my chest rubbed against my T-shirt producing a different kind of irritation.

"I could take my shirt off," I said aloud, looking around. "Who's to see me?"

It had been years since I'd run outside without a top. I remembered when my daddy took me to a park and we chased each other among the trees. Being summer and hot, I took off my shirt without a qualm to climb on a jungle gym. Always carrying a camera, my daddy took my picture, topless and balanced on monkey bars. It was a photo I knew he still kept in his wallet.

Lately, I couldn't change my socks without locking my door. Yet, there was no one around and after turning a complete circle, I pulled off my shirt over my head in time to see a buck deer step from the edge of the trees. He was big as a horse with horns that could have been used to hold four dodge balls. He stared with liquid brown eyes and wiggling his floppy ears before dipping its head.

Hands on my hips I thrust my chest in his direction and shouted, "What are you looking at?"

For an answer, the buck popped his tongue obscenely, wiggled his ears and shook his head before bounding away into the trees.

"Shows what you know," I shouted after him.

The insects regrouped, but I had another idea. Placing my shirt on the high grass beside the trail, I moved three feet to one side of it and kicked the grass. About a cup of water hit my shirt dead center. From different angles I kicked the grass repeatedly until my T-shirt was soaked. Though intending to use my shirt as a cool, wet towel, my efforts made me thirsty again. Overcoming my repugnance, I sucked moisture from the neckline and was surprised there was no grit. I repeated the process and my thirst was quenched. Soaking my shirt again, I rubbed it over my back and chest, blissfully, relieving all irritation. Thirst quenched and semi-reprieved from the bites, I walked on keeping the bugs at bay by slapping my T-shirt over my shoulders and ribs like a martial arts movie I'd seen.

My mood was improved, but I caught sight of my wrist. The area around my *Orion* resembled a garden of active volcanoes. Growling, I concluded that whatever these special moles was supposed to do, they didn't ward off mosquitoes.

"A lot of luck you've brought," I said aloud. "Ana didn't tell me you were bad luck marks from the gods."

Besides what kind of luck had Ana's *Orion* had brought her? She didn't finish college, had not traveled or lived with talented people. She put up with my mother and my uncle, and was now forced to worry for her lost grandchildren.

"Momma is right," I said tapping the Orion. "You are coming off when I get back. If this is the kind of luck you bring, I'd hate to see the bad."

Anger turned into raw resentment and I slapped my shirt over my side.

Not surprising, I caught the wrong spot. Hissing, I swung my stick at the ground, which didn't give. The impact up the shaft stung my fingers, forcing me to drop the stick. I screamed the way Papa did when he hit his finger or lost a paying gig. "Dammit! Dammit! Dammit!"

Fingers in my mouth, I searched for a mountain lion or polar bear, hoping for one of each, mad and ready to tear anything or anybody apart that crossed my path. Eventually, the sting seeped away and I picked up my stick. Understandably, my shirt was dirty from neck to hem, and my *Orion* began to itch. Didn't I have enough problems? I thought, stopping myself from hitting the ground with my stick again.

My self-pity was disrupted when I noticed the trail sloped downhill. Shrugging, I accepted this change and would have returned to grousing about how rotten I thought my life was. Yet, as I rounded a bend I stopped to stare at the sight of an odd rock formation on the horizon. From that distance, it looked like two children's building blocks, their vertical ends placed to lean inward at an angle against one another.

My troubles forgotten temporarily, my progress down the path seemed to take forever with my fascination fixed on the blocks. Yet, the trail led in that direction. By degrees the blocks loomed larger, until I realized they were huge squared boulders the size of a department store tipped on its side. And they weren't connected by their ends, but set side by side. Each boulder was flanked by smaller oblong boulders stacked like fallen dominoes, extending to my left and right into an abyss of brambles and mesquite trees.

I thought the boulders were growing before my eyes until I stood at the edge of a short precipice overlooking a vale twice the size of a large living room. Looking around, I couldn't see a break or path around or over the flanking boulders. However, I noticed steps had been gouged into the rock below me, probably made by animals that used this path. Conveniently, a smaller boulder lay just below these steps providing a short step to the ground. At the other end of this vale was the lower half of the nearest and smaller boulder. Best of all I saw a triangular opening between the two big boulders. Though my view was limited, the space beyond the triangle showed that the trail continued winding into the distance.

There was no other choice, but to climb down to the valley and through that opening. Still, I knew that no matter how careful I was, there was a better than average chance I'd scratch, scrape, bump or make hard contact with something unfriendly to some part of my upper body. Reluctantly, because the bugs were gone and it felt good to be bare-chested, I pulled on my damp T-shirt. Hissing as grit rubbed my sensitive skin, I moved carefully down finding footholds in narrow crevices. Despite my precautions, I still bumped a large bite on my lower back. Instead of cursing again, I poked my stick like a spear at the ledge and broke it.

Forced to lay my back against the moss covered side of a boulder I moved through the open scrapping my shoulder blade and nudging sensitive front parts. "What else can happen?" I said, extending a foot beyond opening. "Can I get a break?"

Nobody I know believes they'll actually get an answer to their wishes at the time they make them. I know I didn't expect one, and I certainly wouldn't have ordered the huge pair of hands, more like paws actually, that grabbed my upper arms. And of all the side orders, a voice like broken glass being ground into hot asphalt wouldn't have been on my menu.

"Be still and you won't be hurt!" The voice growled.

I managed not to scream, but couldn't control my ears ringing or my heart pounding as if it would crash out of my chest. Until the voice spoke into my other ear.

"This reminds me of the story of a cedar hacker's son fishing on this very river, on a day like today."

I wanted to turn around to see who held me, but didn't. The hands holding me were big, really big. Their cucumber sized thumbs rested on the joints of my shoulders and the pinkies, hard as a number one pencil, nuzzled the insides of my elbows

"Fishermen on both shores that day caught nothing," the voice continued. "Only that boy had any luck, an amazing windfall of fish of all kinds including bass, crappie and perch of every size. Eventually, this caused everyone to watch the boy cast."

My heart beat faster even faster, if that was possible, as the voice inhaled and recounted how a curious man asked " the lad" what he used for bait.

"Immediately, the boy produced a coffee can," the voice rasped, and added in a high falsetto voice. "Just these little-bitty, biting worms!" The same terrible voice said, "The can was full of baby-rattlesnakes and the boy's hands had snake bites from his wrists to forefingers." A pause and the mouth shifted to my right ear "They rushed the fool to a hospital. Some believed he wasn't in any danger because the little snakes had little or no venom. Others thought he was simply too stupid to know he was in danger."

I started to turn to my left and found a gray shirt sleeve blocked my view. A thick bicep extended behind my shoulder, but beyond the length of the ruddy arm was a pointing finger extending in the direction of a cedar tree. The tree was just off the trail and some six feet beyond the edge of the boulder. Smaller rocks surrounded the tree like unwrapped Christmas presents.

"Now that old boy wouldn't have any problems in that department," the voice said. "Fact is, I'd bet a million dollars to a donut, there wouldn't be time to take a step, let alone get a doctor."

I was going to turn around to see the man behind me when he gave my right arm a shake.

"Lookie, lookie, oh can't you see, at the base of the bright green cedar tree," the voice sang. "Can't you spy what I found with my ruddy old eye?"

Curious, I postponed looking behind me and strained to see beyond the index finger. I moved my head from side to side, but still only saw the cedar tree and the end of the nearby boulder.

"At the very bottom of the tree," directed the voice. "Look close, see how it blends in perfectly with the trunk."

My forced vision felt as if my eyes would pop from their holes. However, my efforts were in vain and I was reminded of the backs of breakfast cereal boxes. It was those with the games and puzzles on the back that a kid can do while eating breakfast, at least once anyway. On one, I remember were a series of wide eyes situated among a jungle floral background across the box. Shapes there revealed themselves to be happy and smiling little cartoon forest animals. To help in their discovery, as if any help was needed, were written instructions at the bottom of the box. These challenged the reader to find a missing baby orangutan, a cute little zebra, or a smiling toucan with its long multicolored beak.

Yet, it wasn't bright eyes or toothy grins, but rather the bare flutter of an eye lid that froze the breath in my lungs for a second time in as many minutes. I thought of the "all seeing eye" on the back of a U.S. dollar bill. The similarity ended as what lay at the cedar's base didn't blink, but it was animated. Dull yellow eyes glared liquidly from beneath hoary brows as a forked tongue probed the air from a perpetually sneering, lipless mouth.

All that was needed was a magician in a turban to shout magic words for the outline to draw form contours and materialize into definition. But the words spoken had no supernatural power.

"Western diamondback rattlesnakes," the voice announced, "have caused more deaths than any venomous snake in North America." Chuckling, the voice added, "This old booger is triple, extra king-sized, so he probably comes with a double your money back guarantee."

The head was the width of a man's hand and a fly crawled between its eyes. Others flies scooted across a neck thicker than my ankle resting on coils the girth of my legs, all scrunched at the base of a tree inches from the path I would have walked.

"Wouldn't he win a blue ribbon prize at the state fair?" The voice asked. "Still, I wonder if he hasn't gone to seed? Can he do the deed, or will the old timer make liars of us all?"

A sour aroma swabbed my nose as I sensed, rather than felt, the bulk leaning close to my ear.

"I was about to test that theory, which says that he has enough venom to kill more than 40 men. But since you're here I'll forgo the opportunity, at least for now."

The hands left my arms, but I didn't move.

"I'll bet you're as curious as I am to find out what this old rascal is made of, aren't you?" asked the voice, now a short distance away.

I wasn't interested, not a little, and didn't care if every snake in the world went to seed, were made into hand bags, or left town. My concern was being between a crazy person and a monster that fed on pigs and small dogs.

Taking a deep breath, I whirled and braced myself, expecting to be shoved into the snake's maw. Instead, I found a broad shouldered man squatting on his haunches concentrating on gathering pebbles. His face was partially hidden by the wide brim of a brown Stetson hat set on his head. A cinch string attached to the hat dangled beneath his chin. He loosened the cinch and let the hat fall down his back, releasing a thick mane of greasy blonde hair tinged with gray. The split ends flipped like ocean waves in all direction. Loose side tendrils were pushed behind his ears, anchored by the hooks of a pair of reading glasses. Their half-moon lenses rode astride a compact, sunburned nose below eyes the color of a thunderstorm. They were eyes I believed Ana would call "dreamy, that is if their corneas weren't tinted the color of an overripe cherry.

Neither glasses nor hair hid the thin white scar descending from above the right side of his hairline to the center of his face, The jagged lines stretched across his whisker-stubbled cheek and forked with the back tang ending a few inches from the ear in a knob of thick scar tissue. A longer tang veered at a sharp angle toward his nose and ended in a crude, fish hook design below the cheekbone.

The back and chest of the man's gray work shirt were etched with white arrowhead shaped outlines, moist in the center. The sweat stains haloed beyond the breast pockets and drenched the undersides of neatly rolled up sleeves.

With a pile of pebbles cupped in his left hand, the man stood and his back crackled as he arched his spine. The shirt settled over a thick chest above a narrow waist as he dusted his other hand on the leg of multi pocketed shorts. Silently, he moved on sand colored, rubber soled, canvas boots and stepped toward the snake.

He said, "This should be enough," and to my horror, flicked a pebble at the snake. I back peddled and collided with the other boulder, a sharp edge snagging a bug bite. An intense whirring sound reverberated off the sides of the boulders and shivers raced down my tailbone.

"He can see our heat and knows we're here," the man said gleefully. "But, he doesn't know what hit him."

He threw more stones in quick succession and each pebble hit a scale the size of my thumbnail. The tempo of rattles increased, louder with each stone and I even felt sorry for the snake. That is until the harpoon shaped head rose as high as my waist and cocked into a tight striking-S, a sight to knot the stomach and flatten a chest.

"Now this is where the fun begins," the man said. "Let's lock and load old buddy, it's time for the rubber to hit the road."

One, two, three and four pebbles flew through the air striking the snake each time. In response, the big snake weaved and dipped as if offering the offender a last chance to refrain from these indignities to its person and avoid the ultimate consequence. In answer, the man showed teeth and tossed a pebble in an over handed arch and straight down to bounce off the center of the snake's head. Without warning, a blur shot in our direction in three successions. The head was so fast, yet I caught sight of the open mouth, as strike after strike burned the air with no two touching the same space. And while I'm no great judge of distance I know this snake extended itself beyond my height and I'm just over five feet tall.

"Oh, he's really mad now," the man chuckled. " Come on big fella, you can do it!"

He tossed pebbles to either side of the snake while I pressed against the boulder and snake strikes seemed to fly in my direction. In my terror, I willed the snake to focus on the crazy man. Instead, the head was raised in strike position and the coils separated. When the head lowered the snake moved, its head pointed in our direction, rattlers whirring and moved beyond the boulder. The rattlers soon faded like a memory as leaves moved slightly and the big snake moved into the nearby brush.

"Fudge-cookies," the man moaned. "He doesn't want to play anymore. The show's over folks!"

The man's face was creased with melancholy as if he was watching a dear friend depart. He continued to stare long after the snake was out of sight and pebbles slipped out of his left hand forming a small mound beside his boot. With his attention away from me, I edged along the side of the boulder and climbed through the opening. Still on hands and knees I scampered to the rock ledge and found the footholds. Climbing that fast, I was up and gone like an arrow without looking back and never slowed until I reached the spot where I'd seen the deer. What stopped me was realizing there were no footsteps behind me or shouts to stop. Looking over my shoulder, I saw that the path and surrounding area was empty. Stopping to catch my breath, my second thought was for Tommy. I needed to warn him and I recalled, with guilt, how I blamed all my troubles on him earlier. Even so, nobody was going to hurt him while I was around.

That thought in turn made me realize that while the crazy snake man was what Papa might call a nutcase, he was also the only adult in proximity to approach for help, at least for now. Besides, he had stopped me from walking into the world's biggest rattlesnake and driven it off. Even if he had scarred the pee-waddle out of me in the process. He was not the kind of help I would have preferred, but after catching my breath, I found another stick and turned in the direction I had just run.

I scanned either side of the trail hard for more snakes being especially careful climbing down the ledge. Before passing through the opening between the boulders, I poked my stick through and beat the ground as my feet touched down. I continued flailing the surrounding area well away from the boulders until I found the track of a rubber soled canvas boot, its toe pointed in the direction of the river.

CHAPTER 14

Past the big boulders the trail widened to a path of powdery dust where even small footprints were easy to follow, or at least until the path sloped downhill to the fine sand of the riverbank. The tracks disappeared into the weed-strewn bank and I had no idea which direction to turn.

The wrong way could lose him, me and the way back to Tommy. Meantime, I heard running water and was reminded I was thirsty again and wouldn't mind a wash. My bites also ached to be cooled and the swirling waters were inviting. I pulled off my T-shirt and was about to dip it into the water when the lyrics of a song warbled from my left.

> McHale is a mighty man who goes to circus shows,
> leaps into the big cats' cage, to show what he knows.
> For a while he pokes his head in a tiger's mouth,
> takes it out with a smile at the joke and calls the big cat Ralph

Quickly pulling on my T-shirt, I cocked my ear in the direction of the song. "With the ladies the mighty McHale wasn't lazy."

Gravel flew as I followed the sound through a grove of salt cedars and upstream to a stretch of sandy river bank. To my bewilderment, I could not see anyone on either end of the shore, but I could still hear the song. "To the lads, McHale was a cad."

Looking toward the river, I saw the man sitting on what I thought was the roof of submerged car. Smooth and square, the boulder lay about half way into the river. Water swirled and leaped to the rock's top, on its way to the other side. The man sat in the center of the boulder and bounced from one broad butt cheek to the other.

> McHale loved a lawyer's daughter.
> One night he kissed her thirty-three and a third
> and called for mineral water.

As he sang he twirled an object in his right hand like a baton. I watched from the salt cedars ready to duck and my Orion started itching. Fine time for you to start, I thought.

> McHale licks his eyebrows with great agility
> Ties his tongue into a knot, snaps the end
> to spit with supreme facility.

When he stopped singing, the object in his hand ceased twirling and revealed that it was a long bladed knife lying against his palm glistening in the sunlight. It was all I could do to keep from running full tilt back to the tree house. It was a knife that had to have been the most murderous looking instrument I'd ever seen in my life. It was the kind I thought Judas Iscariot, Adolf Hitler or Lonnie's daddy carried.

"Thank you, thank you," the man shouted. "You're too kind, thank you so very much."

Confused, but alert, I looked around to see who he was talking to and could only see and hear the roar of the water around the boulder.

"Really, thank you, thank you. Any requests?"

Nobody was there, either to the left or right, no one, but me.

"Alright how about a ditty about a pessimist?"

Before I could ask, no one in particular, what a pessimist or a ditty was he bellowed.

> Oh, a pessimist he dove from twenty floors
> And passing the open windows ajar
> He yelled to chums and strangers alike,
> "Cover me with mustard and tar."

He sang with elongated flat A's, which also added to my reluctance, as did the sight of the damp, white-fringed stains around his armpits and shirt center. They reminded me of the shadows and shapes on the walls of my room at night. It didn't help I was in broad daylight, wide awake and without my parents or anybody to turn on the lights.

Taking everything into consideration I decided to abandon my plan. But as I started to creep away, I noticed his shirttail had ridden up and caught on a long pouch attached to his belt. Only it wasn't a pouch and, looking closer, I realized it was a funny looking knife sheath, the type always worn by the good guys in Papa's old movies. These heroes included Australians saying G'day, Africans or American Indians in loin cloths, or white hunters in Africa wearing hats with leopard skin hat bands. Ana called them "hotties," like this really old guy-actor named Johnny Weismiller who made Tarzan movies long before Papa was even born.

To know if a guy was the hero hottie, Ana said to look for the guy carrying a big knife with a wicked looking blade. It was the same reason, she added, that the hero got the girl by the movie's end. When I pointed out that the bad guys also had big knives, Ana shrugged looking at Papa with a quirky little smile and said it wasn't always the size, but how the hero wielded it. For some reason Papa laughed and changed the subject, insisting Mr. Weismiller was the only real Tarzan the Ape Man. Why not,

I thought, he ran, jumped, swung on vines, wrestled alligators and lions, and swam like a bullet across raging rivers. Though, I didn't see how a big knife had anything to do with those activities.

Yet, Tarzan always had his knife and never lost it, though not for lack of trying. He was always getting chased by mean looking black men called Wazzuris and Opars. They sang like a church choir before they attacked. Now if that wasn't bad enough he always had to look twice over his shoulder for sneaky white guys named Nigel or Basil. These guys wore shorts, smoked a pipe and talked with snooty voices. They also wore shirts with loops sewn on the breast pockets for bullets they loaded in guns that boomed like cannons. Fortunately, by the end of the movie, despite how devious or mean all the bad guys were, they got theirs. There was always one that got stuck with Tarzan's big knife. Not that the Lord of the Jungle walked up and stuck him. Nope, he threw the knife from way off, and the bad guy always looked surprised to see the knife sticking out of his chest. As if he didn't have it coming through the whole movie. Yet, he'd have this expression like, "Yeah, that's Tarzan's big knife in my chest, no doubt about it. That's really going to hurt to get it out and why did he do that?"

Gritting teeth, the bad guys always grabbed the knife handle like I do when I skinned my knee or elbow. Of course they never yanked it out before falling out of sight. Then Tarzan would throw back his head yelling "Eeeyaah, Eeeyaah, Eeeyaah" and somehow have his knife back from way over there. Afterward he'd tangle with more bad guys, lions or crocodiles.

Like Papa, I had an affinity for Tarzan movies. My problem was that while the man on the rock had good guy certification, a Tarzan-knife, he looked more like a bad guy and sang like a hyena. Worse, he sure didn't look like the suave Nigel, Basil or other snoots. He looked more like lesser bad guys named Jungle Jack, Monk or Knuckles, the same ones leering like maniacs as they performed their dirty work.

I looked hard at the worn and scratched sheath, unable to make up my mind. The sheath showed considerable care with fresh lashings contrasting the oiled leather along the underside. It also interesting that it was made of one piece of leather with a longer pieced looped where a belt could be inserted. The top flap was folded over to make the sheath-pouch and threaded through four slits just above the end of the long belt-loop piece. I'd seen something like this in a history museum with a display of cowboy stuff that including gun holsters cowboys carried their six-shooters. I remember a museum placard calling this design a Mexican Loop. The placard said, "A simple method to make a sturdy holster from one piece of leather without metal brackets."

My interest was drawn to the top strip of leather where the sheath was threaded. There was a Greek alpha symbol stamped in the center. Below it, on the actual sheath, was the infinity sign and the omega symbol was imprinted on the second leather strip. Together they comprised the same design I'd seen on Ana's leather hair stay.

"A New Athenian," I whispered to myself.

He'd have to help us, I thought, and nearly whooped with joy. Yet, I was still fearful of his scruffy appearance and thought of another Tarzan movie. The first one, Papa said, where Maureen O'Sullivan, a very pretty lady, who played Jane first met Mr. Wesmiller's Tarzan.

"Tarzan, Jane, Tarzan, Jane," I remembered the dialogue after Tarzan pulled Jane into the tree. Tarzan pointed his finger at himself and back at Jane.

"Ana, what's he doing?" I asked, tickled with the exchanged.

"Establishing communication," said Ana without looking up. "People have to understand one another, so Jane is finding a way to talk to Tarzan, and he's responding."

Jane needed Tarzan's help, she explained, the ape man was attention starved for his own kind. So, they needed to talk, though it proved difficult in the beginning. It was a start and someone has to make the first move."

I left the salt cedars and walked to the edge of the water. He didn't look around, so I cleared my throat the way I'd seen adults do when they wanted to get someone's attention. The man swayed so far to his right I thought he'd fall in, but never stopped twirling the knife.

"Excuse me," I said loudly. "Hello, please sir, may I talk to you for just a second?"

The sweaty back swayed far left and came close to tipping over as he caught the knife between two fingers, its blade half the width of his hand. He straightened up, tossed the knife into the air again and caught it by the polished bone handle. A real Tarzan knife for sure, but also the type used by ogres and giants I'd seen in illustrations of stories Ana read to us. It was the kind of knife that diced human beings for a stew pot or ground bones to make bread for giants.

He turned and eyed me indifferently before turning back to the river. I counted to five and he looked at me again with an annoyed expression. Grunting, he tossed the knife up and my heart went with it. He caught it, the knife not my heart, and slipped it into the sheath before turning around to face me. His reading glasses hung from a cord around his neck against the center of his chest. With a grimace he pushed his Stetson off his forehead releasing the greasy hair. I know I had heard him talk before, but I almost expected him to leap up and thump his chest. To my relief, he leaned forward and spoke in concise sentences fixing me with cold, red-rimmed eyes.

"The snake-girl!" he said. "Find any more specimens?"

Ignoring and not understanding his question I started to blather. "I need help, my cousin and I are lost, we can't find our grandparents."

"You've got the wrong department, I can't even help myself," he said looking up river. "Besides, I'm going to pull stakes and move on myself. This place is too crowded."

He lowered his head to his chest before looking up. "If you'll retrace your steps I'm sure you'll find your parents," he said. "They can't be far. Where did you camp, that way or that way?" He jerked a thumb up river and a forefinger in the other direction.

"Bandy's Camp," I squeaked.

"Bandy's Camp," he repeated with a curse. "That's a good 40 miles upstream." Rubbing his face with the back of his hand he looked beyond me, raising his head as his eyes searched the surrounding hills and shore line. "How did you get here?"

I told him about the raft and our night in the old deer stand. He grunted and refused to look my way.

"Look uhh, little girl, just follow the river upstream There's got to be a search party looking for you."

I said nothing and didn't move even when he held his palms up.

"I'd help, but I'm busy with a previous engagement, I can't do anything."

Pushing himself up on his hands he scooted his rear and turned back to face the river. Only he didn't break into song or pull out his knife.

"I understand and it's OK," I nearly shouted. "But would you help me get my cousin out of a tree? He's scared of heights and won't come down. If you'll help me get him down, we can be on our way and leave you alone."

The man looked at the sky, the river and land beyond before turning to me again. "All right," he said. "But once he's down, you two vamoose, at least from me."

"Sure," I readily agreed.

He jumped down, wading against the current and splashed ashore without a word. I walked ahead keeping just enough distance and glancing over my shoulder. Finding another stick, I tapped the ground for snakes the whole way to the base of the live oak tree.

I yelled up for Tommy and his head appeared over the side. "This man is here to help get you down."

Tommy looked at me with a puzzled expression. Next to dodge ball, tree climbing was in his blood, as Papa would say. Tommy had climbed considerably taller trees at home and to the consternation of adults had climbed to the tops of more than a few trees. So the confusion on his face was understandable until I jerked my head at the man and, on cue, Tommy recoiled slightly.

"Where have you been Jackie?" Tommy whined. "Did you find Ana, have you got something to eat, I'm awfully thirsty."

The man stared at the tree house and didn't move.

"Tommy," I yelled with my hands on either side of my mouth. "This nice man is going to get you down and it's a short walk to Ana."

"No," Tommy said. "I don't want to!"

"You need help getting down, kid?" The man asked.

"Yeah," Tommy said. "Please, I'm scared."

I had to turn my head and roll my eyes because the tone in Tommy's voice was phony as a three dollar bill, as Papa would say. The man didn't seem to notice. Instead, he leaped to bottom board of the ladder with the ease of an orangutan. Cautiously, Tommy eased himself through the opening in the floor and moved down the rungs until he was within reach of the man's hand and took it. The man stepped over to a nearby branch and held Tommy's hand until he was nearly down the ladder. Once Tommy was there, the man stepped to a rung and jumped down.

"OK, mister, "I said reluctantly. "Thank you, I guess we'll go to the river for a drink now."

I took Tommy's hand and we walked toward the log where I'd used the bathroom. Turning, I waved good-bye and man rubbed his hand against the bristles of his chin.

"Wait, you can't drink that water," the man said. "Come to my camp and I'll give you a cup of clean water to see you on your way."

"Thank you, Mister, uhh...?" I asked.

"Charles," he said hesitantly. "No, Charlie, yeah my name is Charlie." The name must have tasted good, because he rolled it in his mouth, smiled for the first time and said, "Yes, call me Charlie."

" I'm Jackie and this is Tommy."

"Jackie," he said as if sampling my name. "I knew a Jackie once, a good name."

"I've been told that," I replied. "I'm named after my grandmother."

"Do tell, " he replied without interest. "My camp is this way." Without waiting he strode in the direction we'd come. Tommy and I were about to follow when my cousin ran back to the tree.

"Wait, I forgot something," Tommy cried. "The beacon is still up there."

Before I could stop him Tommy scampered up the tree like smoke and wiggled through the opening. Seconds later, he dragged the plastic sheet out and let it drop to the ground before he was down the ladder monkey quick with beacon lanyard dangling from his pocket. Springing to the limb where Charlie had stood to help him down, he dropped to his belly and lowered himself to the next branch before landing in front of Charlie.

With a silent, "uh-oh," Tommy looked at me as Charlie picked up the plastic and handed it to me. "I know you'll need this later."

Again without looking to see if we followed, he turned to the trail. We ran after him and I pulled the plastic sheet to my chest folding it as best I could before stuffing the wad into my shorts' pocket.

Charlie said nothing as he lead the way past the rock noses before veering left to a trail that I had to look twice to notice. We walked for what seemed forever until we topped a rise and started down an incline toward another creek, narrow and filled with deep water. Charlie turned left and we walked for a long time to a spot where the water was shallow and we forded the creek. On the other side was a long canoe turned on its sides. I almost didn't notice it because it was painted a deep forest green with a series of black zig-zag lines from its front to back. The design, I noticed, broke its contours against the landscape and blended with the landscape around it. Charlie passed it without a look and we had to run to keep up as he climbed a rise toward the top of a small hill.

Sweat was pouring off me by the time we reached the top of the rise to a flat area. It was clearing that looked like a photo from a vacation catalogue, the ones with ads showing smiling couples gathered for lunch around a picnic table covered with a red checkered table cloth, while neighbors walked past, carrying fishing poles or pushing bicycles. Other holiday-makers carried the latest accessories necessary for a great time in the great outdoors. The only thing missing from Charlie's camp was a babbling brook and a happy family frolicking nearby.

Pitched in the shade of a tree, was a green dome tent. The carrying straps of two cloth covered jugs hung from a branch of the tree. A cord was tied to another branch with its other end tied to a tree at the edge of the clearing. Colored towels draped across the cord waved like flags.

In the center of the camp was a rock lined fire pit, located a few yards from the tent. A rack of firewood taller than Tommy stood to the far side of the pit, far enough so as not to catch fire. Propped against the wood was what I first thought was a wooden sword. That turned out to be the wooden sheath of a short machete that Charlie called a bolo. Between the tent and fire pit, a big log had been dragged to the edge of the fire pit and draped with a colorful red and green blanket. Beside the log set a large dark green wooden box. Atop the box was a brown leather pouch attached to something with the tapered ends of thin leather strips, and a smaller square pouch was threaded through one of the straps. It was what lay beside the pouch that drew Tommy's attention.

"A gun," he cried. "We can go hunting."

CHAPTER 15

"Stop!" I never thought a spoken word could freeze two kids solid in their tracks. But we knew we didn't dare take another step as Charlie snatched up what had to be the most beautiful weapon I had ever seen. He was even quicker to stuff the folded sheet of paper that had been lying under the pistol, into his shirt pocket.

Growing up in Texas, even at my age, there are opportunities out the kazoo, as Papa would say, to see every kind of gun: hunting rifles, shotguns, BB-guns and, of course, pistols. But I can't recall any gun, before or since, that emanated such a dark and deadly efficiency. Clean and polished, it was black as midnight even in direct sunlight. A color that seemed to manifest from within the metal harmonizing with the swirled ebony grips shaped to the hand and fingers The only color differentiation was a blood red dot set on a sliver of metal at the gun's top end.

"I know all about guns," Tommy declared. "My dad has plenty and Papa taught me how to shoot."

This wasn't true since Aunt Sonia didn't believe in guns and said that owning even a toy one was a half step above owning a slave and using an outhouse.

"Is that so?" replied Charlie without interest.

"Sure is," Tommy bragged. "I've shot hundreds and hundreds of bullets."

"Ever hit anything?" Asked Charlie without looking at him. "Or did you just shoot?"

"Of course I did," said Tommy offended. "I bet I could out-shoot you with that one, if you'll let me."

"You could?" replied Charlie with a tone that didn't care for any answer. "How you figure that?"

"That's a Colt .45 automatic," Tommy said. "Holds seven rounds, one down the pipe."

Charlie closed his eyes as if in prayer and raised the pistol to the sky, parallel to his ear.

"You got the Colt right," he sighed.

"What are you talking about?" Tommy demanded. "That's a Colt .45

automatic, I've shot lots of them."

"Colt .38-Super," Charlie corrected. "Nine and one in the tube for ten."

"No it's not," Tommy insisted. "Thirty-eights are those guns with the round things."

"Revolvers," Charlie said.

Without further comment, Charlie opened his eyes looking as if he was going to shoot the gun in the air, the way I'd seen TV cowboys when they came into town to celebrate. Instead, he pulled a square thing from the gun's bottom, slipped it into his pocket and yanked the gun's top causing an acorn-sized object to jump into the air before he caught it. He held it to his face for a few seconds and I knew it was a bullet. Again it was nothing like I'd seen before, not even the Commemorative's. This bullet had a crater mouth with side splits that reminded me of the sneering lips of playing card jokers. Sighing again, he slipped the bullet into his pocket.

With the drawer thing open, the pipe, or barrel, stuck out. Charlie stared at the gun again before grimacing and turning it sideways to peer into a hole on its top and poke his pinky finger inside. When his finger was clear, the drawer snapped shut, and Tommy and I flinched.

"That's a cool holster," said Tommy pointing at the brown leather pouch. "Where'd you get it?"

Reaching for the thin straps attached to the flap holster, Charlie drew it toward him.

"It's the legacy of a Chinese gentleman I encountered when we found ourselves working together in a Southeast Asian jungle. He willed it to me, you might say."

"Chinese," declared Tommy impressed. "That's a Chinese holster?"

Charlie lifted the flap of the holster revealing a royal purple interior and another pouch sewn into the holster with another square thing inserted into it. "No, it's Russian, or at least they designed it."

Sliding the pistol into the holster, he buttoned the flap and wrapped the carrying straps and smaller pouch into a bundle. Lifting the lid of the box, he placed it inside and took out two large metal cups.

"Still, that's a cool gun," Tommy said. "Did the Chinese gentleman give you his gun too?

"No, that venerable warrior lost his weapon when he…tripped," Charlie said. "This gun was bequeathed to me, at the same time, by a Company man, of questionable character, for guiding him through that same forest."

"Did he trip too?" Tommy asked.

Without answering Charlie set two cups on top of the box and moved to the tree beside the tent. He returned with one of the big plastic square jugs, flipping the jug's stopper, he filled the cups to the brim.

"Drink slowly. You don't need to get sick."

Nothing in my memory ever tasted so good as I drained the water and held out my cup for more and Tommy did the same. Charlie refreshed our cups without raising an eyebrow at the third or even the fourth cup. He watched us with curiosity and I believed he would ply us with water as long as we needed it.

"You wouldn't have anything to eat," said Tommy between gulps. "We haven't had anything since breakfast yesterday."

A cocked eyebrow warned that further courtesies weren't part of our bargain. "Sorry, I forgot to pack groceries for this trip," he said.

By our fifth cup of water, Charlie's mouth pursed randomly and his brow crinkled. He wasn't wearing the watch that had left the pasty circle on his wrist. But if he had, I believe he would have looked at it. Instead, he shaded his eyes as he stood, tilting his head toward the sun. Looking back at us, he seemed as if he was about to say something, when his eyes narrowed. He inclined his head toward Tommy

"Come here, boy," he said motioning like he was calling a dog.

Hesitantly Tommy moved to within an arm's reach of the man. Charlie paid no attention to Tommy's uneasiness as he leaned down and pointed to a row of bug bites covering the length of Tommy's arm.

"What did you do, roll in tenderizer and ring the mosquito dinner bell?" He said this in the same manner I had heard a stranger inform Papa his tire was going flat.

"That's nothing," Tommy said, "look here!"

Lifting his shirt, Tommy revealed a collage of angry bumps imprinted across his belly and chest. He looked like a plucked chicken, and I knew I must look the same.

Shaking his head again, Charlie waved a hand dismissively before sealing the water jug and placing it beside the box. My heart sank, knowing the hospitality was about to end as Charlie turned his back to us, stretching his hands to the sky and bending his arms so that his tensed biceps were next to his ears. Looking around, he frowned as if disappointed at what he saw, but stopped, eyes narrowing and cocking his head toward Tommy again. He resumed his seat and motioned Tommy to toward him.

"Come here, " Charlie ordered again.

Nervously Tommy glanced at me, but obeyed as Charlie moved from his seat to his haunches and placed a hand on Tommy's right shoulder.

Tommy squealed when the hem of his shorts were pulled up. I was about to jump on Charlie's back, when he pointed to the outside of Tommy's thigh where a sickly gray colored berry waved its six legs in tandem.

"You have company," Charlie said.

Tommy and I chorused a squeal as our hands collided reaching to yank the tick off, but Charlie blocked our hands. "There's a better way," Charlie said.

"You're not going to burn it off!" I declared, glancing at the ashes of the campfire. Tommy squirmed and side stepped while Charlie reopened the box.

"Don't be silly, besides that method doesn't work," Charlie said. "That bug would puke and leave a nasty infection."

"What then?" Tommy demanded

Charlie didn't answer as he took items from the box and laid them on the log. These included a plastic baggy containing a pair of tweezers, a green plastic bottle along with cotton swabs and cotton balls. Settling himself comfortably, he closed the box and put the items on top of the box. He motioned Tommy toward him and told him to hold still. Tommy complied, but wouldn't look down as Charlie gently squeezed the skin around the bug between his fingers and dislodged the tick with the tweezers. He held it up for us to see before flinging it into the fire pit ashes. Its death squeal gave me shivers before spewing dark blood to steam onto a hot coal.

"Vile thing," Charlie muttered.

Soaking a cotton ball with the contents of the green bottle, Charlie placed it in Tommy's hand and pressed both against the bite. "Hold that until I tell you otherwise."

A thick aromatic smell made my eyes water reminding me of sick rooms and colored buckets flickering their oily light on summer evenings.

"I suppose," Charlie said with sigh, "we'd better check for any other brush buddies you might have picked up."

Charlie surprised Tommy when he parted his hair, also checking behind and inside his ears, the way I've seen a dog groomer trim the winter shag from a friend's dog. The groomer was nicer. Though Charlie didn't hurt him, he showed no concern to Tommy's hisses and moans as he treated each bite or scratch.

He motioned Tommy to remove his dirty shirt. Complying, Tommy resembled the colored pins on a wall map. Without expression, Charlie used both ends of the cotton swabs until they were nearly black dabbing the boy like he was painting a wall. He was like a car wash Ana used, the type that in a tin voice ordered the driver to pull up before soaking, scrubbing and rinsing. Then, in the same disembodied voice, said, "Please drive forward slowly. Thank you and come again."

Tommy looked anxious when Charlie told him to pull up the right leg of his shorts and I nodded. Charlie took no notice of either of us. The boy couldn't pull the hem up high enough because of his front pocket was full. So, he pulled the beacon from his pocket and laid it on the box. He yanked the cuff of his shorts to his underwear line revealing more bites, but Charlie, even with a hand full of cotton balls, stared at the beacon lying on the box.

Finally he said, "I haven't seen one of these in years." He picked it up with his free hand, twirling the cord and regarded the whistle end.

"So, that's what it was," laughed Charlie without humor. "It sounded so familiar that I swear every time I was about to…"

He caught himself, returned the beacon to the box and motioned Tommy toward him. With a wad of cotton balls soaked from the green bottle, he dabbed the masses of angry bumps on Tommy's thigh and the dingy cotton balls soon made up a dozen individual fires across he fire pit.

Finally Charlie stood and stretched and Tommy let out the breath he'd been holding. Twisting his trunk twice and without looking at me, Charlie ordered flatly, "Next!"

I stepped forward and he repeated the head-to-neck inspection barely touching my scalp.

"Guess you weren't as sweet," he said humorlessly. With only two bites on my neck and a few on my right arm he repeated his hand gestures.

"Shirt, please?" Panicked I wadded the hem of my shirt to my armpits gripping my bunched fists to the center of my chest.

"Now we have a winner."

I tensed, while he soaked cotton balls between his fingers before dabbing my belly with the same impassive disinterest he'd treated Tommy. I was relieved, but also livid at the lack of attention. He'd been more interested in the bug he'd thrown in the fire. Angry, I considered taking off my shirt and dropping my shorts and underpants. I had tried to hide what was under my clothes, the least he could do was extend the interest to justify my modesty. Not that I was actually willing to strip, but it was certainly funny to think how such a move would incite some kind of reaction other than that bored expression.

Fuming, I was not prepared when he turned my left wrist over and stared at it without blinking. Looking at Tommy, I got a return puzzled expression before trying to pull my hand away. I had a better chance of pulling away a nub. He didn't hurt me, but he didn't let go until my jerky movement seemed to break his trance. Still holding my hand, he put on his reading glasses and peered at my wrist again as I tried not to tremble. He licked his thumb and rubbed away the light grime. Naturally, the spit didn't make the marks disappear, nor did swabbing them with cotton balls into a grimy mess. After he pulled off his glasses, he looked into my face.

"That's my *Orion,*" I stammered. "Ancient Greeks believed it to be...."

"A sign bestowed by the gods of those blessed with luck," he finished. Looking away, he grabbed another wad of cotton balls to dab other bites, but avoiding my *Orion.* He'd been efficient with Tommy, but in no hurry. Now there was an urgency similar to kids I seen trying to finish a test before the bell rang. To my relief, he didn't ask me to pull up my shorts cuffs or even treat the bites on my legs. The slosh in the green bottle indicated there was still plenty of gunk left, along with swabs and cotton balls. Without a word he replaced the bottle's lid and stood up with his palm lying on the center of his back.

"Finished?" Tommy yelped. "Everything OK? Something wrong?"

"No," Charlie said. "I've got an idea!"

We tensed as he opened the box and took out a clear plastic squeeze bottle filled with a golden liquid. As an afterthought he retrieved a towel from the nearby clothesline.

"Go to the creek where my boat is," he said. "There's a place where I've stacked some flat rocks into the water. You can get in and out of the water without getting your feet muddy."

He handed me the towel and plastic bottle.

"This is antiseptic soap," he explained. " Wash yourselves from your hair to your toes. It will do a better job sanitizing those bites than I can. You can also use it to wash your clothes."

"But, don't we have to go?" I asked and mentally kicked myself.

"You can go after your clothes dry," he mumbled. "It won't take long in this weather."

He picked up the beacon and sat with his back to us.

CHAPTER 16

We found the rocks where Charlie said they'd be and I laid the towel on the canoe.

"You don't think he expects us to get undressed do you?" Tommy asked. "Maybe he's watching."

My cheeks flushed remembering my first potty experience in the field by the tree house and looked up the hill. There was no sign of Charlie.

"What are we going to do? Tommy demanded.

"I don't know," I answered. "Just be ready to go if I tell you."

"Wish we had swim suits," Tommy said. "Wish we had some food."

"Well we don't," I snapped. "We'll have to make the best of it."

Tommy stomped into the creek until the water was up to his waist before turning to face me and fell back. Surfacing he peeled off his shirt and I threw the plastic bottle at him.

"He's just so weird," Tommy said. "He looks like a bum, but his camp is so neat. We're kids for crying out loud and he wants to get rid of us."

"He hasn't said when we're supposed to leave," I said. "The best thing is to take it easy and not get worked up, like Ana is always saying."

"Maybe so, I just wish we could get that gun," Tommy said. "I've got a bad feeling, I don't like him. I think we should just leave and go back to the tree house."

The yellow soap produced mounds of lather and Tommy used his shirt like a wash cloth rubbing soap across his back. He gave me the bottle and, while I didn't take off my shirt, I rubbed soap under and over and before long was as foamy as Tommy. Charlie was right; after a rinse, I felt a hundred times better.

When I surfaced, Tommy had waded farther downstream where the water was deeper until he took a step and disappeared. He surfaced and sputtered as he splashed toward me where I lay on the bank.

"We've got about all we're going to get out of him," Tommy said. "Since he wants us gone anyway, let's run back to the tree house. We can spot another plane from there."

Feeling so much better, I let my feet bounce off the bottom while my head was partially submerged. I knew we couldn't spend another night in that deer blind, yet Tommy had his mind made up to go in whatever direction seemed easiest. Only he didn't know the right one, and neither did I.

"He still has the beacon," I reasoned. "We can't leave without it."

"Then let's go get it," Tommy said. "We don't even need to wait for our clothes to dry. He gives me the creeps."

"Why's that?" I asked.

"I don't know, the way he doctored our bites," Tommy whined. "Remember what they told us in school? And what is he doing out here? I'll bet he's a crook or a spy."

"No," I said, "he's not any of those, but I know who he is."

"Who?" Tommy demanded.

"Tarzan of the Apes," I said

"Who? Are you kidding?" Tommy nearly shouted. "Jackie, Tarzan is only in books and movies. Besides, why would Tarzan be out here?"

"He's a New Athenian! Didn't you see his knife? It's a Tarzan knife. The scabbard has those same Greek symbols we saw on Ana's leather hair stay. I'll bet he's here on a mission quest."

"Come on," said Tommy, in a tone to convince himself more than me. "Anybody can have a big knife and Greek symbols. It's just one of those things Ana is always talking about when stuff just happens."

"A coincidence?" I said, lying back in the water. "Or is it?"

"Tarzan lives in Africa," Tommy argued firmly. "What's he doing here?"

I knew I had him. "Remember where he said he got his gun?" I asked.

"The jungle…" Tommy answered, "but he wasn't in Africa, it was Southish Azuh, wherever that is."

" How about the way he hopped up that tree."

"He climbed as well as I did, but why would Tarzan come to Texas?"

"Why wouldn't he?" I countered. "Remember the story Ana read about Tarzan coming to America to meet Jane. He drove a car, saved Jane from a forest fire. He rode a ship to his ancestral home in England and went to the Arabian Desert. If he can go there, why can't he come to Texas if he wants too?"

"OK, suppose you're right," Tommy said. "He certainly smells like an ape, but he's nothing like the pictures or movies." Tommy looked up the hill before adding, "What about the way he took that tick off and treated our bites. He could have just as easily given us the soap first."

"But he didn't and he didn't' hurt you," I argued. "He was a lot more interested in my *Orion*, the same way a New Athenian would. Which is why I believe he's on a mission quest."

"Yeah, he was too weird about your *Orion*," said Tommy holding up a finger. "Another thing, I don't remember Tarzan carrying a gun."

"He's got a knife and I remember the ape man uses whatever he has to," I said like I knew. "Remember Papa's movie where Tarzan was in South America, which is just down the road from here? He used a machine gun, tied bombs on the ends of a rope and threw them at a helicopter."

"I still wish we had the gun," Tommy said. "We wouldn't have to worry about anything, or anyone. Wonder why left it out like that and doesn't carry it? There are wolves and bears around here, that's what I'd do."

"Don't forget rattlesnakes," I said glancing around. "Maybe, he was scouting for a sign like they always talk about on TV."

"I just wish there was a sign telling us the way home," Tommy said. "I say let's get the beacon and scat."

I never had another chance to argue. "Hey you guys," called Charlie, standing at the top of the slope, "did you drown or are you building a raft?"

"We're coming," I yelled splashing out of the water.

I wrung my shirt out at the waist and we dried one another with the towel and emptied our tennis shoes. The soles of our shoes squished with every step. Back in camp I draped the towel over the cord between the trees. Charlie made no comment about our wet clothes and pointed at another log he'd placed on the other side of the fire pit. A small fire flickered under a can of water boiling suspended by a branch. With a rag he took the can from the fire and poured the contents into our water cups.

"Tea?" He offered.

My stomach quivered at the thought of any kind of food and Tommy must have felt the same as he grabbed a cup.

"Got any sugar?" Tommy asked.

Charlie indicated a spoon atop a small green plastic box with a sliding lid that set beside several other items on the box.

"There's still nothing to eat," Charlie said. "I didn't expect guests this trip."

Next to the sugar was a plastic salt and pepper shaker and a box containing rice. These, two little cans of tomato juice, bottles of lime juice and olive oil were all of Charlie's groceries.

"We don't want to be any trouble," I said unable to hide my disappointment. "So, we'll be leaving."

Charlie moved to the other side of the tent and returned with a plastic bucket. "We'll go to the store and get a few things."

"There's a store around here?" Tommy blurted. "It should have a phone."

"It's not that kind of store," Charlie said, " and you're standing in the middle of it."

Jerking our heads around, I wondered if this man was really crazy. He picked up the beacon lying on the box and handed it to me. I draped it around my neck.

"You'll need that," he said turning to walk down to the creek. "Let's get moving."

"But where are we going?" I asked falling into step on Charlie's left side.

"Hunting," he said without looking around, " and shopping."

"Aren't you going to take your gun?" Tommy said. "When my dad and I went hunting, we always came home with lots of birds."

"That's not a hunting gun, it wouldn't be any good for hunting birds," Charlie said. "Besides, this will be more appropriate."

Snatching up the machete, he called a bolo, Charlie unwrapped the waxed string threaded through the sheath and draped it over his right shoulder. We walked across the creek and moved upstream. Along the way he found a sapling thick as my two fingers. He cut it with the bolo. When he had hacked away the excess branches and stripped its bark off, he held out a stout stick with a fork at one end.

He led us to a field where a funny colored vine with flowers grew. Using the stick, he unearthed several small pungent smelling bulbs and dropped them into the bucket; Tommy wrinkled his nose and waved his hand in front of his face.

"Whew," Tommy said. "What's that?"

"Meadow garlic," Charlie said.

"You don't expect us to eat that? Tommy demanded.

"You've eaten it before," Charlie answered.

"No way, not me," I said. "I'd remember something that nasty."

"You've eaten pizza and spaghetti?" Charlie asked.

He was right, reminding me of pizzas we shared at Ana's house as he led us to another small meadow. He explained how ancient Greeks and Romans discovered garlic thousands of years ago. That it was supposed to keep away evil spirits, but also warded off mosquitoes and other pests. Somehow, they found it made food taste good, so that was even better.

Again, the smell of garlic reminded me of Ana and I fought back a sob. Absent mindedly, I scratched my wrist, thinking of our collective *Orions*. Looking up, I saw Charlie watching me and he turned taking a couple of steps before stopping.

"Smell that?" He exclaimed.

"Yeah," Tommy said, still walking. "More stinking garlic."

"Something else," Charlie said shaking his head. "Look there!"

He thrust his digging stick into the ground and brought up the results to our faces and waved it. Inhaling through my nose, I thought of Ana grilling hamburgers. Yet, I knew the odor wasn't frying meat.

"Onions," Charlie announced. "Wild onions."

Grinning, he pointed to plot covered with snow-white flower pedals. Using the stick Charlie showed us how to unearth the little bulbs and soon wild onions nearly filled the bucket.

"So," demanded Tommy and wrinkled his nose. "Is this all we're going to eat?"

"It could be," Charlie said, "I read that during the 15th Century, a party of French Jesuits traveled from Green Bay, Wisconsin to Chicago eating nothing but wild onions."

"So let him eat them," Tommy said. "But what is a French Jesuit party and what's Green Bay, Wisconsin anyway?"

Instead of answering, Charlie led us to another trail adjacent to the creek and moved upstream. As usual, Tommy complained, demanding to know where we were going. With a punch to Tommy's shoulder, I put my finger to my lips. He stuck out his tongue and made throat-cutting motions. He was less talkative as we trudged until the sound of rushing water stopped even Tommy's chatter. Putting a finger to his lips, Charlie motioned us to a row of bushes separating the trail from the creek. Dropping to his knees he pointed to a small opening in the shrub.

Through the leaves I saw water gushing over a rock slab the length of my mother's car, it smooth surface sloping into a natural reservoir. Above the slab was another huge, squared boulder lying in the middle of the creek. Water flowed around it and down the slab. Because of the slab's humped design, the rock was wet and slick as a slide as the water ran off either its sides. Sunlight glistened on the wet stone surface while dragonflies floated on the still water just beyond the rush of the current.

"They're here!" Charlie whispered. "Bunches of them."

"Who's here?" Tommy hissed

Charlie dumped the garlic and onions and laid the bolo on top of the pile. Pointing with his stick, he leaned close to our heads.

"Look from the top of the big rock all the way to the edge of the water."

I peered where Charlie pointed and, like the rattlesnake, failed to see what he was talking about.

"They're as long as your hand and black," he whispered. "Look close and they'll move."

Looking again, I felt my mouth drop open at the sight of hundreds of black and red crawfish in the center of the slab. They sauntered across the slab's velvet moss, their long antennas whipping and threatening neighbors with claws the size of jack knives.

"We're going to eat those?" Tommy asked. "Yuck!"

"Maybe," Charlie said with a wink. "If nothing else, we'll have some fun catching them."

With a natural affection for crawly things, Tommy listened attentively as Charlie explained how we must grab the crawfish on the lower half of their body. Otherwise, we'd get pinched. He demonstrated how to reach and grab the crawfish middle between their head and tail.

"We'll approach from the far side," Charlie said. " Don't say anything, the water will cover our approach and the sun will be in their eyes. They won't know until you're right there, step on them if you have to, just don't let them pinch."

He picked up the bucket and led us upstream and around the rocks to a point well behind the big boulder above the slab. At that point, the creek was a flat table, wide as a road with four or five trickles joining together into a shallow pool that flowed into a solid stream around the big boulder. Charlie hunched low, stepping on dry spots, to make his way to the right side of the boulder. We followed his example, picking our way toward the center of the boulder. Stretching out to look around the edge of the boulder, he peeked to one side before pulling his feet under him and nodded. We moved close to the left side of the boulder, crouching chest to back, my chin on Tommy's head looking toward Charlie. Another nod and we leaped around the boulder and moved down the slab where Crawfish carpeted the rock. They seemed to turn as one at our approach and moved like a flying carpet toward the water. Charlie snatched up a crawfish, big as the beacon, and tossed it in the bucket. Two more followed while I wrestled with another, intent more on not getting pinched than getting it in the bucket. Tommy grabbed another, then another, another and another and even tried to step on another.

Our success must have made me over confident as I juggled and tossed three good-sized ones into the bucket. A fourth crawfish sank its claws into my ring finger and white-hot pain shot up my arm. A howl formed in my throat. As Charlie appeared beside me to snap the crawfish's arm off at its body, the claws relaxed, but not my pain. He broke off the other claw before tossing it the bucket.

"Don't look at it and don't think about it," Charlie said. "Then it can't hurt you."

Shaking the soreness out of my finger I intercepted another crawfish with my foot, slipped and landed painfully on my rear, my legs splayed. Hurt and embarrassed, I propped myself up on my hands, at odds which to rub first, my bruised bottom or sore finger. I wondered if the situation could get any more embarrassing. Charlie and Tommy took no notice as they tossed flailing crawfish into the bucket. I got to my feet and managed to grab a few more.

"Great going," Charlie shouted. "Not bad for a first try."

He filled the bucket partially with water before leaping across to the shore to disappear into the brush. I rubbed my sore butt and I shook my hand to flip away the hurt in my finger as Tommy approached me and grinned.

"All right," Tommy cheered.

Laughing, my pains seemed to minimize while Tommy held up both fists in a victory dance. Charlie reappeared with the bolo, the bundled onions and garlic tied around its scabbard, and motioned up stream.

"Come on, there are a few more places."

Chapter 17

Had anyone ever caught so many crawfish at one time? I don't know, but we raided six more nests with the same success. I wondered if Charlie was intent on filling the bucket, but when it was half full he nodded.

"That's all for today," he said and walked to a log near our last raid. He plucked out crawfish to examine and clean. In vain, they tried to pinch him before he dropped most back in the bucket, but others he tossed into the creek.

"Hey," Tommy howled when the third crawfish went flying back into the water. "What was wrong with that one?"

Charlie didn't look at the boy or stop the inspection process. "Female," he said. "She has eggs on her tail, wouldn't make very good eating."

"That one is too small," he said tossing another into the center of the creek. "We'll get him next time."

Like me, Tommy was proud of our catch and reluctant to give up even one. They represented a personal accomplishment and regardless of the reason for the loss, it somehow demeaned the moment. Tommy walked away and leaned against a nearby tree to pout until Charlie finished sorting the crawfish. Oblivious to our moodiness, Charlie unsheathed his bolo and pointed to a grove of cattails near the shore.

"Tommy, can you to cut about a dozen of those and bring them over here?"

Tommy's surliness left him when he took the bolo that looked as big as a Persian scimitar in his hand. He strode purposely toward the nearest cattail and waded into the knee-deep water.

"What do you need these for?" Tommy asked over his shoulder.

"You cut," Charlie said, "and I'll tell you when to stop."

Nodding, Tommy grasped a cattail stalk and swung with all his might. He wasn't prepared for how sharp the big knife was, but managed to avoid slicing his leg. Just like Tarzan, I thought, looking from Tommy to Charlie.

Soon a large sheave of cattails lay on the shore. Using a strip of cattail, Charlie gathered and tied them, along with the onions and garlic, into the bundle. Tommy offered the return of the bolo the same way he'd been offered it, handle first. Nodding, Charlie took and shoved it into its holster before draping the string around Tommy's neck. Inserting the digging stick through the bucket's handle Charlie directed us to take an end while he hefted the bundle and we marched back to camp.

At the crossing, Charlie seated himself on his canoe with the bucket between his feet and twisted crawfish tails and tossed the heads downstream.

"Hey," Tommy shouted. "We swim in this water."

"So do fish and scavengers," Charlie said and arched another crawfish head downstream. "If they don't eat it, something else will, even after the current passes it into the river. Besides, I don't want to leave an invitation to coons and possums to raid our camp."

"Coons," said Tommy turning his head in every direction.

No raccoons appeared and Tommy waded into the water. I was more thrilled to hear Charlie refer to "our camp." I sat beside Charlie and asked to be shown how to clean crawfish. He did and between us we also peeled onions and garlic that he minced with his knife.

"If we had some rosemary sprigs and white wine, we could whip up a good Paella."

Unfamiliar with the word, I stared at him.

"It's a seafood stew they make in Spain," he said. "It's made mostly of the stuff we have here. All we need are some red fish, or even catfish fillets."

"You've been to Spain?" I asked. "Like Columbus sailed the ocean blue from in 1492?"

He nodded and I gazed with greater interest at the ingredients that minutes before had been swimming in the wild. He placed the crawfish in the bucket and the veggies in a blue bandana he pulled from his back pocket.

"Now we'll make an oven," Charlie said.

Tommy and I looked at each other as Charlie picked up the bucket and used the digging stick to hoist the veggie bulged bandana to his shoulder. He started up the slope and I ran and threw myself on Tommy knocking us into the water. Laughing, we got to our feet and caught up with Charlie.

In camp, Charlie put bucket and bundle on the box and took out a folding shovel from one of the box's canvas pouches. Walking a few paces from the fireplace, he broke ground in two places scooping out a hole the size of the bucket. Finished, he handed Tommy the shovel telling him to start another hole beside the first. Tommy struck the earth ineffectively dislodging an earth clod. Charlie handed me some cat tails and demonstrated how to strip their long green leaves. We stacked the results between us. By the time we finished, Tommy had chopped only a few more clods from the ground. Charlie finished the smaller hole leaving a three inch wall separating it from its big brother. He motioned me to bring the stripped leaves and we lined the smaller hole.

"In the Philippines, we dug the oven into the side of a hill," Charlie said. "This way works just as well, don't you think?"

"Pill and beans," Tommy said with a laugh. "What's that?"

"A series of islands in the Western Pacific," Charlie answered, "I worked there for eighteen months."

He placed a bundle of twigs along with some buffalo grass in the hole before taking a slip of paper from his breast pocket. It was the same sheet I'd seen with writing that had been under the pistol when we walked into his camp. For a few seconds, he stared at it before crumpling and placing it in the big hole. Shovel in hand, he walked over to fire pit. Meantime, I peeked down at the scrunched paper. I couldn't read all of what it said, but I managed to make out, "Please forgive me."

Shortly, he returned with a scoop of coals and dropped the hot embers into the big hole. Fire showed above the hole.

"What was that paper?" I asked.

"Tender," he replied and blew harder.

Flames rose from the hole as he added sticks and showed Tommy how to put in wood without getting burned. Returning to the box, he took out a large white cloth and a battered Boy Scout mess kit. He spread the cloth, its center over the mess kit pot, and filled the pot before placing garlic, crawfish and onions on top.

"Are either of you allergic to tomatoes, shellfish or olive oil?"

We shook our heads.

"Good, this particular dish would of awfully bland without them."

He poured tomato juice over the fish and vegetables, added olive oil, lime juice and a dash of salt and pepper. After adding more rice, the small mountain threatened to spill over the pot's lip. Without spilling even a single rice grain, he added more oil, lime juice and salt in the center, tied the four ends into a loose bundle and doused it with water from the jug until it sopped. With cattail leaves he swathed the bundle until only the top knot of the cloth was visible. Thrusting the digging stick through the cloth's loop, he carried it toward the fire holes and eased it into the smaller one. Pouring more water into the hole until I thought it would have filled up.

"I think we've got time for another cup of tea," said Charlie, placing a flat rock over the small hole. The tea was welcome, but my clothes felt clammy from our last swim. The elastic was rubbing my waist and the inside of my legs.

"Could you loan me something to wear?" I asked.

"What's wrong with what you have on?" Tommy asked.

Charlie went to the tent and returned with a nylon bag, he dug two T-shirts from. Thanking him, I took a towel from the line and bundled it and the shirt.

"What kind of card games can you play?" Asked Charlie, tossing the other shirt to Tommy.

"Crazy eight," I said placing the bundle under my arm.

"Go fish, war," Tommy said. "Slap jack!"

"We'll start with war," said Charlie dealing two piles of cards. "Later we'll see how you are with pig, concentration and California Jack."

Leaving them to their game I walked below the rise and glanced back repeatedly until I got to the canoe. After counting to 60, I stepped behind the canoe and wrestled out of my clothes, unhappy with how little concealment the canoe offered. Yet, I didn't care for the idea of what might be hiding in the nearby high grass. I bent down as far behind the canoe as I could get, pulled off the beacon and laid it across the canoe. Yanking my shirt over my head, I wrapped the towel around me, discovering I couldn't peel my shorts and underwear over my sneakers without standing up, and revealing everything. The stress undid the towel, and I squealed before I could recover it. Yet no one appeared at the top of the rise. I scrambled for the towel and nearly jumped out of my skin at the touch of tiny fingers caressing my lower back. Instantly, I slapped my bare skin, bumped my knee against the canoe and fell against the canoe pain shooting like greased razor blades from my chest. Gritting my teeth, determined not to squeal again, I looked behind me and, to my irritation, a yellow butterfly rose from my back and floated toward the water.

"What do you think you're doing?" I said aloud.

For an answer, the butterfly drifted across the creek to the widest part of the green water. I don't know anything about butterflies, but this one seemed to dare me to follow it. Never mind, that I had only planned to step quickly into the ankle deep water, splash myself and get out. Instead, I pulled off my pants and underwear, bundled everything and never taking my eyes off the butterfly on the water's surface. I thought of all the times I'd been told not to go near water without adult supervision and pulled off my sneakers and socks. The butterfly sat on the water, wings pulsating a gentle rhythm.

Without a back glance to the hilltop, I walked to water's edge dropped my clothes and dove into the creek pushing away from the shallows. I walked toward a patch of sunshine until my feet couldn't touch the bottom. Striking out to the center, I sank below the reach of sunlight until I could muss the creek's muddy bottom with both hands.

Ecstatic, I laughed, producing bubbles and looked to the surface, as a cloud of sand enveloped me. I rose effortlessly, fascinated by the multitude of light shimmering through the bubbles about me. Dream-like, I relished the gossamer embrace of the water, caressed with an animal nakedness I'd never known.

The butterfly was waiting not a foot from my head when I broke the surface. Lying back, I gently treaded water with my thoughts also afloat. Unsuccessfully, I reminded myself that I was naked, but couldn't seem to recall why I should be concerned or even bother to look up the hill.

"I wish this day wouldn't end," I told the butterfly. "Things are a lot better than this morning and certainly better than last night, or last week for that matter."

Nearby, the butterfly rubbed its back legs and I remembered reading how butterflies tasted food with their back legs.

"We had the best water I've ever tasted," I said "We're cooking dinner, we caught ourselves, using a dish towel and a hole in the ground."

The butterfly wasn't impressed, probably, I thought, because it caught dinner all the time. It left the water and landed on my chest making me wonder what I tasted like.

"He knows so much, about stuff I never even thought of," I said. "You know, I was kidding Tommy. It was the only way to keep him from taking off. Now I wonder who was kidding who?"

The butterfly climbed to one of the highest perches on my chest and turned round to face me, wings opening and closing. Raising my head, I drained my ears of water.

"So why is he so nasty and his camp so clean, cleaner than my classroom on the first day of school?"

The butterfly opened and closed its wings with a 1-2-3-4 rhythm.

"Maybe he's modest or something? Oh, and by the way?" The butterfly stopped as if giving me its full attention. "This is my first time to go skinny dipping."

Its wings folded in the up position, a warning of danger behind me? Tilting my head back to look behind me. The inverted landscape offered nothing out of the ordinary. Looking back, the butterfly sat with open wings.

"I could get used to swimming this way," I said. "I've done it at home and never thought anything about it. Still being outside is something else all together."

The butterfly turned to profile and resumed its wing exercises: 1-2-3-4-5.

"I wonder if I could do this with other people around though?" I asked.

"It's OK by yourself, you know, the way Charlie was, until we showed up."

The butterfly stopped.

"Sorry, present company excepted."

The butterfly's wings moved 1-2-hold-1-2-hold and I changed the subject.

"And why didn't he pack food, or find onions and crawfish before today?"

The butterfly cleaned its antenna.

"What's he doing here? Why did he leave his gun out like that? That's just dangerous!"

The butterfly vibrated and flew to the top of the tallest tree on the other side of the creek.

I moved back to the shallows and grabbed my clothes. Facing the hill, as I had with the buck deer, I rubbed most of the grime out of them and wrung them dry. "Without looking up the hill, I dried myself and pulled on Charlie's T-shirt, draping the beacon over my neck. Placing my wet things in the towel, I walked back up the hill. Charlie didn't stir when I came into camp or as I hesitantly hung my clothes over the makeshift clothesline.

"I see Spain, I see France, I see…," sang Tommy until Charlie tapped him on the knee with his cards.

"Your play," he growled.

I finished hanging my laundry, Charlie gathered and dealt three new hands as I joined Tommy on the log.

"You go swimming again?" Tommy asked.

I picked up my cards without answering. Tommy grabbed the other T-shirt and towel and moved down the hill. Charlie studied his card hand and, unlike other adults, didn't warn my cousin to be careful. So, I did!

"Yeah, yeah," Tommy called, "I will."

He disappeared down the hill and I picked up my cards. Charlie took the multicolored blanket he'd been sitting on and handed it to me.

"Charlie?" I said after thanking him.

He grunted and stacked his cards for the play.

"Have you really been to all those places?"

"Places?" He asked not looking up. "What places?"

"Spain and the pill and beans."

"Spain and the Philippines," he corrected throwing down the first card.

"Yes," I said taking the trick.

"Yes," he said, tossing another card, adding, "and a few others."

"Others?"

"Other countries besides Spain and Pill-n-Beans," he said. "Though lately I can't tell the difference between them and this one. "

By a few, I knew he meant many, and the more I wanted to hear. "It must be wonderful to go to all those places," I said. "You must have a great job."

"I don't go to those places anymore, I work in an office, " he said in a flat edged tone. "I am a paper pusher."

"That sounds…nice," I said, knowing it didn't.

"No it's not," he replied. "Besides, I might not have gotten the official memo, but I seriously believe my services were no longer needed."

Grimacing, he moved to the woodpile and snatched up a branch and, with the ease I'd break a pencil, broke it and put the ends in the big hole. Returning, he palmed his cards and tapped them against the box.

"So tell me, fair Jackie, what brings you to this far country? I mean besides being separated from your grandparents?"

I wasn't sure what he was asking, or what prompted me. So, I told him everything: about my mother and daddy, problems at school, Tommy's family and bragged about Uncle Theo.

"Sounds like life has not exactly handed you the keys to the kingdom either," he said.

I didn't know what he meant, though his expression reminded me of how Ana looked just two days earlier, though it seemed like 200 years ago. It was my play, only I was afraid to twitch or say anything because his lips moved, again the same way Ana sang her old "united we stand" song. So, I knew he wasn't talking to me.

"I pledge my hands," he began and placed the tip of his finger on his temple, " my head and my heart," and placed the same finger on his chest before holding it up, "and I consecrate myself to truth, justice and humanitarian service. As the first Athenians gave the world architecture, science and government, I will leave my world better through my personal gifts. Rendering freely my talents and resources available without wrong to man or nature."

Glancing at me, he looked away embarrassed. I threw a card, took the trick, he threw another card.

"It's wrong, all wrong," he muttered, "I don't know what to do or where to go."

Charlie's eyes shifted to the box and a sliver of fear danced up my back. Catching my eye, he looked away like this was something he shouldn't do, just as a long, mournful chorus rose from the hills above us.

"What's that?" I said jumping up.

"Coyotes," he said, not looking up. "Local pack is letting us know they're in the neighborhood."

Tommy came running from the creek, nearly tripping on his T-shirt. He caught himself and draped his clothes and towel beside mine on the clothes line. Puffing, he took a seat beside me and Charlie shuffled another hand as the coyotes howled continuously and Tommy looking anxiously in all directions.

"Wolves," Tommy announced, owl eyed. "We heard them last night."

"Coyotes," Charlie corrected, "and they won't come near us."

"Why not?" said a disappointed Tommy. "They sound like they're just behind those trees, ready to tear us a part."

"That's what they want you to think," Charlie said. "Coyotes are cowards, they look for smaller, weaker animals."

"Still," said Tommy his eyes intent. "It sounds like there are so many."

"Coyote packs, like people, are only as big as the food source that can support them," Charlie said. "They howl, like people, to convince themselves, if not others, just how bad they are."

They search out weaker prey, he explained, tear it down. But won't mess with the potential of being eaten. "The rest is just show and hype," Charlie said.

"You could shoot them with your gun if they come around," said Tommy his eyes dropping to the box. "With a gun, nothing messes with you."

"What makes you say that?" Charlie asked.

"It's a fact of life," Tommy said. "Soldiers and police have guns and you don't mess with them. If you have a gun you're somebody."

"Prisons and cemeteries are full of people who might argue with you," Charlie said. "I worked with human coyotes and there's always another ready to join the pack."

"My Uncle Theo has a gun. He's in Iraq," I said. "He's somebody and he's not in jail or a cemetery."

"It's not because he has a gun," Charlie said. "A gun is a tool, no better or worse than the hand holding it. It can be abused depending on what, who, and how it's used."

I wanted to tell Tommy to shut his mouth, only I never got a chance.

"Can I look at your gun?" Tommy blurted.

Horrified, I shook my head, but Charlie winked and cleared off the box. Removing the gun from its Russian-Chinese holster, he performed the ritual of peek, pinky, point, snap the drawer shut and we jumped. Grasping the gun by the long end, Charlie offered the handle to a delighted Tommy. The boy took it with one hand until the weight made him use both.

"Man, oh, man," Tommy said. "I'll bet nobody would mess with me if I had this."

Tommy started to turn the long end toward Charlie, but was stopped by a finger that gently pushed it away.

"Bad Bob could!" Charlie said.

"Bad who?" I asked.

"Bad Bob!" repeated Charlie flipping another card into the box. "You've never heard of Bad Bob?"

We shook our heads and Charlie cleared his throat, tossed another card down before leaning forward.

CHAPTER 18

"B ad Bob was the most NO-torious hombre in the Old West," said Charlie looking at each of us. "The Indians called him *Two Tornadoes That Walked Like a Man.*"

He could ride farther in a day than a bird could fly. He sat on a porch in California and hunted elk in Colorado. It was rumored he'd killed more men than small pox. The James and Dalton gangs, Billy-the-Kid, and Doc Holiday all went on vacation when it was rumored he was in the territory. Sitting Bull stood when Bad Bob came in to his teepee, and Crazy Horse became Silent Snake. There were tales around the camp fire of how mountain lions squawked like chickens at the sight of him, rivers reversed directions, and Yellowstone's Old Faithful was late.

"One day in the town of Sour Springs word came that Bad Bob was on his way," Charlie said. "Panic gripped the people as everyone loaded up their horses and wagons to get out of town."

Unfortunately, the last person to leave was the bar tender Bill Barlow, owner and operator of the Dew Drop Inn Saloon. Bill was loading the last of his gear into his wagon when he chanced to look up the street in time to see a huge man riding a snow white buffalo. The buffalo rider waved at Bill and the poor bar keep could barely lift his hand to return the gesture. He saw the buffalo rider's saddle was made of cactus, the bridle was two live rattlesnakes, tails in the buffalo's nose and their fangs sunk into the man's flesh. He wore a vest carved from solid granite over a belt carrying more bullets than the Seventh Calvary. Revolvers were stuck all the way around his waist and the same number of rifles hung down his back, rolled up like Venetian blinds.

He stopped in front of the saloon where the poor bar tender quaked in his tracks. "Could I get something to eat and drink?" Asked the huge man not impolitely.

"Of course," cried the bartender and ran to unlock the saloon. He threw open the doors, ran to the back and rolled out a barrel of beer, another of wine, a third of whiskey. The stranger nodded happily and poked a hole in the top of each barrels with his pinky finger. Hefting the barrels between his hands he drank their combined contents.

Meanwhile, the bartender ran to the cold meat cellar and wheeled up a freshly roasted side of beef. Parking the half steer at the table, the big man fell on the meat. gnawing it to bones by the time the bar tender returned with a ham, leg of mutton, baskets of onions, corn and apples. The stranger consumed everything, stopping only to swig from another barrel.

When the food was gone the stranger belched and the sound broke a window across the street. He excused himself, wiped his mouth and picked his teeth with a sharpened fence post.

"Is there anything else I can get for you?" the nervous bar tender blubbered.

Shaking his head, the stranger reached into his vest and dropped a clinking Wells Fargo bag on the table.

"No thanks," said the stranger spilling a pile of gold coins taller than the bar tender. "I have to get out of town, Bad Bob is headed this way."

CHAPTER 19

The card game had stopped long into Charlie's story and Tommy rested the gun on the box. Not sure of what we had heard, we stared open mouthed before turning to look at the other and fell over laughing. Stone faced, Charlie took the pistol from Tommy, wiped it with a bandana and replaced in its holster. We fell on the ground laughing so hard we could barely catch our breath.

Silently Charlie went to check our meal. After rolling the flat rock aside, tantalizing smells of garlic and olive oil wafted through the air and my stomach rumbled, which made us laugh even more. Tommy pointed and drummed his heels

Charlie splashed a cup of water into the food hole. After dropping more wood into the fire hole, he resumed his seat and the card.

"Almost ready," he said. "I believe it's my play."

We burst into fresh laughter, Charlie ignored us and studied his cards until our mirth subsided. "Bad Bob is always out there," he said. "Someone bigger and nastier, but that doesn't mean you have to ride the same trail he does."

"Is that what you're doing here?" Tommy asked. "I mean not being on the same trail with those coyotes you work with."

"Tommy!" I cautioned and threw down a card. "He's on a building quest."

"How do you know that?" Tommy demanded, eyes narrowed.

"He's a New Athenian," I said quickly. "He knows the pledge, so he's out here like Ana said, getting his head together on how to use his talent for truth, justice, and an N-light way so he can leave the world better than he found it without causing wrong to man or nature."

Tommy's eyes grew large as he turned to Charlie. "You're following your destiny?" Tommy asked

Snorting, Charlie looked at me and frowned. "What do you think destiny is?" Charlie asked.

"Ana said mine was to go swimming," Tommy answered. "She said Jackie's was to carry the beacon, so I guess it's something you're good at."

"So, what do you think mine is?" Charlie murmured.

I couldn't answer and neither could Tommy.

"I thought it was what I did in the jungle," Charlie said. "I was good at that. I used to think it was my family, until my wife took the kids and left six months ago. There was my job, until I was late to work one day. Nobody even noticed I was missing. That's when I stepped back and realized exactly where I was."

He reminded me of a stuffed monkey I kept on my bed, its arms at its sides, a permanent sad smile and perpetually tired looking.

"Destiny is one thing, survival is another," said Charlie looking embarrassed. "Jobs are not always easy to come by, especially at my age."

"They pay you to work with coyotes?" I asked. "A girl back home offered me five dollars to eat this smelly fishing bait her daddy kept in the refrigerator. There was just no way."

Charlie bent forward, his hat covering his face. Seconds dragged and I was about to ask if he was sick.

"Not enough!" he said. "Not near enough." He threw down his cards and stood up. I expected him to run away.

"Clear the table," he ordered.

Snatching the digging-stick, he went to the fire-pit, pried the rock up with the toe of his boot. Snagging a looped cord with the stick, he brought up the bundle and returned to the box, steam trailing. Slicing away the cattail leaves, he tugged slip knots, pulling back the cloth, and a delicious aroma filled the air. A reddish brown pile mixed with snow-white pieces of steamed crawfish lay before us. With a spoon he heaped portions into the pans of the mess kit and pushed them toward us. Refilling our tea mugs, he handed me the spoon and Tommy a battered fork.

Cautiously, I bit into the best meal I could remember eating. Shoveling a spoonful into my mouth, I almost sputtered watching Tommy do the same. He held out his pot for more and Charlie heaped his plate. That's when I noticed Charlie barely had a palm full of rice and a single crawfish in the frying pan he was using for a plate. Without asking I pulled his plate next to ours and spooned helpings from both until Charlie had an equal portion. He tried to protest until I fixed him with the "Ana-look." He drew back, held his plate up in a toast and scooped food onto the flat of his knife.

We ate until there wasn't a grain of rice left on the cloth. Dropping his fork to his pan with a clatter, Tommy slid down the log, resting his back against it and patting his stomach.

"That was so good," Tommy said, "I couldn't eat another bite."

"That works out fine," Charlie said. "Cause there ain't no more." He picked up the cloth and dropped it and the cookware in the bucket.

"This has to have been the best day of my life," said Tommy still patting his stomach. "If I live to a hundred, I'll will never, ever, forget this day."

"What are you talking about boy?" said Charlie in uncharacteristic irritable tone. "You're lost in the boonies, the whole country is searching for you. You realize you're covered in bug bites. Only a starving cat would slosh the chow you just sloshed."

"I spent the night in a tree house with coyotes ready to eat me. I swam in a creek and washed my clothes," Tommy argued. "Other kids pick on me at school, teachers make me feel stupid, my mom and dad fight all the time and it's just as bad at Jackie's house."

Charlie picked up the cards frowning and turned to me. "This true Jackie?"

I shrugged, not wanting to discuss my problems. While I wouldn't agree that this was the best day of my life, I would rank it in the top ten. Charlie didn't press me as he dealt the cards.

"Ever play rummy?"

Charlie kept score on a piece of toilet paper. Tommy was first to lay down the first matched set, but I won that round and Tommy the second. By the third hand the food, tea and the past two days had caught up with me. The sun going down had the effect of turning off my light switch. Tommy and I sat droopy eyed until Charlie exaggerated a yawn and dropped his cards.

"Time to call it a night," he announced. "You take the tent and sleeping bag. It gets pretty cool around midnight."

"Tomorrow we'll have to leave?" I asked.

"Yes," he said without further explanation. "I'll stay up a while longer. Give me the beacon and I'll fold up the plastic for you."

I removed the beacon from my neck and handed it to him. Taking it, he picked up the wadded sheet of plastic where I'd dropped it.

"Aren't you going to sleep in the tent?"

"No I'm fine here," he said laying wood in the fire pit. "I'll try not to wake you."

Tommy moved to unzip the door, but pointed beyond the tent.

"Jackie look, Orion," he said.

True enough the three horizontal and two slew footed stars glistened against the sky. Hope, food and security filled me with joy as I glanced at my wrist and turned toward Charlie. He stood also looking in that direction just as the wood in the fire pit caught. Firelight revealed how his face had hardened, his mouth similar to a knife slash.

"Good old Orion," he said, "nice to see you again old pal." His tone didn't match his words. He shuffled forward dragging the plastic sheet.

"Orion and me have been talking for the last couple of nights," Charlie said. "Yes sir, very enlightening, only last night…" He looked at us and returned to the fire the plastic sheet making a whisking noises as he walked.

"Tommy," he called. "What if this was the best day of your entire life?"

"Then I'd die really happy," Tommy declared. "It doesn't get any better than this."

"Good night," said Charlie without turning. "I have work to do. "

We bid him goodnight taking off our shoes at the tent door and beating them free of dirt. Inside the tent I found a sleeping bag still rolled in its waterproof carrying bag, next to it was a separate water proof bag containing a foam eggshell mattress. Unzipping the sleeping bag I inhaled a clean smell as though the bag had been packed right after washing. The same was true for another colorful blanket rolled into the sleeping bag and a couple of throw pillows, bedclothes that were considerably sweeter smelling than their owner. So how did they still smell so good and why had he repacked everything from the night before? It wasn't something I'd do if I had been camping for several days.

We laid the blanket over the mattress for a pallet. The blanket, to Tommy's delight, had the woven design of an Indian chief's head with a feathered headdress.

"This is a cool blanket, just like the one on the log," Tommy called. "Where did you get them?"

"Seaport town in Mexico called Mazatlan," Charlie answered. "I met an old Indian on the beach and bargained for them. He fed his family for a week on what I paid."

"You've been everywhere," Tommy declared. "You're so lucky to go to all those places and meet so many people."

"Yeah," Charlie said, "I suppose so."

Again, we wished him goodnight. Tommy was asleep almost before he turned on his side. I lay awake watching Charlie through the tent's screen door. He sat to one side of the fire place and I saw him fold and refold the plastic sheet into a cylinder no thicker than his forefinger, tying it with a piece of fishing line. Reverently, he removed the beacon's cap and took out the items inside before stuffing the folded plastic into the tube. After the other items were reinserted, he replaced the cap and grasped the lanyard with both hands, turning his head and staring in the direction of the tent.

I tried not to move, watching him bow his head. He placed a hand on the box and twirled the lanyard in his other hand before putting the whistle end to his lips. No sound came out as he held it. Holding it out before his face, his lips trembled before he laid the beacon on the box. The fire burned down, so he stoked, put more wood on it and it blazed. He sat staring into it.

He must have known I was awake, I thought, and watching him. So, I shut my eyes tight for a count of ten, opened them and he hadn't moved. I kept trying to doze off. Waking with a snort, I wondered how long I was out and saw Tommy's chest rise and fall, still lying on his side.

The fire died to a few small flames and Charlie still hadn't moved. To make sure I stayed awake, I raked my nails on the mosquito bite on my leg. I wanted sleep so badly and didn't know why I should stay awake. Yet Charlie's face became more drawn, his eyes hard and sunken until he was unrecognizable.

When I couldn't fight off sleep much longer, Charlie rubbed his hands over his forearms, a motion that started slow at first and increased in intensity until I thought he'd rub a layer of hide off. When he finally stopped, he put his head into his hands and sobbed.

I had never seen an adult man cry before and felt I was watching what I had no right to see. I didn't know why he was upset, or what to do. I was afraid when he raised his head, cheeks glistening. Unexpectedly, he popped the gear box lid and withdrew the holster and took out the pistol. He bent forward blocking the light and I heard the familiar sound of loading a bullet. He stood with the pistol hanging by his side and white panic rushed to my toes. We had to run! I laid my hand on Tommy to shake him not knowing where we'd go, but with no doubt where Charlie was headed.

The fire flared as Charlie stepped around the log, Charlie tripped and caught himself. Before he took another step, he bent down to pick something from the ground. I saw it was the beacon and his mouth screwed into a smirk. He tossed it into the air and I thought he would fling it away. Instead his brows narrowed and he brought it closer to his face moving back to the fire. Laying the pistol aside, he put on his reading glasses, tossed some dry tender into the pit, and held the beacon out to the flickering fire.

The flames illuminated his face as he used both hands to twist the beacon by the cord before the light. Unmoving, he stared at the tube for nearly a minute until his face changed into a horrified expression and his hands dropped to his side. He turned toward the tent, the firelight reflecting behind his glasses before he took a step and looked skyward, holding the beacon above his head. Tears glistened in the firelight as they moved down his cheeks. His shoulders shook spasmodically until he snorted and wiped his face on his sleeve. With a last skyward look, he mouthed words and turned to our tent.

Like a spider ready to jump, I nearly squealed when he walked around the fire twice before picking up his gun. My heart seemed to stop and I held my breath until I saw him catch the flying bullet. He replaced the gun in the box, patting the lid like a faithful pet and moved away into the darkness.

Alert and determined not to sleep again, I stared into the darkness until I found myself standing on the front railing of Papa's tree house with Tommy beside me, shading our eyes from the bright sunshine. Only instead of Ana's backyard, we were beside the river, in full torrent. Across the river sat the old fisherman and his elderly wife from Bandy's Camp in their same chairs on dry ground. The old man puffed another of his constant cigarettes like a chimney, whipping a fishing pole that was twice as long as I remembered. Nearby, the old woman sat with a huge book balanced on her scrawny lap, holding a glass of writhing snakes in one hand.

Below us hundreds of coyotes howled in a confused mass. Yapping loudest was a stark white coyote that jumped straight up repeatedly and nearly sunk its jaws into Tommy's hand with each spring. From a rise on the opposite shore, Charlie ran around the old couple down to the edge of the water, his pistol outstretched. The old man frowned irritably swinging his giant fish hook past Charlie's face. The old woman offered her glass of snakes.

Seeing Charlie the coyotes formed a line on the shore and howled. Bloody tears flowed from Charlie's empty eyes dripping down his chin. There was a mocking tone in the coyotes' howl until Charlie's pistol boomed like the guns in a Tarzan movie. Nearby, a cedar tree exploded as if hit by a cannon ball and burst into flames. The old man grimaced and swung his fishing pole. The old woman cooed to the snakes in her glass. She implored Charlie to try one because they were so good. The coyotes howled louder as a frustrated Charlie screamed and shot all around our tree house catching everything on fire. Fire made the coyotes happier and the white one celebrated by jumping with a triple somersault and nearly snapping off Tommy's nose, missing by a freckle. Spent bullets from Charlie's gun landed, smoldering around the old man. He growled at Charlie to watch it, but he didn't get up as fire blazed around us.

The coyotes formed a circle around the tree, howling in chorus, as

Ana walked out onto the balcony. Only she wasn't Ana, my grandmother, but the teenager I'd seen in the old photograph with the New Athenians. She put her hands on our shoulders and the enraged coyotes howled even louder competing with the white one trying to leap the highest and bite us.

Ana sang her old "united we stand" song in a clear voice, inducing an ear splitting howl from the coyotes that couldn't silence her.

Staggering to the river's edge, Charlie stopped shooting and turned his bloody head toward the sound of Ana's voice just as the old fisherman swung his fishing pole toward Charlie. Before it hit him, I shouted a warning and Charlie fell into the water and disappeared. When he surfaced, his face was clean and his eyes clear and blue. Suddenly terrified, the coyotes fell over one another trying to run away and taking the fire with them.

Only the white coyote tried to grab Tommy again. Tommy swung the mess kit's frying pan and knocked the coyote, howling, into the river and it floated toward the old fisherman's line. Charlie waded across to our side of the river and the old woman dropped her glass. Hundreds of snakes slithered down the shore for the river. She jumped to her feet, waving her arms, windmill fashion, as her book fell to the ground with a clap of thunder

"Have a good time now," the old woman called "But be careful, that water is deep."

The white coyote still howled even after I opened my eyes to the sight and smell of Tommy's open mouth. Angry, I jerked and realized I had fallen asleep watching for Charlie's return. An actual coyote's howl cut the silence in the distance though unable to successfully compete with the rasping emanating from the direction of the fire pit. The sound was one I associated with daddy and Papa. A racket that on dark, spooky nights assured me that nothing real or imagined would hurt me.

Crawling to the tent's screen door I strained looking toward the darkened fire pit. Stars provided enough light to see shapes and details of a bulky form lying on the other side of the fire pit between the logs and covered by the other Mexican blanket. I was able to make out the canvas boots protruding from the closest end of the blanket. Shadows danced across the worn soles as a blanket covered head nuzzled against the gear box and the blanket's center mass rose and fell with deep contented snores that might have been heard by Orion.

CHAPTER 20

I loved waking up to Ana bustling in her kitchen making breakfast. The sounds of bacon frying made me smile as I slowly raised my eyelids, a ritual I always tried to make last longer when we stayed with Ana. The general clatter was so nice to wake up to that I never wanted it to end. Only that morning before my eyes were half open I sat bolt upright looking frantically around at the unfamiliar green walls and ceiling. I started to call for Ana when wind rustled the tree outside, imitating the similar sound of frying bacon.

Silly goose, I told myself with my palms on my forehead, as my panic abated at the sight of Tommy's tousled head drooling on his pillow. I scooted next to him for warmth and listened to the morning breeze. The air was cool, not frosty and just right for lulling in bed. So, what better place to be than under a heavy sleeping bag next to my favorite cousin? The sun got brighter outside as the birds waxed eloquent mixing their songs to greet a new day. What I didn't hear was domestic noise, not Ana, of course.

But the events of the previous night came rushing back like a bad dream. I didn't move, but strained my ears and looked through the opening in the tent to locate Charlie. He couldn't still be sleeping, since it was my experience that all old people got up with the chickens, whenever that was. Still, there was no mess kit clanking, crunching boots or sound of wood broken for the fire with its welcome crackle, only the birds and wind strumming the grass and leaves.

Covering Tommy, I crawled to the tent door looking around. Outside, I suppressed a squeak as my feet went into my cold sneakers. Standing up I saw the billycan hanging over a low fire, boiling water and no Charlie in sight.

I retrieved my clothes and a towel, noticing Charlie's grey shirt draped on the line. Turning my head in every direction, I jumped at the sight of Charlie walking up the path. A towel was draped over his shoulder, but he wore no gun. His smile was broad as the sunrise and his hair was clean and combed. The scraggly whiskers were missing and he wore a fresh T-shirt, the other, still wet in his hand.

"Good morning, Jackie," he said. "Sleep well? Where's Tommy?"

What I'd seen the previous night had me uneasy. Yet, his eyes were clear, the whites were pink instead of blood shot and minus the puffy biscuits below them. I forced myself to smile, returned the greeting and told him Tommy was still asleep.

"Great," he nearly shouted. "The soap is by the stepping stones and a comb. I'll have tea ready by the time you're finished."

Not bothering to see if Charlie was looking, I slipped off the T-shirt and my shoes and dove into the creek. To my surprise, the water was warm and I moved into deeper water. Looking down, I saw a minnow nibble one of the moles of my *Orion* until *I* moved my arm and the fish left. I imagined the looks and whispers at school when I told them I'd swam without a bathing suit; not at my house, but outside with my boy cousin and, worse, a crazy man I'd met the day before who played with poisonous snakes. I could imagine what Joyce or Jerri would say, particularly Jerri, since she had the mean streak.

"Uh-oh, there's the pooty naked girl," taunted Jerri in my mind. "Not only does she let winders she won't wear clothes. Look out ladies if she doesn't stink you out, she'll steal your boy friends."

"Shut up," I said out loud silencing the imaginary Jeri. "You're nasty. I didn't do anything wrong. Nothing happened."

Just like nothing happened when Charlie got his gun out last night, I thought. What would have happened, if he had not stopped? Why did the beacon make him happy and cry?

I sort of knew how the girls at school came to the conclusion about who made the winders. It wasn't right, yet it was their only option. Just as mine was to get me and my cousin away from Charlie. Perhaps he would let us leave like he wanted to do in the first place. Whatever, I knew we had to get away, but I needed a plan.

My bug bites were re-scrubbed and I washed my hair. Combing it, I had to remind myself, again, I was naked. What was stranger was the alien feel of my clothes. I wasn't sure if it was because they'd been washed in a creek and dried on clothes line, or it was just me.

Back at camp, Charlie had put on his gray shirt from the clothes line. It was void of yesterday's sweat and grime, pockets buttoned and sleeves rolled neatly. He held out a cup of tea with both hands. I took it and sipped, finding it was already sweetened. How I would have preferred a tall glass of milk or orange juice which Ana squeezed fresh the night before. Still, the tea tasted wonderful.

"Breakfast?" I asked.

"I'm working on that," Charlie replied.

He opened the plastic rice box and placed a small red cardboard box beside it.

"We've got maybe a half cup of rice left and I found this box of raisins in the bottom of the gear box."

Charlie popped a few grains of rice into his mouth and chased them with tea, rolling the grains in his mouth. I did the same, careful not to let a single grain miss my mouth while wishing for buttered oatmeal with brown sugar. I tapped the raisin box edges against my teeth and the most delicious fruit in the world fell into my mouth.

"I guess we could dig more onions and boil them in the mess kit."

The idea of boiled onions for breakfast made my mouth pucker.

"Not the yummiest of entree, unless that's all we had," he concurred. "But finding the raisins reminded me of a wild blackberry bush I saw not far from here. Mind taking a stroll before breakfast?"

And I had my plan! The "stroll" would take us far enough away so we could loose Charlie. Then we could come back and take the canoe to civilization. Simple?

"Yes sir," I said.

"OK," he said draining his tea. "I guess we better wake Tommy."

I knew Tommy was sleeping so deep that thunder wouldn't wake him, which gave me another idea. If I went missing, Charlie would look for me, giving me even more time to get back to camp, wake Tommy and get the canoe in the water.

"Wait" I said. "He's not much of a morning person. So, let him sleep and we'll surprise him."

"All right, if you think he'll be OK," Charlie said. "We shouldn't be gone long. Anytime you're ready!"

I drank my tea and tapped more raisins onto my tongue thinking about the night before. He had been so dark, a picture of anguish and certainly not even close to the man banking the fire. Still, I'd read how people planning to kill themselves were always happiest the time before they did the deed.

I dismissed my doubts, deciding not to take any chances in getting him away from Tommy. But, what about the gun? If he didn't have it, he couldn't shoot me! We could drag the box and throw it into the creek, but we couldn't waste time. In my note, I could tell Tommy to get the gun, and immediately realized what a formula for disaster that was. The problem was knowing exactly where the gun was. That information, and that it was in safe hands, would eliminate the chances of being surprised.

Thus, the odds that I could reduce my surprises if I knew, at all times, where it was, so that it didn't appear from no where.

"I'll leave Tommy a note," said, "and I want you to take your gun."

He looked up in surprise from dusting his hands before reaching into his breast pocket and handed me a small notebook and pen.

"I won't need the gun, it's like I told you before if I hit a rabbit the meat would be ripped up. We'll use the digging stick if we run across snakes."

He handed me the stick, but I wasn't finished.

"That's not the problem, understand that Tommy is fascinated by guns," I said. "My grandparents have a gun they have to keep locked up. They also have to hide its bullets because of Tommy. He's just that way."

It wasn't as though I wasn't telling the truth either, which is why my argument was so acceptable.

"Even if you hide your bullets, he'll look until he gets into trouble," I said. "I know because he's done it before, so it's best if your gun isn't close to where he can find it. I'll tell him you have it with you in my note."

Charlie looked toward the tent and, to my relief, shrugged and nodded as he opened the gear box. As he was pulling the pistol out I scribbled.

Tommy,
I'll be back real soon, be ready to paddle the canoe to the river.
Love, Jackie

I folded the note and stuck inside the lace of Tommy's sneaker, sure he would find it there. Looking up, I watched as Charlie unbuckled the belt at his waist with the New Athenian knife holster and laid it on a log. He took out the holster, but instead of buckling it around his middle, the way TV cowboys on TV and police officers do in real life. He draped the slim belt over his left shoulder and positioned the holster to hang slightly behind his right hip. The smaller square pouch, with bullets, hung conveniently against his right ribs. Holster in place, he buckled the knife belt around his waist above eye hooks of the straps attached to the holster.

This way, I realized the knife belt kept the gun belt straps from sliding, but wasn't forced to carry the extra weight of ammunition and pistol. His knife was located further back on his hip, behind the holster, but didn't impede drawing either knife or gun. When he'd finished adjusting the belts, it was like seeing a different person. By a simple adjustment of the military knife belt at his waist, pistol belt across his chest, everything outside his clean shirt combined with his hat centered. He became what Ana described Uncle Theo wearing his dress blue Navy uniform.

"Dashing," I forced myself to whisper, but wanted to shout. He certainly cut a smart figure, as Ana would say, and I must have been staring, because he asked if something was wrong. I said no, though what I felt was similar to the feeling I had swimming naked in the creek, only this time I wasn't alone.

CHAPTER 21

In the nearby grass, birds were in full voice and bugs hovered in clouds by the time we crossed the creek. We proceeded upstream past the falls we'd caught our first crawfish and alternated walking paths on either side of the creek and the creek bed itself. Stretches were bone dry and made walking easy, while stagnant pools of water, thick with mosquito larva or thatches of high grass, necessitated taking to the shore.

By this time I had the hang of "going potty outside" and past the spot where Tommy cut the cat tails, I needed to go. Despite my veteran status, it wasn't easier telling Charlie, but to my surprise he didn't raise an eyebrow. He pulled a zip-lock bag with a roll of toilet paper inside from one of the pockets in his shorts. I took it and made my way between two trees beside the trail while he looked toward the creek. Once out of his sight, I thought this was the time to take off and get Tommy. Still, I needed to go and privacy was one thing, snakes were my constant concern. Making my way further inland, I found a safe spot beside a grove of bushes. Lowering myself, I found there was a break in the foliage and I could see Charlie. He stared at the point where I had entered the brush. Believing he was going to spy on me, I considered moving away as he drew his pistol.

He stared at it with that same expression I seen the night before. Looking toward the trees he tossed the pistol into the air, caught it by the barrel and swung it over his shoulder as if to throw and stopped. Lowering the gun to chest level, he stared at it again, while he spoke too low to hear. I thought he was talking to the gun. It must have been a one sided conversation, because whatever he had to say, a defiant smile creased his mouth. Chuckling, he inserted the square thing into the pistol's bottom and pulled the drawer. Another click later and the gun was back in its holster.

Cleaning up, I looked behind me and saw there was no easy way through the surrounding brush except back between the two trees I'd entered. I rejoined Charlie and we trekked further to a bend before emerging into a huge amphitheater with a wide stone floor. Sides and floor were cut from one huge rock, Charlie explained, and set in the creek bed.

Impressed, I looked up the rock bank to my left that sloped into the creek in tiered levels like the steps of playing field. Steps created over thousands of years, Charlie said, by combinations of sun, wind and water. Times, he added, that the water level had been as high as the tall grass located at top of the bleachers' some fifteen paces above us.

By contrast the right bank was heaped taller than Charlie with silt, dead limbs, midsize rocks to tiny pebbles forming an embankment and foundation for a stand of cedar trees shading that half of the creek. The trees reminded me of soldiers standing in formation. All except, what had been, the biggest cedar lying inland, its roots exposed to the creek. By falling, the tree had effectively made a break in the embankment ripping open a canal that, since it was dry, offered a narrow path inland. Nearby another tree hadn't been ripped out by its roots, but torn apart mid trunk, its stump upright, its upper half also lying inland, the trees respective ends jagged and sharp enough to prick a finger.

"A big storm with very high winds did this," Charlie said. "It must have snapped these tree trunks like a twig. I'm surprised the others were ripped up too. But these trees didn't give up without a fight."

He pointed to several planks of wood lying about the creek floor like debris from an explosion.

"Why did the wind tear out only two trees? I asked. "Why not the others?"

"I couldn't say, Charlie replied. "Soil, height, branches, or maybe these two were just too proud to bend to the wind. Nature is funny about these things."

I didn't see anything funny about it, but noticed that since the tree had fallen, water, wind, or whatever had also cut a deeper opening into the brush beyond. Trying not to be too interested, I walked toward the center of amphitheater looking up at the bleachers and wondering aloud what it would be like to play dodge ball or volleyball in this place. That's how I almost stepped into a pool, barely managing to stop myself with a squeak. The pool was filled with clear water and Charlie described how a huge notch had been hollowed from the solid rock.

"Eons and eons of rain, wind, sand, probably and even fire made this," Charlie said. "Think how many winters, springs, summers and falls it took to shape this while the rest of the world went its merry little way."

I didn't know what an eon was, but could appreciate Charlie's admiration. The hole was very deep, long enough to park two half-ton trucks on its bottom. So I guess those eons did a good job providing a sheer drop with water clear enough to see its bottom. Still I was surprised to see a school of fish swimming just below the surface moving adjacent to the shore's perimeter. Standing in the shadow of the cedars, we watched them ambling in our direction, but when we stepped to the shore and sunlight, the water erupted as the fish reversed and swam back the way they'd come. I had to laugh as they rounded the other end and swam back to where we stood.

"I'll bet they're asking each other how'd those human get around so fast," Charlie said as the pool's surface rippled again.

With less disorder, the fish reversed to head in the opposite direction and I remembered the string, hooks, and sinkers in the beacon.

"We could catch some," I said, "Only it doesn't look like they'll hang around for us to put a hook in the water."

"And we can't wait all morning for me to make a fish trap, " Charlie replied.

"I guess not," I said. "Besides, fish wasn't exactly what I had in mind for breakfast."

"Don't knock it until you've tried it," Charlie said.

On the embankment side I noticed Charlie concentrate on walking flat-footed upstream. The ground between the pool and bank had a thin, slippery layer of mud. I didn't need to be told to do the same and avoid falling face, or butt first. We left the mud at the pool's upper end. Further upstream I saw that trees and brush closed in forming a curtain beyond that section of the creek. Still, a steady trickle of water made its way to the pool from that direction. We probably could have walked upstream, instead Charlie turned and we climbed the bleachers. At their top we looked across a sloping meadow to a small hill beyond it.

We crossed the meadow to the left side of the hill where a fence stood with rotting wooden posts strung with ancient rusted barbed wire shrouded with thorny brambles. Here, black berries hung, plump and full of juice. I managed to squish my first berry between my fingers. Charlie showed me how to pick them without getting stuck. He also stopped me from popping one into my mouth. Holding out a berry as big as a pecan, he indicated a tiny, almost transparent worm crawling along its surface. My face twisted in disgust as Charlie flicked the worm to the ground.

"Ewww," I squealed, "and we're going to eat those?"

"Yes," Charlie said. "After we've rinsed them.

"In creek water?" I asked. "Isn't that as bad as the worms."

"Not if it's running water," Charlie replied, "which will flush them off the berries and evaporate almost as quick."

I nodded and we began filling the bucket.

"I guess we'll have to leave today?" I said as he dropped berries into the bucket.

"Yes," he said. "But I'm leaving too, so you might as well come along."

"Oh," I said reaching for berries with both hands, "we wouldn't want you to leave early because of us."

"That's fine," he said, "I need to get back and conclude some unfinished business."

"The coyotes?" I asked. "Your job?"

"No, they aren't a problem any more, none of it," he said with a smile. "They were yesterday and a week ago, but only because I let them. It's a situation as messed up as a dirt sandwich, without the bread. I kept believing I could fix things, but I realized that no matter how many times I want to right a wrong of the past, doing the same thing over and over again with the same jerks, expecting different results, it never happens. It's a waste of time, an exercise in insanity, that never works because we're powerless over other people, places, things!"

Glancing at the holster at his hip, I felt goose bumps on my arms recalling his face the previous night as he loaded the gun in the firelight.

"Are you going to shoot them?" I asked, biting my lip and turning ready to run. "Because of what they did?"

"Shoot them? Shoot them?" He said rolling the idea like a piece of meat. "I could do that," he said seriously and the hair on the back of my neck rose. "But it would be like shooting a rabbit, a fleeting thrill, but a bullet and life wasted, particularly mine. It would be a good for nothing situation, especially for me. Considering that, I might just as well shoot myself," I kept my head bent as he paused, my heart racing as he added, "No, I'll accept what's past and let go, because no matter how many times I try to recreate my past with different results, it never happens. It only leads to self-destruction."

Which was almost what happened last night, I wanted to say as he looked to the sky shaking his head before he resumed picking.

"When will I ever stop beating myself up for things I can't control?" He said to no one in particular.

"But don't they deserve everything they get, after what they've done," I demanded wondering how I got so blood thirsty. "For all that and probably worse?"

"We can only keep our side of the street clean," he said. " It's tough to have integrity in this world but with prayer and a willingness to develop strengths, one day at a time, eventually we won't even want to recreate the past, and certainly won't have time to waste on coyotes or their type because the present and future is too exciting."

"What then?" I asked.

"You remember last night when Tommy said he'd had the best day of his life?"

I nodded, still picking berries, dreading and anticipating his answer.

"Well, it wasn't his best day," he said, and dread burned like acid to my toes. "It's one of many he and you will enjoy throughout your lives. Someday, these will fall to the fading memory category. But for Tommy, despite being lost, bug bit, dirty and hungry it was the best day, a day that seemed better than home or school, though he might change his mind."

"You don't understand," I said. "It's been horrible for us."

"I can imagine," Charlie said, "Though I won't say I know how you feel, because I haven't been where you have."

"So how can things get better?" I said stomping my foot. "Tommy and I didn't do anything to deserve how we've been treated."

Angry and careless, I jabbed my finger into a wicked thorn. Squealing, I put my finger in my mouth. Charlie continued picking, but didn't offer to examine my finger.

"Life can be a lot like picking blackberries. That thorn hurts like hell doesn't it?"

I glared, making a "duh" expression with my mouth.

"Before you were a gleam in your granddad's eye, I met a girl," he said. "I can't describe my feelings for her."

I nodded not understanding what that had to do with my abused finger.

"Due to circumstances we parted and I hurt for a long time."

"Wouldn't it have been better if you'd never met that girl?" I asked.

"I thought that at the time," he replied. "It was a feeling a whole lot like what I felt when I came out here. In both cases, I thought I deserved better treatment. Yet, as much as it hurt, I would not trade meeting that girl for all the black berries and crawfish in the world. Instead, I cherish the experience, never to be forgotten or repeated, and all mine."

I wanted to tell him I wasn't a little baby, who could be made to feel better with *they-lived-happily-ever-after-stories*.

"It was the same when my father passed away," he continued. "He wasn't perfect, not my dad, not by a long shot. But who is? I can remember times when he was like a poke in the eye. Yet, as he lay dying, I could only think of those precious moments we'd shared during his life."

"They weren't even major events, he added with a chuckle, most were as insignificant as sitting with him at breakfast or riding to school."

The shock of what my life would be like without my mother and daddy hit me like a brick. Even after recalling how mad they could make me. I only wanted a break, and loosing either one was not what I wanted to think about it.

"Just like berry picking," he said. "Life offers buckets of sweet, plump fruit and," he flicked a huge white worm from a monster berry in his hand, "while life has its stickers and crawlies."

He tapped the end of his ring finger against the point of a curved thorn the size of my thumbnail. He held out his hand and blood pooled across the tip of his finger filling the space under the nail.

"I'm glad for times like those, because no matter how crazy it gets, and life does get crazy, at least I can't say I was bored. I'll get through whatever happens and by this time next year, it will just be a memory."

He flicked the blood off his finger into the nearby grass and pressed his thumb against the wound.

"Some day, you'll be the reason someone looks back, on a time like this," he said, "and they'll say you were the reason for the best day of their life."

Our picking evolved into a berry-picking race that quickly filled the bucket. "Think we can eat all these?" he said, inspecting the finger that had stopped bleeding.

Holding up my punctured pointing finger, I wanted to believe what he said, but couldn't shake the sight of what I'd seen last night. "We'll try," I said.

CHAPTER 22

The bucket brimming with berries, Charlie walked and whistled, singing, and retracing our steps to the creek. I walked beside him, watching for snakes, and keeping the holster in sight, looking for an opportunity to run back to Tommy.

We reached the creek above the amphitheater fish pool and climbed to the creek bed below. I followed as Charlie picked his way upstream toward the sound of falling water to a stack of boulders creating a small ledge half as tall as I was. A trickle of water splattered into a shallow pool on its way down stream. Charlie placed the bucket so the water trickling off the ledge hit the center of the bucket.

"This won't take long," he said, over his shoulder.

Carrying the digging stick, I made my way toward the big pool. But before I could take off running, Charlie appeared. I walked adjacent to the embankment to stand at the lower end of the pool and watch the fish swim their continuous circuit. The fun was moving my shadow into their path just as they were about to make a turn and watch the flutter of water as they reversed directions. Standing there, I considered how to distract Charlie for longer than a second and make my escape.

"We could catch these fish," I called. "There are hooks, sinkers and fishing string in the beacon. But the beacon is back at camp."

I would use that excuse to run back, get Tommy and escape in the canoe. Only I never got a chance for either.

"Our problem is we're hungry now," Charlie said, "and fishing isn't for impatient people with dead lines."

"Too bad, they're just like sheep," I said, moving toward the break in the embankment and the fallen trees. "You could shoot them with your gun, you're bound to hit at least one."

"That's an idea," Charlie said, "only a fish would be in worse shape than a rabbit from the kind of bullets in this gun. Also, they'd probably sink to the bottom."

"You could sharpen a stick into a spear like they do in the movies," I said remembering another movie where Tarzan caught fish with his hands.

"Don't believe everything you see in the movies," he said. "That's one reason man developed nets. I might get one, but the others learn fast."

" But it would be neat to eat fish for breakfast," I said, hoping I sounded convincing, but inspired by my very real hunger. "At least we have the berries."

He tossed a pebble into the pool and I inched toward the dam break watching him. He didn't throw another stone, but looked round toward me. I must have looked guilty of something.

"Herd of sheep," he repeated. "Spear and scatter, but bomb and get the flock."

With a huge smile, he disappeared into the upstream brush and returned holding two plate sized flat rocks. He directed me to walk down stream below the pool where we'd first entered the amphitheater. At his signal he told me I was to move up stream on the step side. I was skeptical, since the fish had proven to be so predictable. Yet, I climbed the steps to a level tier and moved down stream until I could descend to the downstream floor.

"Walk toward me, slow," he called, "and let me know when the fish can see you."

"They'll just swim away," I whined.

"Exactly," he replied, "just like sheep."

Shrugging, I carefully made my way downstream and got into position.

"Ready," I called and started up stream. Charlie called a response, but I couldn't see him as I used the digging stick to pick my way over the sloping rocks. On that side I had to walk close to edge of the water. As expected, the fish saw me, turned and swam upstream. As they entered the shallowest part of the pool, a flat rock sailed through the air from the far end of the cedar trees. It landed in the school's center, inches from shore edge causing a geyser. Three fish went flopping to the bank as Charlie rushed from his hiding place. He couldn't prevent one fish from flopping back to the water, but managed to kick the other two to dry ground. Holding them still with the sole of his shoe, he took out fishing string from his pocket. One fish continued to flop, while the other lay tail curling and gills pulsating. He pushed his fingers through this one and pushed the string through the fish's mouth and gills. He did the same to the other and held them up.

"That's two," he said, " let's try again."

"But they'll be expecting me!" I called.

"They only have two ways to go," he said.

The fish did regroup into a pulsating ball at the pool's center, turning in unison as I made my way downstream. Once out of sight, I counted to ten and picked my way upstream on the bleacher side again. To my surprise the fish headed my way again, but instead of reversing, they raced past me ruffling the water. They averted the downstream end at the last moment and ambled upstream on the embankment side. They rounded the upstream end just as another rock ascended twirling through the air and landed in their center. Another geyser sent three more fish ashore and Charlie bounded after them. None got close to the water.

"That's five," he hooted like a kid out of school. "We'll eat today."

Seeing that he was so absorbed with the fish, I moved downstream toward the opening made by the shattered cedar tree. Now, I thought, was the perfect opportunity with his concern on the fish. By the time he knows I'm gone, I'd be half way back to Tommy. Only I forgot about the mud, my foot slipped and I fell on my seat. My rear smarted and I felt humiliated looking to see if Charlie had noticed me. He hadn't and, feeling almost guilty, I tried to get to my feet when the closest of a pair of rattlesnakes announced its presence. Almost directly in front of me, it lay with its head cocked into a striking-S. The other followed suit and a chorus of rattlers filled the air as I looked to see Charlie adding the last fish on the stringer.

"Snake," I sputtered, wondering why he couldn't hear the rattles, before shouting, "rattlesnake."

Dropping the stringer Charlie moved toward me, his hand on his holster.

He's going to shoot me, I thought, he's going to shoot me. "Shoot it," I pleaded " shoot the snake."

"I can't," he called, "I might hit you."

He side stepped to the edge of the pond where the fish passed behind him. I backed toward him on hands and heels rousing the other snake. He's going to let a snake bite me, I thought, the way he wanted to on the trail. This way he doesn't have to shoot me and Tommy won't be warned by a shot.

"No," I screamed. "Not this time, not again!"

With the digging stick I tried to hit the snake closest to me. It backed away wanting no part of my club while I hopped forward on my tail to hit it again. The head streaked toward my leg and I swung again.

"Jackie," Charlie yelled. "Move aside, get out of the way."

Instead I screamed and hit the snake in the center of its coils. The blow interrupted the rattler rhythm and parried its strike. Growling, I brought the stick down again, again and again effectively forcing the snake to retreat and move sideways. Though it never quite moved out of reach and most times I only hit the ground to its side before it slithered to my right.

I heard Charlie's boots scuff the rock floor, but didn't dare take my eyes off the snake. His intrusion caused the other snake to increase its warning and also move to my right. The nearest rattler rose to half the length of its body, level with my head, and drew back for another strike. I pushed away with my feet, my left hand slipping out from under me. It missed, drew back again and I screamed holding out a palm full of mud and the digging stick in spear fashion.

The gun roared and two shots sounded like one. The snake's neck exploded leaving only a strand of skin connecting the severed head to a frayed body stump. The other bullet knocked the snake twirling to the foot of the shattered cedar tree. The decapitated snake flopped separately trying to raise the ghastly streamer bouncing against its side, the forked tongue continually and vertically tasting air.

Flat footed, Charlie moved forward, his pistol held at waist level, toward the second snake. Rattle tempo increased at his approach and the head drew into a strike. Charlie scooped up a handful of mud and threw it at the snake ordering, "Get out of here!"

In response the snake struck the air twice, uncoiled and eased into the water.

Reaching my side Charlie bent down and said, "You OK?"

"Why didn't you shoot it?" I screamed.

"I would have hit you," he said. "That's why I kept telling you to move."

The other rattlesnake moved to the pond with indecisive direction. The fish fluttered, still swimming in the opposite direction swimming on the rock side. "Shoot, shoot it before it gets away," I said, pointing after the fleeing snake. "Shoot it, shoot it!"

As if it could understand me, the snake slipped into the water and swam toward the opposite shore making zig-zag patterns on the pond's surface. Charlie raised his pistol, lowered it and helped me to my feet.

Thrusting the gun into my hand he said, "You shoot it!"

"I don't know how to shoot a gun," I whined. "Hurry, shoot him."

"It's your snake, you found it, you finish him," he said. "Use the fork of the digging stick as a bench rest."

Wiping my muddy hand on my already muddy shorts, I thought of Ana and the 500 pound hog, wondering if a pistol would knock me on my butt like the Commemorative did to Ana. Charlie stepped behind me and helped me raise the pistol and placed it in the fork of the digging stick. Charlie gave me quick instruction, his fingers on my shoulders to extend my arms. He described how to sight at the snake by putting the gun's red dot between the U at the rear sight.

"The front sight should be a blur," he said.

Catching my breath, I made what Charlie called a bead, or taking aim. The snake was not obligingly and kept swimming past the red dot, so that I had to readjust my aim several times. The snake would not stay still. What a bother, I thought, and more trouble to shoot than it was worth. Readjusting my aim again as the snake crawled out on the far bank. I almost fired when the snake zipped up the rock stair toward a tree. It hit the trunk with a slap and I thought the gun had gone off. Yet there was no recoil or smoke, and to my amazement the snake scurry-swirled up the tree and into the branches. I turned to Charlie, my mouth open.

"Why did it do that?" I demanded.

"You scared it!" He shrugged and directed me to take my finger out of the trigger guard. Clicking the safety lever on the pistol's side, he slipped it back into his holster.

"I scared it," I repeated in amazement.

With the digging stick, Charlie pinned the dead snake's head to the ground, sliced off its head with his knife and flung it into brush.

"It's beautiful," I said pointing at the symmetry of diamond designs across the snake's shattered back. "I almost wish you hadn't killed it."

"They are beautiful," Charlie agreed, "and for all intents, just wanted to be left alone."

"They tried to bite me," I countered.

Dropping to one knee, he sliced off the tail rattlers that tapered to a point and put them in his short's pocket. The snakes, he explained, had chosen that particular spot to sun themselves before they retired for the day. Unfortunately for everybody, I surprised them walking up and they were only warning me not to step on them.

"Any creature defends itself when it's cornered," he said. "It's nothing personal and if you'd known you could have backed away. The snakes would have done the same."

"They aren't much different from us," I said. "I still don't like them, but I see their point."

"Charlie lifted the snake and hung it on one of the lower branches of a tree.

"What are you doing?" I asked.

"Besides not getting bit, you've given some animal a quick meal," Charlie said, 'Unless you'd like rattlesnake with your breakfast menu."

Feeling sad, I didn't bother to react to his teasing and put my fingertips on the dead snake's diamond pattern. Immediately, I jerked my hand back when it moved involuntarily.

Charlie didn't seem to notice as he picked up one of the cedar planks from several that had exploded from the fallen trunk. Picking up another plank the size of a kitchen spatula, he handed it to me and I used it to scrape mud off my rear. Charlie also offered to step out of sight so I could clean my shorts of mud. But that wasn't necessary and I followed him to the tiny waterfall and washed my face and hands. My declining his offer was less out of modesty and more toward not finding another snake. Remembering Tommy, I said we needed to get back since he was probably awake, but didn't mention my fear that he tried to launch the canoe.

CHAPTER 23

The canoe was where I'd last seen it. Charlie dipped the cedar plank in the creek at the spot I had dove after the butterfly. After rinsing away any excess dirt he dipped it again and used his knife to gouge out six holes in the plank.

"Just deep enough to put a peg," he said.

He also cleaned the fish and carried them on the plank back to camp. He handed me the knife and instructed me to whittle five sets of pegs that would fit in the plank's holes. Using the old metal mess kit, he doused the fillets with olive oil, dabbing them with pepper and salt while I whittled the pegs. With those pegs Charlie pierced the fillets to the plank hammering securely with the pommel of his knife.

"An Aleut hunter taught me how to do this when I was in Alaska."

Pegging the fish to the plank, he placed it inside the fire pit's circle and built up the fire.

I noticed Tommy's clothes were gone and the tent flap was open, the inside empty except for the blankets.

"Tommy? Tommy? Where are you?" I yelled. Not even an echo answered.

Charlie grabbed the blanket he'd slept on and shook it out. "Maybe he's watering a tree," he said. "Sit down and have some breakfast."

Charlie poured us a mug of tea and filled one of the mess kit pots with berries, now minus the worms. Meantime, he pulled out the sleeping bag and other bed clothes from the tent, folded and re-packed them in their waterproof bags. He also collapsed the tent, recovered its pegs and reinserted the lot into a little oblong bag. In no time the neat camp had been struck like it had never been there. As he finished policing the camp, the aroma of baked fish filled the air, yet no Tommy. This was very strange, because food would bring my cousin running.

"That's odd," I said between bites of berries. "Tommy should be here by this time."

"The bolo is missing too," Charlie said and moved down the rise carrying bags to the canoe. When he returned, the plank was smoking and I feared it would catch on fire. However, the fish bubbled, flaky and golden brown, as he gripped the plank between two mess kit pots and moved it to the gear box. He lifted the cooked fish off the plank with his knife laying the fillets into the mess kit frying pan and pushed it toward me. I broke off a piece, blew on it and popped it into my mouth. It was my first experience with fish for breakfast and it was the best I ever had. The bacon and egg crowd might knock it, but not when hungry.

Tommy still wasn't in sight by the time I finished my second fish. Charlie put a bandana over the remaining food in the pot and placed it in the fork of the clothesline tree He hung the bucket from another branch and turned to me.

"We better go look for him," he said.

Where, I wanted to ask, and watched Charlie walk the perimeter of the camp in an ever-increasing circle, his eyes on the ground. "What are you doing?" I asked.

"I'm looking for Tommy's trail," he replied.

He walked inland several yards before bending to move something with his finger.

"Here," he said. "This way!"

I joined him beside an animal trail that wound into the brush. Though narrow I made out the heel of a boy's foot print that became even more distinct as we walked on. Though I didn't obliterate a set of cloven hoof tracks headed in the same direction. The trail was wide enough for one person and, for some distance Tommy's prints were clear as a road sign to me before they disappeared.

"Where'd he go?" I asked.

"Off the trial to take care of morning necessities."

"Huh?" I asked.

Charlie pointed to grass that had been pressed down all the way to a mesquite sapling.

"Take a whiff," Charlie suggested.

I inhaled, but unable to figure out what Charlie was talking about.

"Here, " he said. He led me to the mesquite tree with a stain at its base and the fresh aroma of ammonia that told the whole story.

"He had to pee, " I said, finally smelling the obvious.

"Yes, and not too long ago either, he's just ahead of us."

Charlie returned to the trail and we descended into a small valley. At that point, the trail forked. One path curved to our right and around the bottom of a small hill. The other veered into the brush to our left. Charlie considered the hill before turning into the brush and I followed. We had gone only a short distance before Charlie dropped to his haunches and motioned me beside him.

"Tommy didn't come this way," he whispered.

I shook my head at how he knew. With an outstretched arm, he pointed and I hoped it wasn't another rattler as I followed the direction of his finger. To my relief and joy, I saw a spotted fawn nestled in the grass between two trees where it stared curiously at us. I stood to go to it, stopped by Charlie's fingertips on my shoulder.

"We can't bother him," he whispered. "His momma told him to stay put, he'll run off if we get close and coyotes will get him."

"How do you know Tommy didn't come this way?" I asked unable to take my eyes off the fawn's liquid brown eyes.

"Could Tommy resist petting or trying to bring him back?".

Nodding I turned and we made our way back to the fork in the trail and, for once, saw the doe before Charlie did.

"Look," I whispered. "His mother!"

The doe stood where the trail wound round the other side of the hill. Only her attention seemed drawn more to the direction she'd come.

Charlie motioned and we moved away to the opposite base of the hill. Ears twitching, the doe watched our progress before bounding down the path we'd come toward her fawn.

"His momma is going back, " I whispered.

"Yes," Charlie answered. "But something else had her attention. Something on the other side of this little hill."

"Tommy," I hissed.

"Maybe, but doubtful," he replied. "If Tommy were chasing that doe she would have jumped over the moon instead of standing there."

We moved further to our right before climbing up the hill. I kicked rocks and stuff, which couldn't be helped, and saying, unnecessarily, I was sorry and hoping nobody else heard me. By contrast, Charlie never made a sound, even when he dropped to his belly and pushed his hat to his back to crawl the last few feet to the top of the hill. I followed his example, sort of, crab walking to the hill's crest. Peeking over the top, I peered between blades of buffalo grass looking down the other side of the hill.

In the distance was Tommy and I wanted to shout, but Charlie laid a hand on my arm. Beyond the bottom of the hill was a line of brush and a lone oak tree. Under its branches a very animated Tommy gestured with wide arm stretches. Looming over him stood a plain-faced-girl around twenty with palomino-colored, frizzy hair bouncing on her frail shoulders.

She was slender as a pencil and wore a black vest covered with colorful patches. Under the vest, she wore an orange T-shirt with an indistinguishable logo hiding a diminished chest. Black leather wristbands emphasized spindly forearms, contrasted by a big rodeo buckle covering most of her lower front. The belt's tongue hung like drool down the left thigh, while a chain attached to the belt hung in a loop down the right side. Her jeans were old with holes in the knees stuffed into the tops of calve-high biker boots. The bolo dangled from a right hand not much bigger than Tommy's while its wooden scabbard lay at her feet, the waxed string dangling from her other hand.

She seemed mesmerized watching Tommy's arms wind mill and point in our direction. Her head jerked round, curls bouncing as she looked in our direction. She didn't see us and returned to following the ever changing direction of Tommy's hands.

"Unless I call you, stay here," said Charlie surprising me. "If something happens, you scat back to camp."

"What's going to happen?" I hissed.

Without answering Charlie moved further down the right side of the hill and disappeared into the adjoining brush. When he was out of sight, I looked again and made out the fear on the girl's face. The way she stared at my cousin, I thought she expected flying monkeys to carry him off. Again, she scanned the area in front of them again and again, and I thought she saw me, but her head always returned to Tommy. Judging by Tommy's body language, he appeared to have said all he was going to say. This time when the girl scanned the area, a huge smile broke across her face and I could almost hear the "Ah Ha" in her expression. She held up the bolo menacingly and pointed in my direction with her other hand. She stepped forward shouting as I tried to push my face closer to the ground.

Which is why she never saw Charlie appear from behind the tree. Appearing as if conjured, he tapped her on the shoulder and set off a high pitched scream that cut the air. The girl whirled in one motion, dropping the scabbard's string, raising the bolo to grip with both hands

"Baaaad Booooob!" I heard her scream in a broken voice as she rushed Charlie.

Had Charlie been standing closer and not gotten out of her way, she might have grazed him with the bolo. Instead, he took advantage of her motion and pivoted to one side, out of the way of her swing. She recovered, took another step in his new direction, still grasping the bolo with both hands, and stepped forward with her left foot. Her boot tangled the scabbard string midway into her swing, yanking the scabbard toward her calves and it lodged between her ankles. Another step tangled the string around her other foot. Still grasping the bolo, she fell, screaming, unable to stop herself from hitting the tree with a sound like a dropped pumpkin.

I jumped to my feet, running down the hill to join the others just as Charlie holstered his pistol. Bending down on one knee, he gently turned the girl over, pushing away the gauzy hair and placing two fingers on the scrawny neck.

"You brought your gun," squealed Tommy as I joined them.

"Somebody said if I kept it with me, then you'd stay out of trouble," Charlie replied.

Frowning, Tommy cocked his head in my direction while Charlie pulled the girl's eyelids up before prying her lips apart.

"Who's your friend?" I asked Tommy.

"Babes call him Macho Mike," Tommy recited. "He's security chief for this side of the river. Trespassers are not welcome and will be violated."

"He," I cried in disbelief, "this is a guy?"

"Sure," Tommy said "can't you tell?"

Looking down I noticed for the first time the fringe of nearly translucent fuzz above the too full lips. The pointed chin was covered with what reminded me of fungus I once found growing in a coffee cup Papa left on his desk for a week.

"He's more of a M&M," Charlie muttered. "Melts on his feet without the grief."

Charlie opened the left flap of M&M's vest. It was made of plastic that looked like leather. On the front of the vest were embroidered patches with written sayings like, "It's not me, it's you" and "Certified Bad Ass. Beware."

Charlie pulled a crumpled red bandana from inside the vest pocket and a plastic baggy fell to the ground when he unfolded it. Charlie twirled the bandana and gently lifted M&M's head to tie the bandana across the gash on the side of his forehead.

Though I was not glad this man was injured, I stifled a giggle because of the way the ends of the bandana's knot drooped over his forehead to the fuzzy cheeks. They reminded me of bunny ears.

Easing the man's head to the ground, Charlie reached for a scrawny wrist and held it between his palm and fingers. The arms were barely bigger than mine, but my stomach lurched at swirled designs I recognized as badly healed burns. Scars extended from the tops of the bony shoulders down to a pinky finger resembling a melted birthday candle.

"What did you say to him?" I asked Tommy.

"Nothing really, after he told me he was a Navy SEAL, who never lost a fight," Tommy said. "Then I told him about Bad Bob."

Tommy recounted his tale of psycho killer Bad Bob who'd murdered people from Spain to the Pill-n-beans. He recounted all the terrible things Bob had done. He told how the U.S. Government threatened to put TV people in jail if they reported about him because of the wide spread panic if the news got out.

"I told him how I got away from the massacre at Bandy's Camp where Bad Bob shot at me the whole time."

Tommy paused to take a breath and raised his shirt demonstrating how he told Macho Mike his bug bites were wounds inflicted by Bad Bob.

"He mistook a mosquito bite for a bullet hole?" I asked in disbelief. "And the rest?"

Tommy ignored me and recounted telling M&M about a dying policeman telling him, with his last breath, that hundreds of FBI agents were on their way. That he must go and tell the world what happened, because no matter what it took, Bad Bob had to be stopped. "I told him the FBI men had orders to shoot to kill. Only they never had a chance, because Bad Bob had all these rockets, dynamite, and machine guns."

Tommy continued talking as Charlie picked up the plastic bag that had fallen from Macho Mike's bandana. He opened it, smelled and jerked back like he'd been stung. Crumpling the bag, he laid it aside before reaching into M&M's vest and taking out a snot-green-colored glass pipe he also dropped to the ground. I picked it up and caught a reek like Sophie's litter box.

"What is that?" I asked pointing to the bag. "And this?" holding out the pipe and waving my hand in front of my nose. "It smells yucky!"

"Zombie dust," said Charlie taking the pipe and tossing it into the brush where we heard it shatter.

"Is he a zombie?" Tommy asked in a hushed tone. "Was he going to eat my brain?"

"If he's not, he's certainly on his way to being fully qualified," Charlie said. "And it's this stuff that eats your brains," he added indicating the zombie dust.

I thought of another of Papa's old movies of the black and white film of men and women dressed in rags, shuffling and slobbering as they tried to break into a house. There had been a little girl that killed her mother, because she had been bitten by a zombie. The woman cried and wouldn't let other people in the house kill her daughter. As pathetic as Macho Mike looked, I felt shivers at the possibilities.

"So you told him about Bad Bob," Charlie said. "How'd you find him?"

"Totally," Tommy said with a grin. "I think it had something to do with the two gun shots I heard after I left camp to follow a deer I saw. I made it this far when he came out of nowhere yelling and scared the pee-waddle out of me."

"He wasn't yelling when we saw you from up on that hill," I said pointing. "What changed his mind?"

"He grabbed the bolo before I could do anything else," said Tommy remorsefully. "And then I thought of Bad Bob. "

"You took a big chance," Charlie said. "The situation could have turned ugly in at the drop of a hat, and he would have dropped the hat."

"He made me think of that white haired kid at Bandy's talking bad about whole lot of nothing," Tommy said. "I traded him one bull hockey story for another, and he bought it."

"It's sounds like one of Papa's movies," I accused.

"It is, I just changed the characters and places, " Tommy said. "I told him Bad Bob left no witnesses and I was glad to see him, so he could protect me against a psycho killer."

"Those were some whoppers," Charlie said. "Don't you know it's wrong to tell a lie?"

"Well, he was lying to me," Tommy sniffed. "My story just happened to be better."

"Not by a whole lot," I said.

Charlie shook out the bottom of the plastic baggy and the zombie powder drifted to the ground.

"Watch out," Tommy warned. "He'll smell that, wake up and eat our brains."

"That's doubtful," Charlie said. "But it's the main reason this zombie couldn't stand up to Bad Bob."

Charlie continued searching Macho Mike's vest placing everything he found on the ground. From inside his pants' waist Charlie brought out a little silver gun and tossed it into the air, catching it.

"A gun," Tommy said delighted. "Can I have it?"

"This is a piece of junk, " Charlie said. "You deserve better."

Without ceremony Charlie removed the gun's magazine that contained a single bullet. He dropped the magazine to the ground and yanked the gun's slide sending another bullet to the ground.

From two hip holsters Charlie took a curved blade with a series of brass rings for a handle and a dagger with a picture of a lady painted on the handles wearing only stockings and shoes. After tossing the knives to the ground, he traced the long chain on M&M's belt and pulled out a wide leather wallet from his back pocket. Probing its insides with one of the knives, he removed a wad of greasy paper money. From another wallet pocket, Charlie took out another plastic bag with what looked like grass clippings and a pack of small papers. In the middle pocket was a plastic card, its lamentation peeling, but covering the photograph of a boy not much older than Tommy. The photo was of a pale faced boy with a startled expression wearing a badly fitting blue coat, white shirt and broad red tie

"School I.D.," Charlie muttered.

The boy in the photo was Macho Mike, still skinny, though the poodle hair was neatly trimmed. Behind the boy was a school banner with bold faced letters of a name too long to remember. At the bottom of the photo was written "Michael Ebner DeGreif". It was a familiar name I couldn't immediately place.

Again, I was reminded of another of Papa's old movies called "The Invisible Man." I should say the photo reminded me of the movie's ending, when a young woman stared at a headless pair of pajamas covered by a blanket. She reacted to a deep voice punctuated by gestures of the pajama sleeves. Earlier, this invisible man had a long, white bandage wrapped around his head and funny sunglasses. Unclothed, he terrorized the English countryside by strangling a policeman and forcing his friend to wreck his car. At the movie's end, he made amends for his wrongs in the same deep voice before supposedly dying. To my surprise, and disappointment, the head that materialized was of a frail, hooked-nosed young man, appearing first as a skull, followed with muscle and closed eyes. Papa said he was the great actor Claude Rains who'd made bunches of great movies. Maybe so, but I doubted this frail man could wreck the kind of mischief on the larger men that I'd seen in the movie.

I had similar doubts about the young man lying on the ground as Charlie pulled out a folded piece of paper from the big wallet. It was heavy construction paper, and when Charlie unfolded it, there was what looked like a yellow postcard printed in its center. The top of the card was printed in arched, old time letters, the kind I'd seen when I sat in the dentist's chair. Below the old time words was what looked like the picture of a sailing ship and an eagle surrounded by a blue circle. Below the picture at the postcard's center was a name, etched in minute letters and unmistakably the same as the school ID

Well, well, " Charlie sighed. "He really was in the Navy."

"What does 'less than honorable' mean,'" I asked squinting at the olden days style words.

"A lifestyle choice," Charlie said.

Refolding the paper Charlie replaced it along with the card and money. He left the wallet on the ground. After running his hands down Macho Mike's jean legs, he pulled off his boots revealing dingy socks and knives attached by clips to each boot top. He removed the boots and placed the bare feet on one of the tree's roots.

"What are you going to do with him?" I asked. "Aren't you supposed to do first aid?"

"I already have," said Charlie picking up the silver gun. "We'll leave him for now and go get help."

"He's hurt," I said. "Shouldn't we call an ambulance or stay with him."

"No phone, no car, not a single luxury," Tommy sang.

I recognized the tune of an old song from a TV show.

"Unlike Robinson Crusoe, Macho Mike is cold under a big old tree, right here on Jackie's Isle!"

"It's not funny," I said stamping my feet to keep from smiling. "He's hurt!"

"Then we better go find help," Charlie said. "I know where a phone is."

"Shouldn't we take him with us?" I asked.

"No room and I can't carry him," Charlie said with a shrug. "Besides, it's such a nice day, he should be fine until medical attention arrives."

"Won't coyotes eat him," I argued.

"Not until later," Charlie said. "So, we'd better hurry."

Charlie slipped the bolo into the wooden sheath and handed it to Tommy. We followed him toward the brush from where he'd surprised Macho Mike and onto a well-beaten path.

"This isn't the way back to our camp," Tommy said.

"I know," said Charlie looking at the ground. "When I made my way around I noticed this path over here."

"Maybe it's animal path," I said.

"It's too wide," said Charlie pointing to a footprint. "And skunks nor armadillos wear size 13 jogging shoes."

"Those are Macho Mike's," Tommy said.

"He's wearing boots," Charlie said. "And he's like a size 9."

Moving into the undergrowth Charlie disassembled the silver gun. He'd left the magazine with the knives and wallet, but carried the gun that seemed to dissolve between his palms, the parts falling to either side of the trail.

"Hey," Tommy protested. "I wanted that gun."

"It's like I told you," Charlie replied, "it's junk and you deserve better."

He dropped the last part of the pistol as we rounded a corner where the trail forked. One path meandered in the direction of the river, while the other lead inland toward another hill. At its base was a stand of live oaks forming a natural fence. The trail continued between two big trees that formed a covered walkway. Charlie put a hand on our shoulders before we could start forward, dropping to his haunches and motioning us to stand on either side of him.

"Look at that path, real close," he said. "Do you see anything out of the ordinary?"

I squinted, expecting another snake and remembering the fawn. Tommy craned his head before shaking his head.

Charlie pointed and said, "There's something shinning just on the other side of the big trees."

We looked again, following the direction of Charlie extended finger to a patch of sunlight to the left of the left hand tree. A patch of sunlight shone on the bare ground adjacent to the tree barely the breadth of a lawn chair. Looking still harder, I caught the glimmer of a thin line illuminated in the sunshine.

"Something's on the ground," said Tommy pointing.

"No, it's above the ground," Charlie corrected. "Look left and right of that point."

We did and it reminded me of a thin line drawn by a pencil across a sheet of white paper. The ground appeared to have a fold on its surface. "It's a piece of string," said Tommy dismissively.

"Fishing line, new fishing line," Charlie corrected. "And we're a ways from the water. It's pulled tight at ankle level."

Charlie held out a hand and I gave him the digging stick. Cautiously, he walked to within a foot of the invisible line and gently brushed the ground on either side of it, pushing down the patches of grass that hid the line so well. Exposed to the full sun light, it glittered like a Christmas ornament. After probing the ground around the string he motioned us forward.

"What is it?" I asked.

"A booby trap," he answered, "and that's the trip wire."

"Booby trap?" Tommy repeated.

"Are you sure?" I asked hoping he was wrong. "How do you know?"

"I've seen these before," Charlie answered. "Though I'm not sure what kind of booby this trap is designed to catch."

Charlie found a stick that looked like a V and took the beacon from his pocket. He shook out the remaining roll of fishing string and an end to one of the stick's prongs. Tossing the stick to the other side of the trip wire, he moved back playing out the rest of the string and pulled it in until the V stick hooked on the trip wire.

Charlie motioned us to move behind two small trees on the right side of the trail. He laid down on one side of the biggest tree and we joined him. He handed the line to Tommy, nodding. He yanked the string hard with both hands and threw an arm over me. I pressed my face against his, closing my eyes, and...nothing, at least not at first!

Peeking over my arm, I caught sight of a pair of blurs passing over the trail. They emanated a gentle whistle in conjunction with a whine from the branches above. Eventually the blurs slowed, revealing themselves to be two medium sized logs nearly as tall as Tommy hanging from hemp ropes that squealed with a demented musical cord with each pass. The logs' momentum slowed and I saw that each log bristled with wooden spears the length of my arm and sharpened with knitting needle points.

"Cool," Tommy cried, jumping up and moving toward the trap. I followed.

"Wait," warned Charlie also on his feet and holding out a hand. "Not just yet. Let it quit swinging altogether and don't touch it."

Hesitantly we moved closer until the logs hung together like mating pen cushions.

"Cool," Tommy repeated. "How'd they make it?" He stretched his hand out reaching for the nearest of the spiked logs.

"It wouldn't have been cool if these had hit us," I chided. "But why would somebody put something like this out here?"

"It's not hard to construct," Charlie said. "It's already claimed a victim."

"How do you know?" Tommy asked.

Charlie stepped between Tommy and the spike he'd been reaching, and taped the digging stick on the point. Unlike the other spikes, it was black with dried goop and tuffs of brown hair stuck around it.

"A deer walked into this and never had a chance," Charlie said. "It might have avoided one log, but not the other, the same is true for anybody walking that way."

"Who put it here?" I asked. "And why?"

" My guess is Macho Mike and his friends," Charlie answered. "It's to protect what's on the other side of these trees, which I'll bet is a zombie lab." He pointed between the live oaks and the winding trail. A light breeze blew from that direction and a pungent odor had me covering my face with my hand.

"Whew," said Tommy grabbing his nose. "It smells like Ana's mop water, only a hundreds times worse."

"That's what Macho Mike is guarding," Charlie said. "And zombie dust is cooking, but the technical name is methamphetamine. Probably they are using a process called a Nazi lab."

"Cool," Tommy said.

"Why is it called a Nazi lab?" I asked.

"The Nazis in Germany during World War II invented a simple way to make this drug," Charlie answered. "They gave it to their soldiers and factory workers so they could go longer without sleep."

Spooling up the beacon's fishing string, Charlie removed the twig before putting the string in his pocked and turned to the direction we'd come. Tommy didn't move and I could almost hear his imagination whirling into overdrive. The cause, I knew, were more of the old movies he liked to watch with Papa. Those gritty black and white films were of soldiers with domed helmets and scratchy images of a little man with a bad haircut, funny nose and silly moustache. He was always holding his arm in front of him with his palm out as he screamed in a guttural language.

Tommy was mesmerized by images of airplanes, rolling tanks and men marching super fast accompanied by explosions and shooting. There were scenes of burning building and suffering people that made my head hurt.

"A Nazi's lab," said Tommy with a hum. "I've never seen one before." He took a step in the direction between the trees and Charlie held out his hand.

"These aren't actual labs made by Nazis," Charlie said patiently. "It's just the process they used. There's probably a lot of modern plastic jugs, jars and other equipment over there, but the threat is the same."

Tommy turned on Charlie with his fists clenched at his sides, ready to do battle. "I want to see it," my cousin squealed, "and you can't tell me what to do."

"I don't blame you, I'd like to see it too, " Charlie said. "The problem is it might be the last thing we ever see."

"What do you mean?" I demanded.

Charlie explained that to make zombie dust Macho Mike and his friends used materials like camp stove fuel, shredded flashlight batteries, bleach, drain cleaner and match heads mixed together with other drugs for a chemical reaction. "By themselves, these ingredients are harmless, for the most part, " Charlie said, "But during the chemical process these containers emit gases that are flammable and caustic."

"Cause tics?" Tommy said.

"Even without lighting a match, it can burn off your skin or melt out your eyes and lungs," Charlie said. "Whatever is brewing over there could hurt you so fast you wouldn't know it was happening before it was too late.

"Eyes, lungs?" Tommy repeated. "Burn?"

"Your eyes, nose and ears melted out of your head," Charlie said. "Even the police investigating these labs approach them wearing special protective clothes called biohazard suits. I know of a policeman who lifted a trash can lid and got his tongue and eyes burned out."

"You're making this up," accused Tommy glancing at me for confirmation, but not moving. "Aren't you?"

"I wish I was, but I've seen these places before," Charlie said. "Judging from the location and all the trouble Macho Mike and his friends have gone too, they are cooking up a big batch and until the chemical process is complete, anybody or anything going back there stands to loose their hide and are literally taking their lives in their own hands."

"It can't hurt just to look?" Tommy argued. "Would it?"

"You saw those scars on Macho Mike's arms?" Charlie asked. "Those are healed burns. This isn't his first experience making zombie dust. It also explains why he's staying far enough away so he isn't affected by the fumes or risks causing a fire. It's safe to say his camp is a good ways from here."

No one said anything for a full minute.

"What is met-ham-fiend-of-dime," I asked, adding, "zombie dust?"

"It's a drug used for a lot of silly reasons," Charlie said. "It's main draw is how good it makes users feel. So good they're willing to pay a lot of money to become addicted to it. This is why it's called zombie dust, among other names."

He told us how amateur chemists with a fourth grade education saw a way to make a lot of money with a little knowledge and less effort. The problem was zombie chemists couldn't resist sampling their own product. Nor were they immune from the unholy harm the drug did to their insides. It was the equivalent of melting from the inside, Charlie added, over a long period of time."

"Why are they making it here?" I asked feeling silly.

"So they can hide from the police and their competition, most likely," Charlie replied, scanning the bushes, his hand on his holster. "I'll bet my canoe it'll take years to clean up the mess they've made."

These were the byproducts, he explained, toxic waste that more than likely had been dumped into the river.

"After they leave it won't be safe to come close to this area," Charlie said. "Which is why when the police find a lab in a house, or any structure, it's deemed unlivable for years."

A blue jay screeched and Tommy and I jumped, looking toward the source of the sound. We watched the bird fly toward the river and followed Charlie, moving in the same direction.

CHAPTER 24

We returned to where we had left Macho Mike and found he was breathing regularly along with a good pulse.

We left him again, but instead of retracing our steps around the hill. Charlie led us back on the trail to the Nazi lab, and at the fork he turned in the direction of the river. He scanned the trail for more booby traps, and I watched for snakes. We found neither, but I noticed different types of footprints in the dust.

Walking within sight of the river, we found the trail dipped to our left into a gully and wound down a slope to a small, shaded beach. A less used path to our right ascended up a slope into the high area with heavy foliage that shadowed the adjoining beach. Charlie chose the steeper path and we had to climb up on all fours. At the top, we found ourselves on a bluff offering a wide view of the river. The ground sloped to our right into another grove of trees and in the direction of our camp.

Pausing to catch our breath, Tommy cocked his head, being the first to hear the droning of an engine. The sound grew in intensity and we soon spotted a dot approaching from up stream hugging the opposite shore. It was the first boat we'd seen since leaving Bandy's Camp. Remembering the airplane, I wondered if it would pass without seeing us. As if on command to my question, the boat swung round and made toward our position. Soon, the shape changed into a long canoe powered by an outboard motor. A man in the back steered while a large man in the front constantly wiped his face with a rag.

"We can call them," I said.

"I don't think they'd hear you," Charlie said, "besides, let's see where they go."

The canoe continued to cruise directly toward us and the men riding in it became more defined. I was about to call when Charlie's hand lay on my shoulder. His other hand was on Tommy as he gently pushed us down below the tops of a bush.

"Not a word from now on," he whispered. "Be quiet as mice."

"Or ticks," Tommy giggled, "under shorts."

Dropping to his belly, Charlie crawled to the edge of the bluff, but didn't look over. We did the same, listening at the angry hornet drone of the motor before it stopped so suddenly the absence of sound made me jump. The void was filled by the sound of rolling water and the boat's prow slicing the sandy shore followed by a loud splash, and sloshing and dragging sounds.

"Mikey," a voice bellowed. "Yo, yo, yo Mikey, come here!" There was no answer and the same voice, in a lower tone said. "You'd think he would have heard us coming. You told him what time we'd be here."

"I told him, but you know nobody tells Macho Mike what to do," replied a high pitched voice. "Though I'll bet the rent he's probably sleeping, stoned or both, under a tree and totally lost track of time."

"Just so he isn't shooting that gun again," the first voice growled. "This place is made to order. We have to get the only gunslinger in the country that can't figure out gunfire attracts people. "

"Yeah, even that flea shooter barks too loud over here, but doesn't always bite over there," second voice said. "By the way, he wants to be called Macho Mike the Keechi Creek Gunman."

Second voice pronounced the word Keechi as "Key-chu-eye."

"That's Keechi," corrected first voice with softer emphasis on the double E and I producing "Key-chee."

"No it's Key-chu-eye," insisted second voice. "I have a cousin who's a historian and she looked up the pronunciation in a history book."

"That and 90 cents will get you a Coke," snapped first voice dismissively. "Whatever he calls himself, if he brings us any attention, we'll all be up a certain other creek without a paddle."

"I still say it's…"

"Never the hell you mind," first voice interrupted impatiently. "I made sure he only had two bullets."

"You should have given him only one bullet," second voice snorted, "like that old TV show."

"You got to nip it, nip it, nip it in the bud," said first voice in a high nasal inflection. "I never get tired of that line."

"He's heard us," second voice declared flatly. "Only the lazy bastard doesn't want to hump this load up the trail. I'll kick his ass when he shows up."

"Then you can expect him two seconds after everything is at the site," first voice said. "He's too busy playing Navy SEAL protecting the country against black helicopters.'

"Then we better get going," said the first voice with a sigh. "I want to get out of here before dark."

"Suits me," second voice said.

Feet crunching sand and gravel combined with grunts of labor coupled with metal striking metal faded inland. Unable to resist, I crawled to the bluff's edge and saw just the front half of the big canoe on the beach. Around it on the ground were plastic laundry baskets filled with plastic bags snapping in the wind. To the right of the canoe were a dozen squat propane tanks set in rows. These were the kind I'd seen locked in iron mesh pantries at grocery stores.

Stretching further out over the ledge, I saw a black haired head, belonging to the large man, fanning himself with a baseball cap. With a loud sigh he got to his feet, pulling on one of the broad suspender straps that prevented his huge belly from spilling over a pair of shorts.

Moving toward him was another man wearing a straw hat smashed on his head and a gray pony tail, tied in two places, trailing down his back. Despite the warm weather the long sleeves of his work shirt were rolled down and his shirt tails partially stuffed into jeans. His pant cuffs were rolled over pull-on work boots, their steel toe caps exposed and shiny between the rips in the leather.

The second man carried two thick poles balanced on his shoulders and walked to the other side of the beach where a pair of cottonwood trees grew. Dropping one pole, he placed the other between the trimmed branches on each trees. Between them each man threaded the carrying handles of the propane tanks over the ends of the pole. When three tanks were hanging from each end, the big man moved between the trees, ready to shoulder the pole's center. But before lifting the load, he turned suddenly toward the river. Removing his ball cap again, he slowly scanning the area before him. My head went to ground and I nearly squeaked looking through the grass at Charlie.

"What's the matter?" First voice demanded.

"Don't know, I can't really tell you," second voice, the big guy said. "But did you ever get the feeling you're being watched?"

"All the time," said first voice, and laughed. "Just because you're paranoid doesn't mean they aren't out to get you" Then in a serious tone, he said, "Let's get going and out of sight."

I peeked again and saw the big man standing at water's edge looking up stream. He wore thick frame glasses that made his eyes look like oysters in their shell.

"Well," first voice demanded. "Catching anything on your scope?"

With a shake of his head, the big man cursed and snatched a towel from the canoe. He draped it over his shoulders and returned to the cottonwoods. He lifted the pole to his shoulders and lumbered out of sight, his feet crunching gravel. Chancing another look over the edge of the bluff I saw the other man had a pole on the cottonwood trees threading laundry baskets on either their ends. He also looked toward the river, even glancing up before hefting and moving inland in the big man's direction.

We waited for what seemed like forever before Charlie pointed in the direction of our camp. We crawled on our bellies so we wouldn't be seen from the beach or the trail until we were out of sight. Once on our feet, we moved down the slope to the grassy meadow headed for a line of trees. Saying nothing, Charlie took the lead and alternated looking ahead and back.

"Zombie makers," Tommy said loudly. "They are making zombie powder?"

"I'd say so," answered Charlie in a normal voice. "Production and distribution."

"Then let's go get them," said Tommy stopping and I almost ran into his back. "We'll surprise them because they won't expect it. I'll bet there's a reward for their capture."

Cocking his head Charlie looked at Tommy as if he'd grown ten feet tall. "Do what now?"

"You said it yourself, what they are doing is wrong, in fact it's terrible," said Tommy drawing himself up to his full height. "To make their stuff they hurt people and animals with their traps, so it's up to us to stop them." Tommy's voice rose, the way it did when he got excited.

"You have a gun and knife," Tommy said. "I've got the bolo, Jackie's got the digging stick. They'll never know what hit them." My cousin was serious as a black eye and sounded as unrealistic as Aunt Sonia.

"Tommy," I began, hoping to defuse the subject. "Why should Charlie get those guys?"

"You told me he was on a mission quest," Tommy declared. "Tarzan wouldn't think twice about rounding up Macho Mike's gang, or any other bad guys."

At that moment I would have paid for one of those giant condors to swoop down and snatch me away for its lunch. When none appeared, I looked to see Charlie staring at me. "What is he saying?" Charlie asked.

Sheepishly, I recounted my theory of how the legendary lord of the jungle had come to be on the Brazos River. I left nothing out, except what I'd seen the night before and expected Charlie to be mad, before he shot us. Instead, his face relaxed into an bemused expression I hadn't seen before.

"So that's it," he said, more to himself than us, and turned to Tommy. "Now I've got it!"

Tommy gapped, turned to me and I could only shake my head while my wrist itched and my chest ached. Twisting my face into a question I turned to Charlie.

"Destiny, my friends, my mission quest," said Charlie extending his right hand to the sky before thumping his chest. "Tarzan does have a plan," turning to Tommy he added, "Even if he's in a tight jam, right?"

Tommy nodded.

"Tarzan's first priority is to take care of his friends, right. That's over catching bad guys, right."

"Yeah, I guess so," said Tommy blinking. "But..."

"Does Tarzan work alone?" Charlie challenged.

Tommy shook his head hesitantly as if that was the answer expected, but not the one he wanted to give.

"Tarzan can call his elephant or ape friends and even the white commissioner to help him?"

Another boy's head shake, confident this time.

Shaking his head Charlie said, "You can see we're short on elephants or apes now, wouldn't you agree?"

Tommy nodded with a confused expression.

"But there's a county sheriff's office with bunches of deputies and other folks somewhere around here. I'd rather have elephants, but I suppose they'll have to do, at least until the elephants show up."

"Yeah," Tommy whined. "But that's not how Tarzan, I mean you, catch bad guys."

"Nothing says Tarzan has to do it alone," Charlie said. "You have a good plan. Surprise is on our side, but there's also a lot of unknowns, such as who else is out here besides Macho Mike?"

Tommy pursed his lips and shook his head that he wasn't totally convinced until Charlie put his hand on his shoulder. "They might have more guns, more booby traps. That's too many maybes that aren't worth the chance. Understand?'

Tommy nodded.

"Tarzan no ask boy and girl fight bad men. Not if there's an easier way. You OK with that."

Tommy looked disappointed until Charlie extended his right arm and pointed in the direction of our camp.

"Umgawah," he ordered and took off at a trot, "Pacee, pacee!"

CHAPTER 25

Back at camp, I stirred sugar into a mug of tea the way Tommy liked it. Charlie handed down the blackberries and fish and Tommy fell to his breakfast.

Charlie excused himself, after he pulled out a small sack from the gear box, and grabbed the digging stick. He asked me to cover the fire pit with dirt and left camp in the direction we'd just come saying he wouldn't be long.

"Wow, this is great, " said Tommy smacking his lips. " How'd you catch the fish?"

"With a rock," I said. "That's when I wasn't tripping over more rattlesnakes."

Tommy blew tea out of his nose and I filled him in on what else he had missed. Looking in the direction Charlie had disappeared, I lowered my voice. "Did you find my note?" I asked.

"What note?" replied Tommy between bites of fish.

"The one I left in the laces of your shoe," I said.

"I never look at my shoes when I put them on," Tommy whined. "What did it say?"

Irritated, I began circling the camp the way I'd seen Charlie when he was looking for Tommy's tracks, but saw no paper, large or small. "Did you go to the creek before you left," I asked.

Tommy shook his head and I grabbed the shovel and piled dirt into the fire pit. Again, I considered grabbing Tommy and running to the canoe. It had the big water jugs and we had the bolo, though Charlie had the beacon in his pocket. Instead I kept working until Charlie returned carrying the nylon bag, tied to the end of the digging stick with a piece of cord. The bag bulged and I wondered if he'd picked more onions and garlic or other edible plants.

"Whatcha got?" Asked Tommy, all curiosity.

"A little edge we might need for this trip," Charlie said.

Charlie held the bag away from him as he checked the fire pit. With a satisfied nod, he directed us to carry the gearbox to the canoe. Tommy put the bucket and his mug on top of the box and we each took a handle and moved toward the canoe. The whole time Charlie kept the stick and bag held away.

We placed the gear box in the center of the canoe, along with the sleeping bag and tent. Like in the camp, Charlie wanted things stowed and tied down just a certain way. I'm proud to say we made it happen, though Charlie told us how. When he was satisfied, he placed the nylon bag carefully in the back of the boat and pulled out two life vests that had been stuffed behind the canoe's back seat. Tommy recoiled in horror, for he viewed life jackets along the lines of playpens or holding hands going to the park. It was a direct slight to his swimming ability and I thought we would be there all morning. Only Charlie uncharacteristically cut him off.

"Umguawa, boy and girl put on life jacket NOW, pacee, pacee."

Tommy's mouth snapped shut and he put on a life jacket on without another word. After I put mine on Charlie directed me to sit in the front and handed me a paddle. He helped Tommy climb on to the gearbox and tied the sleeping bag up between us as a backrest.

"Why does Jackie get to paddle?" Tommy grumbled.

"I need your sharp eyes to watch my back."

Tommy perked at this compliment and offered no challenge as Charlie pushed the canoe into the shallow water. He jumped into the back seat, snatched up his paddle and nudged the canoe into deeper water. We glided toward the river through no help of mine while I reflected on my "great plan" to take Charlie's canoe. I splashed water, but made very little progress. The reality was that I had never paddled a canoe. My inability became even more evident after my paddle slipped from my hand. Charlie grabbed before it floated past and passed it back without comment, though Tommy said he should paddle.

Again I was faced with a function I had never done before and panic filled my chest. I imagined what The Weed would say I was the perfect example of a lack of comprehension. So, I stabbed and chopped the water ineffectively like a washing machine compared to Charlie's flowing rhythm. He even managed to switch sides with a flip of his paddle, popping the excess water and preventing us from getting us wet. He made it seem so easy while I was silly, poking and scraping the side of the boat offering no contribution to our progress. Just one more thing, I thought, that I was totally rotten doing.

"Grip the shaft tighter," called Charlie with condemnation. There was no reproach in his expression as he smiled and twirled the paddle and said, "It's OK, you're doing fine for a first timer," though I knew I wasn't. "Everybody starts like this, so grip the shaft tighter with your right hand

and rotate your body to your right."

The instructions were simple, the praise priceless.

"Plant the blade in the water all the way to the throat of the paddle and keep the shaft straight up and down."

Naturally, I wasn't perfect the first time, but I dug my paddle again and was amazed at how easy the stroke came as I pulled and turned my body.

"Great," he said. "Keep rotating your torso till your paddle comes to your hip. After a while, you'll find your rhythm."

We neared the river and to my surprise the canoe responded to my movement like my bicycle. I had discovered a super power I never knew I had, though there was little time to gloat. The calm of the creek was replaced by the approaching growl of the river

"Paddle only on your right side for now, Jackie," Charlie called. "When I need you to switch, I'll call *shift*."

Using his paddle like a rudder Charlie guided the canoe into the current and a water level higher than I remembered it two days earlier.

"They must have opened the flood gates on the dam up river," Charlie shouted. "This is good, we won't have to drag the canoe."

Glancing behind me I saw Tommy's head bobbing and Charlie grinned. Turning front, I dug my paddle again and established a rhythm. We made seemingly good time by the way the shore raced past us. Recalling a map I wondered if we could paddle all the way to the ocean, to South America or the Caribbean. We were moving fast enough and had found our own food, great food in fact. Why couldn't we just keep going? What could stop us? I pondered those questions until I felt Tommy stir.

"Hey," he yelled. "There's a boat coming!"

Fully alert, I twisted around and saw a craft moving toward us. I lost my pace and nearly my paddle.

"It's OK," Charlie said. "Keep paddling!"

Forcing myself to look ahead, I did as I was told, hardly able to resist looking behind. The boat was the same canoe that landed the big man and Smash Hat" on the beach below the bluff where we were hiding. As it closed, I turned and made out Macho Mike still wearing the bandana Charlie had tied around his forehead. He stood up holding a rope attached to the boat's front. His kinky hair bounced like cotton candy while his vest flapped in the wind. The big man sat in the boat's middle, gripping the sides, sunlight reflected off his glasses' lenses. Smash Hat gripped the throttle of a little outboard motor and Macho Mike pointed and turned to yell something to the others. The big man pounded the boat sides with both hands before also pointing at us. Smash Hat patted him the way a master might pet a big dog before he spat and wiped his mouth on a sleeve.

"OK, guys," warned Charlie above the din. "Be cool and things will work themselves out."

Macho Mike and the big man hooted and called taunts as Smash Hat twisted the throttle and speed toward our bow, missing it by inches. Charlie paddled into the rising wake looking oblivious to the other boat. Turning, they sped past, circled and crossed our bow again, the three men making animal sounds and silly faces. Still holding on to the rope, Macho Mike whipped a slip of paper from his vest and held it out, laughing. I felt sick realizing it was the note I had written to Tommy about escaping with Charlie's canoe. It must have dropped out of Tommy's shoe near where he ran into Macho Mike. That was how they'd found us so quickly and my *Orion* began to itch.

Macho Mike let the slip of paper flutter away. Charlie appeared oblivious, pointing to his ear and shaking his head. Smash Hat twisted the throttle handle violently, and the motor fell to a hum as their boat slowed and rode abreast of us in the open water between.

"Good morning," Charlie hailed. "How are you?"

"Shove your good morning up your fat butt," Macho Mike spat. "Where's my gun?"

"At the tree where you knocked yourself out," Charlie said. "Along with your knives."

I tried not to giggle remembering how Charlie tossed away the little gun's parts and the cat piss glass pipe.

"You hit me from behind," Macho Mike declared quickly.

"So why is that bump is on your forehead, and not the back of your head?" Charlie asked. "Or don't you remember how you tripped and hit that tree?"

Self-consciously, Macho Mike touched the bandana on his forehead and scowled.

"Terrell, he owes me a new gun," Macho Mike said turning to the two men behind him. "That little boy distracted me while the big guy ran me into a tree and rolled me."

"Never mind," Smash Hat, Terrell, said. "You people were trespassing on private property and will have to come back to answer some questions."

The big man snickered and bounced. Terrell patted him to calm his bouncing movement.

"If it's a matter of reparations," said Charlie laying his paddle across his knees.

"Hey!" the big man cried. "Terrell, tell him to quit using big words."

"Maybe we can agree that I'll pay a trespassing fine," Charlie said. "Something to make up for the damage caused when your boy found our boy.'

Macho Mike bristled and pointed. "That's right," he growled, "and you'll pay it in full." Macho Mike showed teeth, which was meant to frighten and instead made him look even sillier.

"Settle down, Davy," said Terrell still patting the big man. "Mike hush, everything's under control."

"Well if that's the case," Charlie said. "Here's something that will take care of everything."

He reached into the bottom of the canoe and the three men stiffened. Terrell reached behind his back.

"Hold up there partner," Terrell warned. "Don't do anything you'll regret."

Charlie ignored the tone and held up the nylon bag dangling at the end of the digging stick. "There isn't a herpetologist in the world that won't pay at least $500 for this specimen because it's extremely rare. I was on my way back to cash it in. I did harvest it from your property, so you are entitled to it." Their interests perked with the mention of money.

"We'll decide what it's worth," Terrell said "See what's in the collection plate Mikey."

Macho Mike and Terrell exchanged looks and the younger man grabbed the paddle lying at his side. "Give it here," he ordered.

Showing more bad teeth Terrell brought out a scratched cowboy pistol with white plastic handles and laid it on his lap. He throttled the outboard motor and whipped the boat toward our stern.

"Ease that gun over too," shouted Terrell above the engine. "Lay it on the box in front of you. That's part of the fine, too."

Without a word, Charlie ducked his head and pulled the strap of the holster over his head and laid it in front of him. I thought it odd he didn't unbuckle his knife belt to take off the holster, but concluded maybe that was the way he wore it in a canoe.

Grinning, Terrell nodded at Macho Mike as Charlie hunched over the side of the canoe holding the bag above the water with his left hand and his paddle across his knees, the towel still covering his lap. Their canoe drew nearly parallel to us when Macho Mike grasped his paddle with both hands. He stood up with a whining howl, raising the paddle above his head like a broad sword and stepped on to our canoe's gunnels. He started to swing he paddle just as Charlie shoved his paddle across his knees. The blade's end collided hard with the front of their boat like pool stick contacting a billiard ball.

As bumps go, it wasn't much, but enough to disrupt Macho Mike's motion and Terrell had to fight to control the boat. The momentum of M&M's swing carried his foot into mid air above the water. He tossed the paddle away, flailing his arms and trying to regain balance while nearly tipping their canoe over. Shrieking, he fell forward, barely throwing himself into the short space between the two boats and forcing Terrell to push the outboard's tiller a hard left to turn their canoe away and bringing its midsection to within inches of ours. Their canoe passed within inches and Charlie dropped the nylon bag into the front of their boat and yanked the cord free on the digging stick. When the boat was clear Terrell frantically cut the motor's throttle.

"Damn it, Mikey," he screamed, "can't you do anything right."

Macho Mike surfaced, sputtering, just behind our stern

Charlie dropped the digging stick and gripped his paddle.

"Left stroke, Jackie," he commanded. Together we dug our paddles and pulled away.

"Don't go anywhere, you can't outrun us," Terrell snarled. "This ain't over, not by a dammed sight so you better not try to leave."

"He jugged the boat," Macho Mike sputtered, "that bastard don't play fair."

"Shut up, Mikey," Terrell snapped, "I'll take care of this."

Charlie dug his paddle with a twist and our canoe turned bringing us into a T-bone position behind their canoe. Terrell had dropped the cowboy pistol when he turned and cut the throttle. Cursing, he bent over and picked up the gun from the boat's floor, pointing the barrel down to drain it of water until it slowed to a drip. Snarling, he turned and I believe he would have shot us. I also wondered why Charlie didn't get us away?

Terrell twisted round to look over his shoulder in our direction and was about to turn fully around, the gun in his hand, when his eyes widened. His mouth dropped open, I was confused and looked behind me. Charlie held his pistol at waist level, the barrel leveled at Terrell, Charlie's face wearing the dark expression I'd seen the night before. A mocking smile pulled at Charlie's mouth, but he didn't wave his pistol or indicate for Terrell to drop his gun and put up his hands. Instead he inclined his head in a "it's your move" look and Terrell's mouth twisted with outrage.

Don't do it, I warned him silently unable for some reason to bring the words to my mouth. Don't do anything! You didn't see him shoot that snake, and he was farther away than this. Please don't move?

I wanted the top of Terrell's smash hat to open wide to my mental warnings and penetrate. Terrell might have let things slide, only Charlie titled his head in the opposite direction, winked and raised an eyebrow. The color drained from Terrell's face and he started to swing his gun around. Davis' keening drew him up short. The big man was bouncing and holding a quavering finger outstretched toward the canoe's front. From the canoe's forward seat a harpoon shaped head rose, marble sized eyes glistening above sneering lips as the head cocked into a tight striking S and a burring sound filled the air.

"Terrell!" Davis squealed. "S-s-shoot it, s-s-shoot it, please!"

The big man slapped the gunnels, shaking the canoe and instantly drawing the snake's full attention. Before turning around, Terrell spat in Charlie's direction. He turned around, the cowboy pistol grasped in both of his hands.

"Davis! Davis!" Terrell warned. "Sit still like a good boy and I'll get it."

Aiming over the top of Davis' head, Terrell jerked the pistol's trigger and a sound like a hammer hitting wood echoed off the banks. The bullet missed the snake and a geyser erupted to the right of Macho Mike's head.

"Damn it to hell!" Macho Mike screamed. "Terrell what are you shooting at?"

He reached for the canoe, only to fall back in time to stay out of reach of the outstretched fangs. Terrell lifted his gun again, but Davis wouldn't stay still even as he tried to calm him with his other hand

"Get out of the way, Mikey!" Terrell yelled. "Davis sit still, dammit! I'll get it, if you'll just sit still! "

Before Terrell could shoot, the snake's head flashed across the length of the canoe to within inches of Davis' face. In full panic the big man shook off Terrell's restraining hand, twisted to his right, and didn't fall as much as he oozed over the canoe's side. His broad rear barely missed being hit by another snake strike. He twisted and nudged Terrell's gun hand and a bullet bounced across the water thudding into the riverbank. Like a refrigerator being pushed over, the big man tipped the canoe and everything went into the water. The snake was the first to surface and zigzagged across the water toward the nearest shore. Charlie raised a hand in departure.

"Thank you," he called "Please forgive the inconvenience."

The snake swam to the shore and into the brush as Macho Mike splashed toward us ignoring Terrell's cries to help Davis. Terrell and Davis swam to the overturned canoe, a rainbow of oily water produced by the outboard motor around them.

Macho Mike yanked the bandana bandage from his head. His sopping hair shrouded his head with gauze curtains as he splashed toward us. Meanwhile, the current pushed us down stream though, stopping to catch his breath, Macho Mike pointed a finger in our direction.

"I'm going to kill you, " he screamed. "I'll kill your family, your friends and your dog. No matter how long it takes, you are mine, you hear me. You can run, but you can't hide."

With his paddle Charlie kept the canoe level, the front pointed to the bank the snake chose. He made no effort to get underway, but considered Macho Mike while the current continued to move us farther from the other canoe.

"You know, I believe you," Charlie said. "I really do!" There was no sarcasm in his statement, just a cold finality, and his face was horrible to behold. Laying his paddle down, he looked at Macho Mike and grasped the pistol on his lap, scratching his facial scar with the front sight.

"Talk is cheap Mikey baby, just like you," Charlie called. "Wouldn't you agree, oh Navy SEAL wannnabe?"

"I was a SEAL," Macho Mike said. "I can prove it."

"With what?" Charlie taunted. "That big chicken dinner, wash-out ticket next to your stash and your heart?"

"You were in my wallet!" Macho Mike squealed. "You son of a bitch, you'll wish you'd never been born when I get through with you."

"Yeah," Davis yapped. "You'll be sorry."

Terrell hit the big man on the side of his head with an open palm. Holding his face, Davis moaned demanding to know what he'd done. Neither Charlie or M&M paid them any mind.

"You plan to talk me to death, Mikey?" Charlie asked. "Or wait till I die of old age?" He held his pistol over the side of the canoe, the muzzle pointed in M&M's direction.

"Quit pointing that gun at me," M&M ordered. "Turn it away, right now."

"This old thing," drawled Charlie, "I couldn't hit the broad side of a barn from the inside. Come over and get it, Mikey, take it off my hands?"

I thought of the snake Charlie had shot in two while M&M chopped water toward us perhaps twice the distance of the snake shot. I wanted to say something.

"I won't tell you again," M&M whined. "Point it somewhere else."

"Tell you what, you come over here and take it from me. Do it just like a real Navy SEAL, the ones that can swim five miles and fight a battle."

"Keep talking, funny man," called M&M swinging his skinny arm forward. "Just stay right where you are."

"I'm not going anywhere," Charlie said. "We've got all day."

"Damn straight you aren't going anywhere," Macho Mike said. "You're going to get yours."

"Bitch, bitch, bitch," said Charlie with a yawn "Is that all you do?"

"Throw me a rope," Macho Mike said. "Do it if you know what's good for you!"

"Here you go," said Charlie shaking three inches of the stern line above the water with his free hand. "Hurry, come get it."

"You are so dead!" cried Macho Mike between strokes. "Nobody treats me like that, nobody!"

"Mikey, get over here!" Terrell called. "Let's get this boat righted."

"Shut up, Terrell!" spat Macho Mike when his head cleared water. "This is between me and that sorry sack of shit."

"Swim Michael Ebner DeGreif, swim for glory and school spirit!" Charlie taunted. "Otherwise you'll be late for class, and tomorrow the teacher's fool."

New anger seemed to charge Macho Mike's strokes. When he couldn't swim a proper Australian crawl, he submerged and surfaced twice. When he came up again, he held the heavy biker boots and threw them to one side where they sank.

Charlie no longer pointed the gun in his direction, but dangled it carelessly over the side. I thought he would twirl it like a cowboy pistol, but the gun seemed welded to his hand.

"Be careful Mikey," Charlie reproached. "Best go back. Please don't come any closer."

Splashing, Macho Mike chopped the water as Charlie leaned forward, the gun held in a relaxed grip. I wanted to shout, make noise, bang my paddle, do something. Yet, even the bugs were silent as Charlie's eyes and mouth became progressively more cruel. Macho Mike made a little progress as the current carried us just out of his reach. He couldn't swim very much longer, I concluded, and if he was smart, he would turn back before he sank.

"Make him go back!" I wanted to scream. "Or shoot him and get it over with!" Only, Charlie never snuggled the trigger, though his mouth had a cruel twist and a cold gleam filled his eyes.

"I told you Bad Bob was out there," Tommy taunted. "Next time you'll listen."

The gun rose to Charlie's shoulder as if it were attached to a spring-loaded cable. With the muzzle pointed skyward, Charlie blinked and looked around like he just woke up. Taking a deep breath, he shut his eyes and bowed his head. He turned to the grinning Tommy, looked past him and stared as I sat mute-stupid, gripping my paddle with white knuckles. He dropped his eyes while my heart beat so loud I thought everyone within five miles could hear it, but I willed myself not to look away

"Stay put," Macho Mike gasped. "We'll finish this.

Charlie stared at him as if this swimmer had just appeared and the current caught the canoe's bow turning it downstream. With a sigh, Charlie pulled the belt strap of the pistol holster over his head, replaced the pistol and secured the holster flap.

Motioning to Tommy, he said, "Give me your life vest!"

"NO," Tommy protested. "It's mine."

Resisting the urge to slap Tommy with my paddle, I unbuckled my life vest and tossed it to Charlie. He caught it and turned to the struggling Macho Mike and threw it at him. "Here" he shouted, picking up his paddle. "Jackie, full right stroke."

"You can't go," Macho Mike howled. "You yellow, gutless chicken shit, you can't go."

"Don't leave us," Davis called. "Have a heart. What you're doing is illegal! You could go to jail."

Charlie dug his paddle in tandem with mine, and the canoe moved into the current. I glanced over my shoulder and Macho Mike dove forward, a knife gripped in his fist, missing the back of the boat by inches.

"Go back stupid," warned Charlie without looking back. "You'll drown!"

"Come here you son of a bitch!" Macho Mike screamed. "You know what pay back is? Come back and fight like a man, you yellow bastard!"

Macho Mike grabbed the life vest just as it floated past him and before we rounded the next bend.

CHAPTER 26

We returned to the familiar rhythm of paddling and passing scenery. "Why didn't you use your gun?" Tommy complained. "It would have been easier."

"I had it, if we needed it," said Charlie quickly. " Besides, the snake did a better job and was more fun."

"You should have shot them, shot all three," Tommy argued. "That's what they deserved, what they were going to do to us."

Why my cousin was so blood thirsty, I wasn't sure. Ana said it was just the nature of boys at that age. Still, I wanted to smack him for treading so close to the truth. What would Tommy think about Charlie' gun, I wondered, if he knew this was the second time he'd almost killed somebody. I could have shut him up fast if he knew the first had almost been us.

"Tommy," Charlie said. "Wouldn't you have loved to have been here when the Indians roamed this land?"

"Nope," said Tommy crossing his arms. "Then I'd know what was going to happen to the Indians."

"Indians lived here?" I called back, happy to change the subject.

"They aren't called Indians anymore," Tommy said, "you're supposed to call them native Americans."

"The tribe that live here were the Comanche, or as they called themselves, *The People*."

The People, he added, adapted to this country better than any other Indian tribe. Particularly since at one time they were the lowest of low on the totem pole. But they were anything but the "ignorant savages" as the first white men assumed. Their greatness, and their weakness, was that *The People* couldn't conceive of any other way of life. So who could blame them since *The People* had been living free for longer than recorded history.

"What have *The People* got to do with not shooting those drug makers?" Said Tommy with a smart mouth tone that Ana would have slapped his face for using. "I certainly didn't see any Indians when Macho Mike almost brained you."

Where had Tommy gotten such a vicious streak? I wondered. But

Charlie didn't seem to mind.

"I'm getting to that," he said. "*The People* were proud and fierce. They had to be to take this land from other tribes like the Apache. They prospered, growing rich in horses and glory. Yet, for all their ferocity in battle, nothing was held in higher esteem than counting coup on an enemy instead of killing him."

"Counting coup?" I said.

Counting coup, Charlie explained, was what Comanche warriors did during an Indian battle. They touched enemy warriors with a hand or a decorated coup stick. To *The People,* this was greater valor than shooting the same man with an arrow across an open field. To get close enough to count coup, the warrior had to use all his skills of horsemanship, archery and physical agility. He had to cross an open field where other warriors shot arrows, guns and swung clubs. When warriors touched enemy warriors, especially a chief, they reaped their enemy's medicine.

"Counting coup diminished the enemy's power, or medicine. It was a practical, as well as psychological, kick in the head."

The Comanche warrior with coup left the fight with his hair and more medicine. Which was certainly easier to carry than the enemy's weapons, or property, especially if they'd come a long way to fight. The enemy warrior might even be shamed enough to withdraw.

"It didn't always work that way when there were more enemies," Charlie said. "Still, great warriors were known by the number of their horses and a well notched coup stick."

"So, you weren't actually going to shoot those men," said Tommy, sounding disappointed.

"No," said Charlie, and I knew he was lying. But he added, "That's what Tarzan would have done."

"Yeah, but still," said Tommy sounding superior, "I wouldn't have wanted to be here when *The People* lived here."

"Why is that?" Charlie asked.

"If they were so free, I'd know about all those rules and punishments they'd have. Makes me think of what's going to happen to us when we get home."

"What do you think is going to happen to you?" Charlie said. "You'll go back to your family."

"That's true," Tommy said, "but somebody will be mad because we got lost, no matter what. I'll bet the owner of that rubber raft sure won't be happy."

"The point is you've been found," Charlie replied. "The owner can always get a new raft and I'll bet he'd tell you that too."

"Other than counting coup," Tommy countered. "What would you call putting a rattlesnake in Macho Mike's boat?"

"Assault with a scaly weapon," I said with a smirk, "and endangering a helpless animal."

"Laugh if you want too," Tommy said. "I'm saying that, just like *The People*, it won't be nice when we get back. Makes me wish I could stay out here forever."

I had to agree with Tommy. What was I supposed to say when my parents or the police asked what happened in the last three days? Should I tell about last night and the gun? Why couldn't we stay?

What would have happened if Charlie hadn't picked up the beacon? If Tommy hadn't spoken when he did? Would Charlie have shot us, then, or let Macho Mike drown? Never mind that I did nothing to stop him.

"You should have," said the phantom chorus of girls from my class. "Any decent girl would have done something."

"Well I didn't," I muttered.

"You say something Jackie?" Tommy asked.

"No, nothing," I said quickly.

The longer I dwelled on this, the more I wanted to stay on the river indefinitely. The problem was chewing my brain to rags and I had no idea what to do when Charlie steered toward a flat stretch of shore. Its beach was level with the water, and a stand of trees stood not far from the water's edge.

When the canoe beached, we went ashore pulling the bow rope. Charlie stepped out and pushed the boat to dry ground and leaned against an oak tree.

"Arrrrggghhhhhh," he said and stretched his back and legs. We copied his movements finding relief to kinked muscles after sitting for a long time. Tommy wandered a few yards down the beach and pointed to the water

"Look at that," he called.

Following his arm, I caught my breath at the scaly bodies breaking the surface.

"What is it?" I asked. Toothy snouts broke the surface with huge scaly bodies.

"Alligator gar," Charlie said with admiration. "This is a feeding spot."

Nearby a mayfly landed on the water's surface and was immediately snapped up. Before long, the water churned with dozens of fish surfacing with the grace of oil drums.

"Magnificent, " said Charlie and turned to me, "want to go swimming?"

"Are you crazy?" I squealed. "They'll eat me."

"Not if you jump in," said Charlie laughing. "There might be a problem if you grabbed one."

"I'm not going to find out if you're wrong," I said. "What are they doing anyway?

"Feeding," he said. "They're scavengers."

"You mean they eat trash, garbage?" I said.

"Yes," he said, "and do a good job of keeping the water clean."

"I suppose so," I said reluctantly, "but you wouldn't catch me eating one."

"A bug," Charlie laughed, "or a gar?"

I watched the gars dance while Charlie stretched again.

"Bet you'll be happy to get back," he said, "and you'll have lots of stories to tell."

I thought it was as good a time to bring up what I'd seen the night before. Only Tommy came running toward us.

"Somebody's coming," he wheezed. "Somebody funny!"

"Funny?" Charlie said, "you mean funny, ha-ha, or funny, uh-oh!"

"I don't know," Tommy said. "It's just weird, odd and nothing like I ever saw before!"

Looking in the direction Tommy pointed, a man jogged toward us wearing a blue bandana tied around his forehead. It didn't cover the top of his bald head glistening with sweat. A strap strained across his muscled shoulders and a barrel chest was covered with a torn and sopping red T-shirt. He gave no indication he saw us as he moved at a steady trot, his hands gripping the handles of a two-wheeled cart with a platform that reminded me of a Chinese rickshaw I'd seen in Papa's old movies. A black canvas constructed like a retractable accordion covered the cart's platform.

He looked as if he were going to run into the river, cart and all, when he stopped a few feet from the waterline. Two support poles dropped from the handles and the rickshaw's platform was level as the man snatched a long staff tied behind him. He stepped forward, and using the staff for support, he bent forward, catching his breath and pulled another bandana from his back pocket.

"Howdy do," he called, "is it hot enough for you?"

"Oh yeah," Charlie answered. "It's nice to have a river to cool off."

"Just not now," I said pointing to the feeding gar. "I don't think they'd let you."

"They're the reason we're here," the man said.

"We?" Charlie asked.

Instead of answering the big man moved to the rickshaw and pushed back the folded cover revealing a woman lying strapped to the cushioned front half of the platform. She gave us a floppy wave, grinning lopsidedly with her head wobbling against a large pillow.

"This is Flo, my wife," he said proudly. "I'm Bobby Outlaw."

"Pleased to meet you," said Charlie offering a hand to Bobby.

Tommy whispered, "It's Bad Bob!"

I caught him hard with my elbow and Charlie took off his hat and leaned down to Flo to catch her waving hand between his thumb and fingers.

"Nice to meet you folks," he said. "I'm Charlie. This is Tommy and Jackie."

"Hi," Tommy and I hummed.

I avoided looking at the woman and Tommy did the same. We knew special education kids from school and we were told repeatedly not to stare or treat them any differently from other kids. The fact was, they are different, an unavoidable fact since this woman was spread over the platform in caterpillar angles.

Bobby didn't seem to notice our discomfort as he moved to the rickshaw's back and unfolded a wheel chair. Reverently he picked up the rag doll body and placed it in the seat.

"Fishing?" Asked Bobby over his shoulder as he strapped the woman into the wheel chair.

"Camping," Charlie answered. "I found these two along the way, a story in itself."

"You don't say. Well, I got time," said Bobby nodding at Charlie's pistol. "Expecting trouble?"

Charlie glanced at Flo, smiled and motioned Bobby to walk down the shore.

"Let's step over here just a minute?" Charlie said, "and why don't you guys keep Miss Flo company."

Bobby placed the staff on his shoulder and walked with Charlie a short distance with Tommy following. I didn't want to stay either, knowing it would have been rude to just leave the "special ed" lady like she wasn't a person. I stood there, very still, because it was the right thing to do. I also managed to avoid looking directly at her and concentrated on the men. Which is why I nearly jumped out of my skin when she spoke.

"JAAA k,k,k, EEEE," she howled.

Looking around, I found her staring at me, with large brown eyes. A strand of auburn hair was draped across a lopsided grin on her otherwise pretty face. Gracelessly, she brushed the hair back and clapped her hands as if controlled by a puppeteer.

"JAAkkEE, AAre yOOu AAfrAAdd OOf mEE?"

"Of course not," I lied, "why would I be?"

She raised an eyebrow and cocked her head until it was almost sideways.

"MOOst pEEople AAre...wHEN thAAA sEEE me AAAre AAAfrAAid. BU-HUT, ThAAAt's OOO-kay, I,I,I wOOuld bEE scAAAAred of mmmEEE tOOO."

"I'm not afraid," I said crossing my arms. "What's to be scared of?"

"NOOOhing," she answered, rolling her head. "SOOO, wOOuld yOOu dOOO mEE Ah fAAAvor?"

"Sure," I replied thinking it depended on the favor. "Anything!"

"GOOOO tOOO ththth EYE chEEEsss AAAnd BR-Hing mEEE thUUU big sIIIIp bOOttle insIIIde. It hAAAs BIIIll-EEE wrHOAT AHN the sIIIIde."

Happy to put distance between us, I found the ice chest on the rickshaw strapped neatly with other equipment on the back. The ice chest was filled with chipped ice, cans and plastic wrapped bundles. In a corner was a big plastic bottle with a flexible plastic straw and red tip cover and "Flo" written on it in block letters. I brought the bottle to her and put in the cup holder extension of her wheel chair. Bottle in front of her, I removed the straw's cover. Standing back, I thought how she reminded me of a goose trying to grab the straw in her teeth.

"Oh, OOOhhh," she purred. "ThA-A-A-it is gOOd."

"What is it?" I asked, curious, but cautious.

"CIN-ahh-MON EYEsss TEEE," she said. "WAAnt tOOO tr-AYE it-t-t?"

I shook my head, my refusal not impolite but preventative and imagined I'd be in a wheelchair if I stood too close. Heaven knew what direct contact with her spit would do to a body. In response, she pointed a wavering finger at the rickshaw.

"NO, NO-thang cAAAtching, thEEEre Rrrr sOOme cUUps in AHH bO-hox b-b-b-hIIInd thu-thu-thu EYE chEEEs-s-s,"

She took another sip of her drink, looking superior like she knew something funny I didn't.

"If YOOOu're frAAid gEEEt anOOOOther cUUUp-p-p of EYEs-s-s and sOOdA-a-a."

I returned to the rickshaw, pulled the first soda visible from the chest and filled a spare cup with ice. Angry, I was determined to show I wasn't afraid. Back at the wheelchair, I shoved my cup toward her. With a maniac's grin, she twirled her fingers above her sip-cup and I unscrewed the lid. Curiously, my ears had become accustomed to her vowel stretching.

"I make this blend myself and people tell me it's very good," Flo said. "But if you aren't used to it, a little can go a long way."

I'd seen kids in school like Flo. Teachers and student assistants praised them for hanging up their coats, when they could or drawing pictures that I had no idea of what they were supposed to be. So I was prepared that whatever this woman concocted might have a taste equivalent to a crayon slashed messes, but I wasn't backing down. Pouring two finger's worth into my cup, I replaced and repositioned the sip-cup and straw in front of Flo.

"Skoal," she toasted, "and cheers."

Taking a breath, I tipped my cup so the liquid could roll past my tongue. Only the stuff in the cup had a mind of its own and I swallowed, took another swallow, and another. Flo's Cinnamon tea was, well, good. It was better than good, reminding me of cinnamon toast on cold mornings combined with Ana's garden in full spring bloom.

"This is tea?" I huffed, wanting more. "Is that all?"

"Cinnamon iced tea," she corrected. "Different teas blended with spices I mix myself."

Smiling lopsidedly, she took a long pull. I considered ignoring what my taste buds were telling me and my *Orion* started to itch.

"It's like nothing I've ever tasted," I said up ending my cup before turning to her. "You mixed the teas and spices."

"Me and Bobby," she chortled. "I know what and how much and Bobby puts it in the pot."

I looked at Flo for the first time. Her kind had always been "them" to me. She sipped her cup and looked toward the river.

"Aren't they beautiful?" She said surprising me.

"Who?" I asked in alarm looking around. "What?"

Her marionette's arm waved toward the river.

"They're doing ballet."

"Those are alligator gar," I said in my tone for preschoolers. "They have big scales and rows and rows of sharp teeth that will tear you to pieces. They're ugly and eat garbage."

Flo lifted an eyebrow and shook her head. "They're doing what they were created to do, they also do it very gracefully," Flo said. "They are not ugly to other gar. Have you ever eaten garbage?"

"No," I squealed. "Why would I?"

"Don't knock it till you've tried it," she said bobbing the straw. "From their point of view, you're nasty for eating cheeseburgers and pizza with your little bitty flat teeth. But could you give a beautiful show like that?"

"I bet you wouldn't say that if you were in the water with them," I said. My cheeks burned as I realized I had challenged someone who obviously couldn't swim.

"I get in the water with them, and will again," she said. "We watch them until they finish feeding, then Bobby undresses me and carries me into the water. We've gotten to know them, so they swim around us or away. One might let me touch it, if I'm lucky."

I wondered if Flo had the same girl parts I did, unsure as to which question I wanted answered most.

"You get in there naked?" I hissed. "What if someone sees you? What would people will say?"

Flo's head bobble liked a doll's as she laughed. "I have nothing to worry about," she said, "I'm double safe."

"How?" I demanded.

"Most people don't want to think about what I look like without clothes."

"You said double safe," I corrected.

"I don't give a gar's ass about anybody's opinion of me," Flo said. "The water on my bare skin feels so wonderful, that's nobody's business but mine."

"I was naked this morning," I blurted without knowing why. "I swam the same yesterday and a butterfly landed on me. I dove to the bottom of this creek where it was so dark, like being at the bottom of the ocean."

"How wonderful," she said spitting her last syllable. "I would do that all day if I could. You're so lucky."

I nodded and remembered the previous night and Charlie's gun. "There's something else," I said.

"Did he touch you in the wrong places," she demanded sternly as a normal, adult.

"No," I shook my head, considering the idea silly compared to what almost happened. I told her about the previous two days and raised my shirt to show my mosquito bites. When I showed her my left wrist, Flo placed steady fingertips on my *Orion* and her smile was large while her eyes shone.

I recounted about Macho Mike, the Nazi meth lab, booby traps and sinking their boat with a rattlesnake. I didn't tell her about the night before or how close I knew he came to almost shooting Macho Mike and us. Flo laughed, beating her wheel chair arms with spindly fists. Bobby perked like a hunting dog

"What's going on over there?" Bobby called.

"Shut up old man," Flo howled. "This is girl talk."

The big man had the potential of a pitbull dog poised to attack. Yet Flo's rebuke was like a slap with a magazine and he turned back to Charlie.

"What else?" Flo asked.

"What do you mean what else," I replied nervously. "I've told you everything."

"Except," she said holding a wobbly finger to her head.

In panic, I searched and spoke of my fear of the reaction when I got home. What would people say when they heard I ran around naked and ate crawfish with drug makers in the area. They already had plenty to laugh at me. This would be something else. Flo snorted and flopped back hard against her chair before spreading her arms regally.

"If they don't ask," she said, "don't tell."

If my friends didn't have the good sense to come on this trip, she explained, then why share my wealth of experiences. Tell only what I wanted them to know, she added, and nothing else. It wasn't like they had some kind of right to know.

"Would you tell them what you had for breakfast?" Flo said. "Would you tell them you washed your feet and face with the same soap or what you did in the toilet?"

"Of course not," I replied. "That's yucky."

"Exactly, " Flo said.

She couldn't offer more advice before the men returned with Bobby staring intently up river. Flo scolded him for being impolite and not offering us soda and chips before we left. The conversation was about trivial things and when we finished our sodas we got into the canoe. I hugged Flo's neck while she pat-patted me with her doll hands, happily chortling indiscernible syllables. Tommy took that opportunity to sit in the bow. After shaking hands from his seat in the stern, Charlie thanked Bobby as he effortlessly pushed us toward the main stream.

The gar surfaced and gave way to our passing.

CHAPTER 27

Tommy swished water and called it paddling. I stretched out on the gear box using one of the soft bags for a pillow. I propped a T-shirt over my head with a little stick I'd found ashore. I contemplated the danger only a few inches beyond my shoes.

From the corner of my eye I watched Tommy move the paddle with constant banging as his grip slipped the shaft. With each stab, the blade angled at the completion of each stroke rendering it ineffective. Charlie didn't try to instruct him and thanks to Flo's iced tea I managed to push my problems to the back of my mind and fall a sleep despite the racket.

I didn't want to leave this comfy zone even after I felt my foot shaken. Fearing Macho Mike's return, I jolted up as Charlie turned the canoe toward a long dock that extended into the river like a giant toe. Signs on both sides of the dock and beside a shaded picnic table declared the same message.

Tate Landing.
For guests only.
No Trespassing.
Violators prosecuted.
This means you!

Charlie steered past the dock to the shore. "Are we supposed to be here?" I asked.

"Oh yeah," Charlie said. "It has the closest public telephone for miles."

"But, it says for guests only," I argued. "No trespassing."

"We're emergency guests," Charlie laughed. "Emergency takes precedence over paying."

With a stroke of his paddle he guided the canoe broadside to the shore and jumped out.

"You sure they won't mind," Tommy asked "we won't get in trouble."

"Trouble!" Charlie chuckled helping me ashore. "That's been one of my problems. I've avoided that very necessary life mineral when I should have ignored the no trespassing signs."

Charlie pulled the canoe over a path that paralleled the river, up the shore and into a copse of cottonwood trees. Tommy and I walked to the picnic table and noticed a broad and well maintained trail, bordered with railroad ties and carpeted with wood, winding up adjacent hill.

"The natives need to know we come in peace," Charlie called lifting the shoulder strap of the holster over his head. He also unbuckled the knife belt adding, "They don't need to see these."

Charlie pulled off the knife scabbard and laid it to one side as he wrapped the shoulder strap around the holster. He disappeared into the trees shortly before we heard the familiar sound of the gearbox lid being raised. After we heard the solid snap of a padlock, Charlie stepped out smoothing his shirt.

He mounted the trail, stepping on the railroad ties placed to make steps, taking two at a time. Tommy and I had to stop to rest more times than we should. Charlie didn't seem to mind and offered a hand to swing us to the next step.

"We are climbing Jacob's ladder. We are climbing Jacob's ladder."

"What are you singing?" Asked Tommy.

"A hymn we sang when I was a kid at a camp like this," Charlie said. "We sang it after we'd get through swimming and headed back to our cabin. I always found it made chores like climbing or long walks easier."

Charlie sang the first stanza and Tommy and I sang the chorus and without stops we ascended the hill and walked into a small clearing. There was another set of stairs ascending to another level where a building top was visible. We stopped one last time and I caught my breath, taking in the view of the river we'd just paddled. Taking a deep breath, I mounted the steps two at a time the way Charlie had.

At the top of the stairs was a huge cedar tree offering shade to a building with a faded sign attached to its side door declaring "Office & Recreation Hall." A concrete walk extended from the door to a tin roofed pavilion with picnic tables. Adjacent to the tables was another tin shelter with a soda, a snack machine and pay telephone. Beyond the building was a horizontal gravel road, whose border separated the building from a big field containing a swimming pool surrounded by a chain-link fence. To the right of the pool was a big playing field and covered stage. The field to the pool's left included a sand pit for volleyball. Beyond the swimming pool were dozens of campers, recreational vehicles and tents arranged in haphazard rows. Men and women moved around the various shelters or sat on lawn chairs while kids of all ages played nearby.

A woman in a shapeless sundress had her back to us as she swept the concrete walkway. She was humming to herself as we approached, intent on her work, and unaware of us until Charlie cleared his throat. With a yelp, she whirled to face us, the broom held protectively at her front. I smiled, knowing how she felt.

"I'm sorry I startled you," Charlie apologized. "But I need to use your telephone, please?"

The woman stared owl eyed and stumbled stepping off the sidewalk. "Where'd you come from?" She demanded. "Who are you?"

"We just walked up from the river," replied Charlie, ignoring her tone. "These are the lost children from Bandy's Camp. I'm sure you've heard radio reports about them being missing from up river."

"You aren't a guest!" she accused, drawing herself up to her full height. "You aren't supposed to be here."

"Their parents will want to know where they are and search parties must be out," Charlie replied. "So we need to use your telephone."

"I don't know anything about lost kids and I don't want too," the woman snapped. "These facilities are for guests only, you can use the phone at Black Horse Bridge."

"That's more than 20 miles down river," Charlie said. "Their parents need to know where they are."

"Another reason for you to quit wasting my time and yours and get started for Black Horse." she said. "These facilities are for guests only and if you don't leave now, I'll call my husband."

She hadn't finished her threat before Charlie stepped toward the covered area. The door of the office banged and she disappeared. "Ronnie, Ronnie," she screeched from inside. "Ronnie come quick!"

Charlie moved to the other side of the covered picnic tables and picked up the telephone receiver. He had punched two digits when a stocky man in a faded golf shirt and Bermuda shorts banged the office door open.

"Hey, hey you!" Barked the man we assumed was Ron pointing a finger at Charlie. "What do you think you're doing?"

"I'm calling the county sheriff's office about the two children lost from Bandy's Camp."

"No you aren't!" said Ron, his head swinging in long arcs. "This lady told you to get."

At the nearby pool, several people stopped to look our way.

"Martha," said Ron from the side of his mouth, "didn't you tell this joker these facilities are for guests only, right?"

"I certainly did," said Martha, nodding with a now-you're-going-to-get-it-expression, holding her broom like a baseball bat.

"Then in case it isn't crystal clear, partner, these facilities are off limits to you, that includes the telephone you've got your greasy paw on."

"But these children...." Charlie began politely.

"We ain't heard about any dammed kids," Ron spat. "But we know what a smart-ass is. So hustle yourself and those brats off this property like it was your last day on earth, which it just might be."

Sighing, Charlie replaced the phone receiver on the hook and my heart nose-dived to my stomach. Ron crossed his arms a sneer creasing his chunky face. Behind stood a smug Martha holding her broom with an outstretched hand to one side. Charlie stepped toward them and dropped his Stetson and reading glasses on the nearest table. He stopped nearly toe-to-toe looking down at the stocky little man and Ron's superior expression shriveled. Charlie addressed him in that familiar ground glass on hot asphalt voice.

"Other than that, how's it going?"

All color left Ron's face and a twitch danced on the lower ridge of his left cheek. Slowly, he unfolded his arms and Martha's owl expression returned as she hugged the broom to her small bosom.

"I, I, I mean what I say," stammered Ron, turning from Charlie's gaze, the twitch moving faster as he all but ran through the office door. I didn't realize I was holding my breath until the office door slammed. Martha stood quaking as all eyes turned to her.

"How much does tent camping cost?" Charlie asked with a smile. "For one night?"

"We're full up, no room," she stammered adding. "There's no place to camp."

"What about there?" said Charlie pointing at one of the nearby picnic tables. "Nobody has that spot!"

"You can't camp there," she squeaked and gulped, "that's the snack area, it's not for camping."

"Look, Martha," Charlie chuckled, "after I call the sheriff, it'll be thirty minutes to an hour before they get here. Now we're staying, but you can grab a full day's tent fee for no more an hour's use of those picnic tables. What do you say?"

Martha stared at Charlie dubiously, her hands gripping the broom handle.

"I don't even mind sharing," Charlie added, "it will fine by me if somebody wants to sit down right there for a picnic. Deal?"

Loosening the grip on her broom, Martha's face relaxed.

"It's $6 to camp," she quoted, "and $20 for gate fee. We're not responsible for accidents or theft."

I wondered how we rated a gate fee since we hadn't come through a gate, but kept my mouth shut.

"A bargain that couldn't be beat with a stick," said Charlie, reaching into his shorts' pocket and Martha stiffened, until he brought out a money clip. "Twenty-six dollars, that's $20, $5 and $1," he said peeling off the bills, popping each between his thumb and forefinger prompting Martha to flinch three times.

"I'll need a receipt," Charlie said.

"Of course," she said smiling weakly. "I'll be right back."

"We'll be here!"

Chapter 28

Returning to the telephone, Charlie put on his reading glasses as he punched in a number. He turned and we couldn't see his face. He made verbal introduction punctuated with "uh-huhs," "yups," "yeahs," "no, sirs" and "that's right."

We sat drumming our heels on the picnic table seat when Martha returned with a pink receipt. Charlie pointed to me. She dropped the paper and left like I had cooties, but not before Charlie called "Thank you", his hand over the mouth piece, before the door slammed.

"All right then," said Charlie returning to the receiver, "I'll be looking for you anytime."

He took a seat at the picnic table and put his hat on before pulling out a small notebook and pen from his breast pocket.

"Is Ana coming?" Asked Tommy as I handed Charlie the receipt.

"Don't know," Charlie replied. "I was told that sheriff's deputies are on their way, but until then, it's hurry up and wait!"

Charlie offered no other time line and the magnitude of "how long" pressed us.

"Could we have a snack?" Tommy asked.

"Tell you what," Charlie said, "take a walk and get to know the neighbors. Check back with me in a little bit."

My opinion of Tarzan Charlie soured considering he could afford $26 to camp on a picnic table for an hour, but wouldn't spare change for a soda or snack. The situation irked me as we headed for the swimming pool. I noticed a woman and two small children playing in the pool's shallow end. Nearby a blonde girl wearing a tropical print bikini lay next to a brunette girl in a jet black bikini. Both lay on their stomachs on beach towels, their bra straps bunched around the sides of their ample chests. On the other side of the pool sat a portly couple at a table with a metal umbrella, reading books and holding drinks.

No one looked up or greeted us as we hooked our fingers into the chain link fence. A girl swimming in the deep end climbed out on a nearby ladder. Her faded pea green swimsuit hung on her spindly frame like a plastic sack. She approached, using both hands to push water off her suit.

"Hello," she said too formally. "What's your name?"

We returned her greeting and introduced ourselves.

"I am Amy Lynn Sneed, " she said, her name rolling off her tongue like a brand of Italian sports car. I asked her if she'd heard about "the lost children from Bandy's Camp." She shook her head and rung water from the ends of hair and not bothering to close the distance between us and the fence.

"No, I can't say that I have," she added dismissively. "You know you can go swimming only after you've changed into proper swim wear." She turned to go, but looked back, raising her chin as if she'd forgotten something important. "You'll have to have a parent accompany you, otherwise little kids must remain outside the gate."

I didn't miss the emphasis on "little kids."

"That's OK," I said glancing at Tommy. "We've got our suits with us."

For once, Tommy caught my joke.

"Yes, matching outfits," he said and snorted, "and only one way to tell them apart."

"Yeah," I snickered. "One little thing!"

Tommy elbowed me and Amy's mouth puckered as she puffed up. "You kids need to get your daddy before you can come in here," she said, adding acidly, "before you get hurt!"

"Why? Tommy demanded. "My daddy isn't here."

"Or mine," I added.

Smirking, Amy titled her head and pointed at the office. "Who's that?" she said and we turned to see Charlie hunched over his notebook. "Your uncle?"

"Oh him," said Tommy proudly, "That's Tarzan Charlie!"

"Who?" Amy hooted with disbelief. "He's is your uncle, right?"

"No, we're not related," Tommy said. "He's Tarzan Charlie. He found us and took care of us!

"Found you?" Amy repeated.

"He catches giant rattlesnakes," Tommy said proudly. "He lives on crawdads, blackberries, wild garlic and onions. He fights zombies with no hands."

What would you think if you knew he nearly shot us last night? I wanted to ask. And nearly shot three men this morning too. And Amy, you just missed him nearly ripping Ron's arms out, I thought with great satisfaction, delighted to think of the superior Amy Lynn Sneed reaction, if she knew even half of what I did.

"Yes," I added. "We were lost and he found us upriver, doctored and helped us find food in the woods. He tossed a giant rattlesnake into a canoe full of bad men."

The two sunbathing girls turned their heads in unison and looked in our direction. The mother of the two small children looked up with interest.

"So, why do you call him Tarzan Charlie?" Amy asked. "Is he an actor or a wrestler?"

The teenage girls fastened each other's bikini tops and got to their feet. Meanwhile, the older couple put down their books and inclined their heads in our direction.

"Out there, he's more than the Tarzan in the movies," said Tommy pointing toward the river. "The only thing he doesn't do is swing through the trees on vines."

That would have been kind of hard since the trees had no vines, I thought. Nor did this Tarzan get snake bit, not that he hadn't tried. He might shoot people. There was certainly plenty of opportunity. Still, I told what I had told Flo, leaving out certain details, so that by the time we'd recalled the spiked logs the girls, the mom and the couple were standing on either side of Amy.

"I don't believe any of this," Amy said with a sniff, "you're making stuff up."

" What about this?" Tommy asked, holding up a shiny square object.

"What's that supposed to be?" Amy demanded

I stared with the others at what was in Tommy's hand, wondering how he'd gotten it.

"This is the bullet magazine from the zombie Macho Mike's gun, a very bad man," Tommy said. "He tried to cut Charlie with a bolo knife and got knocked out instead. Tarzan Charlie took his gun and dissolved it with his hands. This is all that's left.

"No he didn't," said Amy, her insistence without conviction. "You're making all this stuff up, and you aren't supposed to be near this pool unless a responsible adult is with you."

When the others around her ignored Amy, she dove into the pool. I recounted the story of the snake in a canoe, alligator gar and the barrel-chested man pulling his funny little wife on a rickshaw.

"That sounds like the Outlaws," the reading man said. "That Bobby Outlaw is one stout booger! I heard he hefted a tombstone from the ground that would have ruptured a John Deere tractor. Too bad his woman is the rubber band lady, but they are compatible considering they're definitely freaks."

"I remember him," the reading lady said. "He's built like a brick outhouse and she's afflicted?"

He is, she is and isn't, I thought wondering what these people would think of Flo's cinnamon flavored iced tea and her recreational habits with alligator gar. The expression on the reading lady's face said more than I could.

"That's them," the reading man said. "I heard he takes her for rides all around the country. Nobody has any idea where they go or what they do, but then nobody really cares."

The reading man looked quickly at us and I wanted to tell them about the Outlaws swimming naked with alligator gar.

"It sounds sweet," the reading woman said, "the ladies at the beauty parlor say he takes real good care of her. He must do a good job. She's always smiling."

"Which don't mean anything," the reading man snapped. "She'd grin ear to ear if she was sitting neck deep in snow during a hurricane. Her wires are crossed, nothing goes to her top floor. Her lights might be on, but nobody's home and her mail has been forwarded to another address."

It only goes to show, how little you know I wanted to say.

"She's got one male, special delivery," the reading lady said with a laugh. "Certainly, the way she looks at him isn't goofy and I'd bet the farm he'd attack Tokyo and New York on the same day for her."

The mom also agreed laughing and went back to her kids.

"Ewww," said the reading man, turning to go. "Don't even go there."

The reading lady followed and bikini girls asked more questions. Tommy and I raised our shirts to show our mosquito bites.

"Uh," the blonde girl said," why was Tarzan Charlie giving Turtle Ron a hard time?"

"Who?" We chorused.

The brunette sputtered and both girls broke into giggles.

"He's the, you know, the creepy camp manager," the blonde said, "We saw him and that skinny wife of his, you know, talking to you. They, you know, bought this place last year and now they run it, you know, and act like everybody should be grateful for fire ants and stopped up toilets."

"Why do you call him Turtle Ron?" Tommy asked. "Has he got a pet turtle?"

"What do you think Brandi?" the blond asked the brunette. "Should I tell them?"

"Gloria!" snorted Brandi rolling her eyes. "What'll it hurt? You know!"

"Oh, all right," said Gloria indignantly. "He buys turtles from local goobers and, you know, sells them to China. He also, like you know, sells these paper plans on how to build traps and sells the stuff to catch turtles. He's got like a million turtles, you know, somewhere around here, only, like you know, nobody makes any money."

"Except maybe him," Brandi finished. "He also thinks he's a stud muffin."

"Ewww!" Gloria squealed. "Don't go there!"

We told them how Turtle Ron tried to make Charlie leave. That he paid to use the concession stand paying tent and gate fee, even though we didn't come through the gate, and we were, you know, waiting for the sheriff.

"No way!" Brandi exclaimed. "Like, you know, Ron looked like he was having a cow when Tarzan Charlie got in his face."

"Cool name, by the way," Gloria squealed. "I've got to tell my mom about this." The girls left us and gathered their stuff into a bag before hurrying toward the row of recreational vehicles and trailers.

"What's a stud muffin?"asked Tommy watching them go.

"I don't know, just, you know, let's not go there. OK?"

We walked around the field, crossed the far road walking past the travel homes. Along the way, we were greeted politely, we offered the same, even to those that ignored us. At the farthest end of the row of trailers we saw a playground and moved in that direction walking in the center of the road adjacent to the RV's and trailers parked nose out at the roadside. We were about to pass a large RV, but a woman about Ana's age, stepped out of its side door. She wore a tie-dyed T-shirt and sat down under an awning carrying a large glass. On the nearby table was a fat bellied pitcher brimming with crushed ice and cherry tinted sliced limes. The sight of the drink had my tongue instantly feeling dry, not that it needed much help. The woman took off her sunglasses and motioned for us to come closer.

"Would you like something to drink?" she called. "Limeade?"

We didn't need a second invitation as we moved into the shade to her table. She filled two green plastic cups with ice and topped off each from the pitcher and a slice of lime. We drained the cups and she refilled our glasses a second time. By our third glass, she called toward the trailer.

"Brandi, bring some of those tamales."

The trailer door flew open and Brandi, the brunette from the pool stepped out. She also wore a tie-dyed T-shirt similar to the older woman's and carried a large tray. Blonde Gloria's voice squealed beyond a closed door.

"Help yourselves!" said the woman who had to be Brandi's mom.

Brandi set the platter on the table and took a chair behind her mom and brushed her long hair.

Neither of us had ever eaten tamales. So Tommy's embarrassed first attempts included gnawing the corn husk. Brandi giggled and her mom shushed her as she demonstrated by unrolling a tamale and using the husk like a napkin holder. She took a bite off the end, we followed her example moaning with delight at the taste.

"Brandi says you were lost on the river," Brandi's mom said. "She says a Tarzan Charlie found you."

We nodded, and since Tommy's mouth was full of tamale, I retold most of what happened to us. Again, leaving out certain details.

"Whoa," said a voice behind us and whistling," this Tarzan Charlie sounds mucho bad if he clocked a Navy SEAL."

Looking around I saw that a crowd of about ten people had quietly gathered behind us. A man carrying a plastic drink cup moved to stand beside Brandi's mom. The others crowded closer until they stood shoulder to shoulder between the two RVs. The cup man lifted his drink to the crowd and they became quiet.

"I once heard about a Marine messing with a Navy SEAL," he began. "The Marine was some kind of martial arts master, always pushing the SEAL for a fight. The SEAL tried to avoid him, but the jarhead kept pushing until one day the SEAL slapped the jarhead along his ribs."

For emphasis, the man smacked a broad palm over his ample belly multiple times, producing a firecracker staccato.

"Broke all the Marine's ribs, laid him out flat," the man said morosely. "After that, nobody bothered the SEAL. If Tarzan Charlie took out a Navy SEAL, he isn't just good, he's baaadddd."

Cup can raised his drink again, this time in a toast, turned to us and took a drink.

"Watch that talk about Marines," said a man with an iron gray ponytail. "My son is a Marine."

"Tell him to stay away from Navy SEALS," cup man said between drinks. "And Tarzan Charlie."

Good natured laughter rippled around before a voice with a thick country twang pealed, "That's a bald assed, filthy lie! That's a dirty lie!"

"What?" asked cup man, laughing. "That a sailor can whip a Marine?"

"Arlie," pony tail added also laughing, "these aren't lies, just stories."

The crowd parted and the butter bean colored man we'd seen hit Lonnie stepped forward. With his right hand, missing its thumb, he combed strands of nearly translucent hair from eyes bulging from the sockets of his head. He reminded me of a large horned toad I'd seen get angry and spew blood from its eyes. However, the toad didn't have a faded tattoo of a tear below its left eye.

With all eyes on him, he pulled himself up to his full height as he curled his thick lips back to reveal tobacco-stained-teeth. "I'm not talking about that silly crap," Arlie said. "There's absolutely no way anybody could get the best of Mike DeGrief, not in fair fight anyway."

"You mean Macho Mike. That's what the babes call him" said cup man and the crowd laughed. "Head of Ajax River Bank Security and Loan. Whatever that is!"

"He's more man than you'll ever be Phil," said Arlie stepping toward cup man. "I've worked and drank a lot of beer with that boy. I seen him fight men twice as big as you and lay 'em out like road kill. Hell, he tackled three at once and came out on top."

"I once saw Mikey punch a guy in a parking lot" ponytail said. "He was heavier than Mike by 190 pounds, and just as sloshed. My granddaughter could have knocked that ape down with a fart. Is that the fight you're talking about Arlie?"

"You don't know what you're talking about, Bill," Arlie sneered. "I won't let a buddy like Mike be slandered."

"Slandered?" Phil said. "Do you even know what that term means?"

"I don't know them big words," Arlie spat. "But I know this Tarzan Charlie sounds like a TV kiddy show. If he managed to punch Mike, it was a fluke. More than likely, he snuck up behind poor Mike, who was minding his own business fishing, or something, and ambushed him."

The crowd rumbled and several people left. I listened in disbelief finding myself starting to believe some of these accusations. At least until I realized that, while Charlie may have done some actual crimes, they were nothing close to what this butter bean colored man was telling.

"You weren't there," I said aloud surprising myself. "Macho Mike knocked himself out trying to cut Charlie."

All eyes turned to me. "Charlie helped him," I said, "even if he is a zombie drug dealer."

Arlie's head jerked and turned his bulging eyes at me, pointing the stumpy forefinger of his thumb-less hand. "Is that so?" he drawled. "Well, I'd bet a dime to a B-B Mike caught little missy and that boy doing nasty with this Tarzan Charlie. Fess up missy, you play doctor with nice, old Uncle Charlie?"

Talking to a butterfly sitting on my naked chest flashed in my mind and my cheeks flushed. Had someone been hiding on the opposite bank watching me? But, naked or not, I hadn't done anything wrong. "He's not my uncle," I said, surprising myself with the control. "And how would you know? You weren't there!"

"Don't get smart, missy," Arlie growled. "Mike risked his life to defend his country with honor and distinction."

That's not what that paper in his wallet had written on it, I thought. But before I could reply, Arlie spun and faced the crowd, his stubby finger raised to the sky.

"No matter how long a spoon you use, if you stir shit, you'll get some on you," Arlie said. "Was I the only one who didn't see how that man roughed up poor Mister Ron? "Turning toward me, he dropped to one knee and in a gentle tone said. "I don't know you child, but we won't let him hurt you anymore. Come on missy, tell the truth of what happened out there."

"What about the log trap with the spikes?" I said. "And the Nazi lab?"

Arlie rose to his feet like I had slapped him and stepped back. Feet apart and hands on his sides, he looked like a boy on a playground ready to take on all comers. "You shouldn't lie, missy," Arlie said. "I won't have my friend Mike's reputation smeared."

Friend sounded like a foreign word as Arlie stepped menacingly toward me. I didn't move back, but was ready to move right or left.

"Arlie that's enough," said Phil, stepping in front of me. "Don't start something you can't finish."

Howling, Arlie rushed at Phil and said. "Never tell me what to do, Phil." Before he touched Phil, he jumped back, scanning the rest of the crowd. "That goes for the rest of you," Arlie yelled, "Nobody tells me what to do, not now or ever, but if you're tired of living, go ahead."

No one accepted the challenge and the crowd drew back. With a malicious sneer creasing his jaundiced face, Arlie stepped toward me, only to jump back with an expression of stark terror. Brandi's mother bore down on him hefting the shaft of a long handled spade like an executioner's axe. She pressed the distance and Arlie stepped back even farther.

"I'll chop you into chicken feed if you aren't off my lot immediately," she shrieked. "You may get away with smacking your kid, but I won't allow that here."

Arlie's back-pedaled from the angry woman as people behind him got out of his path. With his thumb-less hand out for balance, his left dug into his shorts' pocket.

"Take that hand out of your pocket, or I'll lop off your other thumb... at the shoulder," Mrs. Gomillion said. "Now get!"

Immediately Arlie's empty hand appeared from his pocket adding to his balance as much to his submission. He shifted his weight, as if to charge, checking himself when the spade whistled past his nose. With her shovel raised like a guillotine, Brandi's mom forged toward her target.

"Keep moving and stay away from these children you twisted bastard," she said.

"Mrs. Gomillion," Arlie begged. "Be careful, look out now."

"I'm looking," Mrs. Gomillion answered, "and I won't put up with it."

Never taking his eyes off the raised shovel, Arlie continued back-pedaling until he stumbled into the road. Laughter broke the tension and the crowd stood together as Arlie got to his feet and stabbed his thumb-less hand at us.

"I won't forget this," he shouted. "You can be sure of that." Smoothing his hair with his thumbed hand, he moved down the road in the direction we'd come.

When he'd gone the crowd, all men, talked and laughed at once. "What are you laughing at?" Mrs. Gomillion snapped. "You would have let that maggot hurt this child."

"No we wouldn't," a voice in the back said without conviction.

Mrs. Gomillion walked to where we stood and put a hand on my shoulder. "That mangy outfit has been getting away with murder," she said, "and when someone stands up to him, like this little girl, you look the other way."

"We're not the police," a man said. "And I'm not a narc."

"Try being a man," Mrs. Gomillion snapped. "I've been bringing my kids here since they were little, and this is the first time I've wanted to leave. We probably won't be back."

"Nobody wants trouble," Phil whined. "Besides, Arlie is essentially harmless."

"Harmless my ass! Just like a drop of strychnine," Mrs. Gomillion snorted. "The harm is ignoring what's been going on here too long. Even Turtle Ron looks the other way because Arlie does odd jobs and keeps the other hard cases away. "

Again there was more muttering among the men with several of them looking as if they wanted to say something, but dropping their eyes.

"So what if he sells a little dope, has wild parties and tries to molest any single girl or married woman he wants?" she said. "If somebody complains, he chases them off. We don't listen and look the other way. After all he isn't bothering us. But let a child offer a story that isn't right with his twisted idea of life and he's ready to pull a knife. That's where I draw the line and so should you."

The muttering grew louder until Mrs. Gomillion ordered them to clear out. They shuffled away talking among themselves. Hearing a voice behind me, I looked around and saw Brandi and Gloria in the door of the RV. Gloria gripped an iron skillet and Brandi held her brush defensively. Mrs. Gomillion sat down breathing hard and reached for her glass.

"Momma," Brandi said. "You were, you know, awesome."

"Brandi sweetie, you really need to quit saying 'you know,' so much," Mrs. Gomillion said. "That bastard will be back tonight to slash our tires. So, go find your daddy and tell him we're leaving."

Turning to us she added, "It would also be a good idea if you went back to Tarzan Charlie."

We finished our limeade and thanked Mrs. Gomillion for her hospitality. Only, we didn't go back to Charlie.

Chapter 29

It made the list of best playgrounds in the world, if I were the one making the list. Four sets of tether ball poles stood like sentinels before us, well away from the swing set for six. The swings were attached to a crossbar so high we had to tilt our heads to see the top. Broad rubbers straps composed the seats attached with long chains that guaranteed marvelous trips into the stratosphere.

Beyond the swings were six teeter-totters, a swirl-a-slide and, at the far end, a covered sand box with red dirt piled taller than I was. Within running distance of the sand box were two separate tree houses set atop telephone poles and connected by a suspended wooden walkway. Each tree house was the size of a small bus, accessible by wooden stair on the outer side. Balconies extended around the cabins and a fireman's pole adjacent to the wood walkway offered an emergency exit.

This was a facility that should have been brimming with children. We'd seen others of all ages around camp, but we were the only kids as far as I could see.

"Where is everybody? Tommy asked.

"Beats me," I said.

We threw ourselves into the rubber seats of the swings holding our arms out like free-fall parachutists. At the teeter-totters, we straddled the center of separate boards, facing one another trying to achieve synchronized movement between the two. We also straddled separate ends bouncing up and down. Tommy raced for the slide before launching into the big mound of dirt. I was content to watch and sit while I dangled my feet over the side of the sandbox digging holes with the toe of my sneaker. Tommy climbed to the top of the mound and rolled to its base.

"I can't believe no one is here playing," he said. "This place is going to waste."

"More for us," I laughed.

We turned at the noise from the tree houses and saw a boy emerge from the left cabin holding a thick magazine open with his finger. Another boy came out of the same cabin and a third emerged from the opposite cabin. They stared at us before nosily moving to the center of the bridge.

We stared back without saying a word, the only discernible sound gum smacking by the boy wearing a baseball cap turned at angle on the side of his head. The boy in the familiar, once white T-shirt with the dried paint leopard spots caught my full attention. The same shirt was dirtier than it had been two days earlier, his shorts, crusted with dried food. His expression was disbelief as his eyes darted left and right. Their momentum seemed to draw his head to look down. When he looked up, his face had the cruel expression I'd seen at the dodge ball wall.

"Look at what the kitty cat done drug out the litter box," Lonnie drawled. "Thank you, Jesus."

Tommy came out of the sandbox and I swung my legs around, picking up two handfuls of dirt as I stood up.

"Well beat the drums and sound the brass," Tommy called. "What's going on, horse's ass?"

Lonnie spat with a jerk of his head and pushed a lock of greasy hair out of his eyes. From behind his ear he pulled a filtered cigarette placing the tip in his mouth, letting it dangle as he spoke.

"I heard you two drowned, but you can't even do that right," he said. "So, looks like I get to finish the job."

Tommy leaned a hand against one of poles in the sandbox. "Does that mean we'll see more French foot fighting?" Tommy asked. "Why don't you just do a swan dive from there and save time."

Lonnie pulled a lighter from his back pocket, flipped it open with his thumb and lit the cigarette. Blowing exaggerated smoke puffs, he snapped the lighter shut, shoving it into his back pocket.

"Not this time, podner," said Lonnie and spat again. "You won't get off so easy. This is gonna be a good, old fashioned ass-whipping."

"That right, podner," Tommy mocked. "You do know that winning a fight isn't a how many times you trip over your big feet and land on your ass?"

"You didn't beat me," said Lonnie, his voice straining and squeaking. "You ran before I could stomp your head in. Besides, you let a girl tell you what to do and my daddy says no real man would ever do that. "

He took another puff of the cigarette and looked at the other boys for approval.

"That's the same daddy that taught you how to break the ground with your head?" Tommy asked.

"You didn't fight fair," Lonnie said. "You were a coward back there and you're a coward now. You ran away, but nobody hits me like that and gets away with it, nobody."

Tommy covered his mouth with a mock yawn.

"Yeah, yeah," Tommy said, "I'll bet that's what you say to everyone who's cored your apple."

Lonnie snapped his fingers at a skinny boy with a silver necklace and he motioned with his thumb to the boy with the ball cap. Both stared uncomprehending until Lonnie barked "Go" and they made a deliberate racket running to the fireman's poles. On the ground silver necklace pumped his arms across his skinny body and said, "What's up, dog?"

"Hey Falcon," called the boy with the cap, not to be outdone. "Take it easy, there's plenty to go around."

"Andrew Edward," Falcon said, "the only easy day was yesterday."

Andrew Edward fell in beside Falcon punching his fist into his palm with each step. Lonnie hooked his thumbs in his belt loops and swaggered over between the other two.

I gripped my dirt ready for total war, while Tommy, to my irritation, watched the approach with disinterest.

"If you were smart, you'd run," Lonnie said.

"What and spoil the big surprise," Tommy said. "That wouldn't be nice!"

Lonnie yanked his hands from his pockets, glancing to either side and finally at me.

"You're gonna show us how to cry," Lonnie said, "or pee your pants when you're scared."

"Whatever smokes your Sunday shorts," Tommy replied. "Come on over, you'll find out."

Confusion crossed the other boys' faces at Tommy' lack of fear. There was something unnatural about his manner and even I didn't know what he was up to.

I was reminded of Papa's Old Western movies where good guys and bad guys stood in the middle of a street for a showdown. The camera panned for a broad shot, a shot of the gunfighters' eyes moving back and fourth until they pulled their guns. It looked silly to fight like that. Besides, Papa told us that historically, Old West shoot-outs were nothing like these movies. Good guys were as likely to shoot bad guys in the back, when they slept, ate supper, or played cards. Worse, I thought, was how boys talked so much and did so little.

Lonnie stopped two arm lengths from Tommy to wave away imaginary gnats. My cousin hadn't moved from sandbox support pole, until, without warning, he bounced toward Lonnie. The older boy stood his ground and even stepped forward, fists raised. I readied my handful of dirt.

"What's going on here?" Yelled a man's voice. We turned in the direction of the voice and saw Turtle Ron moving toward us. "What's going on?" he repeated. "Speak, somebody!"

"Nuthin," Lonnie muttered. "Nuthin."

"You want to speak up boy," Turtle Ron snapped. "And take the mud out of your mouth."

"Nuthin," repeated Lonnie louder. "And you better leave me alone, or my daddy will have the law on you."

"That's a good idea," Turtle Ron said. "Why don't I go call them now? I'm sure the sheriff's office wants to talk to your daddy."

"We'll sue you for everything you've got," Lonnie quoted. "My daddy has a really good lawyer."

"They're called district attorneys," said Turtle Ron, turning to Andrew Edward. "Now, what's going on here?"

"Nuthin," Andrew Edward said. "It's like he said."

"You're just standing here smoking," Turtle Ron said, "and keeping other kids from using this playground."

"That's a lie," said Lonnie, grinding his foot over the cigarette where he'd dropped it. "Who told you that?"

"We're just playing," Falcon said. "We're playing with these kids," he nodded in our direction, " Weren't we?"

I folded my arms and said nothing.

"Nobody is smoking," Lonnie said. "Why should we? That's against the law."

"Then what's this?" said Turtle Ron and snatched a cigarette from behind Falcon's ear.

"I just found that, dog," Falcon said. "I didn't want no little kids finding it and was on my way to turn it in."

"Pup, you can turn yourself into a tree," Turtle Ron said. "Because you're leaving today. I needed an excuse to throw your parents out and this is it. Now, you be long gone by the time I walk by here again."

"I'll think about it," Lonnie muttered.

Turtle Ron grabbed Lonnie's arm and twisted it behind him. The other boys fell back out of reach. Shaking Lonnie like a rag, Ron crumbled Falcon's cigarette under the boy's nose.

"Then you think real hard, sonny buck," Turtle Bob said. "But if that's too much trouble, I can pop your skull off and scoop out that catfish bait you call brains."

Turtle Ron gave the arm another twist and Lonnie gritted his teeth in pain, but kept his lips pressed together. Forcing Lonnie against one of the poles of the tree house Turtle Ron leaned close to the boy's face.

"Better yet, why don't you be here when I get back?" Turtle Ron said. "Just remember, I've got good lawyers too."

Ron yanked Lonnie away from the pole and shoved him hard letting go of his arm. Lonnie stumbled, unable to keep his balance and fell. He looked up and murder was on his face as he tried to regain his feet with doubled fists. His hands to his sides, Ron's expression was unholy, watching the boy approach until Lonnie dropped his eyes. For the second time I felt sorry for him wishing I could help until Ron turned to us. I readied my dirt.

"You two get back to the ape who brought you," Turtle Ron said. "This resort isn't responsible for accidents."

When Turtle Ron had moved out of earshot, Lonnie turned to Tommy. "This ain't over punk," he hissed and spat. "You'll get what's coming to you. I owe you big, and I always pay my debts."

Tommy closed the gap and stood nose-to-nose to the older boy. "Catfish breath, that's the only thing you've got right all day," Tommy said. "You're right, it's not over and I'm going to finish it by stomping your butt, Tarzan Charlie style."

"What the hell is a Tarzan Charlie?" Demanded Andrew Edward with a snort.

"You don't want to meet him, snot head," Tommy said. "He taught me his secrets of fighting. The same one he used to cold-cock a Navy SEAL named Macho Mike this morning."

The mention of Navy SEAL perked the other boys' interest and got an explosive response from Lonnie. "That's a filthy lie!" Lonnie screamed, spraying spittle. "Nobody ever beat Mike DeGrief in a fight, and anybody that says so is a black-tongued-hell-bound liar who'll answer to me in blood."

The name I'd seen printed on the school identification and the Navy postcard flashed in my head like Claude Rains materializing in "The Invisible Man." There was no mistaking the adoration in Lonnie's voice regarding Macho Mike. Evangelists witnessing for Jesus Christ didn't have half of Lonnie's fervor.

"You're a box of rocks, without the box," Tommy said. "And this wasn't nobody."

"You're still a liar," Lonnie shouted, "and I won't stand for it."

Tommy slapped his sides in imitation of Phil the cup man and the other boys tensed. "There's a man here named Phil, he knows how SEALS fight, you ask him. Charlie studied under masters in Spain and Pill-N-

Beans. We saw it, didn't we Jackie? He didn't even touch M&M when he took him out."

"You're full of crap," Lonnie said. "Nobody can knock out a person without touching them."

"You'll find out," Tommy snarled. "You were about to be my first victim, until Turtle Ron showed up."

"So what's stopping you now?" Andrew Edward demanded.

"Nothing," Tommy said, "but we'll take this party where I won't be interrupted, by anybody."

"Like where?" Falcon said.

"There's a sandbar down the hill and upriver a short way, you can't miss it," Tommy said, "There's a cottonwood tree in the middle, know where that is?"

The other boys exchanged puzzled glances.

"Go down to the dock," said Tommy impatiently. "Walk upstream and around the bend about a city block and you can't miss it. It's a piece of land as wide as a basketball court that juts out into the river."

"It's a date, worm dirt," Lonnie said. "You bring the bacon, I'll bring the pain."

"Come alone, your girlfriends have to stay at the dock until I'm finished," Tommy said. "They'll know where to pick up the pieces."

"We're coming," Falcon insisted. "I want to see how a super fighter moves."

"I don't want any witnesses," Tommy growled. "That way it's his word against mine in court. You'll see the end result, or what's left of him."

"He'll see your brains scattered everywhere," Lonnie sneered. "What court is that, the court for whiny losers?"

"Hold that thought, creep," Tommy said, "Just come!"

"Just you make sure you show up," Lonnie countered. "And, just so you know, I've never lost a fight!"

"Wouldn't miss it, twinkles," Tommy said. "Only speak a little louder so they can hear you in Russia."

I could see Falcon and Andrew Edward were trying not to smile. They were having a good time at Lonnie's expense. Lonnie's eyes seemed like they were about to pop out of his skull when he pointed his finger at me.

"What about her?" Lonnie demanded. "I don't want her stopping me again."

"She'll stay here," Tommy said. "Like I said, no witnesses."

Brushing a wisp of greasy hair, Lonnie pulled out a crumpled cigarette pack and put another cigarette in his mouth. He lit it with his lighter and stood back, having regained some of his control. "How far is it down there?" Lonnie demanded.

"Maybe ten minutes walk," Tommy said. "Which reminds me, where's the side bet?"

Lonnie snapped the lighter shut and drew on the cigarette. "The what?" Lonnie demanded. "What are you talking about, or are you trying to pull something?"

"The side bet," Tommy repeated. "It's what real fighters do to make the fight profitable and inspirational. It's a prize like a scalp or a winner's belt. It proves you won, other than just talk."

Smirking, Lonnie winked at Falcon and Andrew Edward and took out a five-cent piece.

"Here you go," he sneered. "There's about all you're worth."

"We're not betting the cost of your only brain cell or your daddy's paycheck," Tommy said. "I'm talking something like this."

Tommy held up Macho Mike's pistol magazine and Lonnie nearly dropped the nickel. Recognition flashed over his face as he swallowed, coughed and drew himself up.

"I been polishing this bright shiny nickel for a month," Lonnie drawled. "It has great sig-f-inance and worth more than that old clip. So what else you got to bet?"

Lonnie tossed the nickel in the air, grinning menacingly. Only no one laughed, the other boys stared at him.

"Clown boy, that won't buy a ticket to this circus," said Tommy, turning to Andrew Edward. "What do you say, lard butt? Lint-head can't even pay attention. Got anything?"

Lonnie's lips folded into his mouth and his eyes narrowed to slits as he stepped between Tommy and Andrew Edward. "I'm going to tell you something," Lonnie screamed. "Nobody slanders me."

"Next window," Tommy yawned. "No food stamps, glass beads, aluminum cans or out-you-butt talk here. Find a stop-and- rob that'll cash your welfare check."

Falcon pointed at Lonnie 's pocket, he nodded and took out the lighter. "How's this," said Lonnie with a smirk. "Is that a bet, doodle bug-ugly?"

"That's more like it," Tommy said. "Jackie, hold the bet."

"Hold it," cried Lonnie and closed his fist around the lighter. "How come she holds it?"

"She'll be up here after the fight," said Tommy handing me the magazine. "Naturally the first one back will be the winner to collect his prizes."

"I don't know, something ain't right!" He said and nodded at the two boys. " Why can't one of these two hold the bet."

"How long have you known these two?" Tommy demanded. "She's my cousin, you can't get much closer than that, and besides, you said it yourself no real man would let a girl tell him what to do."

The other boys shared a sour look, but before they could protest Lonnie tossed the lighter to me.

"Damn straight," Lonnie said, "it's only a formality because I will win."

"In your dreams, drip slick," Tommy said. "You better pack a lunch, you'll be at it all day."

"I won't need it," Lonnie snapped. "Stomping your butt will be more fun than when the hogs ate my little brother."

Lonnie laughed too loud. Tommy ignored him and turned to Falcon and Andrew Edward. "What about you two, you want in on this action? You want to bet on snot head?"

"We aren't fighting," Andrew Edward said. "Unless you want to take us on after Lonnie gets through with you, or all at one time."

"You want to bet on him or not?" Tommy demanded.

"Lonnie already bet his lighter against your bullet clip," Falcon said. "What else have you got to bet?"

I pulled my rubber pirate's knife from my pocket and held it up.

"That's nothing but a kid's toy," Falcon sneered, "and a cheap one at that."

"It was enough back at Bandy's Camp to fake him and the two other boys chasing us," I said.

Lonnie reaped another harvest of looks ripe with suspicion and doubt. "Take it," Lonnie said. "You know that thingy of mine, that you've been wanting? I'll trade you it for the knife after I win."

There was still skepticism in Falcon's expression, but he dug a hand into his pocket. He held up a flat piece of metal nearly as long as my little finger with a figure glued to the front with an Indian in a headdress playing a horn. I realized it was a money clip like the one Charlie had his money when he paid for our camp spot.

"What about me?" Andrew Edward asked.

He held up a new dollar coin with a picture an Indian woman on one side. It was a little bigger than a quarter and looked gold, but wasn't. No one said anything for a few seconds and Lonnie folded his arms over his chest. Neither Tommy or I had anything else, I thought, but Tommy's eyes grew wide and I dreaded, without knowing why, what he'd offer.

"What about this?" said Tommy, offering the arrow head tied with raw hide that Lonnie had thrown at us on the creek.

"Hey, that's mine," said Lonnie, reaching, "It's not yours to bet."

"You threw it at us and I caught it, "said Tommy, holding the arrow head away. "You couldn't catch us to get it back."

Andrew Edward and Falcon looked at Lonnie, expecting an explanation. Instead, Lonnie pointed to me and Tommy and Andrew Edward dropped their "bets" into my hand.

"Just remember, if you chicken out of this rumble, everybody will know you're a yellow bellied coward," said Lonnie and without another strode toward the RV line.

When they were out of hearing, Tommy's shoulders shook. "Rumble?" Tommy snickered. "What is that?"

"I think I heard that word from one of Papa's old movies," I replied. "It was called Rebel Without a Clue. Rumble is a fight, or something I think, I don't really know."

Still laughing, we started in the direction of the office.

"What were you thinking?" I asked. "I believed you were about to walk up his chest and tap dance on his forehead."

"That was the plan," Tommy said. "Only I saw Turtle Ron coming around the corner."

"So, is there a sandbar down there?" I asked.

"Complete with tree," he confirmed. "I saw it just before we got to the dock and thought it would be a great place to swim. We could tie a rope on the tree and swing out into the water."

"You know he won't come alone," I said. "Those two boys will be there and probably everybody else he can find and their sister."

"I'm counting on that, Tommy said. "Look over there!"

Falcon and Andrew Edward ran along the length of the row of trailers and tents. Before they'd reached the last RV at the end of the line, a couple of kids came out of a tent and headed toward the office. From a nearby RV, three small kids, probably first or second graders, approached us.

"They say you're going to fight Booger Head," a little boy said.

"That's right," Tommy responded.

"So, is it OK if we use the playground?" Asked the little boy digging a hole in the dirt with his foot. "We haven't been able to use it since he got here."

"Why not?" I asked.

"He said it's his now, and he'll mash anybody he catches there," said the little boy, on the verge of tears. "He said if we tell, he'll tell his daddy and his daddy will beat up our daddies and mommies, and it'll be our fault."

"Don't worry about it," Tommy said. "Go ahead and help yourself to any of the stuff you find in the tree house."

"Really?" The boy squealed. "That's great, because he stole some of my stuff. He said I owed it to him, he told other kids he found their stuff, though it's got their name written on it."

"It's all yours now," Tommy said.

Instead of going to the playground, the kids ran howling back to the trailers just as Lonnie, Falcon and Andrew Edward came ambling across the field. The kids slowed and gave them a wide berth, but once past them, the kids broke out laughing and ran toward the tents and trailers. Frowning, Lonnie turned to look behind him and caught sight of us. Smirking, he made the cut-throat sign with his finger and, in response, Tommy pushed his little finger into his nose before flicking an imaginary booger in Lonnie's direction.

"Do you think you can beat him?" I asked.

"Bad Bob is coming," Tommy said and my stomach got queasy.

CHAPTER 30

Approaching the office, we saw Charlie sitting at one of the wooden picnic tables in the shade of the concession shelter with an older man sitting opposite him and a younger. Each man had a can wrapped in a paper towel. We saw them talking with Charlie gesturing and the other men nodding in unison, following Charlie's hand motioning toward the river

Our walk wasn't slow and it wasn't hurried, but other kids streamed past us talking excitedly on their way to the river. They passed and a few turned and gave Tommy appraising looks. Unable to avoid moving between the office and concession shelter, they became quiet and avoided adult eye contact. Yet, their sheer number raised attention as more kids appeared, all headed toward the path to the river.

We were nearly to Charlie's table when a boy wearing a cowboy hat passed us. Before he could make his way down the trail the older man stepped into his path demanding where he was going.

"Swimming," swimming!" The boy mumbled and ran past him. The younger man joined the older one and, after shaking hands with Charlie, said they'd see him later and walked down the trail in the direction of the river. We took seats on the picnic bench in front of Charlie.

"What's the good word?" He asked. "Any killings, stealing, or scandals?"

"Nuthin, really," Tommy said. "There's going to be a fight down on the sand bar by the river."

"Oh, ho," Charlie said. "Anybody I know?"

"Yeah, me and this kid named Lonnie," Tommy said. "We got into it at the playground and we plan on settling things on this sand bar by the river."

"Isn't he the one that necessitated your little boat trip from Bandy's Camp?" asked Charlie letting his glasses hang down his chest.

"The one and only," I answered. "He looks like he slept in an aspirin bottle."

"Yes, I saw him and two other boys headed to the river," Charlie said. "Coincidentally, a similar, older looking gentleman offered me the same opportunity not five minutes ago."

"Did he have a tattoo on his face that looked like a horsefly and a thumb missing from one hand?" I asked.

"It wasn't a fly?" Charlie said. "He smelled as if he could draw bugs. Wonder if he lost that thumb swatting gnats?"

"That's him," Tommy said. "His name is Arlie! He's Lonnie's dad and he's Macho Mike's really good friend."

I recounted Mrs. Gomillion's tamales and limeade. Tommy told, in detail, how Arlie threatened us and Mrs. Gomillion's reaction with the spade.

"He kept saying you hit Macho Mike from behind," Tommy said, "and that you were doing something nasty with Jackie."

Shifting his weight, Charlie inhaled deeply before reaching behind him and brought out his knife. He began twirling it slowly. "Technically, he's right," Charlie said. "So that's one point for him, but only on his head."

"What about him saying nasty things about Jackie?" Cried Tommy jumping to his feet to face Charlie with clenched fists. "You know that's a filthy lie."

"It is" replied Charlie tossing the knife twirling into the air. "Considering the source, I believe we should just ignore him. Still, he got it right about M&M cold-cocking himself."

I couldn't stop watching the whirling blade, and neither could Tommy. He also stood mesmerized as Charlie tossed the knife to his other hand and it seemed to slide around his hand.

"You have to admit," he said catching the knife, "that if I hadn't surprised him he wouldn't have turned around. If he hadn't had my bolo, he might not have stumbled over his own feet. So Arlie's right, it is my fault, or at least I provided the means, though not the end."

"So, you're going to fight him," Tommy said, "and make him take back those dirty lies."

"He offered to settled the score right here," Charlie said. "But the presence of the two gentlemen that just left might have been greater odds than he cared for. Still, his offer was very clear."

Charlie twirled the knife, increasing its tempo before tossing it back to his other hand with a dry chuckle. "He also said if I didn't show he'd let everybody know I was a coward," Charlie said. "Talk about a coyote."

"He has a knife too," I said. " At least I think he does. He reached for something in his pocket."

Charlie tossed his knife and spun it back to his other hand. "That was my impression too," Charlie said, "and probably the main reason he didn't want any witnesses."

"Well, at least you have a knife," I said. "Now things are even."

The knife smacked Charlie's hand and he stared at it like it had miraculously appeared from thin air. The blade's edge shone from its needle tip to brass cross guard. Its bone handles were smooth from much handling. The red eye of the lion head pommel twinkled in the sunlight as he pulled the sheath out and holstered it. "I won't need it," Charlie said.

"Why not?" Tommy demanded.

"New Athenians do not defile their sacred blade in trifles with coyotes," Charlie said. "Besides, it's time to pass the duties and responsibly of that office to another."

"What office?" I said feeling sick again. " Who?"

"Why you two," he said. "Step forward ye chosen keepers of the blade."

Tommy and I timidly moved to where Charlie pointed.

"In accordance with the ancient traditions of the New Athenians I pass to you this sacred blade of our noble order," Charlie intoned. "Will you, Jackie and Tommy keep this sacred trust against all coyotes, foreign and domestic, and accept this duty knowingly and faithfully?"

I turned and Tommy looked bug-eyed.

"Will you accept this charge?" Charlie repeated.

I rocked my head and Tommy did the same.

"Then by my power as a New Athenian charter member, I bestow on you this sacred blade," Charlie said. "I charge you with its preservation, protection and use in the time honored ceremonies and pursuit of the noble ideas and purpose of our select fraternity."

"Uh," Tommy stammered. "Which of us is the keeper of the ancient blade? Jackie already has the beacon."

"It's your responsibility to see it to a secure haven."

"Where's that?" Tommy asked.

"Give it to your grandmother when you get home," Charlie said. "I'm sure she'll know what to do with it until you're old enough to take your full responsibility."

Reverently, Tommy took the knife and pulled the sheath from the blade and held it glittering to the sunlight.

"But you won't have your knife when you meet Arlie," I said. "You should keep it, just in case."

"I doubt if we have anything to worry about from him," Charlie replied. "Besides, I have my gun."

"You left your gun at the canoe," said Tommy sheathing the knife. "We saw you take it off and heard you lock the gear box. "

"You did," said Charlie with a wry smile. "Are you sure?"

I saw the angled lump at the front of his shirt just above his waist. "Even in a locked gear box, it's foolish to leave a gun, or anything else valuable by the river," Charlie said. "There are just too many coyotes."

"So you had it when you were talking to Turtle Ron," I said. "You would have used it on him."

"I didn't have to," said Charlie, shrugging. "We worked things out, remember? Besides, like rabbits and fish, I won't waste a bullet on a coyote, unless I have to."

"Do you think it's fair having a gun and he's only got a knife," I argued. "You're not giving Arlie a chance."

"I seriously doubt if Arlie cares about giving anyone a chance," Charlie said. "He'd give about as much a chance as your pal Lonnie."

Amber Snead strolled past, still wearing her ugly green bathing suit, looking straight ahead, but head tilted our way and walking slowly. Our conversation ceased until her head disappeared below the steps.

"Tommy, you can't win against that boy," I said when Amber was out of sight. "He's a head taller than you and a hundred pounds heavier and you've never been in any kind of fight in your life. He won't fight fair and those kids don't care if you're chicken or not, they want to see somebody pounded into pudding."

"But I've got a bet," Tommy said. "I can't back out now."

Charlie looked at me with a "tell me more" expression and I explained, in detail the circumstances of the last hour and emptied my pockets. With all the bets, minus my rubber pirate's knife, were on the table, Charlie whistled.

"WOW, that's a whole lot of coup!"

"Coup," Tommy said, "you mean like *the People* in battle?"

"Pretty much," Charlie replied. "And if we had a shaman he'd say you've been blessed by the spirits of *the People*."

Charlie told us the coin was a Sacajawea dollar with likeness of the woman who helped guide the Lewis and Clark expedition explore lands from the Mississippi River to the Pacific Ocean.

"Ahh and Kokopelli," he said picking up the money clip. " the trickster, master of music and some say of battle. There's heap, strong medicine here little warriors. You've scored like a Comanche."

"I don't care if he's got the key to Fort Knox," I said stamping my foot. "He can't win against that boy."

"Then we need to even the odds," said Charlie getting to his feet and motioning us to do the same. "So, you told them I taught you how to fight. So, let's not make a liar out of you."

Charlie showed us how to make a fist and demonstrated the correct way to stand while protecting our head with our fists held in front of our face. We demonstrated combinations of jabs, right crosses, upper cuts and hooks.

"Use your whole body, not just your arm," he said twisting his torso as he threw a right cross, "and make sure you breathe each time."

Touching shoulders, ribs and belly he explained how these body parts were prime targets compared to the smaller and protected head. He warned against breaking a hand on a thick skull, offering the indented knuckle on his ring finger to emphasis the point.

Jumping around between the picnic tables and office, we must have looked like spastic monkeys trying to imitate Charlie's hunched figure and punching the air. Yet, skeptical as I was, I felt a ray of hope we had a fighting chance.

He waved at Martha and Turtle Ron staring at us through the screen enclosure of the office. I caught sight of Amber Snead ducking below the steps after we had completed a series of combination punches. Anytime, I expected her to run ahead to tell the others we were coming and what we were learning. She gave up all pretense of hiding, stretching her neck out like a turtle's, her eyes round as saucers, but not looking at us.

Following the direction of her stare, I saw a pickup truck with large gold letters and a big star on the side door moving along the road lined with Rvs and campers in route to where we stood. Open mouthed, Amber Snead stood up, craning her whole body, as another truck rolled through the front gate followed by a third. The last truck towed a trailer with a big boat with a big fan on it. The first vehicle crunched to a stop and Amber jumped down the steps, moving for all she was worth in the direction of the river.

"I better get down to the river," Tommy said. "They'll say I'm chicken!"

"Maybe next time," Charlie said, "after you've done a little preparation."

Before Tommy could argue, Charlie stepped toward the first vehicles. I grabbed the knife and slipped it behind my back into my shorts, covering the pommel with my shirt. Tommy looked confused as he scooped up the coup prizes and put them in his pocket. Together we followed Charlie toward the lead vehicle which made a cloud of dust when it stopped. A stubby man wearing a blue polo shirt with a yellow embroidered badge on his chest stepped out. He stood while the other trucks halted and uniformed men and women wearing gun belts poured out and converged around him. They spoke low among themselves before fanning out around us.

The stubby man removed his baseball cap from his bald head and wasn't surprised, like I was, when the office door burst open. The deputies turned like startled cats in that direction and the stubby man held up a hand. Turtle Ron rushed forward and the stubby man walked forward to meet him with arms waving. With a hand gesture, the stubby man indicated Turtle Ron to stay put and walked toward us.

Charlie held out a hand and they shook hands while we watched Charlie nod, point at us, the direction of the river and take out his little notebook, Charlie tore off several sheets and handed them to the stubby man. He glanced at the pages, posed a question and Charlie offered Marlene's pink receipt. Smiling, the stubby man nodded, returned the slip and walked toward us.

"Are you Jackie and Tommy?" Asked the stubby man, his dimpled grin creasing his face.

We nodded.

"I'm Sheriff John Edwards, we're going to get you home," he said. "Your grandmother is waiting in town."

He introduced a woman deputy as "Deputy Cindy" and told us to follow her toward the only car among the convoy of police vehicles. The sheriff and Charlie walked out of earshot.

"But what about the fight?" Tommy whined. "They're waiting for us."

I shushed him and looked over my shoulder at Charlie pointing upstream and talking. The sheriff spoke, Charlie nodded and rejoined us.

"The sheriff wants me to go with his people and show them where Macho Mike capsized," Charlie said. "You guys ride into town and I'll see you later."

Around us, men donned helmets and vests taken from the trucks. The truck towing the big fan boat U-turned and drove toward a side road with a sign that read "Boat Ramp. Cost $5."

I threw my arms around Charlie's waist and collided with the pistol under his shirt. My chest stung and I hissed through clenched teeth, backing away, supported by his fingertips on my shoulders.

"I am sorry, are you hurt?"

"I'm OK," I lied, "thank you."

He smiled sympathetically and offered a hand to Tommy, and he shook it, like boys do.

"What about the fight?" Tommy repeated. "I haven't won the coups."

"Sure you have," Charlie said. "You win by default, the fault being cops are everywhere and you have to go home. The coup is yours fair and square."

Before Tommy could argue, Charlie turned and followed a deputy down the slope toward the direction of the river.

Turtle Ron stood in front of the screen door of his office, moving from one foot to the other as if he would burst. Martha, still holding her broom, gaped at the activity rushing past her. From the camper line, little groups gathered on the field talking and pointing at the sheriff's trucks.

The sheriff walked back toward the direction of the trucks and Ron rushed forward, hands raised and shouting. Draping a thick arm over Ron's shoulder, the sheriff silenced him and drew him to one side. With a pat on Turtle Ron's shoulder, the sheriff continued toward the other trucks. Ron looked as if he would explode until Martha stepped up and whispered in his ear and they went back into the office.

We followed Deputy Cindy to a patrol car and turned with everyone else at the sound of a commotion from the trail to the river. It reminded of the last day of school with kids of every age spilling noisily across the little clearing below the steps. Out of sight for all of three seconds, they reappeared in mass, not bothering with the steps, breaching the hill like an invading army.

At the top of the hill their chatter subsided, and fidgeting took the mob like a plague. Standing in the forefront were Lonnie, Falcon and Andrew Edward looking around as if for an avenue of escape. The mob became quiet and all eyes turned to Lonnie. Without warning the three were roughly shoved and just managed to keep from falling on their faces. Lonnie stumbled a couple of feet regained his balance and whipped around, fists doubled. A cedar pod arched through the air and bounced off his head. Squeaking, he would have rushed them but the bigger kids pushed forward and the mob surged past him.

The deputies, most in battle gear, directed the flow of kids away from their vehicles. Past the office, the kids spread in every possible direction separating into groups of twos and threes.

Lonnie ran, dodging between kids and around the concession stand toward us. Falcon and Andrew Edward moved with the flow of kids and managed to join Lonnie as he tried to move between the deputies' trucks. A tall deputy blocked their path.

"Something I can do for you kids?" The big deputy demanded.

"I want to talk to them," said Lonnie pointing at us and stepping unsuccessfully around the deputy. "They have something that belongs to me."

Forcing the boys back, the big deputy looked over his shoulder
"Hey," he yelled, "you know this boy?"

We shook our heads and the deputy turned to Lonnie.

"They don't know you," he said. "Move on kid."

"They've got something that's mine," said Lonnie with desperation. "I want it and I'm going to get it."

"What it is and I'll get it and bring it to you."

"No, it's mine," Lonnie insisted. "I have to get it myself."

"Some other time, kid," the big deputy said. "Move on."

"I want my stuff," Lonnie shrieked. "I know my rights! They stole my stuff and I want it back."

The crowd by the RV's had grown and moved across the field to lean on the swimming pool fence. They'd been watching and talking among themselves when Lonnie started to fuss. Noticing the attention, the big deputy called to us.

"You kids got something of his?"

Another head shake.

"Move on, kid."

"No, no, I have rights!" Lonnie screamed. "I want what's mine." Without warning Lonnie drove his fist at the deputy's midsection. As if expecting it, the deputy side-stepped and the boy fell, face first, to the ground. Before he could get to his knees the deputy grabbed the scruff of Lonnie's T-shirt, twisting it into a halter. Lonnie struggled and a box fell from his pocket and the deputy retrieved it.

"Ohhhh," moaned Lonnie dramatically, "I've got a concussion, this pig broke my back. Please, I'm begging, somebody call me an ambulance! I'll sue!"

"You're an ambulance," the big deputy said. "Did you know it's not nice to hit people, especially police officers?"

"Get off me, you big goon," Lonnie howled. "Somebody help, call child services, he's molesting me."

Lonnie saw Falcon and Andrew Edward as they moved away, eyes averted.

"Chicken shits," Lonnie called, "I'll get you, I won't forget, you'll be sorry!"

"Bite me," Andrew Edward said over his shoulder as Falcon hawked and spat.

Cursing Lonnie wriggled to get free until the big deputy shook him until I thought his teeth would fall out. When the boy was still the deputy shoved the box he'd picked up under his nose.

"What are you doing with these?" said the deputy holding Marlboro cigarette pack before Lonnie's face.

"Those are mine," Lonnie snapped. "Give them back, let me go."

"It's illegal for minors to have tobacco," the deputy quoted. "Where'd you get these smokes?"

"That's my business," cried Lonnie kicking the air. "You better let go or my daddy will bust your ass. You'll be sorry, that's for sure."

"Is that right?" the deputy said "and who is your daddy, boy?"

"He's whipped bigger men than you for messing with me," Lonnie said." He'll do worse to you, if you don't let me go. He'll mess up your whole sorry bunch."

"Is that right?" The deputy repeated disinterestedly.

"Daddy! Daddy! Daddy!" Lonnie howled. "Daaaddddyyy, help! I need help!"

Lonnie's yowls pierced the air like fingers on a chalkboard, the pitch growing higher for what seemed like a minute. Some smiled, others even laughed, which made Lonnie wail even louder until everyone's attention was drawn to a small house trailer at the end of the row of RV's and closest to the office.

The trailer's door opened like a gun shot. Lonnie closed his mouth, a superior expression creasing his face with a knowing grin. From the open door emerged what looked like a giant yellow eye, its wrinkled, pale blue eye lid, partially open. No Greek monster from Ana's book could have been as horrible. Stepping from the darkness the eye metamorphosed to an image that reminded me of those wooly mammoth elephants from cave man days. The creatures' tousled golden hair shimmered in the sunlight disrupted by the curled lips revealing broken tobacco stained teeth

"You're going to get it now," Lonnie said. "My daddy doesn't take shit or anything off anybody and he's never lost a fight because he knows savate."

Placing one foot outside the door of the trailer, the yellow head swung like a scenting predator until Lonnie howled again. With the direction of the noise targeted, the huge hands gripped the trailer's outer door panels in preparation to launch the huge body into the open. Midway, the head jerked up short, its enraged expression dissolving into bewilderment.

"Arlie," called Sheriff Edwards loud enough for everyone to hear. "Hey everyone, it's Arlie!"

"I'll be dammed, Arlie," cried the big deputy holding Lonnie. "Good ole Arlie."

"Arlie! " repeated Deputy Cindy beside us. "It's been a while! Hi, Arlie!"

Everyone took up the shout that echoed around the field relayed not only by the deputies but soon taken up by the bystanders. With each hail, the wooly head jerked in that direction with a look of stark terror. Without warning, Arlie retreated back into the trailer, pulling the door shut. For the second time since I'd met him, I felt sorry for Lonnie. The confident smirk melted into an expression of total disbelief and the image of probably the most miserable sight I'd seen in my life.

His expression was the look of a little boy discovering Santa Claus stuffing the Christmas tree, the presents, and dinner into his bag and fleeing out the back door.

In desperation Lonnie howled again as the big deputy turned him over to a shorter deputy who walked him to the picnic table and sat him down. The big deputy lead a group of three other deputies wearing bulky vests and helmets and carrying rifles. Other deputies took up positions and directed the onlookers to stay back or go to their trailer or tents. Of course, none did and were content to watch as intently. Only Lonnie wasn't watching the little trailer. He glared at us beside the squad car with Deputy Cindy.

I saw two deputies moved to either side of the trailer, though not directly in front of its door as other helmeted officers disappeared around the other side of the trailer. When everyone gave the high sign that they were in position, the big deputy snapped open a telescopic club and tapped hard on the door.

"AR-LEE," the big deputy sang. "Come out. Come out, we want to talk to you."

Sheriff Edwards finished his phone call and moved to Cindy where she'd been standing by the squad car's driver's door. He muttered words I could not hear before walking toward the deputies surrounding the trailer.

"Anyone want to ride in the front seat?" Deputy Cindy asked.

"I'll sit in the back," said Tommy eyeing the meshed cage that separated the front from back seat. "This is cool."

I took "shotgun" and Deputy Cindy turned the car in the opposite direction of the little trailer, the nose of the squad car passing a short way from where Lonnie sat still glaring. Tommy gave him an arched "so long" wave of his hand and a goofy grin. Screaming, Lonnie tried to jump up and the deputy had to use both hands to hold him. We pulled away as Arlie emerged from the trailer with a wide grin and hands raised as the deputies surrounded him.

The route took us past the playground and Cindy slowed to watch the melee of celebrating kids. The jungle gym and sand box were alive with small bodies with hardly room for a toddler. Screaming kids ran from one tree house cabin to the other dancing and jumping on the suspended bridge. From cabin windows flew a jumble of items, known and unknown, falling to jubilant screams. I saw books and magazines fluttering with their folded middle pictures flapping like game pennants. On the ground, other kids snatched up these magazines and tossed them to the waiting arms of boys and girls arching in the rubber bottomed swings. When the swingers reached the zenith of their ascent, they flung the magazines that fell like eagles with their wings clipped and burst their staples.

CHAPTER 31

At Tommy's insistence, Deputy Cindy turned on the flashing lights and siren. We raced toward town and I watched the flashing landscape as Tommy repeated dialogue he'd heard from a television cop show.

"I was framed," he said laughing, "I want a lawyer."

"Anything you say can be used against you," said Deputy Cindy, also laughing, "If you cannot afford one, a lawyer will be appointed for you."

I listened, but didn't participate.

"You OK, sweetheart?" Deputy Cindy asked. "You sick?"

I told her I was just tired and got a sympathetic smile. I didn't bother to mention the big knife wedged against my tail bone. I didn't want to tell her I wasn't looking forward to answering any questions, particularly about Tarzan Charlie. He was a fictional character I'd created to calm Tommy's fears, though a sillier joke was on me.

Deputy Cindy, I wanted to say, does Sheriff Edwards know the man riding with his other deputies has a loaded gun under his shirt? That he almost shot three men…and me and my cousin? So, how has your day been, Deputy Cindy?

Without knowing my thoughts, Deputy Cindy recounted how we had been reported missing late Saturday afternoon. Guests questioned at Bandy's Camp said the last time we'd been seen was playing dodge ball with a group of kids at the bottom of the hill. A white haired boy had been mentioned more than once.

"That was Lonnie," said Tommy, unnecessarily.

"We looked for him," she added, "but he and his family had disappeared without a trace. Later, an older couple said they'd seen two children floating past them in a rubber raft that morning." I felt some forgiveness for the old fisherman and his wife.

"That's when we started trolling the river and to be honest, we expected…." She glanced at me before she said, "We're just glad we found you."

From the top of a hill we saw housetops. Deputy Cindy switched off the lights and siren long before we turned onto a major state highway and a street that circumnavigated the town square.

Moving along the street I saw a collection of untidy old houses and double-wide trailers and wondered if anyone still lived in this town. The county courthouse did dispute my doubts. It was an unimpressive two-story block structure with the redeeming factor of casting a long shadow across the street. Nearby was another building, built at an angle to, and taller by two stories than, the courthouse. It had iron barred windows and was crowned with a halo of coiled barbed wire on its roof.

Deputy Cindy turned the car onto a street that took us in the direction of the far side of the taller building. Ahead, I saw other police vehicles parked, including an ancient truck with three flat tires and a collection of flotsam between it and the limestone curb. Looking around, the whole town square reminded me of birthday party after the presents had been opened, the cake eaten, and the guests long since gone home. Only no one had bothered to clean up the mess.

I watched sunlight reflect off dirty glass store fronts across the street, all with peeling letters in ancient script advertising furniture, pharmacy, or clothing. Most of the stores were empty, including a former hardware store. Its front panes declared "Antiques" in faded gold letters above shelves with white coats of dust and dead moths. From where I stood, nothing moved in the store's interior. Against the glass front door, stacks of crumpled boxes lay with its detritus spilled across what had been the front entrance floor. Papers with broad, hand written accounts lay yellow and curled in the sunlight that filtered through the bleary window.

The next door was thick glass, its hinges sets solidly into tiled cut stone. Vestiges of peeling clear tape held a "For Lease" sign above the once elegant door handle. A fat-fingered artist had scrawled in the dust of the opposite window "Wash me in 1973." I wondered if anyone actually lived in this town. Were the secrets I carried worth telling and would anyone even care?

Deputy Cindy swung the car in a wide arch and parked in front of a sign that read "Official Police Vehicles Only." Stepping out of the car, I saw a freshly-painted, black and white sign painted on a false front directly across the street that read, "The Whistle Stop Café," underlined with painted railroad tracks. Next door to it were the polished windows of a first "something" bank, shining, as Papa liked to say, like a diamond in a goat's butt compared to its grubby neighbors.

Deputy Cindy opened the back seat for Tommy while I shaded my forehead with my hand against the bright sunlight. Heat reflected from the asphalt into my nostrils, a radical change from the frosty confines of the air-conditioned car. I stretched my back, as I had learned on the river, and side twisted to the cadence of cicadas droning their summer song, being careful not to let the knife slip out of the back of my shorts. Two elderly men sat on a bench in the shade of a Dollar General Store across the street.

After donning a pair of sunglasses, that made her look like a housefly, Deputy Cindy stepped up on the sidewalk and waited for us. We also stepped up just as a high keening drew our attention to a nearby cedar tree against the side of the courthouse with a metal picnic table. Deputy Cindy's hand dropped to the butt of her gun as Ana ran forward and swept us into her arms. Ana cried and Deputy Cindy moved her hand to her mouth. Looking over Ana's shoulder I saw the old men lean forward, hands on their knees while, Dollar General Store patrons with yellow plastic bags stared.

Ana hugged us to her shoulders alternately crying and laughing. "Are you OK?" She sobbed before straightening up and reaching into her purse.

"We're fine," I replied still holding her.

"Where's Papa?" Asked Tommy, his head wagging side to side.

""He's at Bandy's Camp with your parents," she said wiping tears. "I told them to stay put."

"What happened?" she blurted out, but stopped. "When was the last time you ate?"

"Uh, ma'am," Deputy Cindy interrupted. "There's some information we'll need and paper work to fill out"

"Not before these children have had something to eat, "said Ana with finality. You're certainly welcome to come along with us, deputy...?" Without waiting, she took us by the hands and moved past Deputy Cindy toward The Whistle Stop Café.

"It's Youngblood, ma'am, Cindy Youngblood," said Deputy Cindy running to catch up. " Ma'am there are procedures and...."

"There are also priorities," interrupted Ana without breaking stride. "The sheriff's office is in that building?" She pointed to the tall building.

"Yes ma'am," Deputy Cindy said, "but...."

"I knew you'd understand," Ana said. "We'll be over in 30 minutes or however long it takes to eat a hamburger."

Ana lead us through the creaking double inner door where a bell clanged above our heads. Seated at a back table, was an old man showing only three teeth. He raised his coffee cup in a toast before assaulting a slice of high backed meringue chocolate pie. At a nearby table, a middle-aged woman turned from filling salt and pepper shakers. The plastic name tag pinned to the shoulder of her white T-shirt declared "Peggy." Patting the old man's hand, she snatched menus and intercepted us.

"Help you, hon?" Peggy called.

"Could we please get a table in the side room?" Ana replied.

"Sure thing, hon."

We followed Peggy past three rows of tables and a steam table toward a side door. I turned as the front bell rang again and the two old men from Dollar General Store sauntered in. They took a seat opposite chocolate pie eater and watched us disappear into the next room. Peggy seated us beside a window toward the front street. With her thumb she indicated a cork billboard beside the doorway covered with business cards. Below was a chalkboard, like we had in school, with large hand drawn letters listing the special of the day and side dishes.

"We've got a nice lunch special," Peggy said.

"Maybe next time," Ana said. "For now we'll have hamburgers."

Producing a pad and pen, Peggy asked what we wanted to drink and left us with a cheery, "We'll have it right out."

I dreaded Peggy leaving because for the first time in my life I was afraid to be alone and talk with Ana. Pushing myself back against the seat I felt the knife against my backbone. I took and laid it on the table. A perplexed look crossed Ana's face. Hesitantly, she ran her fingers over the scabbard, picked it up and took out the knife, holding it in both hands. Timidly she ran a fingertip over the columns of small triangles on the flat of the blade.

"Hello gorgeous!" She whispered. "Where have you been?"

Lines around her eyes crinkled as she stroked the bone handle with her thumb. At the pommel, she tapped a fingertip against the lion's open maw as if teasing it to bite. Tommy looked at me, puzzled and I shrugged as Ana balanced the knife on the ridge of her hand. Without warning, she tossed it twirling into the air, content to watch its descent like a runaway buzz saw. To our open mouthed amazement, the handle smacked into her palm. Our surprise changed to horror as she ran her thumb along the blade's keen edge. A thin red line appeared below that fingernail which she smeared the length of the blade. Eyes shining, she shifted the blade to her right hand and twirled it. The movement was slow, increasing in tempo with blade and handle merging into a solid haze. Still twirling, again she tossed it, almost to the ceiling this time. It just missed an overhead light before falling with a whisper, the handle smacking her outstretched hand.

It would not have surprised me if my grandmother arched the knife over her shoulder and threw it across the room to stick quivering in the "Today's Special" bulletin board. Instead, she pressed a paper napkin between her index and forefinger, and reverently replaced the knife in its sheath. Laying it between us, her cheeks were bright with color.

"What happened out there?" She asked.

I did most of the talking, this time leaving nothing out. Particularly my concerns about swimming naked and how Charlie nearly shot us, Macho Mike and others. Typically, Tommy interrupted to ask about circumstances he hadn't witnessed, demanding detailed explanations. Ana shushed him and listened without comment until I'd finished my account.

"Did he touch you?" She said.

"He doctored our skeeter bites," said Tommy lifting his shirt. "He held my leg to get a tick off."

"He never touched us that way," I said, understanding her meaning. "When he found us, it was like we were a bag of trash. I thought after he gave us water he'd chase us off."

Tommy stayed quiet, for once, and Ana stared at the knife. "But he didn't," she whispered. "He wouldn't!"

"Tell her about your Orion," Tommy prompted loudly.

"When he saw my *Orion*, it was like he was scared. Afraid to have us around and even more afraid to chase us off."

Ana gazed again into a far away place we couldn't go.

Swallowing hard, I said "Ana, it's true he didn't touch us, but things happened out there that could have turned bad, and I mean really nasty. The fact that they didn't, doesn't excuse that us and other people might not be talking now. It could have been that bad. I'm just not sure about what to do. What if they ask about what I saw or did?"

Ana picked up the knife, but didn't take it out of its sheath. "You know Tommy you're right about this knife," Ana said.

"I...I...I am?" Tommy blurted. "About what?"

"Don't you remember," Ana said, "You told me you wouldn't eat with something that filed horses' hooves. Most people would agree, particularly knowing where it came from. Neither its craftsmanship or the work it took to make a file into this beautiful tool would matter."

I wanted to interrupt.

"They wouldn't know its history either, where it's been, what it's done, how it helped or even saved someone," she said. "Most people would only see an instrument that had manure on it once."

She took a breath and sipped her water glass. "They'd probably say the same thing about my garden," she said. "That is if they knew, because first impressions are the only ones some people use to judge situations or people. Sadly, without the whole story, they don't have the entire truth, so they cheat themselves and others. Which is probably what folks would say if they knew the real story about my garden and the Commemorative."

As a child, Ana said that she lived with her parents on the Texas Gulf Coast, a sunny place by the sea. Her father's job transferred him to San Antonio, but her mother didn't want to go, and, like my parents, they argued. It was one of many reasons Ana's mother decided to return to her parents' Texas Hill Country ranch.

"My parents believed they could work things out, with time," Ana said. "Which just goes to show, the apple doesn't fall too far from the tree."

Yet, the longer her parents were apart, the less inclined they were to settle differences and try to get back together. "There wasn't much that could be done," Ana said, "and I came to misguided conclusion that living on grandpa's ranch was part of the problem."

That was also the time when, just as Ana had done for me, her grandmother had explained about her *Orion*. And, like me, Ana was equally perplexed with her grandmother's explanation about the luck. She saw it another way until her grandpa announced that he was considering leasing the ranch to a cadre of wealthy hunters.

"I thought everything was going to turn out for the best," Ana said. "Not that I hated the ranch, it was fine to visit. Without it I thought there'd be no excuse for my mother not to get back with my daddy."

Besides, and she looked at me, at 14 Ana wanted to be with kids her own age and interests. She had nothing in common with the local kids.

"I was a manicured pinky finger among a bucket full of sore thumbs," Ana said. " They listened to country music and wore jeans. I liked rock-n-roll and wanted a mini skirt. They wanted to run their parents' ranch. I dreamed about New York and Paris. I thought they were hicks. They thought I was stuck up."

All that changed when the lease man called to talk to her grandfather about touring the ranch. He was a tall man around her mother's age and he invited the adults to supper. He needed to collect information for a report he was writing for potential clients and thought a meal would help put everyone at ease. Her mother told her this would be an adults only party and no fun for Ana. So it was best if she stayed home alone.

"I was about to jump with joy," Ana said. "I had my own mini vacation. I planned to gorge on junk food, watch bad TV, and dream of ways to have fun when we moved."

Her parents left and she changed into T-shirt and shorts and watched TV until it was late, not finding a single program that interested her. Noticing the full moon shining through the window, she went out on the front porch sofa, not bothering to turn on the porch light. A light that might have scared off prowling animals, she reflected, and why she couldn't believe the movement in the front yard.

"It was the size of a John Deere tractor," Ana said. "One minute I was looking at the moon, the next this big specter was in my grandmother's garden."

Superstitions about ghosts grew by the millisecond, until the spook snorted. Which didn't quiet her fears. She assumed it was a bear, despite knowing that bears hadn't been seen there since before her grandpa had been born. In fact, she said with a shake of her head, it might have been better if it had been a ghost. The shadow grunted and she recalled a similar sound made by a friend of her grandpa's as he recounted "getting hit last night."

The specter's identity had a multi choice of names, each synonymous with destruction. Wild hogs, razorbacks, rooters or European boar. To local ranchers, it didn't matter, these pigs were capable of destroying up to five acres of ready-to-harvest-crops in a single night. They weren't picky, consuming anything with a calorie.

"They fed beside our horses, ate quail eggs or fawns," Ana said. "They were the ultimate eating machine that could disappear for six months. They weren't discriminating about rooting a farmers' field or a city golf course, resulting in damages costing hundreds of thousands of dollars."

At that time hogs were just becoming a problem in that part of Texas. But this particular hog was a personal threat to Ana that threatened to damage to her grandmother's garden and possibly her escape back to civilization.

"I thought if the lease man saw the front yard ripped up like a bombed field," Ana said, "he'd back out of the deal."

She considered throwing rocks at the pig, but slipped into the house to her grandfather's gun case.

"My grandfather liked to describe himself to his cronies as a crippled old man, saddled with two frail women and a girl on his ranch," Ana said. "Yet, anybody looking for trouble would find it because he had insisted everyone at the ranch learn to shoot a gun."

After all, they were on their own and lived at top of a hill. It was no surprise her grandfather had a shoot-first-and-ask-questions-later policy regarding uninvited guests.

A year earlier he taught Ana to use a .22 rifle. She enjoyed the crack of its report, but wasn't too keen at the goat butt of her grandmother's .410 shotgun, kept behind the kitchen door for snakes or skunks. She knew neither of those guns would do. Hogs were big game, really big, and necessitated a big gun.

"I heard some corporate honcho call them the poor man's Bengal Tiger," said Ana recalling what one of her grandfather's cronies said during a visit. "He said he'd hunted tigers, so he knew, and hog were just as dangerous."

Her grandfather kept a half-dozen rifles in glass fronted gun case. Yet, the only one she was even vaguely familiar with was the Commemorative. She'd seen plenty of rifles like it, loaded and downing various bad guys on the various television western shows. So, she selected the Commemorative and found its ammunition in the bottom drawer. She took pains to be quiet returning outside, but she need not have bothered. The hog never raised its head or took no notice at the long creaking of the opening screen door.

"Orion was out and above the front yard by that time of night," Ana recalled, "with the three main stars of his belt glittering just above the hog's back."

In the dim light, Ana saw how the stiff black hair stood up on the hog's spine like a wheat field from forehead to tail. Enormous curved tusks reflected starlight from their white polished surface.

"I could have thrown a saddle on that pig or hitched it with a chain and pulled cars out of the mud," Ana said. "It was so dammed huge, magnificent and so beautiful."

"A pig," Tommy said. "That must have been some pig Ana!"

Ana nodded, and said that's why she didn't want to kill it. She planned to scare it away. This was definitely not an opinion she would share with her grandfather or his rancher friends, since theirs was a kill all hogs on sight policy.

"So why didn't I just throw a rock at it," said Ana more to herself than us. "I'll never know."

She pushed the long bullets into the gun's loading slot carefully so that the bullet's brass tip didn't mar the gold plating. With the same excruciatingly slowness, she worked the lever and chambered a round, though midway through the action, the massive head turned toward the house. Transforming Ana's admiration to fear of the pig's charge. But the wind to its back, its priority was hunger and with a snort the head returned to its feast.

Ana laid the rifle barrel across the porch rail, the butt stock barely touching her shoulder, the front sight on the right star of Orion's belt that shone directly in front of the pig's snout. It was her plan that after a bullet kicked dust into its face, "this little pig would go wee-wee-wee all the way down the road."

Taking a breath, as she'd been taught, she jerked the trigger, which she had not been taught. The gun thundered, jerked left and slammed her shoulder in the process. She saw a dust puff sprout behind the pig's shoulder before it jumped straight up and wheeled toward Ana. Hooves spread, tusks lowered, its outraged squeal ripped the night silence causing Ana to shudder. Dread turned to terror when the pig stepped forward. With a second step, the pig toppled onto its left side, its back leg kicking like a piston before stopping forever in mid stroke.

Ana sat splay legged on the porch, ears ringing and watching the hog breath its last. Agony raced across her chest when she pulled herself to her knees, but couldn't get to her feet because of the pain in her throbbing shoulder. Her attention was drawn to a scuffling sound from beyond where the hog's lay and three small figures tottered out of the darkness. They formed ranks on the side of the fallen hog to nuzzle its underside.

"It was a sow," explained Ana unnecessarily, "with piglets."

She felt the misery of her bruised shoulder almost justified shooting the magnificent hog. But she knew her pain was nothing to what the piglets could expect without a mother to feed and protect them; slow starvation or predators.

"They were helpless and there was nothing to be done," Ana said. "Actually, yes there was, but I wasn't in exactly the best shape."

She loaded three more bullets into the rifle, expecting, hoping that at any seconds the piglets would flee. Also, knowing a second shot was a zillion to one chance. Like their mother, the piglets' snouts rose quizzically at the mechanical sounds before returning to their meal. Ana moved to a new shooting position on the far side of the porch.

"My grandpa called it a good old boy shot," she recalled. "The kind of marksmanship that men around the coffee shop spoke of with awe, but was unrealistic and seldom, if ever, actually seen. I thought of it as the shortest distance between two points."

Ignoring her pain, Ana laid the rifle barrel on another part of the porch rail. This time she pressed the rifle butt tightly against her aching shoulder. Taking a breath, she forced herself to hold, fine aim and squeeze the trigger. The second report wasn't a surprise and recoil was nearly painless. However, nothing prepared her for the successive leap, squeals and subsequent fall as all three piglets collapsed against their mother. Believing she had hit only one pig, but hoping for time and another shot during the subsequent confusion, she watched for a target. But there was no movement. With one bullet, she had killed all three piglets.

"Wow, Ana," Tommy cried. "Three with one."

"I couldn't make that shot again if my life depended on it," said Ana waving her hand before draining her ice water. "But that was when the fun really began."

She went inside and changed into jeans, sweatshirt and sneakers, located a flashlight, and grabbed a butcher knife from a kitchen drawer. Holding the light outstretched and the knife slash ready, she ran to the barn. Flipping on the lights, she found the small tractor her grandfather kept at the back of the building. She'd learned to drive this tractor almost as soon as her feet could touch the pedals. She had no trouble starting it and while it warmed up, she found a chain and a length of rope putting them behind the seat.

She drove the tractor to the front of the house. In the tractor headlights, the sow and piglets seemed even bigger with shadows. After backing the tractor up to the pigs, she attached the chain to the back of the tractor and looped rope around the necks of the pigs, tying the other end to the hooked chain.

A coppery blood smell filled the air that forced her to breath through her mouth to keep from barfing. She still nearly lost her junk food as she cinched the rope around the dead sow's neck. The nearest piglets were no problem, but the third, the one hit last by her second bullet stirred.

"I put the rope around its neck," Ana said, "and nearly lost a couple of fingers."

"Did you shoot it again?" Tommy asked.

"Couldn't you just leave it?" I asked.

She answered in the negative to both questions.

"I didn't think and left the rifle on the porch," she said. "I panicked."

She considered slashing the piglets' throat with the butcher knife, the way she'd seen a Mexican man butcher a domestic pig. Tommy and I made gagging sounds.

"I felt the same, back then," she said, "and there was already enough blood and carnage without adding to it."

Ball peen hammer in hand she used both hands and raised the hammer high and repeatedly smashed the piglet's skull until it lay still. A chore that required more energy, she reflected, than it was worth.

"Gross," I said, my face twisting in disgust. "And that was better than cutting its throat?"

"If only that was the worst," Ana said. "Those hogs were covered with fleas."

Mounting the tractor, Ana dragged her grisly cargo down the hill from the house toward the property's main gate and the paved county road. To avoid pulling the heads off, she drove slow, stopping twice to re-tie the rope to the trailing chain.

Before reaching the main gate, she turned off the road toward a gully that was part of an unnamed creek. It was located within sight of the main gate, but finding the gully was a matter of looking the post oak trees and briars that formed a seemingly impregnable hedge for most of its length. Yet, the briar patch was accessible through an old animal trail Ana had discovered. Past the briars lay the gully with a stone floor twice as wide as the little tractor. She had been there many times in her life and could have found her way without lights after towing a cart full of odds and ends, like old furniture and a tarp she used to build a shelter, in one of the gully's wide crevices. From the confines of this briar patch she had spied on her grandfather and his neighbor. Neither man, she observed, seemed interested in that section of their adjoining properties, just as cattle rarely grazed near the gully, which was just fine for her needs and privacy.

Being extra careful, she pulled the pigs to the far end of the gully. Though she was loath to leave the gruesome load in her old play ground, that was probably the only spot on the ranch they wouldn't be found until her grandpa completed the sale.

After she stopped, she used the flashlight and undid the chain before turning the tractor around to use the headlights to untie the chain and rope. Only, she could not untie the rope from the pigs' necks. The knots were cinched so tight they wouldn't budge. Worse, the fleas, distinctly visible in the tractors headlights, were coming at her in swarms. Using the butcher knife, she cut the rope closest to the sow, rolling it up and swatting fleas as she got back on the tractor. Returning to the barn, she parked the tractor in its usual place, replaced the chain and hid what was left of the rope. Unfortunately, there was other evidence.

"The fleas were all over me," she said. "I had to get out of those clothes."

Back then, Ana explained, the prescribed method for flea control was to soak the clothes in kerosene. So she stripped down and left her clothes in a brimming pan with the intent of returning early the next morning to rinse them out.

"What did you wear back to the house?" Tommy asked. "A horse blanket!"

"Just my sneakers," said Ana with a shrug, "and a smile."

"You were…," I sputtered, "naked."

Luckily, only the constellations were out. Ana knew they weren't going to tell. Yet that didn't stop her from giving Orion a piece of her mind.

"I would have skinned off my own hide to stop the itching," Ana said. "That's when I yelled at Orion, 'You call this luck?'"

"What did he say?" I asked recalling my own similar situation.

"Not a freaky-leaky thing," she answered. "I asked him to take back his mark, if that was the best he could do."

Back at the house Ana turned on the light in the bathroom and scared herself at the sight in the mirror. She had bites from her neck to ankle with an egg plant colored shoulder.

"All I needed was a single eye and a big white letter right here," she said tapping the area between her shoulder and breast, "and I could have been the alien cheerleader from outer space."

She soaked in the bath tub for an hour and found a long sleeve cotton gown that didn't' irritate the bites. Exhausted, she heard a car's engine in the direction of the front gate after she got into bed and closed her eyes. She opened them even faster.

"The Commemorative," Tommy said.

"The ammunition box," I added.

"Propped on the porch like a broom," Ana finished, "a spent shell in the chamber and two more in the magazine."

Ana stumbled through the living room with car lights illuminating the front corners of the living room and temporarily blinded her. The lights faded as the car drove to the back and she groped for the front door, banging her feet and knees on the front porch. She found the rifle when she bumped it and sent it clattering to the floor. Dropping to her knees, she searched the floor for the ammunition box and found it.

Bumping more furniture, she worked the gun's lever and ejected the bullets that tinkled against the floor tile. Again dropping to her knees, she found the brass and returned them to their box just as the back door to the kitchen was thrown open. Returning to the gun case, she replaced the Commemorative and put the ammunition into the drawer. Lights went on and voices flowed from the kitchen as she locked the case and returned the key. Yawning, she shuffled into the kitchen and the adults turned to look at her rubbing her eyes and asking if they'd had a good time.

"They said yes, only I caught that something was wrong," Ana said. "Grandpa said he had a load of work waiting for him in the morning and it was past his bed time."

I drank deeply from my water glass, staring at Ana with admiration.

"Did they ever find out about the hogs?" I asked.

"Not at first," Ana replied. "What's funny, it didn't even matter."

"Why was that?" Tommy asked.

"Grandma's brown thumb," she answered.

Her grandma had many talents, Ana explained, but gardening wasn't one of them. Her front yard garden had been started by a horticultural genius her grandpa hired one spring. The first year it had been glorious. But every year thereafter her grandma's attempts to emulate the man's talent were dismal successes."

"Ten hogs could not have done any more damage to that piece of earth than my grandma did every year," she said. "Who knows, they might have improved it.

Of course, at that time, that meant nothing to her compared to a bad night's sleep.

"It was worse than when I was expecting your momma," Ana said. "If I wasn't scratching, I'd turn over and my arm felt like it was being ripped out by the roots."

Ana slept late the next morning, but her grandpa didn't and was up before first light. He liked to sit on the front porch with his first cup of coffee.

"That's where he found the other spent casing lying on the porch sofa, bold as, well, brass."

With the break of a new day, Ana's shoulder throbbed beyond any pain she'd known. The misery wasn't helped because she couldn't resist touching the flea bites, a practice she tried to avoid with her grandma watching her from anywhere in the room.

"She had her eye on me," said Ana, jabbing a finger at me, "always, always watching."

Which is why she couldn't go to the barn for her clothes, just as going to the garden was impossible without raising questions. Not that her suffering or worry mattered. It was the lease man who discovered the dead hogs.

The previous night, her grandpa had given the lease man a key for the front gate with instructions to telephone when he was on his way. That way he wouldn't call and interrupt grandpa working or necessitate waiting by the front gate.

That afternoon the lease man drove to the property and as he re-locked the gate he couldn't help notice the large number of buzzards flying and landing. A shift of wind brought a smell that could knock a buzzard off a gut wagon, but the lease man was a curious cuss. He also drove a bright red car and wore an expensive western suit and cowboy hat with Tony Llama boots. Since he had another appointment, he planned to make this visit brief, with no intention of getting off the road. However, despite the lease man's fashion sense, he drove as close as he could before finding the break in the briars and made his way into the gully. Rounding a bend, he surprised a pack of coyotes and buzzards squabbling over carcasses.

Carrion was a poor reward for the lease man's investigation. He should have been satisfied with his first glance and left right there. The coyotes and buzzards took off and so would have he, if he hadn't seen the rope, a rope that linked the four pigs like a string of pearls. Handkerchief over his face, his other hand waving away the clouds of blue flies, the lease man walked a wide circle around the carnage.

It was after they'd shook hands that her grandpa noticed the beggar's lice and burrs covering the lower half of the lease man's expensive slacks. He suggested they adjourn to the porch swing on the porch and asked Ana to bring a small trash can. Ana was about to leave as the lease man explained how he came by the burs and she felt like a thief caught with the goods. Using his pocket knife to dislodge the burrs without pricking his fingers, the lease man recounted finding the roped hogs. He added, with a tone of admiration, that though the scavengers had started on the soft parts. The only mark on the big pig's otherwise golden fleece was a single well-placed bullet. It was the same with the piglets, which were obviously her offspring. sharing their mother's distinctive ridge of mane.

"The sow," he told Ana's grandpa, "had to have been one of the biggest animals I've ever seen and certainly the largest hog, alive or dead."

He added, "Somebody did some fine shooting. Whoever the guy was, he was better than good. He was a professional to pop the whole brood."

Ana was offended and hoped the topic would turn to other business. But the lease man gushed with admiration.

"In my experience," he said, "when you shoot one hog the rest of the herd will take off like scalded apes in as many directions. I'm almost tempted to believe a single bullet killed all four pigs."

Still, he said flipping the last of the beggar's lice into the trash can, these were just feral pigs and not a 12-point buck deer.

"That's when grandpa educated the lease man about wild boar," said Ana with girl's chuckle. "By the time grandma called us, that poor man knew more than he ever wanted to know about feral piggies, and nothing out of a nursery rhyme."

After lunch, her grandpa drove the lease man around the ranch. When they returned, the lease man talked about opportunities with the right investment money. He mentioned he had to talk to some money people and would her grandpa call later.

Even before the big car was out of sight, grandpa called everyone into the living room. He recounted the lease man's account about finding the dead hogs and held out the spent cartridge he'd found in the front porch couch. Ana's mother and grandmother stared and Ana wanted to look anywhere but into her grandpa's eyes. With no choice but to fess up, she told them everything and unbuttoned her shirt to reveal her battered shoulder. Her grandpa raised an eyebrow, while her grandma was up and calling her into the kitchen where she was soaking brown wrapping paper in vinegar to wrap her shoulder.

"She also dabbed my flea bites," Ana said, "and refused to let grandpa or momma near me until she'd dabbed every last chomp."

"Was your grandpa mad because you shot the Commemo-rative?" Tommy asked. "Is that why he couldn't sell it?"

"He knew it had been fired. He left me to grandma and went back to work," Ana said. "After supper that evening, I learned how to clean a rifle."

The next day her grandpa telephoned the lease man. She also heard him tell him how Ana shot the hogs. Ana had been standing nearby when her grandpa held the telephone receiver out and the brays of the lease man's laughter filled the room

"He wouldn't believe it," Ana said. "He wanted to know what was the joke? Grandpa said he didn't make jokes, not like that, and I even wore a silk night gown."

The lease man made other noise before grandpa ended the conversation and said good-bye. The old man said nothing and went outside. Thanks to her grandma's vinegar poultices, the maroon colored shoulder bruise faded within a day. By the following afternoon, the full momentum of her arm returned and grandpa asked her to take a ride. They drove to the far side of the ranch, parking on the dam side of a stock pond.

"He took out grapefruit juice cans," Ana said, "and told me to fill each with water from the tank."

"Grapefruit juice cans," said Tommy wrinkling his nose. "What for?"

Ana recalled that her grandpa was a deep believer in the medicinal properties of grapefruit juice. He claimed it cleaned out impurities and kept his blood pressure down.

"So there was always plenty of quart cans for all kinds of uses," Ana said. "In this case for targets."

She carried the filled cans to where her grandpa stood. He placed them on the lower ridge of the dam and walked the thirty paces to where he had parked the truck. He took out the Commemorative, laid blanket on thee truck's hood along with two boxes of ammunition. Handing Ana the loaded rifle, he recounted the basic fundamentals of shooting, particularly a heavy gun.

"My first lesson was controlling a rifle's recoil," she chuckled dryly. "If only I'd known earlier."

Patiently, her grandpa talked of breathing, sight fining and caressing the trigger. Ana's first few shots menaced rocks and the alligator skin cracks she remembered in the side of the dam. But before they drove home, she could hit five out of five cans. It was an afternoon, she added with sad smile, that was one of her fondest memories with her grandpa.

The lease man returned the following week wearing another expensive suit and a smile to match. To her surprise her grandpa asked her to ride between them on another tour of the ranch. Listening with half an ear, Ana's mind wandered until she found herself asked about hog hunting.

"I told him everything I knew, which wasn't much, " Ana said. "I didn't tell about the flea bites and bruised shoulder."

The lease man seemed impressed and congratulated her grandpa that Ana was such a clever girl.

"I know men who'd be intrigued at even the idea of a mere slip of a girl bringing down a 500 pound wild boar," said Ana imitating the lease man. "What is it you call them?" She repeated and answered, "Ahh yes, the poor man's Bengal tiger."

Her grandpa drove to the stock pond and instructed Ana to set up fresh grapefruit cans. She did and her grandpa made a show of loading the Commemorative before handing the rifle to Ana. The lease man crossed his arms and looked bemused watching Ana take the rifle. After sending four cans spiraling up the dam with a fifth dinked between the can opener holes, his arms were at his side. Her grandpa nodded approval and the lease man continue to stare.

"I didn't think he was happy and wasn't sure he approved," Ana said. " I think he might even have been a little afraid of me."

Her grandpa suggested readjustments on her sight picture as the men examined the cans and set them up again. Returning to the firing line grandpa offered the Commemorative to the lease man. Pushing his big cowboy hat off his forehead, the lease man took the rifle, loading it as he told them about an African safari a friend from college had invited him on the previous year. Ready, he took a wide stance and jacked the Commemorative's lever like it offended him before snapping the stock to his shoulder, firing and cranking the lever with one movement.

"A spent cartridge was mid way to the ground before another was in the air," Ana said. "He dinked a can and plowed a lot of dirt."

With another too wide grin, the lease man refused another try, but didn't return the rifle. Instead, he placed the barrel on his right shoulder, D-ring up and pulled his cowboy to his forehead.

"I have to be honest," the lease man said, "after crunching some numbers, this property didn't seem worth my time. Others have considerably more deer and hospitable topography for high dollar lease hunters."

Ana remembered her grandpa's gnarled fingers shoved partially into his jeans pockets watching the lease man cradle the Commemorative in his left arm.

"But after checking with certain sources and briefing them about the potential of wild boar hunts," he paused for effect and said, "I believe next season we could make a truck load of money."

"Grandpa only tilted his head, the same way he did when he wanted to hear better," Ana said. "For me it was Thanksgiving, Christmas, my birthday, and Independence Day rolled into the same hour."

"That's why I believe," continued the lease man, "that with a little investment, some renovation and first class advertisement this property could become a hunter's Mecca."

"Is that right?" said grandpa without enthusiasm.

"Yes sir," the lease man said. "Why, you could give up ranching altogether. Because the money you'd make could be invested and make another fortune."

"Is that right?" her grandpa repeated.

"But only if we move fast," said the lease man beaming. "We can literally have every hour reserved for the next hunting season. Hell, for the next ten years."

Ana wanted to shout and turn somersaults, she felt like singing and dancing right there. Here was the big time. Her Grandpa said nothing.

"I've already talked to a well known architect about plans for a hunting lodge," the lease man said. "How soon could your family be out of your house."

"Can't say," grandpa said. "But, why should we move?"

"We'll be using your house as command central during the refurbishment," the lease man explained. "Naturally we'll find you suitable accommodations elsewhere."

"Is that right?" her Grandpa repeated again, "Suitable accommodations elsewhere!"

"Yes sir, you won't want to live here once things start jumping," the lease man said. "This will be one hopping place when things get going. In a year's time you won't recognize the place. Besides a four star hotel, we're talking horse stables, swimming pool and every luxury accommodation. Folks will come from all over the world and you'll be rolling in dough."

"I was ecstatic, I could have burst," Ana recalled. "Until the lease man let the other boot drop in a cow pie."

"Naturally, you and your family will stay on when the facilities are finished, " the lease man said. "We particularly want to hire the girl here, and, of course, her mother."

"I felt like one of those survivors climbing out of the rubble of a city that had been bombed without warning," Ana said. "Grandpa never blinked or asked the lease man why he wanted to keep me on and I didn't care for his tone when he spoke about my mother."

"She'll be the main attraction," the lease man gushed. "That will draw hunters like bees to honey."

"I beg your pardon," her grandpa said. "I don't appreciate where this is going."

"Don't misunderstand,' the lease man said. "These city hunters will chomp at the bit to match her."

"You mean shoot a hog," said her grandpa, "which she shot by pure dumb luck."

"Not from what I've seen today," the lease man said. "When I introduce this little lady at some shooting demonstrations by other experts, word will fly like a grass fire. We'll have a waiting list of hot shot shooters from across the country before the end of summer."

"Swimming pools, four star hotels and every luxury was what I thought I wanted," Ana said. "But those things didn't belong on my grandpa's land. Property his grandpa first settled. Worse, this was completely wrong in a way I could not even put into words. Yet, I was a part of it. I had killed a beautiful animal to avoid ruining the deal. Even though it was unintentional, and even beneficial by rancher standards, my justification was my belief that it was the only way to get off the ranch. That was when I had a true understanding of why I had an *Orion*. "

"So did your grandpa let the lease man do everything he wanted?" Tommy asked.

"No," Ana said. "He told him he'd think about it and get back to him."

The lease man accepted grandpa's answer and asked for something else. "He wanted to buy the Commemorative. He offered a bunch of money, much more than it was worth."

"Why didn't he sell it," I asked.

"He said, 'Because this rifle belongs to my granddaughter,'" Ana repeated, "and she doesn't want to sell it!'"

They never saw the lease man again and for good reason. They learned he had been a swindler cheating landowners and hunters out of thousands of dollars. So she and her mom stayed on her grandpa's ranch. Ana got in involved and made it a point to know the local kids. She attended events and tried to appreciate what the community had to offer

"Once I got to know them," Ana said, "I had a lot of fun and found I had a lot in common. I still wanted to see Paris and New York. I just didn't tell them about it."

"Did your parents get back together?" I asked.

"Yes they did," Ana replied, "and, for a while, things were fine."

They broke up later and when her parents finally realized they couldn't live together, her mom returned to her grandpa's ranch. She got a job in town and they were happy until Ana went away to college."

"What has your garden got to do with the hogs?" Tommy demanded.

"That garden is how I see life through *Orion's* perspective," Ana said. "It's a place hogs can root, kids can play or ladies of the tour of homes can criticize."

I wanted to argue, only Peggy banged through the doorway with a full tray. Ana slipped the knife into her purse and looked around at Peggy's toothy grin.

CHAPTER 32

It was the best hamburger I could remember eating. Of course, I was very hungry. The meat was juicy, crispy on the sides, the buns lightly toasted with just a touch of mustard consecrating a marriage of lettuce and tomato to patty.

Ana also liked her hamburger and told Peggy as much with a wad of bills. Beaming, the waitress escorted us to the front. Deputy Cindy sat talking to the old men and catching sight of us, laid a handful of coins on the table as payment for her coffee and moved with us to the door. The old men I saw dug frantically into their pockets spilling out dimes and nickels onto Cindy's contribution.

We were in the middle of the street when the old men tried to leave the café and collided shoulder to shoulder. They might have been funny if not for the red pickup truck that pulled to a stop in an official space beside Deputy Cindy's cruiser. In the back of the truck sat Macho Mike, Davis and Terrell, their eyes barely showing above the truck's tailgate. The driver door opened and Bobby Outlaw jumped out, pulling his long staff behind him. He loosened a rope nearest to the driver's side and walked back untangling the end to the truck's tailgate.

Macho Mike's eyes lit and he called to Deputy Cindy.

"Deputy, arrest this animal," he howled. "He assaulted and kidnapped us."

Terrell and Davis bobbed their heads in agreement. Deputy Cindy didn't seem to notice them, turning her attention to Bobby Outlaw. "Hello Bobby," she hailed. "Whatcha got?"

Bobby only smiled as he tossed the rope end towards the pickup cab.

"Deputy," said Macho Mike holding up his wrists swathed in gray duct tape. "This maniac beat us senseless with that stick and forced us to drag a woman he was assaulting."

Cindy still ignored him and he looked as if he were about to repeat himself when he saw us approaching from behind her. "Arrest those kids too," he ordered. "They assaulted me, left me to die and nearly got me bit by a rattlesnake. Arrest them, dammit!"

After loosening all the ropes, Bobby returned to the open driver's door and stripped off his T-shirt. Using a rag he doused with water from a jug, he dabbed his chest and back before reaching behind the seat. He brought out a pressed beige shirt with a gold nameplate on one and a big badge on the other pocket. The badge declared "Constable" in black letters.

Balancing the staff on his shoulder, he walked to the truck's tailgate buttoning his shirt. "Ah ha, police brutality," said Macho Mike, pointing with his duct taped hands. "I'm a victim of police brutality. Get me a lawyer."

Bobby didn't bother to tuck in his shirt tail as he greeted us and unlatched the pickup's tailgate. The other men's hands were also bound with gray duct tape. Without being told they scooted to the edge of the tailgate and swung their legs out. Macho Mike's feet hung with what had been my life jacket, resembling a badly wrapped Christmas present. Slipping off the tailgate, Macho Mike's bare toes touched hot asphalt and he promptly hopped back up on the tailgate.

"It's police brutality, I'm telling you," he screamed again. "I'm going to sue this town for a million dollars and I won't move until I get some proper footwear."

I wanted to laugh, and would have, if I hadn't heard my name called from the passenger side of the truck and Flo Outlaw bobbing her head as she called, "HELLOOO, JAAAACKIEEEEE!"

I ran to the cab and hugged her while Macho Mike raised new protests. "I said, I ain't moving until I get proper foot wear," he said defiantly. "I know my rights."

M&M's mouth closed as Bobby 's staff came off his shoulder.

"Shut up Mikey," Terrell said. "It's hot, we want to get out of the sun."

Shaking his frizzy hair, Macho Mike pushed off the tailgate and the others followed moaning about needle and pin sensations down their legs.

"I told you Bad Bob was out there," Tommy mocked, "but would you listen?"

Macho Mike tried to step toward Tommy and nearly collided with the end of Bobby's staff. Snarling, he moved back and the unspoken directions of the staff to the building adjacent to the courthouse.

"Would you help Flo out of the truck?" Bobby called over his shoulder.

He and Cindy escorted the trio toward a double door. Cindy keyed a button on the microphone clipped to her shoulder connected to squiggly cord to her belt radio. Tommy hopped into the truck for Flo's folded wheelchair as two more deputies appeared from the courthouse. Bobby saluted them with his staff and they nodded taking position on the sides of the three. I made introductions.

"HOOOOOW DOOOO YOOOUUU DOOO?" Flo said.

Flo's hands waved uncontrollably until Ana caught her right and shook it. Tommy moved the unfolded wheelchair toward us and Ana undid the truck seatbelt. Together we moved Flo to her chair and she pat-patted us, cooing in her synthesized language.

"I see you made it," she said. "Where's Tarzan Charlie?"

I told her about Tate's Landing and the deputies asking Charlie to go up river, and strapped her into her wheelchair. I also asked how they found the three zombie men.

"They found us," answered Bobby, joining us. "They showed up about an hour after you left."

"And you arrested them," said Tommy with malicious glee.

Bobbie shook his head and explained he had no cause to detain any of them as they stumbled into the camp, just as he had no reason to believe Charlie's story. Still, he was alert to the three men walking toward them. He and Flo had enjoyed the morning, he hoped the three would push on so they could enjoy the afternoon.

"So why did you bring them in?" Tommy demanded.

"They wanted my shoes," Bobby said. "They threatened Flo."

Chapter 33

Bobby and Flo were lying on the bank enjoying a cool drink when they heard the clatter up river. With the warning of loud noise, Bobby had plenty of time to dress Flo and himself. They waited but were still unprepared for the sight of the miserable looking trio that stumbled into the clearing. A man with a straw hat made customary salutations, yet it was the curly haired boy with a girl's face who turned rude and mean.

"He's Macho Mike. Charlie calls him M&M," Tommy said. "Straw hat is Terrell."

His feet were wrapped with what had been the sections and straps of a life jacket. The whole apparatus was shredded and looked as if it might fall apart at any time. Limping toward Bobby the boy looked him up and down, then leaned close.

"What size shoe do you wear" Mike demanded.

"Too big for you," Bobby told him.

"I don't need a smart ass answer. My feet are nearly in shreds," Macho Mike said. "I need shoes and you're the only store in town. Get 'em off!"

"How'd you manage to do that?" Asked Bobby ignoring Mike's manner. "It's not good to leave home without proper footwear in this country."

"None of your business," M&M replied. "And I've told you about being a smart ass. I won't repeat myself, get those shoes off."

He hopped toward Bobby, mouth puckered, brows arched when he noticed Flo lying on her blanket. "What's that?" Mike asked. "Who's that?"

"A woman," Bobby told him. "My wife."

"Jeez, what happened to her?" asked the chunky guy the others called Davis-you-dumb-ass. "She been in an accident or something?"

"Yeah something. It's called Cerebral Palsy," replied Bobby without apology, "She's been this way since she was a child."

"Jeez Louise, talk about freaky shit," said Davis, wiping his hand on his pants and stepping back. "She looks like she was born without bones."

The straw hat guy joined Davis to eye Flo with obvious disgust. "That's just too bad," said Terrell, without sincerity. "So what's up dwarf? What are you and the…little lady doing out here?"

"Besides your act," snorted Davis, slapping his knee with a laugh. "You know one more freak and we could have a circus."

"Enjoying a beautiful day," said Bobby ignoring Davis, "And what brings you folks to these parts?"

"We'll ask the questions," Terrell snapped. "Did you see a big guy in a canoe come by here with a couple kids?"

Bobby confirmed we'd stopped and continued down river. He never mentioned what Charlie had told him and they didn't ask. Macho Mike hobbled to the rickshaw and flipped the lid on the ice cooler.

"Get out of there," Bobby warned. "Those aren't yours."

"Who's going to stop him, dwarf?" Terrell demanded. "You?"

When Bobby didn't answer, Mike flipped the cooler's lid shut with his middle finger and picked his way toward Flo.

"You two doing something dirty?" Mike snickered.

"Ewww," Davis moaned. "That is just gross. No, that's nasty."

"Beats making meth," Bobby said. "I understand some no account druggies cooking on this river."

All humor left the other men's faces. "Look little guy, if you know what's good for you, shuck the shoes, like yesterday," Terrell said. "In fact lose everything from your pockets, including car keys and point us in the direction of your ride. That way you and the little lady can avoid trouble, and even more hurt."

"So this is a robbery," Bobby said. "Maybe assault?"

"You catch on fast dwarf," Terrell spat. "Give the little guy a cigar and a gold star."

"You still have those damn shoes on?" Mike howled. "I won't tell you again." He moved toward Bobby with a hand on one of his knives.

"I just wanted to make sure," replied Bobby, shifting the staff from his shoulder to both hands.

Only Flo wasn't surprised as Bobby closed the distance on Terrell and rammed the staff into the bigger man's midsection. Breath knocked out of him, Terrell fell to the ground and rolled from side to side grasping his chest.

Bellowing, Davis charged, arms outstretched and missed Bobby by a whisker as the smaller man pivoted. Bobby alternately rapped the ends of his stick against Davis' ribs, before swinging it in an arch across the big man's broad back.

Wheezing for breath, Terrell crawled and grabbed a stick lying just out of reach and used it to get unsteadily to his feet. Grasping the stick like a baseball bat, Terrell advanced to a waiting Bobby, whose parry disintegrated Terrell's club. Throwing away what was left of his stick at

Bobby, Terrell reached for the staff and Bobby whipped it out of his reach, before tapping the ends across Terrell's shoulders, thighs and knees. A final tap to Terrell's unguarded solar plexus and he crumpled to the ground like a tossed wrapper.

An outraged Mike whipped out his knives and moved toward Bobby in a tiger's crouch, the dagger extended the full length of his left arm. Hopping forward making "ha-ha-ha" sounds, Mike's right hand coiled against his chest, the fingers threaded through that knife's brass loops, the curved edge outward.

Bobby advanced, thrust and parried Mike's awkward dagger strike. Before Mike could recover, a series of sharp taps rattled his skinny chest with a tom-tom drum beat. Shifting his staff, Bobby pressed his attack with quick feigns before double taping his opponent's hands. The knives clattered to the ground. Howling like he had been skinned, though suffering no broken skin, Mike held his hands out to his sides waving the sting from both hands.

"Son of a bitch," Mike yowled. "That hurt!"

Growling, Mike dropped to retrieve the knives. Bobby rammed the staff toward the younger man's foot, forcing Mike to jump back barely in time to avoid loosing a toe. He was forced to back peddle in a jerky jig with Bobby stabbing repeatedly at one foot, then the other. Predictably, Mike tripped over his feet and hit the ground hard, breath rushing from his lungs. He tried to get up, only to be forced back with Bobby leaning against the staff on Mike's chest.

"Nuff, nuff," Mike screamed. "Oh please! Nuff, I give!"

Davis got to his feet, obvious to the strings of spit trailing down his lower lip catching in his beard stubble. Seeing his fallen friends, he growled and took an uneasy step.

"That's when I clapped," said Flo, with one of her deep in the chest laughs. "Foolish maybe, but I learned why they called him Davis, you dumb ass."

Davis brought a knife from his pocket, popped open the blade and ran toward Flo.

"He wanted to take me hostage, I think," Flo said. "Oh, lucky, lucky me."

An honor for Flo, a mistake for Davis as Bobby galloped to head him off. Laughing, Davis saw his goal and with a burst of energy closed the distance. He only had to grab the woman and put his knife to her throat, like he'd seen in TV shows.

Davis heard a soft whistling and turned his head in time to see what resembled, to him, a gigantic butterfly. It was baring down on him and Bobby was a distance behind it, empty handed.

The spinning staff hit Davis in the shins and sent him sprawling. Before he could get to his knees, a foot stomped the center of his back and to ground. When the tip of the staff pressed to his ear, a groaning Davis stretched his arms wide, fingers splayed.

Staff at the ready, Bobby motioned for Davis to get to his feet. The big man stumbled toward the others where Bobby ordered them to sit with their backs to Mike and not to move.

Gathering the knives, Bobby tossed them into the rickshaw. Scooping Flo into a blanket in one arm, he placed her in the rickshaw and strapped her in. He directed the trio to grab the trace poles of the rickshaw.

"We ain't your slaves," Davis whined.

The others also raised their voices, until Bobby lifted the staff off his shoulder.

"And hEEEERE wEEE AAAre," Flo said, her head weaving, with a broad smiled.

CHAPTER 34

Bobby held the door open to the sheriff's office building while Tommy and I pushed Flo inside. Deputy Cindy told us to follow her and Flo howled, "LEEEEt thEEEEmm gEEEEEt clEEAned Up. ThEy bEEn in thEEE BOOOndOOOcks AAAAll wEEEk."

"Not just yet, Flo," Deputy Cindy explained. "A doctor needs to see them first."

Ana followed us into a nearby room where a doctor wearing a dark blue smock and pants and stethoscope around his neck stood. Nearby, an older woman wearing a cartoon character smock laid out various packages.

Doctor Jones' dark hair was cut short, his eyes were bright, and he smiled as he introduced himself and Nurse Jones. He asked me to "please" go behind a nearby screen, undress and put on a paper gown. While I was happy to get out of my dirty clothes, having my rear exposed by the open back was nothing to smile about.

I sat on a table covered with a paper sheet as Nurse Jones took my temperature, blood pressure and pulse. She measured and weighed me on a scale, poked my ears and shined a light up my nose and in my eyes. Having just accepted the paper gown, I was told to pull it down to my waist. Keeping my eyes on the nearby door, I still managed to "ahh" and "oh" on cue. I also coughed, when I wasn't taking deep breaths, including a really deep one when Doctor Jones put his very cold stethoscope on my bare back.

Told to sit back on the edge of a paper draped table, Doctor Jones raised the paper gown to look *down there*. And by look down there, I mean really look and touch. Red faced, I complied after a reassuring glance from Ana. This procedure wasn't a ride I wanted to make a habit of, but Doctor Jones was gentle and only mildly intrusive. So, it wasn't as bad as it sounds. Thankfully, his hands were warm and he wore rubber gloves. He didn't make any noises indicating he found anything wrong, though my concern was what was he looking for in the first place.

As if that wasn't bad, or good enough, the doctor also wanted to look *back there*. Later Tommy told me he got the same experience so I didn't feel as if I'd gotten special treatment. Finally Doctor Jones told Nurse Jones to list me as a "normal, developing pre-adolescent female."

Hearing that I was normal, my opinion of Doctor and Nurse Jones improved considerably. Never mind, they examined me with the same dispassion Charlie had dabbed disinfectant on my bug bites. I always thought doctors and nurses should be more caring. Which I suppose they were. Doctor Jones asked if I felt dizzy or sick. I gave no to both questions and the nurse checked a clipboard. However, when asked what I had to drink or eat in the last 48 hours, I got their full attention.

"He made you eat that?" the nurse squeaked glancing at the doctor as if she should have asked permission.

"Nobody made us eat anything," I said indignantly, "because it was the best meal I ever ate, and we caught everything ourselves."

To dispel any doubt, I pushed out my finger the crawfish had pinched. Fascinated, Doctor Jones applied a white cream to my finger and an adhesive strip as he asked for particulars about cooking meals in a towel using a hole in the ground for an oven. Nurse Jones shook her head disapprovingly. Dr. Jones laughed handing Ana a tube of the white cream and more bandages, and told me he'd like to hear more, if I had time.

Tommy walked in as I jumped off the table, though I tried to keep the back of my gown closed, my cousin pointed and laughed until told him to hush. Ana helped me tie it before stepping into the hall and following Cindy to an alcove where, beyond the "ladies room" sign, there was a row of sinks and stalls. I never thought a toilet could feel so good on my rear.

In a nearby room was a long bench, separate shower stalls, and the second best experience with water in my memory. I adjusted the shower spray so it was hot enough to nearly peel my skin off and stood on the drain letting the spray gush over me. I would have stayed until the hot water ran cold and beyond. Only Ana ordered me out, before, as she put it, I melted.

Ana held out a big white towel as I pulled the shower curtain back, the same as she'd done since before I could walk. She dried my back, rubbed my hair and examined my head as if it contained hidden weapons. Using a washcloth like a plumber's snake, she grubbed my ears clean and showed me the results. All indignities were forgiven as she smeared me with sweet smelling body lotion.

"Some bug bites won't go away," she said looking at my chest. "We'll have to take you shopping."

Red cheeked, I pulled the towel up to my chin, wincing as it brushed my chest. Ana took no notice and picked up a brush, combed and tied my hair into a ponytail. From a Dollar General Store bag she brought out new underwear, stiff jeans and a lime green T-shirt with "Girls just want to have fun" printed on the front. A pair of matching lime-green sandals completed my ensemble.

"Deputy Cindy got these for you," Ana explained.

So I dressed and admired myself in the mirror, surprised at the absence of the wild savage in a paper gown who glared from the mirror only minutes before. To my surprise, Ana tipped my head and painted my lips with lip gloss from her purse and sprayed my neck with a pencil sized atomizer. The perfume stung my bites. Ana's prideful expression made me forget all my discomfort and recall how she'd stood with me looking into a mirror only two days before. This, I knew, was different, maybe because I was different.

"Shakespeare said clothes make the man," she said. "You clean up pretty good, as we used to say on the ranch."

Stuffing my dirty clothes into the yellow bag, we left the rest room, stepping into the hall where Tommy, dressed in new boy's clothes, sat with a similar bag at his feet.

Carrying a yellow legal pad, Deputy Cindy directed us to follow her to the end of the hall. On the way, my heart hammered thinking of those television police shows with suspects in dingy rooms confessing to their alleged crimes within five minutes.

"Where we going?" Tommy asked.

"We just need to get your statements," Deputy Cindy said. "Nothing is done until the paperwork is done, so I'm told."

Deputy Cindy opened the door to a room with a long mirror on the wall to our left and a long metal table bolted to the floor. On each side of the table were four chairs. An air conditioner blocked the lower panes of the room's only window while the panes above it were painted the same dull green as the walls.

Deputy Cindy indicated Tommy and I sit at the table facing the mirror. Without being told Ana took a seat beside Tommy. Deputy Cindy moved a chair the far end of the table allowing her to talk to us and watch the door. Placing her yellow pad and a pen in front of her, she leaned back and asked Ana if everything was OK. Ana responded that everything was fine and thanked Deputy Cindy again for getting us the new clothes. Thereafter, we struggled through small talk for what I knew was longer than usual. Deputy Cindy desperately tried not to look at her wrist watch. I made it a point of asking a question about the air conditioner and watching from the corner of my eye. It was during one of these impromptu diversions, that Deputy Cindy lifted her watch to her face. Sighing, she got up and moved to the door and it was thrown open. She jumped back to avoid colliding with a stringy man with a big moustache. He wore a uniform like Deputy Cindy's, with gold chevrons on the left sleeve and a gray cowboy hat tipped over one eye. A cigarette dangled between his thin lips wafting a smoky halo around his hat. He regarded Deputy Cindy, but wouldn't retreat as he took the cigarette between the fingers of his right hand and let it drop to his pistol holster. Without word, Deputy Cindy returned to her chair at the end of the table and the man put the cigarette back in his mouth.

The man moved into the room carrying a file and a tape recorder under his left arm. His right hand grasped the bottom half of the black pistol holster attached to his belt. Moving into the room he yanked the holster downward every other step as if it might float away. He exhaled smoke from a crooked nose with a bump on its ridge that, Ana told me later, had been broken at least twice.

"I didn't expect you this early," he drawled.

"The doctor finished his examination," Deputy Cindy said. "They even had time for shower."

With an impatient glance in Deputy Cindy's direction, he turned to us and announced, "I am Sergeant Austin Drumhead, the sheriff's department criminal investigator and I will be taking your statements about the alleged incidents. I ask that you please be totally honest, fourth coming and answer all my questions to the utmost of your recall. Understand that the truth will be revealed in the end, so I need you to do the right thing."

Feeling uneasy, I immediately disliked Sergeant Drumhead. His words, like his hat, were too big. Though he took the hat off and carefully placed it, crown down, to his left toward Deputy Cindy about three-quarters down the table.

He yanked his holster again before sitting down, placing the file and tape recorder between us. His head wagged searching for something on the table until Deputy Cindy got up and pulled a drawer open from our side of the table. She took out an aluminum ashtray and slid it toward him. He eyed Deputy Cindy as he viciously crushed out the cigarette before turning to us and jabbing the tape recorder's play button.

"For the record," he began, "I need all of you to state your full name and address, then give a brief description about what happened to you. Please include everywhere you went, all the activities you witnessed between the time you left home until you came into this room. Deputy Cindy will be making notes, so don't mind her."

He shoved the tape recorder's microphone toward an unprepared

Tommy. The boy stared at it as if it had an eye. Meantime, my chest ached and my *Orion* itched as I pulled the microphone between us. Taking a deep breath, I recited my version of "the activities." Drumhead peered at me with runny eyes, tapped his pen, wrote a little and said nothing. He alternated looking from me to Tommy, who shifted in his chair like a tree caught in a high wind.

Reaching when Charlie grabbed me before I walked into the snake, I had grown comfortable as spokesperson. My *Orion's* itch had dropped to a mild irritation and Tommy relaxed enough to interject a fact or two, keeping with Sergeant Drumhead's directions. I didn't bother with minor details like the "little bitty biting worm" story, Bad Bob or the fish pool. I talked believing I had told an accurate story.

"Why did you take the raft?" Drumhead demanded quietly. "The men who own that raft said the only way it could have been found was if the thieves had watched where they put it.

The way he said "take" echoed of the tone kids at school used when they meant steal, swipe or rob. He didn't call us thieves but my *Orion* went into overdrive itch. Ana sat with her hands folded and cleared her throat. Irritated, Sergeant Drumhead glanced in her direction and Deputy Cindy scribbled.

"We didn't take it," I said firmly. "We fell in and it took us."

"It just got loose by itself," Drumhead declared.

Nodding, I recounted Tommy prank of pulling me into the raft and grabbing the wrong end of the rope, untying us from the tree. Drumhead asked Tommy if he intended to take the raft for a short ride and if the current was heavy. Tommy shook his head and Drumhead wanted to know how it got away from us in such a weak current.

"We had no paddles," Tommy said. "We couldn't have taken it even if we knew how or wanted too."

"What happened to get that boy Lonnie so riled?" Drumhead asked.

I was tempted to say it didn't take much to get Lonnie mean, particularly if the offender was smaller and weaker than him. Instead I recounted Lonnie's savate kicks at Tommy's head, our footwork and run down the trail to the creek.

"Mighty slick, mighty slick indeed," said Drumhead, nodding his head with a grin that didn't reach his eyes. "Why didn't you run to your parents or some other adult?"

My *Orion* prickled as I re-explained how our way was blocked and we took the only escape open to us.

"And you're sure you didn't know the raft was down there?" Sergeant

Drumhead asked.

"We only arrived at Bandy' Camp a few hours earlier," Ana said, "and they've never been to this part of the country before, so how could they know?"

Drumhead's mouth pursed, but he didn't reply as he gave Ana a look and Cindy scribbled on her pad.

"On the raft," Drumhead said, "why didn't you yell for help?"

"We did call, we even yelled for Lonnie," I said. "We yelled and I blew my whistle, but nobody heard us."

"Whistle," Drumhead said. "What whistle, where is it?"

I told him about the beacon and his moustache twitched.

"Where is this whistle?" he asked again. "Can I see it? Do you have it?"

I remembered leaving the beacon with Charlie and told Drumhead as much. He mumbled and Cindy scribbled.

"So of all the hundreds and hundreds of people in and around Bandy's Camp, you couldn't get anybody's attention," Drumhead said shaking his head. "You just decided to go for a row-row-row your boat ride."

I repeated how we'd passed the old man and his wife on the dock, which happened to be when Papa's band started to play. Without prompting, Cindy confirmed that the old folks had come forward when they heard about the missing children. She added that Lonnie and his family had also been at Bandy's Camp. Inhaling, Drumhead shot Deputy Cindy a disapproving look and nodded his head. Cindy dropped her head and scribbled.

"Now, how'd you meet this Charlie character," Drumhead said, and why did you go to his camp?"

Character was another one of those word with a different meaning I didn't care for.

"He stopped me from walking into a rattlesnake," I replied, "I asked for a drink of water and he took us back to his camp."

"But you said you ran away from him after he saved you," Drumhead said.

I looked at Tommy and even turned to look at Ana before I answered.

"I don't know, I guess it was because he had red eyes, was dirty and smelled," I said. "I didn't sleep good and I was scared."

"Red eyes," said Drumhead with a glance at Cindy, "so, did you find him, or did he catch you?"

Again I recalled how I went looking for Charlie, glad for my Orion's itch and the soreness in my chest.

"Didn't your mother ever tell it's not a good idea to talk to strangers,"

Drumhead demanded.

Yes, I replied with control, my mother and Ana warned me every time I went anywhere. There was also a program at school, called Stranger Danger.

"He was the only grown up out there," I said my voice quavering. "I thought he was our only chance of getting found."

"Yet you ran away," Drumhead said.

"Because," I said biting my lip, "he was a stranger."

"But you found him again," Drumhead said. "To be clear, did you find him or did he find you?"

"I found him sitting in the river," I said, my *Orion* feeling like a worm burrowing out of my wrist.

"Doing what?" Drumhead demanded. "Swimming, fishing, something else?"

"He was sitting on a rock and…singing," I said. "It was a good thing too, because if he hadn't been singing, I wouldn't have found him."

"Singing?" Drumhead repeated like I'd said Charlie was water skiing.

"McHale is a mighty man who goes to circus shows," I sang, " leaps into the big cats' cage, to show what he knows."

"OK, I get it, said Drumhead impatiently. "I get the idea."

"For a while he pokes his head in a tiger's mouth," I continued singing, "and takes it out with a smile at the joke and calls the big cat Ralph."

"Alright, already," Drumhead growled, "now look little lady, fun and games are over. This is serious business, so you need to sit up and fly right because a lot of time, money and man power went to rescuing you, so I suggest you drop any more foolishness."

We were rescued by Tarzan Charlie, I thought, and you wouldn't have known where to find us if he hadn't called you. My thoughts were interrupted when Ana's chair scraped. Drumhead glared in her direction. I didn't have to look to know Ana was returning Drumhead's look with a vengeance. The sound of Cindy's scribbling seemed to bring his eyes back to us.

"He was sitting on a big rock that was out in the river and singing," Drumhead repeated. "Where was he looking?"

"At the river," I said not understanding the question.

"You sure he wasn't watching or waiting for somebody?" Drumhead asked.

Again, not understanding the question, I shook my head.

"You said he had drinking water?" Drumhead asked.

We nodded, Cindy wrote.

"Did he offer you anything else?" Drumhead asked.

"Only as much water as we could drink, " I said. "We were really thirsty."

"Why didn't he kill that big rattlesnake you nearly walked into?" Drumhead demanded. "It could have bitten you."

I explained that considering I'd almost stepped on the snake, what else would a snake do? And besides, it was pretty!

"Pretty," Drumhead hooted. "You know what would have happened if a snake that size bit you? That would be enough reason for me to kill it, enough reason to kill every snake in the whole country."

"Yes, pretty," I repeated, ignoring his last statement, "and I'd bite somebody who tried to step on me."

"You would" he said. "Is that what Charlie told you?"

No, I answered and added I was still glad Charlie didn't kill the snake, though he was certainly capable. "What makes you say that?" Asked Drumhead in a subdued tone.

"He drove the big snake away with pebbles," I said. "He certainly could have done worse with a rock or stick."

Cindy scribbled

"Did he say what he was doing out there?" Drumhead asked.

"Teasing rattlesnakes," I said without knowing why.

Ana and Deputy Cindy laughed, Drumhead looked irritated. "Is that's what he told you?" He said.

"No, that's what he was doing," I said, weary of that particular question.

"I've warned you about being silly," Drumhead chided. "Is THAT what he told you?"

No, I repeated again without the commentary, and so it went, back and forth with me answering truthfully, 90 percent of the time, as Papa would say. But only because Drumhead didn't ask the right questions, and I didn't care to help. By the time Drumhead asked about our crawfish, and rice supper, I was more than a little irritated.

"It was the best meals I've ever ate," I said. "I can't remember ever being so hungry."

"Food cooked in a towel!" Said Drumhead with toilet sarcasm. "Sounds gunky, not something I would ever eat."

"You would if you were hungry," Tommy said. "How can you say it doesn't sound like something you'd eat if you've never tried it?"

"I'll ask the questions," snapped Drumhead and turned to me. "Why did you go to the creek alone? Why didn't Charlie go with you? Did he watch you undress?"

"We rubbed soap on our wet clothes," I said unable to hide my indignity. "The water wasn't deep," at least not in some places, I thought with satisfaction.

Drumhead also wanted to know what Charlie's camp was like? Glad for the change of topic, I described the orderly layout from fireplace to inside the tent, emphasizing the overall tidiness and order. Though I wondered what any of that had to do with the price of crawdads.

"Did he say why he made his camp so far away from the river and even the creek?" Drumhead said. " From what you've said the spot where he beached his canoe would have been just right."

I told him we didn't know, and he'd have to ask Charlie since neither Tommy or I had ever been camping before then.

"Don't get smart," he said, reminding me of Lonnie and Macho Mike.

Ana's chair scrapped, but Drumhead's eyes never left me as he demanded to know if we'd seen anything else in Charlie's camp. Anything unusual, funny, odd objects that might have been out of place.

"Like what?" Tommy asked.

"Stuff like jars, hoses, propane tanks," he recited. You've know what coffee filters look like, you've seen ice coolers before? Were there a lot of those?"

We knew of these things, but we stared at Drumhead in confusion. We hadn't seen any of those things in Charlie's camp. They would have stood out like sore thumbs and toes if they had.

"Do you remember any odd sounds, funny odors, say before you walked into his camp?" Drumhead asked. "Could you recall anything you might have thought later that was nasty, weird or out of the ordinary?"

"Yes," Tommy said, "he had this gunk in a green bottle."

"Gunk," said Drumhead with triumph. "What kind of gunk, how big was the bottle?"

"About this size," said Tommy forming a C with his forefinger and thumb in front of his face. "He dabbed that gunk on our bug bites."

The gunk, Tommy explained, smelled like the goop his mom slathered on his chest when he got a cold. Charlie's gunk also kept the mosquitoes away while we hunted crawdads, he added. Cindy continued scribbling, smiling. Drumhead's mouth disappeared behind his moustache before asking why Charlie and I had left Tommy alone.

"Breakfast," I replied. "We went to pick wild blackberries and caught fish."

I recounted, again filling the bucket with plump blackberries, soaking away the worms and the unique way Charlie fished. It was my hope that

Drumhead, like the doctor, would be impressed.

"Who decided to leave Tommy alone?" He repeated. "Was it you or Charlie?"

No one, I lied, explaining Tommy's penchant for sleeping late, adding that we, or I, didn't expect to be gone very long.

"To hear Charlie talk," I said, "he expected to pick a bucket of blackberries and come right back in 30 minutes or less."

"Is that what he told you?" Drumhead asked. "Are you sure it wasn't his idea to leave Tommy?"

No, I answered, adding that I didn't believe he even knew about the fish, let alone fishing with a rock, until I gave him the idea.

"A rock?" Said Drumhead as if he were repeating a 28 letter Russian word. "A rock?"

"Actually rocks, big ones," I bragged. "He threw three or four flat rocks and got fish each time."

I described herding the fish, the magnificent splashes an the stringer of fish. Unimpressed, Drumhead demanded to know "exactly" where I was when those "big" rocks were falling? A safe distance, I answered, without mentioning the rattlesnakes or Charlie using his gun.

"During this berry picking and fishing time did Charlie ever put his hands on you?" Drumhead asked.

All eyes turned to me and again I answered Tarzan Charlie hadn't touched me. I was so tired of hearing that question and almost recounted how Charlie and I pricked our fingers on the thumbnail sized thorns and pressed them together. The itch of my *Orion* kept my mouth shut as Deputy Cindy scribbled and Drumhead sighed before shifting subjects to focus on leaving Tommy alone with the bolo.

"I left him a note," I said. "I thought we'd be back sooner."

"I never found it," Tommy said.

"There was no note," Drumhead said flatly, "like the whistle."

"Yes, there was, I left it in his shoe," I said. "It must have fallen out when he chased after that deer." And found by Macho Mike and company I added silently to myself.

"That so," Drumhead replied. "Must have!"

I wanted to kick myself for sounding so desperate to convince this man, not that I really cared. But Drumhead had a obnoxious knack for turning everything around to make it sound bad, if not worse than it could ever be.

"You found Tommy missing and Charlie tracked him?" Drumhead said. "Why did he take you instead of leaving you in camp with your breakfast of …blackberries and fried fish."

"Baked fish," I corrected. "Cooked on the side of a cedar wood plank."

"Mighty slick, mighty slick," drawled Drumhead again, though I don't think he saw the joke I did. Obviously slick was another different meaning word. Like the question about being touched. I was fed up with double-meaners.

Why Charlie took me, I thought, I didn't know, but I was glad he did. I concentrated on the recollection of walking the trail, the baby deer, climbing the hill. I hoped Drumhead could read the emotion I felt at the shock at seeing Tommy with Macho Mike. Nor did I hide my admiration at how quietly Charlie moved behind Macho Mike before tapping him on the shoulder.

"And that's when Charlie hit Macho Mike," Drumhead said. "Did you see what he hit him with?"

"He didn't hit him with anything," I said my voice rising. "He didn't touch him, Macho Mike tripped and fell."

"But you just said Charlie tapped Mike on the shoulder," Drumhead challenged. "People don't get knocked out by nothing, unless somebody hits them with a club. But you say he just tapped him. Don't you mean, he hit that man with his fist?"

"He tapped him on the shoulder with a finger, I was there, I saw him," said Tommy not mentioning the gun in Charlie's other hand. "Macho Mike raised the bolo to chop Charlie."

"That would have been justification to hit Macho Mike, "Drumhead said. "Probably with a stick or rock?"

Tommy and I shook our heads.

"Maybe he moved so fast, you only think you saw him tap this man on the shoulder," Drumhead said. "He could have tossed his weapon away, couldn't he, like while you were watching Macho Mike fall?"

Instead of answering, I described the attention Charlie gave to Mike's wounds. Which was more than Macho Mike would have done, I thought, considering he tried to chop Charlie with a bolo.

"Are you sure Macho Mike was actually hurt?" Asked Drumhead ignoring my statement. "Maybe he was playing possum, faking it?"

Again, I confirmed Macho Mike had truly knocked himself out.

"Slick, mighty slick indeed " said Drumhead again, crossing his arms over his chest, "and Charlie didn't try to make a litter or hoist this poor man on his back? From what you say, Macho Mike couldn't have weighed much, since he was so skinny."

"No, Charlie did not," I repeated. "He did make him as comfortable as possible by propping his feet on the root of a tree. The idea was to go for help."

"But Charlie didn't immediately go for help," Drumhead said, "did he?"

Anxiously, Tommy described how Charlie searched M&M

"He didn't have time to carry a man to safety," Drumhead said, "but he could rob an unconscious victim."

Cindy scrawled as I recalled the stuff from M&M's pockets and wondered why anybody would want, let alone, care about that junk. There was money, but Charlie replaced it and everything else, all except the knives and gun and I did not see why any of this was important.

In desperation I described Charlie replacing the school I.D. and navy bad postcard before dumping the zombie power from the plastic bag.

"Zombie powder?" Drumhead exclaimed. "Charlie knew what that powder was?"

"It smelled funny," Tommy said.

"I thought you said you didn't see or smell anything funny?" said Drumhead leaning over the table. "Did you forget something?"

"We said there was nothing funny at Charlie's camp," I said, my voice pitched higher than normal. "Tommy is talking about what we found on Macho Mike."

"But Charlie knew what zombie powder was, didn't he?" Drumhead said," and he took Mike's gun."

More double meaning words.

"He took it apart," Tommy said. "I wanted it, but he said I deserved better and tossed the parts into the bushes."

"Are you sure," Drumhead demanded?

I was so close to screaming, "Hell yes, you son of a bitch, we were two feet from where everything happened."

But I didn't, and alternated with Tommy describing the discovery of the trip wire, booby trap and Charlie's description of a Nazi lab. Tommy's voice quavered as he did when trying to relate too many facts tried to include every little fact, though I didn't see the point. I also realized that no matter how good our answers were, it didn't matter to Drumhead. For every question this deputy asked, he interposed two possible situations that didn't or could not have happen. Just as he ignored the logistics of trying to carry Mike and was scornful of Charlie's tracking ability. As a last ditch, I thought that describing how the other canoe turned over, we were home clear. Silly me!

"Did Charlie have a gun?" Drumhead asked. "A rifle or a pistol?"

"Macho Mike and Terrell had guns," Tommy quipped.

"So you told me," Drumhead said. "What about Charlie?"

My *Orion* itched so much I wanted to tear my wrist off.

"He has a Colt .38 Super with a 10 round clip," Tommy recited, "and he let me hold it."

"He told you this," said Drumhead triumphantly and repeated. "And he let you hold it."

"It was unloaded," I interjected, sounding desperate even to me. "He never let Tommy point it at anything or anybody."

"That's beside the point," said Drumhead leaning back in his chair, " and very interesting, very interesting, indeed."

"Interesting how, Sergeant Drumhead?" Asked Ana for the first time since we'd sat down. Drumhead looked away and Ana repeated the question louder. Drumhead gave his pistol a little tug and sighed looking at Ana with that look for people too stupid to comprehend.

"That particular caliber happens to be the preferred weapon of certain drug cartels to the south," Drumhead said. "Since it's not a military weapon, ammunition is easy to come by or transport in those hemispheres. These same men are known to deal in the same funny smelling white powder your friend Charlie knows so much about."

"Just having a particular gun doesn't automatically mean a man is in a drug cartel member," Ana defended. "I'll bet thousands of gun owners in this state own a.... She turned to Tommy.

"A Colt .38 Super automatic," beamed Tommy knowing he had the right answer.

"Yes, a Colt .38 Super," Ana repeated, " and as far as I know it's not a crime to openly carry a gun in the woods. I personally know a gun is an excellent deterrent against varmints and rattlesnakes. Don't you need a little more information to even suspect a man of that kind of association."

"No, it's not," said Drumhead though neither his tone, nor his eyes matched his words, "but you know, where there's smoke there's usually fire. The sheriff radioed for a 10-29, a check for warrants or prior criminal history, on your Tarzan Charlie."

"And what in particular did you find out?" Ana asked. "If anything?"

"A couple of traffic tickets," replied Drumhead shrugging with a little disappointment, followed by glee rising in his voice. "But the sheriff also included the company and telephone number where he worked. I gave them a call."

"Being Memorial Day weekend did anyone even answer?" Ana asked.

"That was my first thought," said Drumhead, obviously proud of himself, "but I gave them a shout and a guy happened to be there, doing some catch up work."

"What kind of guy," I asked before I could stop myself.

"I don't know," said Drumhead waving his hand dismissively. "I got his name. He sounded young, probably a college boy. He said he was the assistant, assistant something."

A coyote, I thought and forced myself not to say.

"That's not the point," Drumhead said. "You know the first word out of this guy's mouth, after I mentioned who and why I was calling?" We shook our heads.

"Scarface," he said and his moustache tipped upward. "Scarface, like the 1920s Chicago gangster or that movie about the drug lord starring.... uh."

"Al Pacino," Tommy finished, "and Michelle Pfeiffer."

"That's the one," said Drumhead pointing at Tommy with his finger like a gun. "The one where the guy has a mountain of zombie dust on the table in front of him."

Ana shot Tommy a look that told me my cousin would have some explaining to do later, but turned to Drumhead and said, "Scarface, a movie, and this person actually referred to Charlie as Scarface?"

"Yes, and that wasn't all," Drumhead said, "he said Scarface had a reputation with that company for being a rough, no nonsense guy, nobody likes him. He even described how he was a lot like the Al Pacino character in getting things done. Tough and ruthless, I believe were the words he used. He also said the office gossip was Scarface had personal and money problems and he was this close to being let go. Overall the guy didn't have anything good to say about your friend Charlie."

"And you took this information at face value," Ana said, "from somebody you happened to get doing catch up on Memorial Day Weekend."

"Well no, there are still other sources to consider," Drumhead said. "But as I said where there's smoke, there's fire."

"Bad Bob is on his way," I muttered, " it's time to get out of town."

Now," said Drumhead and turned back to me, "tell me more about this gun."

"Charlie kept his gun put up most of the time," I protested. "He even took out the square thing with the bullets and made sure it was unloaded."

Drumhead produced a square thing from a pouch on his belt and held it up before asking, "Like this one?"

We nodded and he replaced the square thing and double yanked his gun holster in the process.

"You say he never pointed his gun at anyone or shot it."

"He shot a snake!" I answered.

"I thought you said he didn't shoot the snake," Drumhead said.

"It was another snake," I said, wanting to add "you idiot," and how anybody wouldn't know there was more than one snake nearby. My voice was louder than usual because everyone stared at me and Drumhead triple tugged his holster.

"Take it easy young lady, " Drumhead cooed. "Neither you or your cousin have done anything wrong we're just trying to ascertain certain facts about this man who calls himself Charlie."

Yet, this questioning was all too familiar to me, and it wasn't right, none of it. It reminded me of The Weed, Jeri and Joyce and even Lonnie.

"You're a lucky kid," Lonnie had said, "most people don't like lucky kids."

I remembered what the reading man beside the pool had said about Flo. "Don't go there!" the reading man's voice echoed in my mind. None of what Drumhead said was relevant or factual, just rumor and assumptions. He hadn't been out there, how would he know? The reader man didn't know Bobby and Flo. The Weed and her stupid election. Coyotes and their movies. This wasn't the truth and this shouldn't happen to Tarzan Charlie, or anyone. Bad Bob was just a story and somebody should do something

"He was going to shoot you and those three men," I heard my own voice say in my head. "You can't allow him to get away with that."

But he didn't, I argued, he took us in, gave us water, gathered food, let us sleep his tent and rescued Tommy.

"Does that really excuse him for almost killing somebody," argued the voice in my head. "You were there both times, if hadn't been for…"

Then there's no excuse for me not shooting that other rattlesnake at the fish pool, I thought. Even Sergeant Dumb Drumhead, as I'd come to call him, would agree on that

"But that's different," my voice said. "That was just a dirty rattlesnake."

Not to the rattlesnake, I thought, and not to me. Intent is one thing, doing is another.

"All right," said my voice, exasperated, "what are you going to do about Sergeant Dumb Drumhead and how can you help Charlie?"

What could I do? I wasn't big and powerful, there was no gun or knife under my shirt. Ana had her Commemorative and Mrs. Gomillion her little spade. There was nobody to back me up this time, I didn't even have a handful of sand box dirt. All I had was me!

"Charlie did nothing wrong," I said in a voice I had never talked to an adult before, especially a police officer. "You seem to only want to talk about bad stuff and none of it had anything to do with Charlie. You haven't asked about everything he did to help us."

"We'll get to that," Drumhead said. "Now when the boat turned over."

"He didn't have to help us, " I said ignoring Drumhead. "He could have just as easily chased me away with that rock or stick. He didn't hit Macho Mike, but you keep trying to make us believe he did."

Drumhead looked like I had slapped him in the face with a fish.

"He didn't have to cook us supper in a towel, or anything else," I said. "But he did and it was great eating, especially after we hadn't had anything to eat for a while. Do you think someone bad could do something like that?"

"Look here young lady, I'll ask the questions here," growled Drumhead before adding in a softer tone. "No one is doubting he helped you. Now, tell me about what happened after the boat turned over."

"I can paddle a canoe now," I said ignoring his question. "He gave me his gun to shoot another rattlesnake, but I couldn't do it."

"I don't see what that has to do with what happened when the boat turned over," said Drumhead beginning to sound desperate.

"I'm not afraid of snakes anymore," I said. "Charlie never saw those men before today, but he knew they were bad. He might know about zombie powder, but he kept us from becoming zombies or getting our eyes burned out."

Drumhead glared and tugged on his pistol holster but I wouldn't look away.

"You think Tommy and I stole that raft?" I said. "For all those fun and a games you were talking about?"

Deputy Cindy quit writing and looked from me to Drumhead.

"Young lady," began Drumhead his voice rising, "please try to control yourself…"

"I can tell you there are a whole lot of better ways to have fun," I said, pushing my chair back and yanking the hem of my T-shirt up to my chin, painfully brushing my skin.

"Does this look like we were having fun?" I demanded. "Well, does it?"

In the mirror, behind Drumhead, a sunburned savage stood with blazing eyes and a mouth pursed into a snarl. She scrunched her new green T-shirt to her collar bones with "Girls Just Want to Have Fun" written on the front and could have ripped it in two. The skin of her naked torso was taunt over a flat belly and ribs that could be counted. It would not be so easy to count the dozens of star burst tattoos that puckered from her throat to her pants line in varying shades of infection red. The product of multiple healing bug bites that contrasted like a constellation of tiny suns and stars against the twin brown moons of the developing areolas of her heaving breasts.

CHAPTER 35

Ana was beside me the next moment pushing my hands and shirt down. Looking up I saw that her eyes blazed with the same intensity I'd seen the girl in the mirror. Drumhead couldn't seem to find his holster as Deputy Cindy moved to his side and said, rather than suggested, we take a break.

Drumhead mumbled something that sounded like "stock-home-sin-drum" and left the room, forgetting his hat, with Deputy Cindy behind him. Later, she returned alone carrying sodas for everyone and asked that we excuse Drumhead. She would continue the interview.

She was thorough, without Drumhead's what if situation and it seemed to take no time for her to finish. After reminding us where the rest rooms where, she left and returned with a set of typed sheets of paper. We were asked to read the typed sheets and point out anything wrong before signing. Neither Tommy nor I read anything we didn't like. Ana found a few errors in punctuation and spelling, but also signed it.

Again, I wondered if what I had done was right. I knew Charlie had been on the verge of shooting us the night before. He might have only shot himself, but he did neither. He had helped us and brought us back safe. He also could have shot Macho Mike and Arlie. I could have shot that rattlesnake swimming across the fishpond. Neither of us did, though people like Dumbhead Drumhead would have probably said we were both justified. For my part, I just wanted to go home

As for swimming naked, in retrospect I was surprised I hadn't done it sooner and wondered why more people didn't make it a habit. Later, Ana would tell me private skinny dipping was nothing compared to flashing my boobies at a cop. How would I ever live that down? I thought shaking my head and dismissing the idea.

It was late by the time we finished the paperwork and walked out of the sheriff's building. Outside, Flo sat in her wheel chair with Bobby at a nearby picnic table. His staff was across the back handles of her wheelchair as he pushed her toward us. Across the street sat two of the old men on the Dollar General Store bench, along with the chocolate pie eater. Seeing us, they nudged one another as I hugged Deputy Cindy and Flo. An unenthusiastic Tommy stiffened accepting Flo's embrace with his finger tips on Flo's slender shoulders.

"Come back and we'll swim with the gars," she said in her singsong language, "and drink more iced tea."

"That would be nice," I replied and looked past her toward the parking lot where Ana's van was parked. A sheriff's department pickup truck pulled into a for official use only parking spot." Two men sat in the front seat, their heads bobbing in animated conversation. Lashed to the bed of the truck was a green, black striped object, protruding off of the tail-gate with a red rag attached to its end. A sheriff's deputy, I'd seen at Turtle Ron's, slid out of the driver's side holding a big notebook and a familiar flap holster and bullet pouch slung over the same shoulder, its thin strap meant to be worn across the chest. From the passenger side, Tarzan Charlie mounted the curb still smiling as he talked with the deputy.

They have his gun and canoe, I thought, in panic. But, they can't put him in jail, he's done nothing wrong. I cried out his name and raced across the yard full force. Looking up and seeing me, Charlie's face broke into a huge grin as I sprang into his arms wrapped mine around his neck. Burying my face into his shoulder I inhaled the heady smell of river and man sweat mingled with smells of wild flowers, wind and wood smoke.

"I didn't rat you out," I whispered into his neck. "I didn't vote for you."

He bent his head holding me against his chest. I wrapped my legs around his waist. His big hands supported my back as he rocked me, his fingers drumming a gentle tattoo. My eyes welled with tears looking at the old men across the street staring. Holding me with one brawny arm against his chest, Charlie brushed my tears away and I caught the smell of rattlesnake musk on his hand.

"We have to quit meeting like this," he said laughing. "People will think we know each other."

I slid down his chest, taking care not to snag his folded reading glasses and my feet hit the ground, his hands resting on my shoulders.

"I didn't think I'd see you again," I said. "I didn't want to go without saying thank you and good-bye."

"Not a problem," he said and added, "and don't you clean up nice?"

Blushing, I stepped back and looked over my shoulder.

"I also wanted you to meet my...."

Before I could say her name Ana was behind me and Charlie pushed his Stetson off his head. The shocks of gray-blonde hair sprang up and he slid a trembling hand from my neck to smooth it before laying it on my upper arm. Ana stepped closer and placed her hands on my shoulders where his had been. Judging by the extra weight, her touch was less for affection than for physical support as she absently smoothed stray wisps of her hair behind her ears. A gesture I'd seen her make a thousand times before Papa came home.

Standing up straight and clearing my throat, I said formally, "Ana, this is Charlie."

Neither spoke, for what seemed forever while they stared at one another, until Ana whispered, "Hello, I am so very happy to meet you."

"Hello," he rasped, "the pleasure is all mine."

Both reached for their respective reading glasses, hanging by cords down their fronts. Seeing the action of the other, they chorused dry laughter and simultaneously dropped them.

"You look like an old hippie," she said without rancor.

"Takes one to know one," he replied with a shy grin.

I felt Ana's hand leave my shoulder and looked up to see her lips part in a silent moan as she reached over my head. Her shaking fingers brushed the raised scar on Charlie's face. He didn't draw back as she caressed the scar's ridge with her fingertips, an agony pursing her mouth and adding lines to her eyes. Tears rolled down her cheeks as he turned his head to her hand like a cat wanting its ears rubbed.

It's nothing, was the expression on his face. Nothing to cry about, the hurt is gone, it's all better now.

I felt his hand leave my arm and saw him grasp Ana's fingers and gently turned her palm up. My *Orion* itched as he turned his eyes to her upturned wrist and his tears brimmed. Closing his fingers over Ana's hand, a smile quivered on his lips and he reached into his back pocket with the other hand for a bandana.

"Thank you for my children," she said taking the bandana. "Thank you for so much."

"Thank you for sending them," he said.

Ana dabbed her tears and his before offering the bandana back, only she didn't turn it loose. Looking down at me, Charlie released her hand and reached into one of the side pockets of his shorts.

"I believe this is yours," he said, holding out the beacon by the lanyard before me.

I took it and the tube crackled under my fingers as I turned it and found the rattlesnake rattlers attached by a thread to the lanyard.

We must have stood there for a long time because the deputy from the truck cleared his throat and I found Tommy standing just outside my peripheral vision, though I hadn't heard him approach. Deputy Cindy,

Flo and Bobby were also there and the old men across the street helped each other up, grins creasing their wrinkled faces. Peggy the waitress stood outside the Whistle Stop Café, a cigarette in her hand watching us. The same way other townspeople were, and I thought for a town devoid of life, there seemed to be a lot going on.

Stepping to our other side, the deputy said, "Hate to bug you Charlie, but I'd really like to get this report done before my shift is over. Then we'll find you a motel and I'll go home."

"Sounds like a plan," Charlie said and Ana released the bandana.

Her hand returned to my shoulder and I draped the beacon's lanyard over my neck with a clack of the snake rattle.

"Not a problem," Charlie added, "I'll be with you in just a second."

"Thank you again," Ana said. "Their folks will be happy to see them, so I guess we'd better go."

"I'm sure they will," Charlie said with resignation. "Take care."

I hugged Charlie again and he shook Tommy's hand before we piled into Ana's van. Charlie took his place on the curb and waved goodbye with the others. Peggy saluted with her cigarette hand, and others I didn't know waved.

Before we were on the highway, Ana tuned the radio to her oldie and moldy channel, as Tommy called it. He said that station played the kind of music that put him to sleep, so he stretched out on the back seat. He was fast asleep before the first song had ended.

"How that boy does that I'll never know," Ana said. "Especially after all that's happened."

We drove and listened to one golden oldie after the other for many miles. We could have ridden like that all the way back to Bandy's Camp, I suppose, only my *Orion* itched and for a distraction I let my mind wander. Naturally, my mind wandered into the dark recesses and I looked at Ana.

"Ana are we in trouble?" I asked. "We didn't do anything wrong, but are we in trouble?"

"Yes," she replied to my disappointment, "We're both in trouble."

"What did you mean both of us? " I demanded. "You didn't do anything, other than come to get us."

"Your mom and dad are madder than a chicken with an egg broke inside it," she said. "Aunt Sonia talks of committing me to a nut house. M.J. might lock my cell door."

"But you did nothing wrong," I said in defense. "They have no right."

Ana switched off the radio and glanced back at the sleeping Tommy.

"Your grandfather is none too happy with me either," she said, "and you probably won't like me before the day is out."

"I don't understand," I stammered.

"Uncle Theo is coming home," she said in a dry voice. "I don't know exactly when, but he's on his way and very soon."

"But he wasn't supposed to be home till Christmas," I said as the truth closed around my stomach.

CHAPTER 36

The soreness of my breasts was like a fond memory. Swallowing, I found my throat was bone dry. My skin had no sensation and the blood roaring through my ears drowned out passing cars and the car's air conditioner.

"What happened?" I croaked. "Is he … is he all right?".

Ana stared at the highway, her knuckles white on the steering wheel.

"He was shot," she said, "shot in the shoulder, with a big hole on both sides of his body. The bullet missed vital arteries, but thankfully the bullet's impact also spun him around. If he hadn't been turning when he did, another bullet would have hit him in the heart, instead of his hip."

"Is he all right?" I repeated in a steadier voice.

"I don't know," she said with quivering lips. "They flew him to Germany and Michelle left to go see him Thursday morning."

"How, how did it happen?" I asked.

"There was an attack at Theo's base," Ana said, "at least that's what these Navy men told your Aunt Michelle. It's their job is to tell families bad news. They told Michelle what they knew, which wasn't much, because information was still being gathered. About the only sure thing they could say was that Theo led some Army men in a counter attack that drove the enemy away and saved a lot of lives. He did that before he got shot."

We rode in silence for many miles.

"But why should anybody be mad at you?" I demanded. "You got a letter from Uncle Theo just three days ago."

"I got that letter Wednesday," she said flatly. "And I was re-reading it when Michelle called."

"You knew about Uncle Theo when momma dropped me off, and we went to Bandy's anyway?" I asked not wanting to hear the answer.

Nodding, she said she had been so angry with Uncle Theo. Mainly, because he'd gone back into the military, when he didn't have to. The bitter truth was she had been angry with all her children, angry the most at the sorry lot she thought life had given her. What was the thing, she sighed and laughed, is there was no real reason to be mad at anyone. Yet, she needed, wanted to blame someone for the wrong in her life. Which is how the situation seemed to snow ball.

After the Navy men left, Aunt Michelle telephoned Ana to tell of her plans to fly to Germany. Aunt Michelle didn't invite Ana to go, nor asked her to mind my cousins. Instead, she had asked her mother to keep them and said she would call when she got to Germany.

"All I could think was who in hell did she think she was?" Ana said, "And what claim did the stinking U.S. Navy and this sorry world have on my son. Why couldn't they all have the decency to remember who I was, that this was my son for crying out loud?"

Tears streamed down her cheeks as she pounded the steering wheel with the flat of her right hand.

"If there was ever an award for a pity party, I had the grand bam slam, thank you mum, blue ribbon complete with candles and balloons," she said. "But you want to know the worst part?" She didn't wait for my answer. "I felt justified because I had told Theo this would happen. I knew it, as sure as I knew the sun would rise." Sobbing she added, "I begged him not to go, because I could not go through that pain again. I did not want to be right again. Beside, he had no business being there, not when he had so much to live for and do with his life."

"Uncle Theo wasn't supposed to be near any fighting," I said to console her and convince myself. "So it wasn't his fault."

"I was talking about another boy," she said flipping tears from her eyes with her finger. "The boy in that photo with those other talented people. Theo, like that boy, was where he was supposed to be," she added with a snort. "Just as you were where you were supposed to be."

Pulling the van over to the side of the road, she admitted that what was ironic was that she never intended to have kids or raise a family. "I wanted to go to college, travel and accomplish things I'd read about," Ana said. "The main reason I got married was to get away from my mother."

Yet, once she had those kids and a family, they were hers and she wasn't about to let anyone, or anything hurt them, including the kids themselves. And lately, everyone, Theo, my mother, and M.J. seemed hell bent to jump through the hurdles of life carrying scissors in each hand. They did it even as she ran along side screaming at them to drop them.

She had sacrificed so much and they still messed up their lives with problems she believed could have easily been avoided. Aunt Michelle's phone call was the straw that broke the camel's back leaving Ana drained, bitter and determined to set things right. She'd been stewing about these issues when my mother and M.J. dropped us off.

"It wasn't fair since I had played by the rules and was a good citizen.

And what did it get me?" She said. "But who said life was fair?"

Right there, she decided she wasn't going to take any more guff and the world could go to hell without her. She convinced herself that her sacrifice for her children had been a cruel joke. Her justification for withholding the information about Theo could force amends and rewrite some history.

"The more I though about it, the madder I got, but resentment is only good for so long," she said. " I guess that's why it was so easy to try to escape back to the wonderful world I had known in college. That's why I brought out the memory box filled with all its mythical hope of yesterday and fabulous tomorrows. I actually hoped I could climb inside that box and pull the lid shut."

Which is where Tommy and I had found her, listening to her music and reminiscing about how much better things could have been.

"Only it's like my grandmother used to say," Ana said, "the good old days weren't that good even back then. And when you went missing, reality slapped me back to the present. Still, I wanted to know why me? Why was Theo shot, why not someone else? The answer was why not me?"

As a parent she thought she owned her kids, but the truth was she was just preparing them for life. Though Aunt Sonia wouldn't agree, sometimes as a parent, you just had to let them make their own way and mistakes. Theo was where he was needed for those who needed him and God only knows what might have happened if he hadn't been there. My Theo was every bit the New Athenian."

I recalled what Charlie said as we picked black berries. "No matter how many times we want to right the wrongs of our past, doing the same thing over and over with the same jerks and expecting different results," I said. "It won't work because we're powerless over other people, places, things! It's pure self-sabotage. We need to stop beating ourselves up for things we can't control because we can only keep our side of the street clean."

Without looking at me, Ana said, "He told you that didn't he?"

I nodded, knowing she meant Charlie, and said, "He said he forgot how foolish it is to try to recreate the past with different results. That with prayer and willingness to develop strength, one day at a time, we eventually won't even consider recreating the past, because the present and future are too exciting."

Inhaling deeply she nodded her head, dried the rest of her tears. She told me that after we went missing, she and Papa waited at Bandy's Camp and watched the volunteers organizing to search for us. As if Papa didn't have enough eating him, she told him about Theo. His reaction was typical and better than any she expected.

"I've seen that man pissed before," Ana said, "but nothing close to this."

In a poor mimic of Papa she repeated, "Woman, what the hell were you thinking? He's my son, I had a right to know, dammit we all had a right to know."

"I don't think I was ever so glad to have somebody mad at me," Ana said. "Your mom and M.J. went typically nuclear. My children, my destiny and nothing will ever change that."

She took some wet naps out of the side compartment and looked in the rearview mirror as she finished cleaning up her face. "There's a lot of mad going around, but at least we're talking," she said. "Something we haven't been doing as a family for too long. It's not much, but it's a start and there's no going back."

"What about Tarzan Charlie?" I asked.

Ana blew her nose again, my *Orion* itched and my breasts throbbed. "Men go to war, the lucky ones come home and given time their wounds heal," she said. "They can never be as they were, and we shouldn't expect them to be. Yet, we're blessed to have them home again. Just as you're coming home and so is Theo."

Yet, I had one more question.

"Ana, we owe Charlie a lot, he took us in and saved us, but I know as sure as I'm sitting here he was going to kill us last night," I said. " I didn't want to tell Drumhead because I don't like him. I just can't understand what happened after Charlie picked up the beacon. Whatever meanness was eating him seemed to drain away."

"Give me the beacon," she commanded.

I gave it to her and she placed it on the dash in the direct sunlight. Slowly she turned the cylinder so that the whistle end toward the windshield and angled so that the curved portion, that spot below the whistle's mouthpiece, was in the direct sunlight. Impatient, I could have told her I had looked over every inch and snitch of the beacon. She held up a hand for silence and tapped the beacon's mouth piece with her finger, turning it to an irregular angle. A series of marks flashed and disappeared. She rotated the beacon again, in the opposite direction, and I saw the minute scratches of "JKC + CTW" appearing plainly in the direct light. These were the same initials that I'd seen on Ana's hair stay.

"We can't go back to the past," Ana said, "but sometimes we need a reminder of where we've been, what we have and how far we've come, before we know where we are going."

For the second time I saw my grandmother in a new light and another guise. She would never be put her back on that phantom pedestal I think every kid puts their grandmother on. She was wise, yet fallible, and very human, and she wasn't the same, but neither was I.

She draped the beacon over my head and turned the van onto the empty highway as the radio announcer said, "Here's a number one song from a long ago summer."

Again the female vocalist spoke longingly of her need without the scratchiness of Ana's old record.   After the male vocalist answered, Ana and I joined the chorus, and a confused Tommy woke and automatically added his voice.

CHAPTER 37

I arrived at my first day of middle school knowing only acquaintances. I recognized faces the way I knew there was going to be rain. The former didn't respond and there were no clouds to indicate the later. The evening of the second day of school my mother and father sat with me on our front yard as I pointed to the various constellations in the clear night sky.

A heavy front moved in sometime after I went to bed without thunder and gently spinning a soft lullaby of windy rain for a dreamless sleep. The next morning, I opened my eyes at my usual time, but my room was so dark, like the middle of the night. I settled back into my pillow sighing contentedly at the sound of rain and extra sleep. The next moment, my bedroom door flew open with my mother ordering me to get up because it was later than it seemed.

Through my bedroom window I saw rain falling in dancing sheets and knew my summer was over. I dressed and for the first time reflected on the events of a spring and summer I would always remember.

Back home, few people had any idea about our adventures over the Memorial Day weekend. I didn't know why other than maybe they had better, worse or more exciting stuff happening elsewhere. Certain people broached the subject innocently and received mild explanations and a change of subject.

At the insistence of my mother and Aunt Sonia Tommy and I were told not mention what happened outside the family. Typically, Tommy asked why and, for once, Aunt Sonia didn't bother to reason. "Because I said so," she said, and the topic was closed.

The situation between our parents and grandparents was tense, to use a mild description. But Ana and Papa came to our house a week after we got home. A few days later we went to their house and week later we met at Tommy's house. Still, we were like residents of different countries located on the opposite ends of the earth learning a new culture. What irritated me was how everybody was so polite. I knew I was fed up with being everybody's whipping girl and wasn't going to be take anymore disrespect or abuse from anybody or thing.

So, it was a surprise when my mother recommended we take a girls day out for some shopping, but didn't invite Ana. I didn't think she was being fair and said so when I telephoned Ana. Another surprise shut me up when Ana chided me and stressed how my mother was taking one of her sick days from work. Thus, I should be grateful and enjoy the day as it was intended.

Maybe it was the river or standing up to Lonnie and Sgt. Drumhead, I don't know, but her answer chaffed me. Feeling a thousand percent independent, I had the confidence to walk up a wall, so making my own decisions was nothing. It didn't help that days before the trip I caught my mother staring at me with a silly expression. When I asked what she was looking at, she sighed and said, "You're growing up to be such a pretty girl."

Excusing myself, I went in to the bathroom and stared at myself in the mirror, looking extra close this time. To my horror, my ears hung even lower and under my bangs my forehead was far too high. One of my eyes was lower than the other reminding me of a weird Spanish painting. Equally disturbing was my discovery that my right boob was bigger than my left. I resembled a side drawer pulled out of a desk. Add pointy elbows, knobbier knees, and ribs that could have been mistaken for accordion keys. Then there was the discovery of the dark-blonde mini hairs that covered my forearms and legs like moss. Angry, I concluded I wasn't pretty or handsome; just plain everyday homely, though I stopped myself short of adding ugly.

On the river I learned to use those resources available, the what-you-see-is-what-you-get. Well so be it, and instead of trying to pass myself off as something I wasn't, I would be exactly what I was, and the world could choke. Ana said even a prize hog with a blue ribbon is still just a swine, or something like that.

On the way to the shopping mall my mother talked more than she had in the past year, using her normal, friendly voice. Automatically, I suspected ulterior motives, concluding besides selling me a pack of lies, this trip was an opportunity to get back a Ana. It was a plot I was determined to sabotage, as I had decided I was through taking abuse from anybody. Here was the perfect time to take my stand. It would also be good practice for going back to school to stand up to Jeri and her gang.

Thus for every really cute blouse, pair of pants or dress my mother pulled off the rack, I found two others in neutral or earth colors, including sweatshirts and billowy pants, generally a size larger. Of course the selection wasn't the same for bras. She'd held up a couple for my consideration, along, to my horror, for the rest of the store to see, asking what I thought.

Instantly, I ordered, her to just put them in the shopping cart.

I sullenly followed toward the check out counter whining that we had enough clothes and we could leave now, if not sooner. Of course, we couldn't go without trying them on. At a sales counter a sales lady saw us approach, smiled, stepped out and was gorgeous.

As if the day wasn't bad enough, I fumed. Why couldn't she be one of those frumpy types. Instead, she was everything I knew I would never be. Slighter taller than my mother and younger than Ana, she wore her lustrous dark brown hair shaped to curl below her perfect jaw. A tone of cinnamon kissed her peaches and cream complexion, while her nail polish matched the full lips parted just enough to show even, white teeth.

A pair of half moon reading glasses, similar to Charlie and Ana's, set on a small pointed nose, their ear hooks attached to a thin gold colored chain draped around her long neck and the lapels of a charcoal gray jacket. The matching knee length skirt over dark seamed hose and black stilettos completed the picture.

Her only jewelry was a wedding ring and small gold chain and cross centered on her chest. She removed her glasses revealing molten brown eyes. Absently, she let the glasses hang to the neckline of her white, silk blouse forming a bracket around the brief cleavage formed by her full breasts. Her voice was soft and musical with a slight accent and I wondered if she'd ever met Charlie.

"Hel-LO, may I help you," she said looking at my mother and smiling at me.

My eyes dropped to the floor, I was determined to hate her while my mother asked her to help me try on some of the clothes. A basket full "we" had chosen and helped me mix and match outfits.

"Vous êtes une belle fille," said the sales lady fixing me with those intense eyes.

"Uh, uh, excuse me?" Stammered my mother, and I realized she was as intimidated as I was.

"I say she is a beautiful girl," she said, "and pardon me, please, I sometimes speak ze language I am thinking. However, ze meaning is ze same in either language, she is very pretty. I would be most happy to assist."

My mother gushed as she introduced us and the woman bowed slightly.

"Berthe Emilie Mercier," she said, extending a right hand with a cool palm and firm grip. I was about to excuse myself for the bathroom, when my mother told me she'd be right back. After my mother was gone, I took a deep breath and parked my hands on my hips.

"Uh look, Berthe Emilie, uh Mercier, let's be honest," I said, cringing at my terrible mispronunciation of her name. "I can dress myself and I already know what I like and what looks good. So, you can go take a coffee break, or something, because we both know I am not a beautiful girl, I'm not even pretty. So, you go do your thing and I'll do mine, and I'll see you when we're ready to check out. "

She didn't look offended or amused, but my *Orion* itched and I had to stop myself from stepping back from the perfectly manicured index finger she held before my eyes.

"Pas encore, le bien-aimé !" She said barely parting her lips. "Not yet, sweetheart!"

"Uh, excuse me, I don't understand," I replied, adding quickly. "Where are the dressing rooms?"

"You will be beautiful," she said. "Vous êtes une oeuvre d'art dans le progrès. A work in progress, zere is no doubt, and, one day, men will stare as you walk past."

"Are you kidding?" I said, almost stamping my foot. "Look at me, I'm hideous. My ears are like open car doors, my eyes look like one of those weird Spanish paintings by, by…"

"Picasso," she finished for me.

"Yes, I mean whatever, my eyes are off center," I said, "my head's funny shaped and my elbows make sharpened pencils look dull."

"Zhere is nothing wrong with your head or body," she said, with a dismissive wave of her hand. You'd thought I'd told her I became a werewolf. "Actually, your features are striking, especially for a girl of," looking down her nose, she hesitated a moment before saying, "11, oui."

"Yes," I replied taken back at the guess, but not willing to concede. I leaned close and whispered, "My right boob is bigger than my left." Smirking, I crossed my arms over my chest.

"You are right handed, oui," she said not impressed. "Virtually all right handed women are bigger on zhat side, because zhose are ze muscles of ze particular arm zhey use ze most. Development of zhat side of ze body is quite natural. So you must remind yourself to use your left arm, more often, and ze boobies will even out."

Stunned, I struggled to make sense of these facts particularly since they messed up my plans to get back at everyone who'd done me wrong. My *Orion* took that moment to start itching and I didn't know why. I was reminded of how difficult it had been to aim Charlie's pistol at the other rattlesnake and the trouble with "drawing a bead." The *Orion* continued to itch and Ana's words came back to me about how Orion's belt could be used to find the direction to other planets or holy places. Or, by choice or ignoring the true direction it could lead to the opposite path into a void.

What was it Charlie had said? "Hard right turn, Jackie!"

"Choosing clothes is a skill zhat must be learned," said the French woman, interrupting my thoughts with her clicking heels to step toward our shopping basket. "Some women never master the nuances, even as taste and styles change, and believe me," she said, holding up a bra, "zhere is much more to choosing a lady's lingerie than many would believe."

With the only French word I knew, I asked, "Mademoiselle, could you show me? Like I said, I know how to dress myself, but I don't know anything about nuisances."

Smiling, she pushed the shopping cart toward a nearby dressing rooms.

"Address me as MA-dame," she said holding up her wedding ring, " and I shall be only too happy. In the meantime, we will work on your French and English."

I soon learned to say "merci beaucoup," which is "thank you very much" and the difference between a nuance and a nuisance. Before my mother returned, I had tried on, mixed and matched a dozen dresses, tops and pants. We culled most of the dull colors I had chosen, and Madame was so right: There was more to choosing lingerie. She set aside all the bras my mother chose and though I won't go into details, I left with others, including a black one, I told myself I wouldn't wear in a hundred years.

"It is something every lady should have in her dresser," Madame Mercer lectured.

When my mother returned I wore denim Capri pants and a short sleeve plaid shirt with front pockets. I didn't see the Picasso model I'd seen at home, just like I couldn't see the sunburned savage girl exposing herself to Sgt. Drumhead in the interrogation room. Meantime, my mother giggled and wiggled like it was Christmas as Madame rang up the bill. Before we parted, Madame kissed me on both cheeks, which I returned saying, "Merci beaucoup Madame Berthe Emilie Mercier," in what Madame called horrid French. She told me to keep practicing and come back again.

We ate at a nice restaurant where waitresses with crisp embroidered aprons poured from porcelain teapots. They served us fruit salad and sandwiches with paper-thin sliced meat and veggies pressed tightly together between toasted bread baked there in the restaurant. During lunch, I asked my mother if I could get my hair cut to neck level. After all, I was entering middle school and fixing my hair every morning was becoming a problem. I didn't mention this was also the style the other girls were getting theirs cut.

We walked to a big window store front where several women sat getting their hair fixed and stepped inside. Before the girl at the front desk could say a word, a brawny man with a flattop haircut called to her. All eyes were drawn to him as his thick chest strained his black T-shirt with "Bill" written on the left pectoral. He grinned as he introduced himself and gave the swivel chair, he stood beside, a twist. He stopped it to face me with huge arms stretched open to announce that I was next.

Bill gave me a great haircut, but the fun was watching those huge hands gently encase my entire head as the corded muscles of his arms flexed and worked the shampoo on my hair into piles of lather. The results made my mother as happy as I was and I pressed the advantage.

"Please, can we show Ana?" I asked in the car. "Besides, she said she was looking for a new hair dresser, we need to tell her about Bill."

Without having to think, my mother started the car and we soon arrived at Ana's house amid mutual excitement. I wanted to hammer the front door trick-or-treat style, but knew better. I saw that my mother was divided with her emotions as we walked to the front door and I knocked.

The front door flew open and Ana squealed and fumbled the screen door open. Motioning us into the living room, my mother took the couch. Ana clapped her hands and told me to turn around so she could see every angle of my new clothes and hair style. Both women beamed as I twirled. For me, I noticed something out of the ordinary on Ana's coffee table.

"Ana, what's that," I asked stopping in my second twirl. "They look like school books."

"They are college textbooks, " she confirmed, "I've signed up for a couple of college classes this Fall."

"Momma, what are you thinking?" My mother demanded. "What classes?"

My mother had lost the frivolity she'd brought from the store.

"I've decided to go back to college and finish my degree," Ana said. "I'm starting with some night classes."

"Momma, be serious," my mother said. "Do you realize the average age of the kids you'll sit in class with? You'll be at a disadvantage because, after a certain age, a person can't learn anything. Just imagine what your friends and neighbors will say? You'll be a laughing stock, besides how will you pay for this?"

"More non-traditional students are going back to school, so I won't be alone," Ana said. "My friends and neighbors have their own fish to fry and the government has grants for geezers like me, and you don't know what you can do until you try."

"But you haven't set foot in a classroom for 30 years," my mother chided "Education has changed, students are totally different, they'll make fun and won't have anything to do with you."

"The objectives are the same, to get an education," Ana said, " and if they make fun, what do I care? I have a date for Friday night and drank my first beer."

Irritated, my mother and said, "Even if you managed to make it through a semester, how long will getting a degree take? Have you considered how old you'd be if you finally got a diploma?"

"Yes, " Ana replied, "and, unless there's a youth serum I haven't heard about, I'll be just as old without a diploma. The difference is I'll have the college degree I've always wanted. If I die before I'm finished, at least I tried."

"But momma," my mother said. "Be reasonable, this is so out there. Shouldn't you find something traditionally in keeping with your age and present interests?"

"But nothing sweetheart," Ana said. "You're my daughter and I love you, but sometimes you just don't get it. Recently, this family nearly lost three precious people. Well, we have them back, and I, for one, don't intend to take any of life's precious moments for granted again. There too many opportunities that will pass if not seized."

"Momma," said my mother with less resolve.

Ana put her hands on my mother's shoulders and said, "Sweetheart, I've got a box full of memories and regrets. One I'll cherish, the others I'll toss or do something about making them happen. Regardless, I can do it easier if I have your support."

My mother looked stunned before she hugged Ana.

"You have it momma," said my mother laughing. "I'll even help you with your home work, if you want."

Tearfully, Ana returned the hug, also laughing.

"I may take you up on that," Ana said, "as you said, I am a little rusty, so I can use all the help I can get."

"We'll get Jackie to help," my mother said holding out an arm for me to join the embrace.

"There's an idea," Ana said, "we'll certainly need her when Theo comes home."

"Theo," my mother said looking around. "Theo is back in the U.S., he's home?"

Ana explained that Uncle Theo had been flown from overseas to a military hospital only a few hours away. Aunt Michelle had been to see him and now his doctors thought it would all right for the rest of his family to visit.

"I want to go," I said without thinking.

"Now, Jackie, no," said my mother in the tone she tried to dissuade Ana. "You can see him when he's better and comes home."

"But he very much wants to see her," Ana said. "Michelle told him about what happened on the river and he's really looking forward to talking to her."

"But, momma, be reasonable," my mother repeated. "Don't they have rules about age limits?"

With a wry smile, Ana said, "They have their rules, and I have mine about getting Theo well again. A visit would do him a world of good."

"But momma," my mother repeated.

"She's got a new do and super threads," Ana said, "she came through an ordeal that could have killed a grown man. What's a trip to visit her uncle hurt?"

"But momma," my mother said, "can she even get on base, let alone the hospital?"

"She won't be smuggling guns or on a beer run," Ana said. "Just sidestep a few silly bureaucracies to visit a sick sailor."

Before my mother could say another "but momma," Ana ordered all my new clothes be brought in. I did and we laid everything around the living room. Unfortunately, these included, to my utter mortification, the new bras, including the black one. Ana didn't seem to notice, only nodded, holding each outfit in front of me.

She complimented us on our good taste and my mother gave credit to Madame Berthe Emilie Mercier. Nodding her approval, Ana said she'd have to make Madame's acquaintance before she disappeared into a back room. She returned with a camera instructing us to hold up the various outfits while she snapped our photograph.

While my mother folded and returned the clothes and underwear to the store bags, Ana directed me to stand against a wall with no pictures or decorations. I started to smile, but she said don't before snapping my photograph.

A week later I was jumping on pins and needles expecting to be left home at the last minute. However, the morning before we left, Ana telephoned and asked me to wear the same Capri pants and plaid shirt with front pockets I wore when we first showed her my new clothes. Happily I agreed, but wasn't comfortable with her request to wear my black bra. Like I said, I thought I'd never wear it in a hundred years. Yet, red faced, I agreed before Ana asked to speak to my mother.

Hanging up the phone, my mother told me Ana needed help putting a package together for Uncle Theo and would be over soon to pick me up. I ran to take my shower and fix my hair. There was enough time to iron my clothes, though I locked my door to put on my black bra.

When Ana honked, I ran to her car. Only when we got to her house a cardboard box set on the coffee table with "Theo" written on the sides and sealed with a single strip of duct tape. Before I could ask, she told me to take off my shoes and give them to her. Sitting on the couch, I complied and my mouth dropped open as she wrote with a heavy black ink marker on the soles of my shoes. When she'd finished she held them toward me and the bottom of each shoe had the number 13 written in huge block letters at the widest part.

"If anyone asks how old you are," Ana said, "you can honestly say you are over 13."

I giggled at this clever mischief and slipped my 13 shoes on. I lost all humor when grandmother ordered me to remove my top and my bra. Without waiting for my compliance, she disappeared into the back of the house. When she returned shortly. I was topless, with my back to her, a palm over each breast. I peered over my shoulder and saw her place what looked like a raw chicken cutlet into each cup of my bra.

"Ewww," I said, turning around and forgetting my nakedness "Ana are you crazy? You can't put raw meat in my bra."

She didn't respond and I moved toward her to prevent the violation of my lingerie.

"This isn't meat," said Ana patiently. "These are silicone bra inserts."

"I don't care what they are," I said shuddering, "get those creepy things away."

"You're friend Madame Mercier recommended these," Ana said, "she thought they would be better than stuffing Kleenex."

The mention of Madame Mercier's name defused my outrage just as I realized I was topless before my grandmother. I started to raise my hands, but putting my hands over my boobs again seemed silly.

"What are they are for?" I asked with equally redundancy.

"For the same reason I got that card made that's lying next to the box," said Ana indicating with her chin. "Now come here and let's check these bandicoots out."

Forgetting my nudity again, I picked up the laminated card with the photograph I recognized as the one Ana took of me last week against the wall. My photo filled the card's right hand side. At its top was a white lettered logo written on a black background with the name of my middle school. Below the logo, and left of my photograph was my name in bold-faced letters. Beneath the name was my birth date, minus two years, which would make me thirteen. The last line declared "Eighth Grade." It was all very impressive, and while there was nothing shoddy about this card, its similarity to Macho Mike's "school ID" was unsettling.

Holding my bra before her, cups down, inserts, up, Ana motioned for me to turn around.

"Ana," I said, my back to her, "My middle school doesn't give I.D. cards, and this says I'm two years older and in the 8ᵗʰ grade."

"You know that, and I know that," Ana said. "But a soldier at that hospital isn't going to know unless you carry your birth certificate. Besides, nothing says official like a picture I.D."

Ana pressed my bra against my chest and though I was expecting it, the cool feel of the plastic inserts made me jump. She directed me to hold them in place as she hooked me from behind. She told me to bend forward so the inserts could drop into place and helped me adjust my shoulder straps. When everything felt comfortable, or as comfortable as one can feel with two bowls of Jell-o on one's boobs, she led me to a mirror, smiling. I marveled at my cleavage, which wasn't on the scale of Madame Mercer, but there was some. Again, the memory of the boy who became Macho Mike in the school identification, left me with a growing discomfort I couldn't explain. It wasn't so much we were doing something wrong, but it wasn't exactly right.

I buttoned my shirt and just had time to put the I.D. card in my back pocket before the door bell rang and door flew open. M.J. barged in declaring we needed to make tracks with my mother and Aunt Michelle behind him. Ana said she had to visit the bathroom one more time and without being told M.J. grabbed the cardboard box and carried it out to the car. Michelle took a seat on the couch and took a handkerchief out of her purse. Meantime, my mother stood in the hallway staring at me.

"Something wrong?" I asked innocently. "Or did you forget something."

"No," she said, "it's just that there's something…."

Before she could finish Ana was back and shooing everyone toward the front door.

Only my mother, Michelle, M.J., Ana and I went on this trip. My daddy and Papa had to work and Aunt Sonia and Tommy had to go to an appointment. I sat in the middle in the back seat. Michelle, on my left, told me how pretty my new hair style and outfit were before dabbing her eyes again with her handkerchief. M.J. agreed, though he wasn't looking at me as he twirled the steering wheel and swung the car into the street. My mother's eyes seemed to bounce over me before looking at the back of Ana's head sitting in the front passenger seat. I avoided my mother's gaze until she pulled a paper back book from her purse. The only problem was when I happened to look in her direction, she was gazing at me over the top of her book.

Still, she was the least of my problems and the trip to the military hospital didn't take long enough with my apprehension growing with each mile. The entrance to the base wasn't manned by a soldier, but by an older man wearing a white combination cap and a nondescript uniform with broad scripted patches on the shoulders. He did wear a pistol and police accoutrements and smiled warmly as he asked how we were? Michelle responded in kind, handing him the typed pass that identified us as guests of a military member and our restricted access to the base. Showing tobacco stained teeth, the guard asked for our personal identification to verify the names on the guest pass. Everyone dug into wallets, but I was the first to pass my new identification card through the window. My mother raised her eyebrows in surprise, but said nothing as the guard took my bogus card.

The guard's bemused expression seemed filled with suspicion to me. I readied myself to confess my deception and take my punishment, but not reveal my accomplice. Instead, after a quick peek, the guard handed my card back faster than I had delivered. His scrutiny was longer with the adults' cards before he waved us through and told us to have a wonderful day.

Out of earshot of the gate guard, M.J. uttered a "whew" and a nervous laugh.

"It's like I'm back in high school when I talk to those guys," M.J. said. "I haven't done anything wrong, I checked the car before we left to make sure there wouldn't be any problems, but still."

"Yes, it takes some getting used to," Michelle said, "but for the most part those men are nice people and I've never had a problem. They are basically first line defense."

But they didn't catch me, I wanted to say, stuffing my I.D. card into my expanded breast pocket and feeling the squish from the insert because of the extra pressure.

At Michelle's direction, M.J. drove to a large parking lot located between three tall buildings. M.J. carried the gift box and we followed Michelle toward the largest buildings and climbed the steps to the entrance, making room for a man to go through first. His head was swaddled in bandages and he lay on a gurney pushed by two men in white clothes. As they passed I saw the injured man's eyes were open, staring into nothingness. I had to force myself not to look at him and fought the desire to dash back to the car.

Beyond a rotating glass door, we entered a cavernous hall with dull blue carpet and wood paneling. Men and women in camouflage uniforms passed us murmuring between themselves as Michelle lead us toward a desk. A burly looking man sitting behind the desk with a face like a bulldog watched her approach with interest. He wore a white smock that emphasized his beefy arms and asked us to sign and print our names on a form attached to a clipboard.

Waiting my turn I noticed a sign behind the burly man listing hospital rules. My eyes were drawn to the restriction of "children under 12." The other stood round me as I filled in my information, but that didn't stop the burly man from looking intently at me, or so it seemed Self-consciously I found the strap of my black bra, that was visible against my collar bone, and moved it toward my shoulder, feeling the slight and silent squish of the inserts.

"How old are you?" He asked.

"I'm over 13," I said, shuffling from one foot to the other.

"Really," he said, sounding disappointed, "I would have taken you for older."

Shrugging the burly man used a paper diagram map and traced directions to Uncle Theo's room with a yellow highlight marker. We walked a short way to an elevator that took no time to reach any particular floor. Though, before I stepped into the hall, I knew I didn't want to be there.

The big hall that lead to another information desk was wide, clean and cheerful with plants along the walls and paintings. I could also have cut the sanitized air with a knife. Yet, beyond the antiseptic smell was a shadow of putridity and pain that I sensed with each step. I kept my head down, trying not to look at the grim faced men and women in smocks or white coats, a stethoscope hanging from their necks like an alien appendage. Some reminded me of Dr. Jones in the sheriff's office medical examination room. Most only glanced at our passing and I shuddered at the groans emitting from some of the rooms we passed.

The situation didn't improve inside Uncle Theo's room. For me, just stepping into the door, it was everything I could do to keep from running full speed all the way to the bottom floor. I wanted to confess my fraud to the burly man at the information desk, and, if necessary, declare crime involvement, that is if it could get me out of there. Anything was preferable to seeing the shriveled husk lying in the raised hospital bed. No way, something told me, was this pitiful creature the fabulous man who had modeled Persian pants and cartoon hats for me.

Smiling, his sunken eyes watched our approach. I tried not to stare at the fresh scab on the end of his nose, or the gray hair at his temples, that hadn't been there when he left. Every pore, wrinkle and sore seemed magnified against a translucence yellow skin that I desperately wanted to believe had been painted on.

A spider web of wires and tubes stretched from nearby monitors to his body giving him android appearance. My fingers opened and closed at the sight of the needle stuck in the top of his wrist while I controlled the temptation to pull it out. My eyes dropped to the side of the bed and my stomach churned at seeing a tear shaped plastic bag; partially filled with copper colored pee oozing through a tube thick as an entrail, its other end covered by a blanket.

Greetings were exchanged and M.J. awkwardly, but gently shook the undamaged left hand, patting the same shoulder. In accordance with seniority, each woman leaned forward for a brief hug, pat and kiss on the cheek, again extra careful to avoid his right arm. Unable to mesmerize myself through the closed door I tipped, touched, made smack noises with my lips and backed up.

Smiling, Uncle Theo looked at me and said, "Ain't like the movies, huh Jackie?" I shook my head in answer and he chuckled dryly. "That's the way I thought too, until I got here."

A nervous chuckle rose among the adults and I hoped someone would redirect the conversation and I could blend into the wall. Instead, Uncle Theo motioned me to come closer.

"Jackie, you're looking fine, there's definitely something different about you," he said, "we're going to have to spray you with boy repellent."

My cheeks blushed and the adults laughed again as I prayed that anything would take his attention off me. Instead, Uncle Theo motioned me closer and dropped his good arm to the side of the bed.

"C'mere, I got something for you," he said bringing up a brown bag with looped handles and setting it on a nearby table that was beside his bed. "I heard about your adventures on the river and thought this might be just the gift for a girl like you."

He held out the bag and I took it, hesitantly, noticing the adults smiling with uncertainty. Carefully, I thrust my hand inside the sack, felt cloth. Grasping it, I pulled out a long olive green length of cloth embroidered with checkered designs of bars and lines with tassels attached to the four corners.

"Uh, thanks," I said holding it in two hands. "What is it?"

"It's a Shemagh or Keffiyeh, depending on which Arab state you're in," Uncle Theo said. "We used them for protection against the sun and sand, but it also keeps the head warm in cold weather. It's a design that originated in ancient Mesopotamia and has been a social, political and fashion accessory for centuries. Some famous figures like Yasser Arafat, T.E. Lawrence and Field Marshal Erin Rommel wore them."

"They didn't wear this one, did they?" I demanded, feeling new panic and holding the cloth by two fingers and away from me.

"Don't be silly," Uncle Theo laughed. "And don't' worry, it's new and clean. Now try it on."

With a nervous smile, I looked around the room before Uncle Theo rolled his eyes and directed me to fold the cloth into a triangle, place it on my head and wrap it around my neck.

"What do you think?" Asked Theo, looking at everyone in the room. "Give her an M-4, a helmet and a bandoleer and stand back."

My mother laughed too loud and knew it, and everyone looked toward Ana. Using his hands to gesture, Uncle Theo told me to pull the top of the Shemagh off my head and onto my neck

"It's something you could have used on the river, and it's great against mosquitoes," Uncle Theo said. "Besides, I hear you packed a gun out there. What was it?"

"A Colt .38 Super automatic," I recited. "It belonged to a company man in the jungle."

"Sounds interesting," said Uncle Theo moving to straighten up and gritting his teeth as an expression of pain creased his face. The others took a collective step toward him, but he waved the back and said, "Hold that thought. I've got some people I want to hear this."

There had to have been a fool's smile on my face because I wanted desperately to rip the Shemagh off my neck. I had the panicked belief that touching a wounded man's things was contagious. Of course that desire was nothing compared to not wanting to meet anybody else in this hospital. Yet, with a grin to match mine, Uncle Theo leaned forward and adjusted the folds of my Shemagh before gesturing to M.J. to bring him a wheel chair from against the wall. He waved away the protests leaving no choice, except to help him into the chair without twisting his tubes or wires. Seated, he pointed to the door and M.J. pushed him toward it while Michelle moved the blinking box on its rolling stanchion and we trooped into the hallway.

He asked me to walk beside him and directed M.J. to proceed in the opposite direction we'd come in. In route, he raised his good hand to greet staff and patients on either side of the white corridor before we entered a large room with broad windows.

A group of men and women sat in wheelchairs or laid on gurneys looking in our direction. Trying to keep from stumbling, I knew that if I didn't want to be in Uncle Theo's room, these people were worse. They included a man missing both his legs, a woman, actually a girl not much older than me, with only one arm and the top of her head bandaged. Others were similarly swathed and missing limbs, while some had exposed scars crisscrossing healing flesh, with stitches prominent as cat's whiskers.

"Hey guys meet my family!" Uncle Theo announced. " Family meet The Regulars!"

Mumbled greetings were exchanged by the people in the room, most looking away until Uncle Theo called for their attention.

"Guys, you've got to hear this. This young lady is my niece Jackie, tell them about what you and Tommy did on the Brazos River with Tarzan Charlie."

This couldn't be happening I thought, while Uncle Theo used his good hand to move in a semi-circle and beamed with pride. Hands clasped at my waist, I felt perspiration develop between my chest and the inserts. Small sweat driblets moved down my ribs.

"Hello, I'm Jackie," I said nervously. "I'm happy to be here."

No I wasn't, but instead of focusing on these injured people I thought of blue flowing water and buffalo grass. I almost felt the dichotomy of sunbaked earth beneath my feet and creek water on my skin. The howls of coyotes faded before the cooing of morning doves mingled with the rustle of wind and leaves and the stroke of a wooden paddle against the side of a canoe.

Looking around I found everyone including the medical staff, looking at me, smiling and all were interested. Remembering Flo, I recalled nearly walking into the giant rattlesnake. The sudden grasp of Charlie's hands on my shoulders prompted a collective intake of breath around the room. But when I'd finished, everyone applauded and made their way toward us. Uncle Theo held his good hand over his face and told me I was a natural born storyteller.

I answered their questions the best I could as their interest in me wound down and many of the soldiers engaged Ana, my mother and M.J. in conversation. Holding Michelle's hand, Uncle Theo sat a little taller in his wheel chair beaming with new color coursing his sallow skin as he spoke to another man in a wheel chair.

Naturally, interest in me dwindled, but to my delight a young soldier hobbled over with eyes the color a spring sky. Running his right hand over his corn colored head, he introduced himself as Sam. I wondered if he wasn't part of the hospital staff since instead of a hospital gown and robe, he wore a logo T-shirt, gym pants and running shoes over his lanky frame.

We shook hands, I smiled, he opened his mouth, and metal reflected light from between his lips. Seeing my astonishment, he shrugged and recounted being wounded by the shock of a bomb that killed most of the men in his patrol. Widening his mouth extra wide he revealed studs sunk into his gums and connected by wire.

"I'm being fitted for dentures," he said, before telling me how much he enjoyed canoeing the lakes near his home in Michigan. Thereafter, I didn't notice his metal teeth and I couldn't say what we talked about.

We found we had a lot in common with the same video games and grooving to some of the same music. Though we hadn't known each other fifteen minutes, I toyed with the embrace of my potential and unspoken status of a girl with a boyfriend. Not that boys, particularly my own age, were a priority. Most of them were too stupid and to full of themselves to grasp what having a girl friend meant. For them it was more like knowing the latest dirty joke. Of course, I wasn't in love with Sam, at least not yet and he hadn't actually asked me to be his girl friend. The possibility made me giddy of being the first girl, I knew, to have a serious relationship.

Yet, my "tryst" ended before it started when he asked what grade I was in school. Without thinking I told him I'd be starting middle school in the fall and his eyes widened with shock at the reality that I wasn't even 12. Thereafter, he started fidgeting and topics shriveled to compliments and stuttering between sentences. Finally, he asked to be excused and hobbled in the direction of a rest room. The light heartedness of having a boyfriend went with him, replaced with the equally new, and bitter, experience of being dumped. It was a feeling worse than when Jeri and Joyce shunning me.

Sam left my life forever and I plopped down on a couch hoping to hide my disappointment and praying neither my mother or Ana would notice. In the movies I'd seen spies hide behind newspapers to camouflage their presence while traveling. Seeing a stack of newspapers lying on a nearby coffee table I grabbed a paper and opened it the way my daddy and Papa did and rattled the pages extra hard to hide my sighs. Hoping we'd leave soon, my eyes wandered across the page not intending to read anything, until my eyes were drawn to a three-inch article on a back page. Its headline struck like a rattlesnake as I read the article piece meal to its end.

"Texas man dies fleeing Kansas police.

Coffeyville, Kan.-- Suspect, man, 22, of ---driving south, Highway ---, routine traffic stop, Coffeyville Police, Kansas State troopers-------, armed stand off, highway blocked,---small caliber pistol ---self inflicted head wound---pronounced dead at...Believed to have fled --- released on bond from Texas ---, charged with alleged illegal manufacture.... Suspected of returning to Texas after----- Police continue to investigate."

Michael E. DeGrief was written once, DeGrief was repeated throughout the little article. Yet in my mind "Macho Mike" or "M&M" inserted themselves into the words swirling from the article. Again I read it, this time slowly absorbing each detail. It filled me with a sadness I couldn't describe. I took out my school I.D, and with it, the image of the scared boy wearing a tie and school blazer.

Reading the article a third time the words seared themselves into my memory. I considered tearing the article out for Tommy before tossing the newspaper back on the coffee table. Lonnie Fant hung in the air like smoke and a deep sense of pity amplified my recollection of Lonnie's admiration for Macho Mike. This worship was echoed in the boy's voice anytime he spoke about Macho Mike. He was the only hero, the only substance in Lonnie's life. It was a loyalty he wore like a medal. Now what was left for Lonnie?

There was no way I could articulate my emotions other than what I might feel watching a kitten hit by a car and left to twitch its life out. Compared to Lonnie, my tragedies weren't even close. What was losing a boyfriend I never had in the first place?

"You're not even 12," I silently admonished myself, "and he's from where?"

Michigan, I answered, not even sure where that was and, with a quick look around, realized Sam was no where in sight. Nearby, Ana sat with Uncle Theo. with Michelle looking at him like an unopened Christmas present. Seeing me, Uncle Theo motioned me over. The movement also attracted my mother and M.J. who said good-bye to the soldiers they'd been talking to and joined us.

Trying not to cry, Ana told Uncle Theo we needed to go and asked if there was anything he wanted next time and hugged him. Laughing through gritted teeth, Uncle Theo said how glad he was we'd come. Being last, and with real appreciation, I thanked him for my Shemagh and asked if I could do or get him anything.

"Yes Jackie," he said, looking more like the Uncle Theo I remembered. "I want you to write down what happened on the river. I'd like to read it when you get through, if you'll let me."

I said I would before excusing myself. I took the gift bag with the Shemagh and went into the ladies' room. Behind a locked stall I removed the bra inserts, not only because I didn't need them, but because they made me sweaty. It was a relief to get them off my chest in more ways than one. Wrapping them, in the Shemagh, I put them in the gift bag. Looking into the mirror above the sink, I saw I wasn't as big as I was, but felt so much better.

Sam never appeared before we left, but I left him a note with a nurse saying how glad I was to have met him, wished him a speedy recovery and included my name and address. I wasn't disappointed when I never heard from him.

CHAPTER 38

For the rest of the summer, my parents tried to be civil, at least in front of me and particularly at the marriage counselor's office. I went with them, but sat in the waiting room while they discussed, or cussed. I used the time to start my story for Uncle Theo.

I helped with the housework and my daddy taught me how to mow a lawn, after starting the lawn mower for me. He also took me swimming, to movies and taught me to drive his car while I sat on his lap. Eventually these social invitations were extended to my mother and before the summer was over my daddy moved back home, for a little while.

Summer days were stifling during most of the daylight hours, so after finishing my chores I read or wrote my account for Uncle Theo. After lunch, we spent whole afternoons swimming at the city pool. In the evening I played with neighborhood kids until the sun went down and my mother had to call me to come in. Days fell into weeks and months. Each was filled with little league baseball games, garage sales, stage plays and programs at the public library.

In between days, Ana attended college classes and Papa collected more classic movies that he insisted we see outside on a big screen plasma television he moved outside on rollers. This weekly event drew neighbors to Ana's back yard by the dozens to spread blankets and sit in lawn chairs for another mystical experience.

I received the first of many letters and post cards from Charlie and Billie. Charlie wrote from a place called Brazil. He explained that the "corporate honchos" weren't happy to learn about his adventures on the Brazos River and his involvement with drug makers and law enforcement. While his rescue action of lost children were commendable, he had also besmirched the company's name.

"They wanted to let me go without so much as a blackberry or a crawfish," he wrote, "but I pointed out the development of a public relations nightmare. Plus, there was that coyote's statement on record at the local sheriff's department. Since he represented the company when he referred to me during an official call as Scarface and offered a slanted if not dubious account that was not true. I told them the name of a lawyer who said I had an excellent case for libel as well as unfair termination of employment."

However, he pointed out that transferring him to their branch office in Brazil might be the best for everyone. Which is where he went.

Billie, or I should say Bobby, wrote that they were buying Tate's Landing and during the winter months the place would undergo a major refurbishment before it was reopened as the B&F Campground.

"We can't turn away customers like Arlie Fant and Macho Mike," he wrote, "but they'll certainly know they aren't welcome."

Again, I felt sorry for Lonnie realizing yet another door was being slammed in his face. Flo said she hoped to see me and my family next summer for a visit when she would bestow on me the secret of making cinnamon flavored iced tea.

The appointment Aunt Sonia and Tommy had, while we were visiting Uncle Theo, was to discuss Tommy joining a local Boy Scouts troop. Being Aunt Sonia, she asked more than a few questions about activities and qualifications for being a scout then should have been legal. These were questions that inspired Tommy to want to crawl under his chair as she questioned Scout Master Spenser Stroud with the skill and persistence of an inquisitor. Tommy reported that Scout Master Stroud quietly answered all her questions, but unlike most people seemed more intrigued with Aunt Sonia than impatient. After asking what Tommy called the zillionth question, Scout Master Stroud asked Aunt Sonia if she would be interested in becoming an adult volunteer for the troop.

For once Aunt Sonia was at a loss for words, but to Tommy's humiliation, she agreed. Tommy and Aunt Sonia attended meetings and no one minded Aunt Sonia taking charge of troop organization and planning. Before the summer was out, she had done such a good job, and with a glowing recommendation from Scout Master Spenser, she was offered a job at the national headquarters.

"I think this was the only way Scout Master Stroud could get her out of his hair," Tommy confided to me.

Her new job didn't stop her from being outraged when M.J. announced he had agreed to let Tommy take karate lessons. She counted on her fingers a list of logical justifications why "her son" shouldn't participate, adding threats of what she'd do if Tommy were hurt. For once, M.J. didn't argue, perhaps following the Boy Scout example, and asked her to join him for the adult class held by a different karate instructor the same time as Tommy's class. My mother also agreed to let me take karate lessons and by the end of the summer we all had our yellow belts.

The first two days of school were too rushed to acknowledge or even notice other kids. I didn't share classes with any from my old school. Though I caught glimpses of Joyce and Jeri clustered in a corner with their old crowd and a few more. Typically, they gathered or moved in a herd, just as they did the day it rained.

My mother dropped me off in the school driveway and I ran with my bag above my head to the big portico sheltering the broad walk extending from the double, front doors. Standing in the center of the walkway, away from the water dripping on either side, stood the J's as I'd come to know them. No other kid was within 12 feet of the group as if an unseen barrier couldn't be crossed unless by invitation only. Individual boys and girls drifted past them giving a wide berth as they shuffled from one group to the other asking for acceptance.

I stepped under the portico and no one greeted me, which was fine with me since I was still waking up. Passing the J's prompted a titter of giggles above the drumming of the falling rain.. Ignoring them, I walked to a solitary corner to the right of the front doors. Leaning against the wall I stared beyond the groups, watching cars queue in the driveway where kids ran giggling and splashing up the walk and into the portico. With the absence of rain on their heads they became quiet, while soft murmurs of conversation were drowned by the sound of the rain.

Shortly before the first bell, a female figure wearing a maroon raincoat emerged from a car and walked toward the portico while others ran past her. When she was standing on dry concrete, she loosed the belt of her raincoat and simultaneously swept a clear plastic rain scarf from her head. From an inside pocket she produced pair of black-square-framed glasses that wrapped around her face like a mask. Glasses weren't something any boy or girl wanted to wear, not at that time. But she could have been a bandit queen or a super heroine. She only needed Charlie's Chinese-Russian pistol holster as an accessory to complete her ensemble.

Wadding the rain scarf, she put it away and with a shake of her head, each strand of her Dutch boy trimmed hair seemed to settle into place. Using the same economy of motion, she slipped off the bulky backpack, carrying it effortlessly by her left side. She walked and flipped the buttons of her raincoat open, revealing a light green pant suit over a white turtle neck. Her black boots cracked as she strode through the portico and all eyes, including mine followed her.

She greeted boys and girls alike, offering a wave, accepting a hug and receiving positive replies with only the hopeless dropping eyes. She smiled at those too shy to say anything and called to those with their backs turned. Even stranger were a pair of teachers that happened to round the corner from an adjoining porticos. Before they even stepped into the main portico they were greeted with a series of tin-whistle pitched shouts.

"Hell-ohoooooo, Mrs. JOOOnes, Hiiiiiii Mrs. SmIIIth."

I smiled thinking of Flo, though even she couldn't have made those kinds of sounds.

With a slight grimace the women forced a smile and returned the greetings until they were adjacent to the girl.

"Good morning, Mrs. Jones and Mrs. Smith, " said the girl without the juvenile plea for adult approval. The greeting was made to equals and the teachers acknowledged in kind. "Beautiful morning, even with the rain, which we certainly need."

"Good morning, Wendy," they chorused, smiling in tandem, hurrying toward the double door and replying. "Yes it is, we certainly do!"

"Who's that," asked one of the original J's too loudly.

"I don't know," Joyce said. "And don't care."

There was an edge of uncertainty, tinged with fear, in Joyce's tone, barely discernible to those actually listening. As the leader of fashion and trend, she might welcome handmaidens, but rivals weren't tolerated. Jeri, the brains of the outfit, so to speak, and privy to "scads of details" flashed Joyce dire facial warnings.

Ignoring Jeri, Joyce turned her head toward Wendy and raised her chin. A gesture, I knew from first hand experience, that was the equivalent of an empress extending her scepter to an unworthy minion. It was a summons equivalent to placing a biscuit on a dog's nose in my opinion. Without breaking stride, a tiny smile tugged the corner of Wendy's full mouth and Joyce was dismissed.

"Hi Wendy," called Jeri desperately trying to mend a burning bridge, her eyes darting to Joyce. "Join us. You won't believe what we've heard."

"Maybe later," said Wendy without breaking stride. "I have something to do right now."

Wendy glided past them and Joyce shot Jeri a silent look conveying they would have words later. Light reflected off Wendy's glasses from the light behind me while the eyes of the Js' watched Wendy walk to my corner. Jeri muttered a comment and all heads turned like a switch into the circle.

Neither Wendy or I looked at the other until she complained about rain so early in the school year. She'd had a great time this summer, she said and could have gone for another year without rain or school. I agreed and she introduced herself with an outstretched hand.

"You got your outfit from Madame Mercer," said Wendy, staring straight ahead. "And Bill did your hair."

"How did you know?" I almost shouted, closing my mouth at her raised hand.

"Bill can bench press 300 pounds and has a six pack," she said. "He once shattered a beer bottle over his upper arm."

I huffed disbelief and she recounted her last time at the beauty shop. She'd punched Bill, at his invitation, in his stomach and as hard as she could with both her fists.

"I might as well have been hitting packed sand," she said. "He never flinched."

She was impressed with my family taking karate together and raised an eyebrow about my almost boyfriend, a soldier. I didn't bother mentioning the boob inserts, we'd just met after all. Wendy was bigger than me, up there, even with the inserts. She asked about when my birthday was and lamented she was nine months my senior and envied a birthday during warm months.

In a short time our conversation expanded to music, celebrities and expectations of the coming school year. The bell rang and we shouldered our backpacks just as the Js moved as one and forced their way through the double doors. We stood watching other kids squeeze through before making our way into the main hallway walking shoulder to shoulder around a corner.

In the center of the hallway Jeri and Joyce were bivouaced near a water fountain making no move to get to class. The circle of heads rose like one of those "Wack-A" games at an arcade smirking in our direction. Despite another of Jeri's warning looks, Joyce stepped into our path. Wendy didn't seem to notice her as she moved and talked. The den of J's fell silent and watched like a bull fight crowd for the moment of truth. I had to force myself not to look in their direction.

"So Jackie, does your four-eyed friend know about your little problem," Jerri crooned, "or have you pu-pu- put it to her yet?"

"Shut your mouth," Wendy barked, "or I'll close it for you."

Joyce's mouth clamped shut and she nearly collided with Jeri shuffling to get out of our way. Confusion spread through the Js like plague until they hefted their backpacks ambling away in different directions without another word.

We moved around the next corner and Wendy asked, "Did you do anything this summer?" "

ABOUT THE AUTHOR

Christopher T. Hunnewell was raised in north central Texas near the Brazos River and its tributaries. This area is rich in folklore and characters and he grew up appreciating a well-told tale.

After completing his first two years of college, he served over twenty years in the U.S. Navy, circumnavigating the globe three times and visiting over thirty countries. During the Iranian Hostage Crisis, he was on station in the Indian Ocean and later was a member of the Multi-National Peace Keeping Force in Beirut. He was also there "when all hell broke loose," assisting United Nations troops withdrawing from Somalia. He documented these experiences in journals and penned a personal newsletter to friends. One friend said that getting these letters was like reading an adventure novel.

After military service, Hunnewell returned to Texas and completed his degree at Midwestern State University. He became an award winning staff writer and photographer for newspapers in Texas and Oklahoma before deciding to concentrate on writing fiction. *By the Light of Orion's Belt* is his first novel. He resides in his hometown with his wife Carolyn.